Johnny Ludlow by Mrs Henry Wood

The Third Series

"God sent his Singers upon earth
With songs of sadness and of mirth,
That they might touch the hearts of men,
And bring them back to heaven again."

I0691737

Ellen Price was born on 17th January 1814 in Worcester.

In 1836 she married Henry Wood, whose career in banking and shipping meant living in Dauphiné, in the South of France, for two decades. During their time there they had four children.

Henry's business collapsed and he and Ellen together with their four children returned to England and settled in Upper Norwood near London.

Ellen now turned to writing and with her second book 'East Lynne' enjoyed remarkable popularity. This enabled her to support her family and to maintain a literary career.

It was a career in which she would write over 30 novels including 'Danesbury House', 'Oswald Cray', 'Mrs. Halliburton's Troubles', 'The Channings' and 'The Shadow of Ashlydyat'.

Sadly, her husband, Henry died in 1866.

Ellen though continued to strive on. In 1867, she purchased the magazine 'Argosy', founded two years previously by Alexander Strahan. She was a prolific writer and wrote much of the magazine herself although she had some very respected contributors, amongst them Hesba Stretton and Christina Rossetti. Although she would gradually pare down writing for the magazine she continued to write novel after novel. Such was her talent that for a time she was, in Australia, more popular than Charles Dickens.

Apart from novels she was an excellent translator and a writer of short stories. 'Reality or Delusion?' is a staple of supernatural anthologies to this day.

Ellen Wood died of bronchitis on 10th February 1887. He estate was valued at a very considerable £36,000.

She is buried in Highgate Cemetery, London.

A monument to her in Worcester Cathedral was unveiled in 1916.

Index of Contents
CHAPTER I - THE MYSTERY OF JESSY PAGE
CHAPTER II - CRABB RAVINE

CHAPTER III - OUR VISIT
CHAPTER IV - JANET CAREY
CHAPTER V - DR KNOX
CHAPTER VI - HELEN WHITNEY'S WEDDING
CHAPTER VII - HELEN'S CURATE
CHAPTER VIII - JELLICO'S PACK
CHAPTER IX - CAROMEL'S FARM
CHAPTER X - CHARLOTTE AND CHARLOTTE
CHAPTER XI - THE LAST OF THE CAROMELS
CHAPTER XII - A DAY IN BRIAR WOOD
CHAPTER XIII - THE STORY OF DOROTHY GRAPE: DISAPPEARANCE
CHAPTER XIV - THE STORY OF DOROTHY GRAPE: IN AFTER YEARS
CHAPTER XV - LADY JENKINS: MINA
CHAPTER XVI - LADY JENKINS: DOUBT
CHAPTER XVII - LADY JENKINS: MADAME
CHAPTER XVIII - LADY JENKINS: LIGHT
CHAPTER XIX - THE ANGELS' MUSIC
MRS HENRY WOOD (aka ELLEN WOOD) – A CONCISE BIBLIOGRAPHY

CHAPTER I

THE MYSTERY OF JESSY PAGE

I

Our old grey church at Church Dykely stood in a solitary spot. Servant maids (two of ours once, Hannah and Molly), and silly village girls went there sometimes to watch for the "shadows" on St. Mark's Eve, and owls had a habit of darting out of the belfry at night. Within view of the church, though at some distance from it, stood the lonely, red-brick, angular dwelling-house belonging to Copse Farm. It was inhabited by Mr. Page, a plain worthy widower, getting in years; his three daughters and little son. Abigail and Susan Page, two experienced, sensible, industrious young women, with sallow faces and bunches of short dark curls, were at this period, about midway between twenty and thirty: Jessy, very much younger, was gone out to get two years' "finishing" at a plain boarding-school; Charles, the lad, had bad health and went to school by day at Church Dykely.

Mr. Page fell ill. He would never again be able to get about much. His two daughters, so far as indoor work and management went, were hosts in themselves, Miss Abigail especially; but they could not mount a horse to superintend out-of-doors. Other arrangements were made. The second son of Mr. Drench, a neighbouring farmer and friend, came to the Copse Farm by day as overlooker. He was paid for his services, and he gained experience.

No sooner had John Drench, a silent, bashful young farmer, good-looking and fairly-well educated, been installed in his new post, than he began to show a decided admiration for Miss Susan Page—who was a few months younger than himself. The slight advances he made were favourably received; and it was tacitly looked upon that they were "as good as engaged." Things went on pleasantly through the spring, and might have continued to go on so, but for the coming home at Midsummer of the youngest daughter, Jessy. That led to no end of complications and contrariety.

She was the sweetest flower you ever saw; a fair, delicate lily, with a mild countenance, blue eyes, and golden hair. Jessy had never been very strong; she had always been very pretty; and the consequence was that whilst her sisters had grown up to be useful, not to be idle a minute throughout the long day, Jessy had been petted and indulged, and was little except being ornamental. The two years' schooling had not improved her taste for domestic occupation. To tell the truth, Jessy was given to being uncommonly idle.

To John Drench, who had not seen her since her early girlhood, she appeared as a vision of beauty. "It was like an angel coming in at the door," he said of the day she first came home, when telling the tale to a stranger in after years. "My eyes were fairly dazzled."

Like an angel! And unfortunately for John Drench, his heart was dazzled as well as his eyes. He fell desperately in love with her. It taught him that what he had felt for Miss Susan was not love at all; only esteem, and the liking that so often arises from companionship. He was well-meaning, but inexperienced. As he had never spoken to Susan, the utmost sign he had given being a look or a warmer handshake than usual, he thought there would be no difficulty in transferring his homage to the younger sister. Susan Page, who really loved him, and perhaps looked on with the keen eyes of jealousy, grew at last to see how matters were. She would have liked to put him in a corn-sack and give him a good shaking by way of cure. Thus the summer months went over in some silent discomfort, and September came in warm and fine.

Jessy Page stood at the open parlour window in her airy summer muslin, twirling a rose in her hand, blue ribbons falling from her hair: for Jessy liked to set herself off in little adornments. She was laughing at John Drench outside, who had appeared covered with mud from the pond, into which he had contrived partially to slip when they were dragging for eels.

"I think your picture ought to be taken, just as you look now, Mr. John."

He thought hers ought to be: the bright fair face, the laughing blue eyes, the parted lips and the pretty white teeth presented a picture that, to him, had never had its equal.

"Do you, Miss Jessy? That's a fine rose," he shyly added. He was always shy with her.

She held it out. She had not the least objection to be admired, even by John Drench in an unpresentable state. In their hearts, women have all desired men's flattery, from Eve downwards.

"These large roses are the sweetest of any," she went on. "I plucked it from the tree beyond the grass-plat."

"You are fond of flowers, I've noticed, Miss Jessy."

"Yes, I am. Both for themselves and for the language they symbolise."

"What language is it?"

"Don't you know? I learnt it at school. Each flower possesses its own meaning, Mr. John Drench. This, the rose, is true love."

"True love, is it, Miss Jessy!"

She was lightly flirting it before his face. It was too much for him, and he took it gently from her. "Will you give it me?" he asked below his breath.

"Oh, with great pleasure." And then she lightly added, as if to damp the eager look on his face: "There are plenty more on the same tree."

"An emblem of true love," he softly repeated. "It's a pretty thought. I wonder who invented—"

"Now then, John Drench, do you know that tea's waiting. Are you going to sit down in those muddy boots and leggings?"

The sharp words came from Susan Page. Jessy turned and saw her sister's pale, angry face. John Drench disappeared, and Miss Susan went out again, and banged the door.

"It is high time Jessy was put to some regular employment," cried Susan, bursting into the room where Miss Page sat making the tea. "She idles away her time in the most frivolous and wasteful manner, never doing an earthly thing. It is quite sinful."

"So it is," acquiesced Miss Page. "Have you a headache, Susan? You look pale."

"Never mind my looks," wrathfully retorted Susan. "We will portion out some share of work for her from to-day. She might make up the butter, and undertake the pies and puddings, and do the plain sewing."

William Page, a grey-haired man, sitting with a stick by his side, looked up. "Pretty creature!" he said, for he passionately loved his youngest daughter. "I'll not have her hard-worked, Susan."

"But you'd not have her sit with her hands before her from Monday morning till Saturday night, I suppose, father!" sharply returned Miss Susan. "She'll soon be nineteen."

"No, no; idleness brings nothing but evil in its train. I didn't mean that, Susan. Let the child do what is suitable for her. Where's John Drench?"

"In a fine mess—up to his middle in mud," was Miss Susan's tart answer. "One would think he had been trying to see how great an object he could make of himself."

John Drench came in, somewhat improved, his coat changed and the rose in his button-hole. He took his seat at the tea-table, and was more shy and silent than ever. Jessy sat by her father, chattering gaily, her blue ribbons flickering before his loving eyes.

But the butter-making and the other light work was fated not to be inaugurated yet for Jessy. Charles Page, a tiresome, indulged lad of twelve, became ill again: he was subject to attacks of low fever and ague. Mr. Duffham, peering at the boy over his gold-headed cane, said there was nothing for it but a dose of good seaside air. Mr. Page, anxious for his boy, began to consult with his daughters as to how it might be obtained. They had some very distant connections named Allen, living at Aberystwith. To them Miss Page wrote, asking if they could take in Charles and one of his sisters to live with them for a month or so. Mrs. Allen replied that she would be glad to have them; since her husband's death she had eked out a scanty income by letting lodgings.

It was Jessy who went with him. The house and farm could not have spared Abigail; Susan said neither should it spare her. Jessy, the idle and useless one had to go. Miss Susan thought she and John Drench were well rid of the young lady.

September was in its second week when they went; November was at its close when they returned. The improvement in Charles had been so marked and wonderful—as Mrs. Allen and Jessy both wrote to say—that Mr. Duffham had strongly urged his staying as long as the weather remained fine. It was a remarkably fine late autumn that year, and they stayed until the end of November.

Charles came home well and strong. Jessy was more beautiful than ever. But there was some change in her. The light-hearted, talking, laughing girl had grown rather silent: she was often heard singing snatches of love songs to herself in a low voice, and there was a light in her eyes as of some intense, secret happiness that might not be told. John Drench, who had begun to show signs of returning to his old allegiance (at least, Miss Susan so flattered herself), fell a willing captive again forthwith, and had certainly neither eyes nor ears for any one but Jessy. Susan Page came to the conclusion that a shaking in a sack would be far too good for him.

The way of dressing the churches for Christmas in those past days was quite different from the new style of "decoration" obtaining now. Sprays of holly with their red berries, of ivy with its brown clusters, were stuck, each alternately into the holes on the top of the pews. It was a better way than the present one, far more effective—though I, Johnny Ludlow, shall be no doubt laughed at for saying so. Your woven wreaths tied round the pulpit and reading-desk; your lettered scrolls; your artificial flowers, may be talked of as "artistic," but for effect they all stand absolutely as nothing, in comparison with the more simple and natural way, and they are, perhaps, the least bit tawdry. If you don't believe me, pay a visit to some rural church next Christmas morning—for the old fashion is observed in many a country district still—and judge for yourselves. With many another custom that has been changed by the folly and fashion of these later days of pretension, and not changed for the better, lies this one. That is my opinion, and I hold to it.

The dressing in our church was always done by the clerk, old Bumford. The sexton (called familiarly with us the grave-digger) helped him when his health permitted, but he was nearly always ill, and then Bumford himself had to be grave-digger. It was not much trouble, this manner of decoration, and it took very little time. They had only to cut off the sprays almost of the same size, trim the ends, and lodge them in the holes. In the last century when a new country church was rebuilt (though that did not happen often), the drilling of these holes in the woodwork of the pews, for the reception of the "Christmas," was as much a matter of course as were the pews themselves. Our Christmas was supplied by Mr. Page with a liberal hand; the Copse Farm abounded with trees of holly and ivy; one of his men, Leek, would help Bumford to cut it, and to cart it in a hand-truck to the church. It took a good deal to do all the pews.

On this Christmas that I am telling you of, it fell out that Clerk Bumford and the sexton were both disabled. Bumford had rheumatic gout so badly that getting him into church for the morning service the past three Sundays had been a marvel of dexterity—while the sexton was in bed with what he called catarrh. At first it seemed that we should not get the church dressed at all: but the Miss Pages, ever ready and active in a good work, came to the rescue, and said they would do it themselves, with John Drench's help. The Squire was not going to be behind-hand, and said we boys, for Tod and I were just home for the holidays, should help too.

And when Christmas Eve came, and Leek had wheeled up the holly, and we were all in the cold church (not I think that any of us cared whether it was cold or warm), we enjoyed the work amazingly, and decided that old Bumford should never be let do it again, gout or no gout.

Jessy Page was a picture to look at. The two elder ladies had on tight dark cloth dresses, like a riding-habit cut short, at the ankles: Jessy was in a bright blue mantle edged with swans-down, and a blue bonnet on her pretty head. She came in a little late, and Miss Susan blew her up sharply, for putting on that "best Sunday cape" to dress a church in: but Jessy only laughed good-naturedly, and answered that she would take care not to harm it. Susan Page, trimming the branches, had seen John Drench's eyes fixed on the girl: and her knife worked away like mad in her vexation.

"Look here," said Jessy: "we have never had any Christmas over the pulpit; I think old Bumford was afraid to get up to do it; let us put some. It would hide that ugly nail in the wall."

"There are no holes up in the wall," snapped Miss Susan.

"I meant a large bunch; a bunch of holly and ivy mixed, Susan. John Drench could tie it to the nail: it would look well."

"I'll do it, too," said John. "I've some string in my pocket. The parson won't know himself. It will be as good as a canopy over him."

Miss Page turned round: she and Charley had their arms full of the branches we had been cutting.

"Put a bunch there, if you like, but let us finish the pews first," she said. "If we go from one thing to another we shall not finish while it's daylight."

It was good sense: she rarely spoke anything else. Once let darkness overtake us, and the dressing would be done for. The church knew nothing about evening service, and had never felt the want of means to light itself up.

"I shall pick out the best sprays in readiness," whispered Jessy to me, as we sat together on the bench by the big christening bowl, she choosing branches, I trimming them. "Look at this one! you could not count the berries on it."

"Did you enjoy your visit to Aberystwith, Jessy?"

I wondered what there was in my simple question to move her. The branch of holly went anywhere; her hands met in a silent clasp; the expression of her face changed to one of curious happiness. In answering, her voice fell to a whisper.

"Yes, I enjoyed it."

"What a long time you stayed away! An age, Mrs. Todhetley says."

"It was nearly eleven weeks."

"Eleven weeks! How tedious!"

Her face was glowing, her eyes had a soft light in them. She caught up some holly, and began scattering its berries.

"What did you do with yourself, Jessy?"

"I used to sit by the sea—and to walk about. It was very fine. They don't often have it like that in November, Mrs. Allen said."

"Did Mrs. Allen sit and walk with you?"

"No. She had enough to do with the house and her lodgers. We only saw her at meal times."

"The Miss Allens, perhaps?"

"There are no Miss Allens. Only one little boy."

"Why, then, you had no one but Charley!"

"Charley? Oh, he used to be always about with little Tom Allen—in a boat, or something of that sort. Mrs. Allen thought the sea breezes must be so good for him."

"Well, you must have been very dull!"

Jessy looked rather foolish. She was a simple-minded girl at the best. The two elder sisters had all the strong sense of the family, she the simplicity. Some people called Jessy Page "soft": perhaps, contrasted with her sisters, she was so: and she was very inexperienced.

The dusk was gathering, and Charley had gone out tired, when John Drench got into the pulpit to tie the bunch of holly to the wall above it. Tod was with him. Drench had his hands stretched out, and we stood watching them in a group in the aisle below, when the porch-door was burst open, and in leaped Charles.

"Jessy! I say! Where's Jessy?"

"I am here," said Jessy, looking round. "What do you want?"

"Here's Mr. Marcus Allen."

Who Mr. Marcus Allen might be, Charles did not say. Jessy knew: there was no doubt of that. Her face, just then close to mine, had flushed as red as a June rose.

A tall, dark, imposing man came looming out of the dusk. His handsome, furred great-coat was open, his waistcoat was of crimson velvet; he wore two chains, three rings, and an eye-glass. And I'll leave you to judge of the effect this vision of grandeur made, dropping down on us plain church-dressers in our every-day clothes. John Drench leaned over the pulpit cushion, string in hand; the two Miss Pages stood staring; Jessy turned white and red with the unexpected amazement. It was to her he approached, and spoke.

"How do you do, Miss Jessy?"

She put her hand out in answer to his; but seemed to have been struck as dumb as the old stone image on the monument against the wall.

"These are your sisters, I presume, Miss Jessy? Will you do me the honour of introducing me to them?"

"Mr. Marcus Allen," murmured Jessy. "My sister Abigail; my sister Susan."

Mr. Marcus Allen, bowing over his hat, said something about the pleasure it gave him to make their acquaintance personally, after hearing so much of them from Miss Jessy at Aberystwith, and begged to be allowed to shake their hands. Miss Page, when the hand-shaking was over, said in her straightforward way that she did not know who he was, her young sister never having mentioned him. Jessy, standing like a little simpleton, her eyes bent down on the aisle bricks, murmured in confusion that she "forgot it." John Drench had his face over the cushion all that time, and Tod's arms began to ache, holding up the bunch of green.

Mr. Marcus Allen, it turned out, was related in some way to the Allens of Aberystwith: he happened to go to the town soon after Jessy Page and her brother went there, and he stayed until they left it. Not at the Allens' house: he had lodgings elsewhere. Mrs. Allen spoke of him to Jessy as a "grand gentleman, quite above them." An idea came over me, as we all now stood together, that he had been Jessy's companion in the walking and the sitting by the sea.

"I told Miss Jessy that I should be running down some day to renew my acquaintanceship with her and make that of her family," said Mr. Marcus Allen to Miss Page. "Having no particular engagement on my hands this Christmas time, I came."

He spoke in the most easy manner conceivable: his accent and manner were certainly those of a gentleman. As to the fashionable attire and the rings and chains, rather startling though they looked to us in the dark church on that dark and busy evening, they were all the rage for dandies in the great world then.

Noticing the intimation that he had come purposely to see them, Miss Page supposed that she ought, in hospitably good manners, to invite him to stay a day or two at the farm, but doubted whether so imposing a gentleman would condescend to do so. She said nothing about it then, and we all went out of the church together; except John Drench, who stayed behind with Leek to help clear up the litter for the man to carry away. It was light outside, and I took a good look at the stranger: a handsome man of seven-or-eight-and-twenty, with hard eyes, and black whiskers curled to perfection.

"In what way is he related to the Allens of Aberystwith, Jessy?" questioned Miss Page, drawing her sister away, as we went through the coppice.

"I don't quite know, Abigail. He is some distant cousin."

"How came you never to speak of him?"

"I—I did not remember to do so."

"Very careless of you, child. Especially if he gave you cause to suppose he might come here. I don't like to be taken by surprise by strangers; it is not always convenient."

Jessy walked along in silence, meek as a lamb.

"What is he?—in any profession, or trade?"

"Trade? Oh, I don't think he does anything of that kind, Abigail. That branch of the family would be above it, Mrs. Allen said. He has a large income, she says; plenty of money."

"I take it, then, that he is above us," reasoned Miss Page.

"Oh dear, yes: in station. Ever so much."

"Then I'm sure I don't care to entertain him."

Miss Page went straight into the best kitchen on arriving at home. Her father sat in the large hearth corner, smoking his pipe. She told him about the stranger, and said she supposed they must ask him to stay over the morrow—Christmas-Day.

"Why shouldn't we?" asked Mr. Page.

"Well, father, he seems very grand and great."

"Does he? Give him the best bedroom."

"And our ways are plain and simple, you know," she added.

"He must take us as he finds us, Abigail. Any friend of Mrs. Allen's is welcome: she was downright kind to the children."

We had a jolly tea. Tod and I had been asked to it beforehand. Pork-pies, Miss Susan's making, hot buttered batch-cakes, and lemon cake and jams. Mr. Marcus Allen was charmed with everything: he was a pleasant man to talk to. When we left, he and Mr. Page had gone to the best kitchen again, to smoke together in the wide chimney corner.

You Londoners, who go in for your artistic scrolls and crosses, should have seen the church on Christmas morning. It greeted our sight, as we entered from the porch, like a capacious grove of green, on which the sun streamed through the south windows. Old Bumford's dressing had never been as full and handsome as this of ours, for we had rejected all niggardly sprays. The Squire even allowed that much. Shaking hands with Miss Page in the porch after service, he told her that it cut Clerk Bumford out and out. Mr. Marcus Allen, in fashionable coat, with the furred over-coat flung back, light gloves, and big white wristbands, was in the Pages' pew, sitting between old Page and Jessy. He found all the places for her in her Prayer-book (a shabby red one, some of the leaves loose); bowing slightly every time he handed her the book, as if she had been a princess of the blood royal. Such gallantry was new in our parts: and the congregation were rather taken off their devotions watching it. As to Jessy, she kept flushing like a rose.

Mr. Marcus Allen remained more than a week, staying over New-Year's Day. He made himself popular with them all, and enjoyed what Miss Abigail called their plain ways, just as though he had been reared to them. He smoked his pipe in the kitchen with the farmer; he drove Miss Susan to Alcester in the tax-cart; he presented Miss Abigail with a handsome work-box; and gave Charley a bright half-sovereign for bullseyes. As to Jessy, he paid her no more attention than he did her sisters; hardly as much: so that if Miss Susan had been entertaining any faint hope that his object in coming to the Copse was Jessy, and that in consequence John Drench might escape from bewitching wiles, she found the hope fallacious. Mr. Marcus Allen had apparently no more thought of Jessy than he had of Sally, the red-armed serving-girl. "But what in the world brought the man here at all?" questioned Miss Susan of her sister. "He wanted a bit of country holiday," answered Miss Page with her common sense.

One day during the week the Squire met them abroad, and gave an impromptu invitation to the Manor for the evening. Only the three Miss Pages came. Mr. Marcus Allen sent his compliments, and begged to be excused on the score of headache.

One evening at dusk we met him and Jessy. She had been out on some errand, and he overtook her in the little coppice path between the church and the farm. Tod, dashing through it to get home for dinner, I after him, nearly dashed right upon them. Mr. Marcus Allen had his face inside her bonnet, as if he were speaking in the ear of a deaf old lady of seventy. Tod burst out laughing when we got on.

"That fellow was stealing a sly kiss in the dark, Johnny."

"Like his impudence."

"Rubbish," retorted Tod. "It's Christmas-tide, and all fair. Didn't you see the bit of mistletoe he was holding up?" And Tod ran on, whistling a line of a song that the Squire used to sing in his young days:

"We all love a pretty girl, under the rose."

Mr. Marcus Allen left the Copse Farm with hearty thanks for its hospitality. He promised to come again in the summer, when the fields should be sweet with hay and the golden corn was ripening.

No sooner had he gone than John Drench asked Jessy to promise to be his wife. Whether he had felt any secret jealousy of Mr. Marcus Allen and his attractions, and deemed it well to secure Jessy as soon as the coast was clear, he spoke out. Jessy did not receive the honour kindly. She tossed her pretty head in a violent rage: the idea, she said, of her marrying him. Jessy had never flirted with John Drench since the Aberystwith journey, or encouraged him in any way—that was certain. Unpleasantness ensued at the farm. Mr. Page decidedly approved of the suitor: he alone had perceived nothing of Susan's hopes: and, perhaps for the first time in his life, he spoke sharply to Jessy. John Drench was not to be despised, he told her; his father was a wealthy man, and John would have a substantial portion; more than double enough to put him into the largest and best farm in the county: Mr. Drench was only waiting for a good one to fall in, to take it for him. No: Jessy would not listen. And as the days went on and John Drench, as she said, strove to further his suit on every opportunity, she conceived, or professed, a downright aversion to him. Sadly miserable indeed she seemed, crying often; and saying she would rather go out as lady's-maid to some well-born lady than stay at home to be persecuted. Miss Susan was in as high a state of rapture as the iniquity of false John Drench permitted; and said it served the man right for making an oaf of himself.

"Let be," cried old Page of Jessy. "She'll come to her senses in time." But Miss Abigail, regarding Jessy in silence with her critical eyes, took up the notion that the girl had some secret source of discomfort, with which John Drench had nothing to do.

It was close upon this, scarcely beyond the middle of January, when one Monday evening Duffham trudged over from Church Dykely for a game at chess with the Squire. Hard weather had set in; ice and snow lay on the ground. Mrs. Todhetley nursed her face by the fire, for she had toothache as usual; Tod watched the chess; I was reading. In the midst of a silence, the door opened, and old Thomas ushered in John Drench, a huge red comforter round his neck, his hat in his hand.

"Good-evening, Squire; good-evening, ma'am," said he in his shy way, nodding separately to the rest of us, as he unwound the comforter. "I've come for Miss Jessy, please."

"Come for Miss Jessy!" was the Squire's surprised echo. "Miss Jessy's not here. Take a seat, Mr. John."

"Not here?" cried Drench, opening his eyes in something like fear, and disregarding the invitation to sit down. "Not here! Why where can she have got to? Surely she has not fallen down in the snow and ice, and disabled herself?"

"Why did you think she was here?"

"I don't know," he replied, after a pause, during which he seemed to be lost. "Miss Jessy was not at home at tea: later, when I was leaving for the night, Miss Abigail asked me if I would come over here first and fetch Jessy. I asked no questions, but came off at once."

"She has not been here," said Mrs. Todhetley. "I have not seen Jessy Page since yesterday afternoon, when I spoke to her coming out of church."

John Drench looked mystified. That there must have been some misapprehension on Miss Page's part; or else on his, and he had come to the wrong house; or that poor Jessy had come to grief in the snow on her way to us, seemed certain. He drank a glass of ale, and went away.

They were over again at breakfast time in the morning, John Drench and Miss Abigail herself, bringing strange news. The latter's face turned white as she told it. Jessy Page had not been found. John Drench and two of the men had been out all night in the fields and lanes, searching for her. Miss Abigail gave us her reasons for thinking Jessy had come to Dyke Manor.

On the Sunday afternoon, when the Miss Pages went home from church, Jessy, instead of turning indoors with them, continued her way onwards to the cottage of a poor old woman named Matt, saying Mrs. Todhetley had told her the old granny was very ill. At six o'clock, when they had tea—tea was always late on Sunday evenings, as Sally had leave to stay out gossiping for a good hour after service—it was discovered that Jessy had not come in. Charley was sent out after her, and met her at the gate. She had a scolding from her sister for staying out after dark had fallen; but all she said in excuse was, that the old granny was so very ill. That passed. On the Monday, soon after dinner, she came downstairs with her things on, saying she was going over to Dyke Manor, having promised Mrs. Todhetley to let her know the real state of Granny Matt. "Don't thee get slipping in the snow, Jessy," said Mr. Page to her, half jokingly. "No danger, father," she replied: and went up and kissed him. As she did not return by tea-time, Miss Page took it for granted she was spending the evening with us. Since that, she had not been seen.

It seemed very odd. Mrs. Todhetley said that in talking with Jessy in the porch, she had incidentally mentioned the sickness of Granny Matt. Jessy immediately said she would go there and see her; and if she found her very ill would send word to Dyke Manor. Talk as they would, there was no more to be made of it than that: Jessy had left home to come to us, and was lost by the way.

Lost to her friends, at any rate, if not to herself. John Drench and Miss Page departed; and all day long the search after Jessy and the speculation as to what had become of her continued. At first, no one had glanced at anything except some untoward accident as the sole cause, but gradually opinions veered round to a different fear. They began to think she might have run away!

Run away to escape Mr. John Drench's persevering attentions; and to seek the post of lady's-maid—which she had been expressing a wish for. John stated, however, that he had not persecuted her; that he had resolved to let a little time go by in silence, and then try his luck again. Granny Matt was questioned, and declared most positively that the young lady had not stayed ten minutes with her; that it was only "duskish" when she went away. "Duskish" at that season, in the broad open country, with the white snow on the ground, would mean about five o'clock. What had Jessy done with herself during the other hour—for it was past six when she reached home,—and why should she have excused her tardiness by implying that Granny Matt's illness had kept her?

No one could fathom it. No one ever knew. Before that first day of trouble was over, John Drench suggested worse. Deeply mortified at its being said that she might have run away from him, he breathed a hasty retort—that it was more likely she had been run away with by Mr. Marcus Allen. Had William Page been strong enough he had certainly knocked him down for the aspersion. Susan heard it with a scared face: practical Miss Abigail sternly demanded upon what grounds he spoke. Upon no grounds in particular, Drench honestly answered: it was a thought that came into his mind and he spoke it on the spur of the moment. Any way, it was most unjust to say he had sent her.

The post-mistress at the general shop, Mrs. Smail, came forward with some testimony. Miss Jessy had been no less than twice to the shop during the past fortnight, nay, three times, she thought, to inquire after letters addressed J. P. The last time she received one. Had she been negotiating privately for the lady's-maid's situation, wondered Abigail: had she been corresponding with Mr. Marcus Allen, retorted Susan, in her ill-nature; for she did not just now hold Jessy in any favour. Mrs. Smail was asked whether she had observed, amongst the letters dropped into the box, any directed to Mr. Marcus Allen. But this had to be left an open question: there might have been plenty directed to him, or there might not have been a single one, was the unsatisfactory answer: she had "no 'call' to examine the directions, and as often did up the bag without her spectacles as with 'em."

All this, put together, certainly did not tend to show that Mr. Marcus Allen had anything to do with the disappearance. Jessy had now and then received letters from her former schoolfellows addressed to the post-office—for her sisters, who considered her but a child, had an inconvenient habit of looking over her shoulder while she read them. The whole family, John Drench included, were up to their ears in agony: they did not know in what direction to look for her; were just in that state of mind when straws are caught at. Tod, knowing it could do no harm, told Miss Abigail about the kiss in the coppice. Miss Abigail quite laughed at it: kisses under the mistletoe were as common as blackberries with us, and just as innocent. She wrote to Aberystwith, asking questions about Marcus Allen, especially as to where he might be found. In answer, Mrs. Allen said she had not heard from him since he left Aberystwith, early in December, but had no doubt he was in London at his own home: she did not know exactly where that was, except that it was "somewhere at the West End."

This letter was not more satisfactory than anything else. Everything seemed vague and doubtful. Miss Page read it to her father when he was in bed: Susan had just brought up his breakfast, and he sat up with the tray before him, his face nearly as white as the pillow behind him. They could not help seeing how ill and how shrunken he looked: Jessy's loss had told upon him.

"I think, father, I had better go to London, and see if anything's to be learnt there," said Miss Page. "We cannot live on, in this suspense."

"Ay; best go," answered he, "I can't live in it, either. I've had another sleepless night: and I wish that I was strong to travel. I should have been away long ago searching for the child—."

"You see, father, we don't know where to seek her; we've no clue," interrupted Abigail.

"I'd have gone from place to place till I found her. But now, I'll tell ye, Abigail, where you must go first—the thought has been in my mind all night. And that is to Madame Caron's."

"To Madame Caron's!" echoed both the sisters at once. "Madame Caron's!"

"Don't either of you remember how your mother used to talk of her? She was Ann Dicker. She knows a sight of great folks now—and it may be that Jessy's gone to her. Bond Street, or somewhere near to it, is where she lives."

In truth they had almost forgotten the person mentioned. Madame Caron had once been plain Ann Dicker, of Church Dykely, intimate with William Page and his wife. She went to London when a young woman to learn the millinery and dress-making; married a Frenchman, and rose by degrees to be a fashionable court-milliner. It struck Mr. Page, during the past night-watch, that Jessy might have applied to Madame Caron to help her in getting a place as lady's-maid.

"It's the likeliest thing she'd do," he urged, "if her mind was bent that way. How was she to find such a place of herself?—and I wish we had all been smothered before we'd made her home here unhappy, and put her on to think of such a thing."

"Father, I don't think her home was made unhappy," said Miss Page.

To resolve and to do were one with prompt Abigail Page. Not a moment lost she, now that some sort of clue was given to act upon. That same morning she was on her way to London, attended by John Drench.

A large handsome double show-room. Brass hooks on the walls and slender bonnet-stands on the tables, garnished with gowns and mantles and head-gear and fal-lals; wide pier-glasses; sofas and chairs covered with chintz. Except for these articles, the room was empty. In a small apartment opening from it, called "the trying-on room," sat Madame Caron herself, taking a comfortable cup of tea and a toasted muffin, after the labours of the day were over. Not that the labours were great at that season: people who require court millinery being for the most part out of town.

"You are wanted, if you please, madame, in the show-room," said a page in buttons, coming in to disturb the tea.

"Wanted!—at this hour!" cried Madame Caron, as she glanced at the clock, and saw it was on the stroke of six. "Who is it?"

"It's a lady and gentleman, madame. They look like travellers."

"Go in and light the gas," said madame.

"Passing through London and requiring things in a hurry," thought she, mentally running through a list of some of her most fashionable customers.

She went in with a swimming curtsy—quite that of a Frenchwoman—and the parties, visitors and visited, gazed at each other in the gaslight. They saw a very stylish lady in rich black satin that stood on end, and lappets of point lace: she saw two homely country people, the one in a red comforter, muffled about his ears, the other in an antiquated fur tippet that must originally have come out of Noah's ark.

"Is it—Madame Caron?" questioned Miss Abigail, in hesitation. For, you see, she doubted whether it might not be one of Madame Caron's duchesses.

"I have the honour to be Madame Caron," replied the lady with her grandest air.

Thus put at ease in regard to identity, Miss Page introduced herself—and John Drench, son of Mr. Drench of the Upland Farm. Madame Caron—who had a good heart, and retained amidst her grandeur a vivid remembrance of home and early friends—came down from her stilts on the instant, took off with her own hands the objectionable tippet, on the plea of heat, conducted them into the little room, and rang for a fresh supply of tea and muffins.

"I remember you so well when you were a little thing, Abigail," she said, her heart warming to the old days. "We always said you would grow up like your mother, and so you have. Ah, dear! that's something like a quarter-of-a-century ago. As to you, Mr. John, your father and I were boy and girl sweethearts."

Over the refreshing tea and the muffins, Abigail Page told her tale. The whole of it. Her father had warned her not to hint a word against Jessy; but there was something in the face before her that spoke of truth and trust; and, besides, she did not see her way clear not to speak of Marcus Allen. To leave him out altogether would have been like bargaining for a spring calf in the dark, as she said later to John Drench.

"I have never had a line from Jessy in all my life: I have neither seen her nor heard of her," said madame. "As to Mr. Marcus Allen, I don't know him personally myself, but Miss Connaway, my head dressmaker, does: for I have heard her speak of him. I can soon find out for you where he lives."

Miss Page thought she should like to see the head dressmaker, and a message was sent up for her. A neat little middle-aged woman came down, and was invited to the tea-table. Madame turned the conversation on Mr. Marcus Allen; telling Miss Connaway that these country friends of hers knew him slightly, and would be glad to get his address to call upon him; but she did not say a syllable about Jessy.

Mr. Marcus Allen had about two hundred a year of his own, and was an artist in water-colours. The certain income made him idle; and he played just as much as he worked. The few pictures he completed were good, and sold well. He shared a large painting-room somewhere with a brother artist, but lived in chambers. All this Miss Connaway told readily; she had known him since he was a child.

Late though it was, Miss Abigail and her cavalier proceeded to Marcus Allen's lodgings; or "chambers," as they were ostentatiously called, and found him seated at dinner. He rose in the utmost astonishment at seeing them; an astonishment that looked thoroughly genuine.

Jessy missing! Jessy left her home! He could but reiterate the words in wondering disbelief. Abigail Page felt reassured from that moment; even jealous John Drench in his heart acquitted him. He had not written to Jessy, he said; he had nothing to write to her about, therefore it could not have been his letter she went to receive at the post-office; and most certainly she had not written to him. Miss Abigail—willing perhaps to offer some excuse for coming to him—said they had thought it possible Jessy might have consulted him about getting a lady's-maid's place. She never had consulted him, he answered, but had once told him that she intended to go out as one. He should imagine, he added, it was what she had done.

Mr. Marcus Allen pressed them to sit down and partake of his dinner, such as it was; he poured out glasses of wine; he was altogether hospitable. But they declined all. He then asked how he could assist them; he was most anxious they should find her, and would help in any way that lay in his power.

"He knows no more about her than we know," said John Drench as they turned out into the lighted streets, on their way back to the inn they had put up at, which had been recommended to them by Mr. Page. "I'm sorry I misjudged him."

"I am sorry too, John Drench," was Miss Abigail's sorrowful answer. "But for listening to the words you said, we should never have had such a wicked thought about her, poor child, and been spared many a bitter moment. Where in the wide world are we to look for her now?"

The wide world did not give any answer. London, with its teeming millions, was an enormous arena—and there was no especial cause for supposing Jessy Page had come to it.

"I am afraid it will be of no use to stay here any longer," said Miss Abigail to John Drench, after another unsatisfactory day had gone by, during which Marcus Allen called upon them at the inn and said he had spoken to the police. It was John Drench's own opinion.

"Why, you see, Miss Abigail, that to look for her here, not knowing where or how, is like looking for a needle in a bottle of hay," said John.

They reached home none too soon. Two unexpected events were there to greet them. The one was Mr. Page who was lying low in an attack of paralysis; the other was a letter from Jessy.

It gave no clue to where she was. All she said in it was that she had found a situation, and hoped to suit and be happy in it; and she sent her love to all.

And the weeks and the months went on.

II

Snow was falling. At one of the windows of the parlour at Copse Farm, stood Susan Page, her bunch of short dark curls fastened back with a comb on both sides of her thin face, her trim figure neat in a fine crimson merino gown. Her own portion of household-work was already done, though it was not yet mid-day, and she was about to sit down, dressed for the day, to some sewing that lay on the work-table.

"I was hoping the snow was over: the morning looked so clear and bright," she said to herself, watching the large flakes. "Leek will have a job to get the truck to the church."

It was a long, narrow room. At the other end, by the fire, sat Mr. Page in his arm-chair. He had dropped asleep, his cheek leaning on his hand. As Miss Susan sat down and took up her work, a large pair of scissors fell to the ground with a crash. She glanced round at her father, but he did not wake. That stroke of a year ago had dulled his faculties.

"I should uncommonly like to know who did this—whether Sally or the woman," she exclaimed, examining the work she had to do. One of Mr. Page's new shirts had been torn in the washing, and she was about to mend the rent. "That woman has a heavy hand: and Sally a careless one. It ought not to have been ironed."

The door opened, and John Drench came in. When he saw that Mr. Page was asleep, he walked up the room towards Miss Susan. In the past twelvemonth—for that amount of time had rolled on since the trouble about Jessy and her mysterious disappearance—John Drench had had time to return to his first allegiance (or, as Miss Susan mentally put it, get over his folly); and he had decidedly done it.

"Did you want anything?" asked Susan in a cold tone. For she made a point of being short with him—for his own benefit.

"I wanted to ask the master whether he'd have that ditch made, that he was talking about," was the answer. "There's no hurry about it: not much to be done anywhere while this weather lasts."

She made no reply. John Drench stood, waiting for Mr. Page to wake, looking alternately at the snow and at Miss Susan's steel thimble and nimble fingers. Very deftly was she doing the work, holding the linen gingerly, that the well-ironed bosom and wristbands might not get creased and unfit the shirt for wear. He was thinking what a good wife she would make: for there was nothing, in the shape of usefulness, that Susan Page could not put her hand to, and put it well.

"Miss Susan, I was going to ask you a question," he began, standing uncomfortably on one leg. "I've been wanting to do it for a good bit now, but—"

"Pick up my cotton," said Miss Susan tartly, dropping a reel purposely.

"But I believe I have wanted courage," resumed he after doing as he was bid. "It is a puzzling task to know how to do it for the best, and what to say. If you—"

Open flew the door, and in came Miss Page, in her white kitchen apron. Her sleeves were rolled above her elbows, her floured hands were lightly wiped. John Drench, interrupted, thought he should never have pluck to speak again.

"Susan, do you know where that old red receipt-book is?" she asked, in a low tone, glancing at her sleeping father. "I am not certain about the proportions for the lemon cake."

"The red receipt-book?" repeated Susan. "I have not seen it for ever so long."

"Nor I. I don't think I have had occasion to use it since last Christmas-Eve. I know I had to look at it then for the lemon-cake. Sally says she's sure it is somewhere in this room."

"Then you had better send Sally to find it, Abigail."

Instead of that, Miss Page began searching herself. On the book-shelves; on the side-board; in all the nooks and corners. It was found in the drawer of an unused table that stood against the wall.

"Well, I declare!" she exclaimed, as she drew it out. "I wonder who put it in here?"

In turning over the leaves to look for what she wanted, a piece of paper, loosely folded, fell to the ground. John Drench picked it up.

"Why!" he said, "it is a note from Jessy."

It was the letter written to them by Jessy, saying she had found a situation and hoped to suit and be happy in it. The one letter: for no other had ever come. Abigail, missing the letter months ago, supposed it had got burnt.

"Yes," she said with a sigh, as she glanced over the few lines now, standing by Susan's work-table, "it is Jessy's letter. She might have written again. Every morning of my life for weeks and weeks, I kept looking for the letter-man to bring another. But the hope died out at last, for it never came."

"She is a heartless baggage!" cried Miss Susan. "In her grand lady's-maid's place, amongst her high people, she is content to forget and abandon us. I'd never have believed it of her."

A pause ensued. The subject was a painful one. Mortifying too: for no one likes to be set at nought and forgotten by one that they have loved and cherished and brought up from a little child. Abigail Page had tears in her eyes.

"It's just a year ago to-day that she came into the church to help us to dress it," said John Drench, his tender tone of regret grating on Miss Susan's ear. "In her blue mantle she looked sweeter and brighter than a fairy."

"Did you ever see a fairy, pray?" asked Miss Susan, sharply taking him up. "She acted like a fairy, didn't she?"

"Best to forget her," interposed Abigail, suppressing a sigh. "As Susan says, she is heartless. Almost wicked: for what is worse than ingratitude? Never to write: never to let us know where her situation is and with what people: never to ask or care whether her poor father, who had nothing but love for her, is living or dead? It's best to forget her."

She went out of the room with the note and receipt-book as she spoke, softly closing the door behind her, as one does who is feeling trouble. Miss Susan worked on with rapid and angry stitches; John Drench looked out on the low-lying snow. The storm had passed: the sky was blue again.

Yes. Christmas-Eve had come round, making it just a year since Jessy in her pretty blue mantle had chosen the sprays of holly in the church. They had never had from her but that one first unsatisfactory letter: they knew no more how she went, or why she went, or where she was, than they had known then. Within a week or two of the unsatisfactory journey to London of Miss Abigail and John Drench, a letter came to the farm from Mr. Marcus Allen, inquiring after Jessy, expressing hopes that she had been found and was at home again. It was not answered: Miss Page, busy with her father's illness, neglected it at first, and then thought it did not matter.

Mr. Page had recovered from his stroke: but he would never be good for anything again. He was very much changed; would sit for hours and never speak: at times his daughters thought him a little silly, as if his intellect were failing. Miss Page, with John Drench's help, managed the farm: though she always made it a point of duty to consult her father and ask for his orders. In the month of June they heard again from Mr. Marcus Allen. He wrote to say that he was sorry not to fulfil his promise (made in the winter's visit) of coming to stay with them during the time of hay-making, but he was busy finishing a painting and could not leave it: he hoped to come at some other time. And this was now December.

Susan Page worked on: John Drench looked out of the window. The young lady was determined not to break the silence.

"The Dunn Farm is to let," said he suddenly.

"Is it?" slightingly returned Miss Susan.

"My father has some thoughts of taking it for me. It's good land."

"No better than other land about here."

"It's very good, Susan. And just the place I should like. There's an excellent house too, on it."

Susan Page began rummaging in the deep drawer of the work-table for her box of buttons. She had a great mind to hum a tune.

"But I couldn't take it, or let father take it for me, unless you'd promise to go to it with me, Susan."

"Promise to go to it with you, John Drench!"

"I'd make you as good a husband as I know how. Perhaps you'll think of it."

No answer. She was doubling her thread to sew on the button.

"Will you think of it, Miss Susan?"

"Well—yes, I will," she said in a softer tone, "And if I decide to bring my mind to have you, John Drench, I'll hope to make you a good and faithful wife."

He held out his hand to shake hers upon the bargain. Their eyes met in kindliness: and John Drench knew that the Dunn Farm would have its mistress.

We were going to dress the church this year as we did the last. Clerk Bumford's cough was bad, and the old sexton was laid by as usual. Tod and I got to the church early in the afternoon, and saw the Miss Pages wading their way through the coppice, over their ankles in snow: the one lady having finished her cake-making and the other her shirt-mending.

"Is Leek not here yet?" cried they in surprise. "We need not have made so much haste."

Leek with his large truck of holly was somewhere on the road. He had started, as Miss Page said, while they were at dinner. And he was not to be seen!

"It is all through his obstinacy," cried Susan. "I told him he had better take the highway, though it was a little further round; but he said he knew he could well get through the little valley. That's where he has stuck, truck and all."

John Drench came up as she was speaking. He had been on some errand to Church Dykely; and gave a bad account of the snow on the roads. This was the third day of it. The skies just now were blue as in spring; the sun, drawing towards the west, was without a cloud. After waiting a few minutes, John Drench started to meet Leek and help him on; and we cooled our heels in the church-porch, unable to get inside. As it was supposed Leek would be there sooner than any one else, the key of the church had been given to him that he might get the holly in. There we waited in the cold. At last, out of patience, Tod went off in John Drench's wake, and I after him.

It was as Miss Susan surmised. Leek and his truck had stuck fast in the valley: a low, narrow neck of land connecting a byeway to the farm with the lane. The snow was above the wheels: Leek could neither get on nor turn back. He and John Drench were hard at work, pulling and pushing; and the obstinate truck refusing to move an inch. With the help of our strength—if mine was not worth much, Tod's was—we got it on. But all this caused ever so much delay: and the dressing was begun when it ought to have been nearly finished. I could not help thinking of the other Christmas-Eve; and of pretty Jessy who had helped—and of Miss Susan scolding her for coming in her best blue mantle—and of the sudden looming upon us of the stranger, Marcus Allen. Perhaps the rest were thinking about it as I was. One thing was certain—that there was no liveliness in this year's dressing; we were all as silent as mutes and as dull as ditch-water. Charley Page, who had made enough noise last year, was away this. He went to school at

Worcester now, and had gone to spend the Christmas with some people in Gloucestershire, instead of coming home.

The work was in progress, when who should look in upon us but Duffham. He was passing by to visit some one ill in the cottages. "Rather late, shan't you be?" cried he, seeing that there was hardly any green up yet. And we told him about the truck sticking in the snow.

"What possessed Leek to take it through the valley?" returned Duffham.

"Because he is fonder of having his own way than a mule," called out Miss Susan from the aisle.

Duffham laughed. "Don't forget the gala bunch over the parson's head; it looked well last year," said he, turning to go out. And we told him there was no danger of forgetting it: it was one of our improvements on old Bumford's dressing.

Darkness overtook us before half the work was done. There was nothing for it but to get candles from the Copse Farm to finish by. No one volunteered to fetch them: a walk through the snow did not look lively in prospective to any one of us, and Leek had gone off somewhere. "I suppose it must be me," said John Drench, coming out from the holly to start: when Miss Page suddenly bethought herself of what the rest of us were forgetting—that there might be candles in the church. On a winter's afternoon, when it grew dark early and the parson could not see through his spectacles to finish his sermon, Clerk Bumford would go stumping into the place under the belfry, and re-appear with a lighted candle and hand it up to the pulpit. He ought to have a stock of candles in store.

John Drench struck some matches, and we went to explore Bumford's den—a place dimly lighted by the open slits in the belfry above. The first thing seen was his black gown hanging up, next a horn lantern on the floor and the grave-digging tools, then an iron candlestick with a candle end in it, then a stick half-a-mile long that he menaced the boys with if they laughed in church; and next a round tin candlebox on a nail in the wall. It was a prize.

There were ten candles in it. Leaving one, in case it should be wanted on the morrow afternoon, the nine others were lighted. One was put into the iron candlestick, the rest we stuck upright in melted tallow, wherever one was wanted: how else could they be set up? It was a grand illumination: and we laughed over Clerk Bumford's dismay when he should find his store of candles gone.

That took time: finding the candles, and dropping the tallow, and talking and laughing. In the midst of it the clock struck five. Upon that, Miss Abigail told us to hinder no more time, or the work would not be done by midnight. So we set to with a will. In a couple of hours all the dressing was finished, and the branches were ready to be hung over the pulpit. John Drench felt for the string. He seemed to take his time over it.

"Where on earth is it?" cried he, searching his pockets. "I'm sure I brought some."

He might have brought it; but it was certain he had not got it then. Miss Abigail, who had no patience with carelessness, told him rather sharply that if he had put it in his pockets at all, there it would be now.

"Well, I did," he answered, in his quiet way. "I put it in on purpose. I'm sure I don't know where it can have got to."

And there we were: at a standstill for a bit of string. Looking at one another like so many helpless noodles, and the flaring candles coming to an end! Tod said, tear a strip off the tail of Bumford's gown; he'd never miss it: for which Miss Abigail gave it him as sharply as if he had proposed to tear it off the parson's.

"I might get a bit of string at old Bumford's," I said. "In a few minutes I'll be back with it."

It was one of the lightest nights ever seen: the air clear, the moon bright, the ground white with snow. Rushing round the north and unfrequented side of the church, where the grass on the graves was long and no one ever walked, excepting old Bumford when he wanted to cut across the near way to his cottage, I saw something stirring against the church wall. Something dark: that seemed to have been looking in at the window, and now crouched down with a sudden movement behind the buttress, as if afraid of being seen.

"Is that you, Leek?" I called out.

There was no answer: no movement: nothing but a dark heap lying low. I thought it might be a fox; and crossed over to look.

Well—I had had surprises in my life, but never one that so struck upon me as this. Foxes don't wear women's clothes: this thing did. I pulled aside the dark cloak, and a face stood out white and cold in the moonlight—the face of Jessy Page.

You may fancy it is a slice of romance this; made up for effect out of my imagination: but it is the real truth, as every one about the place can testify to, and its strangeness is talked of still. Yet there are stranger coincidences in life than this. On Christmas-Eve, a year before, Jessy Page had been helping to dress the church, in her fine blue mantle, in her beauty, in her light-hearted happiness: on this Christmas-Eve when we were dressing it again, she re-appeared. But how changed! Wan, white, faint, wasted! I am not sure that I should have known her but for her voice. Shrinking, as it struck me, with shame and fear, she put up her trembling hands in supplication.

"Don't betray me!—don't call!" she implored in weak, feverish, anxious tones. "Go away and leave me. Let me lie here unsuspected until they have all gone away."

What ought I to do? I was just as bewildered as it's possible for a fellow to be. It's no exaggeration to say that I thought her dying: and it would never do to leave her there to die.

The stillness was broken by a commotion. While she lay with her thin hands raised, and I was gazing down on her poor face, wondering what to say, and how to act, Miss Susan came flying round the corner after me.

"Johnny Ludlow! Master Johnny! Don't go. We have found the string under the unused holly. Why!—what's that?"

No chance of concealment for Jessy now. Susan Page made for the buttress, and saw the white face in the moonlight.

"It's Jessy," I whispered.

With a shriek that might have scared away all the ghosts in the churchyard, Susan Page called for Abigail. They heard it through the window, and came rushing out, thinking Susan must have fallen at least into the clutches of a winter wolf. Miss Susan's voice trembled as she spoke in a whisper.

"Here's Jessy—come back at last!"

Unbelieving Abigail Page went down on her knees in the snow to trace the features, and convince herself. Yes, it was Jessy. She had fainted now, and lay motionless. Leek came up then, and stood staring.

Where had she come from?—how had she got there? It was just as though she had dropped from the skies with the snow. And what was to be done with her?

"She must—come home," said Abigail.

But she spoke hesitatingly, as though some impediment might lie in the way: and she looked round in a dreamy manner on the open country, all so white and dreary in the moonlight.

"Yes, there's no other place—of course it must be the farm," she added. "Perhaps you can bring her between you. But I'll go on and speak to my father first."

It was easy for one to carry her, she was so thin and light. John Drench lifted her and they all went off: leaving me and Leek to finish up in the church, and put out the candles.

William Page was sitting in his favourite place, the wide chimney-corner of the kitchen, quietly smoking his pipe, when his daughter broke in upon him with the strange news. Just in the same way that, a year before, she had broken in upon him with that other news—that a gentleman had arrived, uninvited, on a visit to the farm. This news was more startling than that.

"Are they bringing her home?—how long will they be?" cried the old man with feverish eagerness, as he let fall his long churchwarden pipe, and broke it. "Abigail, will they be long?"

"Father, I want to say something: I came on to say it," returned Miss Page, and she was trembling too. "I don't like her face: it is wan, and thin, and full of suffering: but there's a look in it that—that seems to tell of shame."

"To tell of what?" he asked, not catching the word.

"May Heaven forgive me if I misjudge her! The fear crossed me, as I saw her lying there, that her life may not have been innocent since she left us: why else should she come back in this most strange way? Must we take her in all the same, father?"

"Take her in!" he repeated in amazement. "YES. What are you thinking of, child, to ask it?"

"It's the home of myself and Susan, father: it has been always an honest one in the sight of the neighbours. Maybe, they'll be hard upon us for receiving her into it."

He stared as one who does not understand, and then made a movement with his hands, as if warding off her words and the neighbours' hardness together.

"Let her come, Abigail! Let her come, poor stray lamb. Christ wouldn't turn away a little one that had strayed from the fold: should her own father do it?"

And when they brought her in, and put her in an easy-chair by the sitting-room fire, stirring it into a blaze, and gave her hot tea and brandy in it, William Page sat down by her side, and shed fast tears over her, as he fondly stroked her hand.

Gay and green looked the church on Christmas morning, the sun shining in upon us as brightly as it shone a year before. The news of Jessy Page's return and the curious manner of it, had spread; causing the congregation to turn their eyes instinctively on the Pages' pew. Perhaps not one but recalled the last Christmas—and the gallant stranger who had sat in it, and found the places in the Prayer-book for Jessy. Only Mr. Page was there to-day. He came slowly in with his thick stick—for he walked badly since his illness, and dragged one leg behind the other. Before the thanksgiving prayer the parson opened a paper and read out a notice. Such things were uncommon in our church, and it caused a stir.

"William Page desires to return thanks to Almighty God for a great mercy vouchsafed to him."

We walked to the Copse Farm with him after service. Considering that he had been returning thanks, he seemed dreadfully subdued. He didn't know how it was yet; where she had been, or why she had come home in the manner she did, he told the Squire; but, anyway, she had come. Come to die, it might be; but come home, and that was enough.

Mrs. Todhetley went upstairs to see her. They had given her the best bed, the one they had given to Marcus Allen. She lay in it like a lily. It was what Mrs. Todhetley said when she came down: "like a lily, so white and delicate." There was no talking. Jessy for the most part kept her eyes shut and her face turned away. Miss Page whispered that they had not questioned her yet; she seemed too weak to bear it. "But what do you think?" asked Mrs. Todhetley in return. "I am afraid to think," was all the answer. In coming away, Mrs. Todhetley stooped over the bed to kiss her.

"Oh don't, don't!" said Jessy faintly: "you might not if you knew all. I am not worth it."

"Perhaps I should kiss you all the more, my poor child," answered Mrs. Todhetley. And she came downstairs with red eyes.

But Miss Susan Page was burning with impatience to know the ins and outs of the strange affair. Naturally so. It had brought more scandal and gossip on the Copse Farm than even the running away of the year before. That was bad enough: this was worse. Altogether Jessy was the home's heartsore. Mr. Page spoke of her as a lamb, a wanderer returned to the fold, and Susan heard it with compressed lips: in her private opinion, she had more justly been called an ungrateful girl.

"Now, then, Jessy; you must let us know a little about yourself," began Susan on this same afternoon when she was with her alone, and Jessy lay apparently stronger, refreshed with the dinner and the long rest. Abigail had gone to church with Mr. Page. Susan could not remember that any of them had gone to church before on Christmas-Day after the morning service: but there was no festive gathering to keep them at home to-day. Unconsciously, perhaps, Susan resented the fact. Even John Drench was dining at his father's. "Where have you been all this while in London?"

Jessy suddenly lifted her arm to shade her eyes; and remained silent.

"It is in London, I conclude, that you have been? Come: answer me."

"Yes," said Jessy faintly.

"And where have you been? In what part of it?—who with?"

"Don't ask me," was the low reply, given with a suppressed sob.

"Not ask you! But we must ask you. And you must answer. Where have you been, and what have you been doing?"

"I—can't tell," sobbed Jessy. "The story is too long."

"Story too long!" echoed Susan quickly, "you might say in half-a-dozen words—and leave explanations until to-morrow. Did you find a place in town?"

"Yes, I found a place."

"A lady's-maid's place?—as you said."

Jessy turned her face to the wall, and never spoke.

"Now, this won't do," cried Miss Susan, not choosing to be thwarted: and no doubt Jessy, hearing the determined tone, felt something like a reed in her hands. "Just you tell me a little."

"I am very ill, Susan; I can't talk much," was the pleading excuse. "If you'd only let me be quiet."

"It will no more hurt you to say in a few words where you have been than to make excuses," persisted Miss Susan, giving a flick to the skirt of her new puce silk gown. "Your conduct altogether has been most extraordinary, quite baffling to us at home, and I must hear some explanation of it."

"The place I went to was too hard for me," said Jessy after a pause, speaking out of the pillow.

"Too hard!"

"Yes; too hard. My heart was breaking with its hardness, and I couldn't stop in it. Oh, be merciful to me, Susan! don't ask any more."

Susan Page thought that when mysterious answers like these were creeping out, there was all the greater need that she should ask for more.

"Who found you the place at first, Jessy?"

Not a word. Susan asked again.

"I—got it through an advertisement," said Jessy at length.

Advertisements in those days, down in our rural district, were looked upon as wonderful things, and Miss Susan opened her eyes in surprise. A faint idea was upon her that Jessy could not be telling the truth.

"In that letter that you wrote to us; the only one you did write; you asserted that you liked the place."

"Yes. That was at first. But afterwards—oh, afterwards it got cruelly hard."

"Why did you not change it for another?"

Jessy made no answer. Susan heard the sobs in her throat.

"Now, Jessy, don't be silly. I ask why you did not get another place, if you were unable to stay in that one?"

"I couldn't have got another, Susan. I would never have got another."

"Why not?" persisted Susan.

"I—I—don't you see how weak I am?" she asked with some energy, lifting her face for a moment to Susan.

And its wan pain, its depth of anguish, disarmed Susan. Jessy looked like a once fair blossom on which a blight had passed.

"Well, Jessy, we will leave these matters until later. But there's one thing you must answer. What induced you to take this disreputable mode of coming back?"

A dead silence.

"Could you not have written to say you were coming, as any sensible girl would, that you might have been properly met and received? Instead of appearing like a vagabond, to be picked up by anybody."

"I never meant to come home—to the house."

"But why?" asked Susan.

"Oh, because—because of my ingratitude in running away—and never writing—and—and all that."

"That is, you were ashamed to come and face us."

"Yes, I was ashamed," said Jessy, shivering.

"And no wonder. Why did you go?"

Jessy gave a despairing sigh. Leaving that question in abeyance, Susan returned to the former one.

"If you did not mean to come home, what brought you down here at all?"

"It didn't matter where I went. And my heart was yearning for a look at the old place—and so I came."

"And if we had not found you under the church wall—and we never should but for Johnny Ludlow's running out to get some string—where should you have gone, pray?"

"Crawled under some haystack, and let the cold and hunger kill me."

"Don't be a simpleton," reproved Susan.

"I wish it had been so," returned Jessy. "I'd rather be dying there in quiet. Oh, Susan, I am ill; I am indeed! Let me be at peace!"

The appeal shut up Susan Page. She did not want to be too hard upon her.

Mr. Duffham came in after church. Abigail had told him that she did not like Jessy's looks; nor yet her cough. He went up alone, and was at the bedside before Jessy was aware. She put up her hand to hide her face, but not in time: Duffham had seen it. Doctors don't get shocks in a general way: they are too familiar with appearances that frighten other people: but he started a little. If ever he saw coming death in a face, he thought he saw it in that of Jessy Page.

He drew away the shading hand, and looked at her. Duffham was pompous on the whole and thought a good deal of his gold-headed cane, but he was a tender man with the sad and sick. After that, he sat down and began asking her a few things—where she had been, and what she had done. Not out of curiosity, or quite with the same motive that Miss Susan had just asked; but because he wished to find out whether her illness was more on the body or the mind. She would not answer. Only cried softly.

"My dear," said Duffham, "I must have you tell me a little of the past. Don't be afraid: it shall go no further. If you only knew the strange confidences that are sometimes placed in me, Jessy, you would not hesitate."

No, she would not speak of her own accord, so he began to pump her. Doing it very kindly and soothingly: had Jessy spent her year in London robbing all the banks, one might have thought she could only have yielded to his wish to come to the bottom of it. Duffham listened to her answers, and sat with a puzzled face. She told him what she had told Susan: that her post of lady's-maid had been too hard for her and worn her to what she was; that she had shrunk from returning home on account of her ingratitude, and should not have returned ever of her own will. But she had yearned for a sight of the old place, and so came down by rail, and walked over after dark. In passing the church she saw it lighted up; and lingered, peeping in. She never meant to be seen; she should have gone away somewhere before morning. Nothing more.

Nothing more! Duffham sat listening to her. He pushed back the pretty golden hair (no more blue ribbons in it now), lost in thought.

"Nothing more, Jessy? There must have been something more, I think, to have brought you into this state. What was it?"

"No," she faintly said: "only the hard work I had to do; and the thought of how I left my home; and—and my unhappiness. I was unhappy always, nearly from my first entering. The work was hard."

"What was the work?"

"It was—"

A long pause. Mr. Duffham, always looking at her, waited.

"It was sewing; dress-making. And—there was sitting up at nights."

"Who was the lady you served? What was her name?"

"I can't tell it," answered Jessy, her cheeks flushing to a wild hectic.

The surgeon suddenly turned the left hand towards him, and looked at the forefinger. It was smooth as ivory.

"Not much sign of sewing there, Jessy."

She drew it under the clothes. "It is some little time since I did any; I was too ill," she answered. "Mr. Duffham, I have told you all there is to tell. The place was too hard for me, and it made me ill."

It was all she told. Duffham wondered whether it was, in substance, all she had to tell. He went down and entered the parlour with a grave face: Mr. Page, his daughters, and John Drench were there. The doctor said Jessy must have perfect rest, tranquillity, and the best of nourishment; and he would send some medicine. Abigail put a shawl over her head, and walked with him across the garden.

"You will tell me what your opinion is, Mr. Duffham."

"Ay. It is no good one, Miss Abigail."

"Is she very ill?"

"Very. I do not think she will materially rally. Her chest and lungs are both weak."

"Her mother's were before her. As I told you, Jessy looks to me just as my mother used to look in her last illness."

Mr. Duffham went through the gate without saying more. The snow was sparkling like diamonds in the moonlight.

"I think I gather what you mean," resumed Abigail. "That she is, in point of fact, dying."

"That's it. As I truly believe."

They looked at each other in the clear light air. "But not—surely, Mr. Duffham, not immediately?"

"Not immediately. It may be weeks off yet. Mind—I don't assert that she is absolutely past hope; I only think it. It is possible that she may rally, and recover."

"It might not be the happier for her," said Abigail, under her breath. "She is in a curiously miserable state of mind—as you no doubt saw. Mr. Duffham, did she tell you anything?"

"She says she took a place as lady's-maid; that the work proved too hard for her; and that, with the remorse for her ingratitude towards her home, made her ill."

"She said the same to Susan this afternoon. Well, we must wait for more. Good-night, Mr. Duffham: I am sure you will do all you can."

Of course Duffham meant to do all he could; and from that time he began to attend her regularly.

Jessy Page's coming home, with, as Miss Susan had put it, the vagabond manner of it, was a nine days' wonder. The neighbours went making calls at the Copse Farm, to talk about it and to see her. In the latter hope they failed. Jessy showed a great fear of seeing any one of them; would put her head under the bed-clothes and lie there shaking till the house was clear; and Duffham said she was not to be crossed.

Her sisters got to know no more of the past. Not a syllable. They questioned and cross-questioned her; but she only stuck to her text. It was the work that had been too much for her; the people she served were cruelly hard.

"I really think it must be so; that she has nothing else to tell," remarked Abigail to Susan one morning, as they sat alone at breakfast, "But she must have been a downright simpleton to stay."

"I can't make her out," returned Susan, hard of belief. "Why should she not say where it was, and who the people are? Here comes the letter-man."

The letter-man—as he was called—was bringing a letter for Miss Page. Letters at the Copse Farm were rare, and she opened it with curiosity. It proved to be from Mrs. Allen of Aberystwith; and out of it dropped two cards, tied together with silver cord.

Mrs. Allen wrote to say that her distant relative, Marcus, was married. He had been married on Christmas-Eve to a Miss Mary Goldbeater, a great heiress, and they had sent her cards. Thinking the Miss Pages might like to see the cards (as they knew something of him) she had forwarded them.

Abigail took the cards up. "Mr. Marcus Allen. Mrs. Marcus Allen." And on hers was the address: "Gipsy Villas, Montgomery Road, Brompton." "I think he might have been polite enough to send us cards also," observed Abigail.

Susan put the cards on the waiter when she went upstairs with her sister's tea. Jessy, looking rather more feverish than usual in a morning, turned the cards about in her slender hands.

"I have heard of her, this Mary Goldbeater," said Jessy, biting her parched lips. "They say she's pretty, and—and very rich."

"Where did you hear of her?" asked Susan.

"Oh, in—let me think. In the work-room."

"Now what do you mean by that?" cried Miss Susan. "A work-room implies a dressmaker's establishment, and you tell us you were a lady's-maid."

Jessy seemed unable to answer.

"I don't believe you were at either the one place or the other. You are deceiving us, Jessy."

"No," gasped Jessy.

"Did you ever see Mr. Marcus Allen when you were in town?"

"Mr. Marcus Allen?" repeated Jessy after a pause, just as if she were unable to recall who Mr. Marcus Allen was.

"The Mr. Marcus Allen you knew at Aberystwith; he who came here afterwards," went on Susan impatiently. "Are you losing your memory, Jessy?"

"No, I never saw the Marcus Allen I knew here—and there," was Jessy's answer, her face white and still as death.

"Why!—Did you know any other Marcus Allen, then?" questioned Susan, in surprise. For the words had seemed to imply it.

"No," replied Jessy. "No."

"She seems queerer than usual—I hope her mind's not going," thought Susan. "Did you ever go to see Madame Caron, Jessy, while you were in London?"

"Never. Why should I? I didn't know Madame Caron."

"When Marcus Allen wrote to excuse himself from visiting us in the summer, he said he would be sure to come later," resumed Susan. "I wonder if he will keep his promise."

"No—never," answered Jessy.

"How do you know?"

"Oh—I don't think it. He wouldn't care to come. Especially now he's married."

"And you never saw him in town, Jessy? Never even met him by chance?"

"I've told you—No. Do you suppose I should be likely to call upon Marcus Allen? As to meeting him by chance, it is not often I went out, I can tell you."

"Well, sit up and take your breakfast," concluded Susan.

A thought had crossed Susan Page's mind—whether this marriage of Marcus Allen's on Christmas-Eve could have had anything to do with Jessy's return and her miserable unhappiness. It was only a thought; and she drove it away again. As Abigail said, she had been inclined throughout to judge hardly of Jessy.

The winter snow lay on the ground still, when it became a question not of how many weeks Jessy would live, but of days. And then she confessed to a secret that pretty nearly changed the sober Miss Pages' hair from black to grey. Jessy had turned Roman Catholic.

It came out through her persistent refusal to see the parson, Mr. Holland, a little man with shaky legs. He'd go trotting up to the Copse Farm once or twice a-week; all in vain. Miss Abigail would console him with a good hot jorum of sweet elder wine, and then he'd trot back again. One day Jessy, brought to bay, confessed that she was a Roman Catholic.

There was grand commotion. John Drench went about, his hands lifted in the frosty air; Abigail and Susan Page sat in the bedroom with (metaphorically speaking) ashes on their heads.

People have their prejudices. It was not so much that these ladies wished to cast reflection on good Catholics born and bred, as that Jessy should have abandoned her own religion, just as though it had been an insufficient faith. It was the slight on it that they could not bear.

"Miserable girl!" exclaimed Miss Susan, looking upon Jessy as a turncoat, and therefore next door to lost. And Jessy told, through her sobs, how it had come to pass.

Wandering about one evening in London when she was very unhappy, she entered a Catholic place of worship styled an "Oratory."—The Miss Pages caught up the word as "oratorio," and never called it anything else.—There a priest got into conversation with Jessy. He had a pleasant, kindly manner that won upon her and drew from her the fact that she was unhappy. Become a Catholic, he said to her; it would bring her back to happiness: and he asked her to go and see him again. She went again; again and again. And so, going and listening to him, she at length did turn, and was received by him into his church.

"Are you the happier for it?" sharply asked Miss Abigail.

"No," answered Jessy with distressed eyes. "Only—only—"

"Only what, pray?"

"Well, they can absolve me from all sin."

"Oh, you poor foolish misguided child!" cried Abigail in anguish; "you must take your sins to the Saviour: He can absolve you, and He alone. Do you want any third person to stand between you and Him?"

Jessy gave a sobbing sigh. "It's best as it is, Abigail. Anyway, it is too late now."

"Stop a bit," cried sharp Miss Susan. "I should like to have one thing answered, Jessy. You have told us how hard you were kept to work: if that was so, pray how did you find leisure to be dancing abroad to Oratorios? Come?"

Jessy could not, or would not, answer.

"Can you explain that!" said Miss Susan, some sarcasm in her tone.

"I went out sometimes in an evening," faltered Jessy. And more than that could not be drawn from her.

They did not tell Mr. Page: it would have distressed him too much. In a day or two Jessy asked to see a priest. Miss Abigail flatly refused, on account of the scandal. As if their minister was not good enough!

One afternoon I was standing by Jessy's bed—for Miss Abigail had let me go up to see her. Mrs. Todhetley, that first day, had said she looked like a lily: she was more like one now. A faded lily that has had all its beauty washed out of it.

"Good-bye, Johnny Ludlow," she said, opening her eyes, and putting out her feeble hand. "I shall not see you again."

"I hope you will, Jessy. I'll come over to-morrow."

"Never again in this world." And I had to lean over to catch the words, and my eyes were full.

"In the next world there'll be no parting, Jessy. We shall see each other there."

"I don't know," she said. "You will be there, Johnny; I can't tell whether I shall be. I turned Roman Catholic, you see; and Abigail won't let a priest come. And so—I don't know how it will be."

The words struck upon me. The Miss Pages had kept the secret too closely for news of it to have come abroad. It seemed worse to me to hear it than to her to say it. But she had grown too weak to feel things strongly.

"Good-bye, Johnny."

"Good-bye, Jessy dear," I whispered. "Don't fear: God will be sure to take you to heaven if you ask Him."

Miss Abigail got it out of me—what she had said about the priest. In fact, I told. She was very cross.

"There; let it drop, Johnny Ludlow. John Drench is gone off in the gig to Coughton to bring one. All I hope and trust is, that they'll not be back until the shades of night have fallen upon the earth! I shouldn't like a priest to be seen coming into this door. Such a reproach on good Mr. Holland! I'm sure I trust it will never get about!"

We all have our prejudices, I repeat. And not a soul amongst us for miles round had found it necessary to change religions since the Reformation.

Evening was well on when John Drench brought him in. A mild-faced man, wearing a skull-cap under his broad-brimmed hat. He saw Jessy alone. Miss Page would not have made a third at the interview though they had bribed her to it—and of course they wouldn't have had her. It was quite late when he came down. Miss Page stopped him as he was going out, after declining refreshment.

"I presume, sir, she has told you all about this past year—that has been so mysterious to us?"

"Yes; I think all," replied the priest.

"Will you tell me the particulars?"

"I cannot do that," he said. "They have been given to me under the seal of confession."

"Only to me and to her sister Susan," pleaded Abigail. "We will not even disclose it to our father. Sir, it would be a true kindness to us, and it can do her no harm. You do not know what our past doubts and distress have been."

But the priest shook his head. He was very sorry to refuse, he said, but the tenets of his Church forbade his speaking. And Miss Page thought he was sorry, for he had a benevolent face.

"Best let the past lie," he gently added. "Suffice it to know that she is happy now, poor child, and will die in peace."

They buried her in the churchyard beside her mother. When the secret got about, some said it was not right—that she ought to have been taken elsewhere, to a graveyard devoted to the other faith. Which would just have put the finishing stroke on old Page—broken all that was left of his heart to break. The Squire said he didn't suppose it mattered in the sight of God: or would make much difference at the Last Day.

And that ended the life of Jessy Page: and, in one sense, its episode of mystery. Nothing more was ever heard or known of where she had been or what she had done. Years have gone by since then; and William Page is lying beside her. Miss Page and Charley live on at the Copse Farm; Susan became Mrs. John Drench ages ago. Her husband, a man of substance now, was driving her into Alcester last Tuesday (market-day) in his four-wheeled chaise, two buxom daughters in the back seat. I nodded to them from Mr. Brandon's window.

The mystery of Jessy Page (as we grew to call it) remained a mystery. It remains one to this day. What the secret was—if there was a secret—why she went in the way she did, and came back in what looked like shame and fear and trembling, a dying girl—has not been solved. It never will be in this world. Some old women put it all down to her having changed her religion and been afraid to tell: while Miss Abigail and Miss Susan have never got rid of a vague doubt, touching Marcus Allen. But it may be only their fancy; they admit that, and say to one another when talking of it privately, that it is not right to judge a man without cause. He keeps a carriage-and-pair now; and gives dinners, and has handsome daughters growing up; and is altogether quite up to the present style of expensive life in London.

And I never go into church on a Christmas morning—whether it may be decorated in our simple country fashion, or in accordance with your new "artistic" achievements—but I think of Jessy Page. Of her sweet face, her simplicity, and her want of guile: and of the poor wreck that came back, broken-hearted, to die.

CHAPTER II

CRABB RAVINE

I

"Yes! Halloa! What is it?"

To be wakened up short by a knocking, or some other noise, in the night, is enough to make you start up in bed, and stare round in confusion. The room was dark, barring the light that always glimmers in at the window on a summer's night, and I listened and waited for more. Nothing came: it was all as silent as the grave.

We were staying at Crabb Cot. I had gone to bed at half-past nine, dead tired after a day's fishing. The Squire and Tod were away: Mrs. Todhetley went over to the Coneys' after tea, and did not seem in a hurry to come back. They fried one of the fish I had caught for my supper; and after that, there being no one to speak to, I went to bed.

It was a knocking that had wakened me out of my sleep: I was sure of that. And it sounded exactly as though it were at the window—which was very improbable. Calling out again to know who was there, and what was wanted—though not very loudly, for the children slept within earshot—and getting no answer, I lay down again, and was all but asleep when the noise came a second time.

It was at the dining-room window, right underneath mine. There could be no mistake about it. The ceilings of the old-fashioned house were low; the windows were very near each other, and mine was down at the top. I thought it time to jump out of bed, and take a look out.

Well, I was surprised! Instead of its being the middle of the night, it must be quite early still; for the lamp was yet alight in the dining-room. It was a cosy kind of room, with a bow window jutting on to the garden, of which the middle compartment opened to the ground, as French windows do. My window was a bow also, and close above the other. Throwing it up, I looked out.

There was not a soul to be seen. Yet the knocking could not have been from within, for the inside shutters were closed: they did not reach to the top panes, and the lamplight shone through them on the mulberry tree. As I leaned out, wondering, the crazy old clock at North Crabb Church began to tell the hour. I counted the strokes, one by one—ten of them. Only ten o'clock! And I thought I had been asleep half the night.

All in a moment I caught sight of some one moving slowly away. He was keeping in the shade; close to the shrubs that encircled the lawn, as if not caring to be seen. A short, thin man, in dark clothes and round black felt hat. Who he was, and what he wanted, was more than I could imagine. It could not be a robber. Robbers don't come knocking at houses before people have gone to bed.

The small side-gate opened, and Mrs. Todhetley came in. Old Coney's farm was only a stone's-throw off, and she had run home alone. We people in the country think nothing of being abroad alone at night. The man emerged from the shade, and placed himself right in her path, on the gravel walk. They stood there together. I could see him better now: there was no moon, but the night was light; and it flashed into my mind that he was the same man I had seen Mrs. Todhetley with in the morning, as I went across the fields, with my rod and line. She was at the stile, about to descend into the Ravine, when he came up from it, and accosted her. He was a stranger; wearing a seedy, shabby black coat; and I had wondered what he wanted. They were still talking together when I got out of sight, for I turned to look.

Not long did they stand now. The gentleman went away; she came hastening on with her head down, a soft wool kerchief thrown over her cap. In all North Crabb, no one was so fearful of catching face-ache as Mrs. Todhetley.

"Who was it?" I called out, when she was under the window: which seemed to startle her considerably, for she gave a spring back, right on to the grass.

"Johnny! how you frightened me! What are you looking out at?"

"At that fellow who has just taken himself off. Who is he?"

"I do believe you have on nothing but your nightshirt! You'll be sure to take cold. Shut the window down, and get into bed."

Four times over, in all, had I to ask about the man before I got an answer. Now it was the nightshirt, now catching cold, now the open window and the damp air. She always wanted to be as tender with us as though we were chickens.

"The man that met me in the path?" she got to, at length. "He made some excuse for being here: was not sure whose house it was, I think he said: had turned in by mistake to the wrong one."

"That's all very fine; but, not being sure, he ought to mind his manners. He came rapping at the dining-room window like anything, and it woke me up. Had you been at home, sitting there, good mother, you might have been startled out of your seven senses."

"So I should, Johnny. The Coneys would not let me come away: they had friends with them. Good-night, dear. Shut down that window."

She went on to the side-door. I put down the window, opened it at the top, and let the white curtain drop before it. It was an hour or two before I got to sleep again, and I had the man and the knocking in my thoughts all the time.

"Don't say anything about it in the house, Johnny," Mrs. Todhetley said to me, in the morning. "It might alarm the children." So I promised her I would not.

Tod came home at mid-day, not the Squire: and the first thing I did was to tell him. I wouldn't have broken faith with the mother for the world; not even for Tod; but it never entered my mind that she wished me to keep it a close secret, excepting from those, servants or others, who might be likely to repeat it before Hugh and Lena. I cautioned Tod.

"Confound his impudence!" cried Tod. "Could he not be satisfied with disturbing the house at the door at night, but he must make for the window? I wish I had been at home."

Crabb Ravine lay to the side of our house, beyond the wide field. It was a regular wilderness. The sharp descent began in that three-cornered grove, of which you've heard before, for it was where Daniel Ferrar hanged himself; and the wild, deep, mossy dell, about as wide as an ordinary road, went running along below, soft, green and damp. Towering banks, sloping backwards, rose on either side; a mass of verdure in summer; of briars, brown and tangled, in winter. Dwarf shrubs, tall trees, blackberry and nut bushes, sweet-briar and broom clustered there in wild profusion. Primroses and violets peeped up when spring came in; blue bells and cowslips, dog-roses, woodbine, and other sweet flowers, came later. Few people would descend except by the stile opposite our house and the proper zigzag path leading down the side bank, for a fall might have broken limbs, besides bringing one's clothes to grief. No houses stood near it, except ours and old Coney's; and the field bordering it just here on this side belonged to Squire Todhetley. If you went down the zigzag path, turned to the right, walked along the Ravine some way, and then up another zigzag on the opposite side, you soon came to Timberdale, a small place in itself, but our nearest post-town. The high-road to Timberdale, winding past our house from South Crabb, was twice the distance, so that people might sometimes be seen in the Ravine by day; but no one cared to go near it in the evening, as it had the reputation of being haunted. A mysterious light might sometimes be observed there at night, dodging about the banks, where it would be rather difficult for ordinary human beings to walk: some said it was a will-o'-the-wisp, and some said a ghost. It was difficult to get even a farm-servant to go the near way to Timberdale after dark.

One morning, when I was running through the Ravine with Tod in search of Tom Coney, we came slap against a man, who seemed to be sneaking there, for he turned short off, into the underwood, to hide himself. I knew him by his hat.

"Tod, that's the man," I whispered.

"What man, Johnny?"

"The one who came knocking at the window three nights ago."

"Oh!" said Tod, carelessly. "He looks like a fellow who comes out with begging petitions."

It might have been an hour after that. We had come up from the Ravine, on our side of it, not having seen or spoken to a soul, except Luke Mackintosh. Tod told me to stay and waylay Coney if he made his appearance, whilst he went again to the farm in search of him. Accordingly, I was sitting on the fence (put there to hinder the cattle and sheep from getting over the brink of the Ravine), throwing stones and whistling, when I saw Mrs. Todhetley cross the stile to go down the zigzag. She did not see me: the fence could hardly be gained for trees, and I was hidden.

Just because I had nothing to do, I watched her as she went; tall, thin, and light in figure, she could spin along nearly as quick as we. The zigzag path went in and out, sloping along the bank until it brought itself to the dell at a spot a good bit beyond me as I looked down, finishing there with a high, rough step. Mrs. Todhetley took it with a spring.

What next! In one moment the man with the black coat and hat had appeared from somewhere, and placed himself in front of her parasol. Before I could quit the place, and leap down after her, a conviction came over me that the meeting was not accidental: and I rubbed my eyes in wonder, and thought I must be dreaming.

The summer air was clear as crystal; not a bee's hum just then disturbed its stillness. Detached words ascended from where they stood; and now and again a whole sentence. She kept looking each way as if afraid to be seen; and so did he, for that matter. The colloquy seemed to be about money. I caught the word two or three times; and Mrs. Todhetley said it was "impossible." "I must, and I will have it," came up distinctly from him in answer.

"What's that, Johnny?"

The interruption came from Tod. All my attention absorbed in them, he stood at my elbow before I knew he was near. When I would have answered, he suddenly put his hand upon my mouth for silence. His face had a proud anger on it as he looked down.

Mrs. Todhetley seemed to be using entreaty to the man, for she clasped her hands in a piteous manner, and then turned to ascend the zigzag. He followed her, talking very fast. As to me, I was in a regular sea of marvel, understanding nothing. Our heads were hardly to be distinguished from the bushes, even if she had looked up.

"No," she said, turning round upon him; and they were near us then, half way up the path, so that every word was audible. "You must not venture to come to the house, or near the house. I would not have Mr. Todhetley know of this for the world: for your sake as well as for his."

"Todhetley's not at home," was the man's answer: and Tod gave a growl as he heard it.

"If he is not, his son is," said Mrs. Todhetley. "It would be all the same; or worse."

"His son's here," roared out passionate Tod. "What the deuce is the meaning of this, sir?"

The man shot down the path like an arrow. Mrs. Todhetley—who had been walking on, seeming not to have caught the words, or to know whose the voice was, or where it came from—gazed round in all directions, her countenance curiously helpless. She ran up the rest of the zigzag, and went swiftly home across the field. Tod disentangled himself from the brambles, and drew a long breath.

"I think it's time we went now, Johnny." It was not often he spoke in that tone. He had always been at war tacitly with Mrs. Todhetley, and was not likely to favour her now. Generous though he was by nature, there could be no denying that he took up awful prejudices.

"It is something about money, Tod."

"I don't care what it is about—the fellow has no business to be prowling here, on my father's grounds; and he shan't be, without my knowing what it's for. I'll watch madam's movements."

"What do you think it can mean?"

"Mean! Why, that the individual is some poor relation of hers, come to drain as much of my father's money out of her as he can. She is the one to blame. I wonder how she dare encourage him!"

"Perhaps she can't help herself."

"Not help herself? Don't show yourself a fool, Johnny. An honest-minded, straightforward woman would appeal to my father in any annoyance of this sort, or to me, in his absence, and say 'Here's So-and-so come down upon us, asking for help, can we give it him?'—and there's no doubt the Squire would give it him; he's soft enough for anything."

It was of no use contending. I did not see it quite in that light, but Tod liked his own opinion. He threw up his head with a haughty jerk.

"You have tried to defend Mrs. Todhetley before, in trifling matters, Johnny; don't attempt it now. Would any good woman, say any lady, if you will, subject herself to this kind of thing?—hold private meetings with a man—allow him to come tapping at her sitting-room window at night? No; not though he were her own brother."

"Tod, it may be her brother. She would never do anything wrong willingly."

"Shut up, Johnny. She never had a brother."

Of course I shut up forthwith, and went across the field by Tod's side in silence, his strides wide and indignant, his head up in the air. Mrs. Todhetley was hearing Lena read when we got in, and looked as if she had never been out that morning.

Some days went on. The man remained near, for he was seen occasionally, and the servants began to talk. One remarked upon him, wondering who he was; another remarked upon him, speculating on what he did there. In a quiet country place, a dodging stranger excites curiosity, and this one dodged about as much as ever the ghostly light did. If you caught sight of him in the three-cornered plantation, he vanished forthwith to appear next in the Ravine; if he stood peering out from the trees on the bank, and found himself observed, the next minute he'd be crouching amongst the broom on the other side.

This came to be observed, and was thought strange, naturally; Hannah, who was often out with Hugh and Lena, often saw him, and talked to the other servants. One evening, when we were finishing dinner, the glass doors of the bow-window being open, Hannah came back with the children. They ran across the grass-plat after the fawn—one we had, just then—and Hannah sat down in the porch of the side-door to wait. Old Thomas had just drawn the slips from the table, and went through the passage to the side-door to shake them.

"I say," cried Hannah's voice, "I saw that man again."

"Where?" asked Thomas, between his shakes of the linen.

"In the old place—the Ravine. He was sitting on the stile at the top of the zigzag, as cool as might be."

"Did you speak to him? I should, if I came across the man; and ask what his business might be in these parts."

"I didn't speak to him," returned Hannah. "I'd rather not. There's no knowing the answer one might get, Thomas, or what he's looking after. He spoke to the children."

"What did he say to them?"

"Asked if they'd go away with him to some beautiful coral islands over the sea, and catch pretty birds, and parrots, and monkeys. He called them by their names, too—'Hugh' and 'Lena.' I should like to know how he got hold of them."

"I can't help thinking that he belongs to them engineering folk who come spying for no good on people's land: the Squire won't like it if they cut a railroad through here," said Thomas; and the supposition did not appear to please Hannah.

"Why you must be as silly as a turkey, old Thomas! Engineers have no need to hide themselves as if they were afraid of being took up for murder. He has about as much the cut of an engineer as you have, and no more: they don't go about looking like Methodist parsons run to seed. My opinion is that he's something of that sort."

"A Methodist parson!"

"No; not anything half so respectable. If I spoke out my thoughts, though, I dare say you'd laugh at me."

"Not I," said Thomas. "Make haste. I forgot to put the claret jug on the table."

"Then I've got it in my head that he is one of them seducing Mormons. They appear in neighbourhoods without the smallest warning, lie partly concealed by day, and go abroad at night, persuading all the likely women and girls to join their sect. My sister told me about it in a letter she wrote me only three days ago. There has been a Mormon down there; he called himself a saint, she says; and when he went finally away he took fifteen young women with him. Fifteen, Thomas! and after only three weeks' persuasion! It's as true as that you've got that damask cloth in your hand."

Nothing further was heard for a minute. Then Thomas spoke. "Has the man here been seen talking with young women?"

"Who is to know? They take care not to be seen; that's their craft. And so you see, Thomas, I'd rather steer clear of the man, and not give him the opportunity of trying his arts on me. I can tell him it's not Hannah Baber that would be cajoled off to a barbarous desert by a man who had fifteen other wives beside! Lord help the women for geese! Miss Lena" (raising her voice), "don't you tear about after the fawn like that; you'll put yourself into a pretty heat."

"I'd look him up when I came home, if I were the Squire," said Thomas, who evidently took it all gravely in. "We don't want a Mormon on the place."

"If he were not a Mormon, which I'm pretty sure he is, I should say he was a kidnapper of children," went on Hannah. "After we had got past him over so far, he managed to 'tice Hugh back to the stile, gave him a sugar-stick, and said he'd take him away if he'd go. It struck me he'd like to kidnap him."

Tod, sitting at the foot of the table in the Squire's place, had listened to all this deliberately. Mrs. Todhetley, opposite to him, her back to the light, had tried, in a feeble manner, once or twice, to drown the sounds by saying something. But when urgently wanting to speak, we often can't do so; and her efforts died away helplessly. She looked miserably uncomfortable, and seemed conscious of Tod's feeling in the matter; and when Hannah wound up with the bold assertion touching the kidnapping of Hugh, she gave a start of alarm, which left her face white.

"Who is this man that shows himself in the neighbourhood?" asked Tod, putting the question to her in a slow, marked manner, his dark eyes, stern then, fixed on hers.

"Johnny, those cherries don't look ripe. Try the summer apples."

It was of no use at any time trying to put aside Tod. Before I had answered her that the cherries were ripe enough for me, Tod began at her again.

"Can you tell me who he is?"

"Dear me, no," she faintly said. "I can't tell you anything about it."

"Nor what he wants?"

"No. Won't you take some wine, Joseph?"

"I shall make it my business to inquire, then," said Tod, disregarding the wine and everything else. "The first time I come across the man, unless he gives me a perfectly satisfactory answer as to what he may be doing here on our land, I'll horse-whip him."

Mrs. Todhetley put the trembling fingers of her left hand into the finger-glass, and dried them. I don't believe she knew what she was about more than a baby.

"The man is nothing to you, Joseph. Why should you interfere with him?"

"I shall interfere because my father is not here to do it," he answered, in his least compromising of tones. "An ill-looking stranger has no right to be prowling mysteriously amongst us at all. But when it comes to knocking at windows at night, to waylaying—people—in solitary places, and to exciting comments from the servants, it is time some one interfered to know the reason of it."

I am sure he had been going to say you; but with all his prejudice he never was insolent to Mrs. Todhetley, when face to face; and he substituted "people." Her pale blue eyes had the saddest light in them you can well conceive, and yet she tried to look as though the matter did not concern her. Old

Thomas came in with the folded damask slips, little thinking he and Hannah had been overheard, put them in the drawer, and set things straight on the sideboard.

"What time tea, ma'am?" he asked.

"Any time," answered Mrs. Todhetley. "I am going over to Mr. Coney's, but not to stay. Or perhaps you'll go for me presently, Johnny, and ask whether Mrs. Coney has come home," she added, as Thomas left the room.

I said I'd go. And it struck me that she must want Mrs. Coney very particularly, for this would make the fifth time I had gone on the same errand within a week. On the morning following that rapping at the window, Mrs. Coney had news that Mrs. West, her married daughter, was ill, and she started at once by the rail to Worcester to visit her.

"I think I'll go and look for the fellow now," exclaimed Tod, rising from his seat and making for the window. But Mrs. Todhetley rose too, as one in mortal fright, and put herself in his way.

"Joseph," she said, "I have no authority over you; you know that I have never attempted to exercise any since I came home to your father's house; but I must ask you to respect my wishes now."

"What wishes?"

"That you will refrain from seeking this stranger: that you will not speak to or accost him in any way, should you and he by chance meet. I have good reasons for asking it." Tod stood stock-still, neither saying Yes nor No; only biting his lips in the anger he strove to keep down.

"Oh, very well," said he, going back to his seat. "Of course, as you put it in this light, I have no alternative. A night's delay cannot make much difference, and my father will be home to-morrow to act for himself."

"You must not mention it to your father, Joseph. You must keep it from him."

"I shall tell him as soon as he comes home."

"Tell him what? What is it that you suspect? What would you tell him?"

Tod hesitated. He had spoken in random heat; and found, on consideration, he was without a case. He could not complain to his father of her: in spite of his hasty temper, he was honourable as the day. Her apparent intimacy with the man would also tie his tongue as to him, whomsoever he might be.

"You must be quite aware that it is not a pleasant thing, or a proper thing, to have this mysterious individual encouraged here," he said, looking at her.

"And you think I encourage him, Joseph?"

"Well, it seems that you—that you must know who he is. I saw you talking with him one day in the Ravine," continued Tod, disdaining not to be perfectly open, now it had come to an explanation. "Johnny was with me. If he is a relative of yours, why, of course—"

"He is no relative of mine, Joseph." And Tod opened his eyes wide to hear the denial. It was the view he had taken all along.

"Then why do you suffer him to annoy you?—and I am sure he does do it. Let me deal with him. I'll soon ascertain what his business may be."

"But that is just what you must not do," she said, seeming to speak out the truth in very helplessness, like a frightened child. "You must leave him in my hands, Joseph: I shall be able, I dare say, to—to—get rid of him shortly."

"You know what he wants?"

"Yes, I am afraid I do. It is quite my affair; and you must take no more notice of it: above all, you must not say anything to your father."

How much Tod was condemning her in his heart perhaps he would not have cared to tell; but he could but be generous, even to his step-mother.

"I suppose I must understand that you are in some sort of trouble?"

"Indeed I am."

"If it is anything in which I can help you, you have only to ask me to do it," he said. But his manner was lofty as he spoke, his voice had a hard ring in it.

"Thank you very much, Joseph," was the meek, grateful answer. "If you will only take no further notice, and say nothing to your father when he comes home, it will be helping me sufficiently."

Tod strolled out; just as angry as he could be; and I ran over to the farm. Jane Coney had received a letter from her mother by the afternoon post, saying she might not be home for some days to come.

"Tell Mrs. Todhetley that I am sorry to have to send her bad news over and over again," said Jane Coney, who was sitting in the best kitchen, with her muslin sleeves turned up, and a big apron on, stripping fruit for jam. The Coneys had brought up their girls sensibly, not to be ashamed to make themselves thoroughly useful, in spite of their education, and the fair fortune they would have. Mary was married; Jane engaged to be. I sat on the table by her, eating away at the fruit.

"What is it Mrs. Todhetley wants with my mother, Johnny?"

"As if I knew!"

"I think it must be something urgent. When she came in, that morning, only five minutes after mamma had driven off, she was so terribly disappointed, saying she would give a great deal to have spoken to her first. My sister is not quite so well again; that's why mamma is staying longer."

"I'll tell her, Jane."

"By the way, Johnny, what's this they are saying—about some strange man being seen here? A special constable, peeping after bad characters?"

"A special constable?"

Jane Coney laughed. "Or a police-officer in disguise. It is what one of our maids told me."

"Oh," I answered, carelessly, for somehow I did not like the words; "you must mean a man that is looking at the land; an engineer."

"Is that all?" cried Jane Coney. "How foolish people are!"

It was a sort of untruth, no doubt; but I should have told a worse in the necessity. I did not like the aspect of things; and they puzzled my brain unpleasantly all the way home.

Mrs. Todhetley was at work by the window when I got there. Tod had not made his re-appearance; Hugh and Lena were in bed. She dropped her work when I gave the message.

"Not for some days to come yet! Oh, Johnny!"

"But what do you want with her?"

"Well, I do want her. I want a friend just now, Johnny, that's the truth; and I think Mrs. Coney would be one."

"Joe asked if he could help you; and you said 'No.' Can I?"

"Johnny, if you could, there's no one in the world I'd rather ask. But you cannot."

"Why?"

"Because"—she smiled for a moment—"you are not old enough. If you were—of age, say—why then I would."

I had hold of the window-frame, looking at her, and an idea struck me. "Do you mean that I should be able then to command money?"

"Yes, that's it, Johnny."

"But, perhaps—if I were to write to Mr. Brandon—"

"Hush!" she exclaimed in a sort of fright. "You must not talk of this, Johnny; you don't know the sad mischief you might do. Oh, if I can only keep it from you all! Here comes Joseph," she added in a whisper; and gathering up her work, went out of the room.

"Did I not make a sign to you to come after me?" began Tod, in one of his tempers.

"But I had to go over to the Coneys'. I've only just got back again."

He looked into the room and saw that it was empty. "Where's madam gone? To the Ravine after her friend?"

"She was here sewing not a minute ago."

"Johnny, she told a lie. Did you notice the sound of her voice when she said the fellow was no relative of hers?"

"Not particularly."

"I did, then. At the moment the denial took me by surprise; but I remembered the tone later. It had an untrue ring in it. Madam told a lie, Johnny, as sure as that we are here. I'd lay my life he is a relative of hers, or a connection in some way. I don't think now it is money he wants; if it were only that, she'd get it, and send him packing. It's worse than that: disgrace, perhaps."

"What sort of disgrace can it be?"

"I don't know. But if something of the sort is not looming, never trust me again. And here am I, with my hands tied, forbidden to unravel it. Johnny, I feel just like a wild beast barred up in a cage."

Had he been a real wild beast he could not have given the window-frame a much worse shake, as he passed through in his anger to the bench under the mulberry-tree.

When you have to look far back to things, recollection sometimes gets puzzled as to the order in which they happened. How it came about I am by no means clear, but an uncomfortable feeling grew up in my mind about Hugh. About both the children, in fact, but Hugh more than Lena. Mrs. Todhetley seemed to dread Hugh's being abroad—and I'm sure I was not mistaken in thinking it. I heard her order Hannah to keep the children within view of the house, and not to allow Hugh to stray away from her. Had it been winter weather I suppose she'd have kept them indoors altogether; there could be no plea for it under the blue sky and the hot summer sun.

The Squire came home; he had been staying some time with friends in Gloucestershire; but Mrs. Coney did not come—although Mrs. Todhetley kept sending me for news. Twice I saw her talking to the strange man; who I believed made his abode in the Ravine. Tod watched, as he had threatened to do; and would often appear with in-drawn lips. There was active warfare between him and his step-mother: at least if you can say that when both kept silence. As to the Squire, he observed nothing, and knew nothing: and no one enlightened him. It seems a long time, I dare say, when reading of this, as if it had extended over a month of Sundays; but I don't think it lasted much more than a fortnight in all.

One evening, quite late, when the sun was setting, and the Squire was smoking his pipe on the lawn, talking to me and Tod, Lena and her mother came in at the gate. In spite of the red rays lighting up Mrs. Todhetley's face, it struck me that I had never seen it look more careworn. Lena put her arms on Tod's knee, and began telling about a fright she had had: of a big toad that leaped out of the grass, and made her scream and cry. She cried "because nobody was with her."

"Where was mamma?" asked Tod; but I am sure he spoke without any ulterior thought.

"Mamma had gone to the zigzag stile to talk to the man. She told me to wait for her."

"What man?" cried the Squire.

"Why, the man," said Lena logically. "He asks Hugh to go with him over the sea to see the birds and the red coral."

If any one face ever turned whiter than another, Mrs. Todhetley's did then. Tod looked at her, sternly, ungenerously; and her eyes fell. She laid hold of Lena's hand, saying it was bed-time.

"What man is the child talking about?" the Squire asked her.

"She talks about so many people," rather faintly answered Mrs. Todhetley. "Come, Lena dear; Hannah's waiting for you. Say good-night."

The Squire, quite unsuspicious, thought no more. He got up and walked over to the beds to look at the flowers, holding his long churchwarden pipe in his mouth. Tod put his back against the tree.

"It is getting complicated, Johnny."

"What is?"

"What is! Why, madam's drama. She is afraid of that hinted scheme of her friend's—the carrying-off Master Hugh beyond the seas."

He spoke in satire. "Do you think so?" I returned.

"Upon my honour I do. She must be an idiot! I should like to give her a good fright."

"Tod, I think she is frightened enough without our giving her one."

"I think she is. She must have caught up the idea from overhearing Hannah's gossip with old Thomas. This afternoon Hugh was running through the little gate with me; madam came flying over the lawn and begged me not let him out of my hand, or else to leave him indoors. But for being my father's wife, I should have asked her if her common-sense had gone wool-gathering."

"I suppose it has, Tod. Fancy a kidnapper in these days! The curious thing is, that she should fear anything of the sort."

"If she really does fear it. I tell you, Johnny, the performance is growing complicated; somewhat puzzling. But I'll see it played out if I live."

The week went on to Friday. But the afternoon was over, and evening set in, before the shock fell upon us: Hugh was missing.

The Squire had been out in the gig, taking me; and it seems they had supposed at home that Hugh was with us. The particulars of Hugh's disappearance, and what had happened in the day, I will relate further on.

The Squire thought nothing: he said Hugh must have got into Coney's house or some other neighbour's house: and sat down to dinner, wondering why so much to-do was made. Mrs. Todhetley looked scared to death; and Tod tore about as if he were wild. The servants were sent here, the outdoor men there: it was like a second edition of that day in Warwickshire when we lost Lena: like it, only worse, more commotion. Hannah boldly said to her mistress that the strange man must have carried off the boy.

Hour after hour the search continued. With no result. Night came on, with a bright moon to light it up. But it did not light up Hugh.

Mrs. Todhetley, a dark shawl over her head, and I dare say a darker fear upon her heart, went out for the second or third time towards the Ravine. I ran after her. We had nearly reached the stile at the zigzag, when Tod came bounding over it.

"Has not the time for shielding this man gone by, think you?" he asked, placing himself in Mrs. Todhetley's path, and speaking as coolly as he was able for the agitation that shook him. And why Tod, with his known carelessness, should be so moved, I could not fathom.

"Joseph, I do not suppose or think the man knows anything of Hugh; I have my reasons for it," she answered, bearing on for the stile, and leaning over it to look down into the dark Ravine.

"Will you give me permission to inquire that of himself?"

"You will not find the man. He is gone."

"Leave the finding him to me," persisted Tod. "Will you withdraw the embargo you laid upon me?"

"No, no," she whispered, "I cannot do it."

The trees had an uncommonly damp feel in the night-air, and the place altogether looked as weird as could be. I was away then in the underwood; she looked down always into the Ravine and called Hugh's name aloud. Nothing but an echo answered.

"It has appeared to me for several days that you have feared something of this," Tod said, trying to get a full view of her face. "It might have been better for—for all of us—if you had allowed me at first to take the affair in hand."

"Perhaps I ought; perhaps I ought," she said, bursting into tears. "Heaven knows, though, that I acted from a good motive. It was not to screen myself that I've tried to keep the matter secret."

"Oh!" The sarcasm of Tod's short comment was like nothing I ever heard. "To screen me, perhaps?" said he.

"Well, yes—in a measure, Joseph," she patiently answered. "I only wished to spare you vexation. Oh, Joseph! if—if Hugh cannot be found, and—and all has to come out—who he is and what he wants here—remember that I wished nothing but to spare others pain."

Tod's eyes were blazing with angry, haughty light. Spare him! He thought she was miserably equivocating; he had some such idea as that she sought (in words) to make him a scape-goat for her relative's sins. What he answered I hardly know; except that he civilly dared her to speak.

"Do not spare me: I particularly request you will not," he scornfully retorted. "Yourself as much as you will, but not me."

"I have done it for the best," she pleaded. "Joseph, I have done it all for the best."

"Where is this man to be found? I have been looking for him these several hours past, as I should think no man was ever looked for yet."

"I have said that I think he is not to be found. I think he is gone."

"Gone!" shouted Tod. "Gone!"

"I think he must be. I—I saw him just before dinner-time, here at this very stile; I gave him something that I had to give, and I think he left at once, to make the best of his way from the place."

"And Hugh?" asked Tod savagely.

"I did not know then that Hugh was missing. Oh, Joseph, I can't tell what to think. When I said to him one day that he ought not to talk nonsense to the children about corals and animals—in fact, should not speak to them at all—he answered that if I did not get him the money he wanted he'd take the boy off with him. I knew it was a jest; but I could not help thinking of it when the days went on and on, and I had no money to give him."

"Of course he has taken the boy," said Tod, stamping his foot. And the words sent Mrs. Todhetley into a tremor.

"Joseph! Do you think so?"

"Heaven help you, Mrs. Todhetley, for a—a simple woman! We may never see Hugh again."

He caught up the word he had been going to say—fool. Mrs. Todhetley clasped her hands together piteously, and the shawl slipped from her shoulders.

"I think, madam, you must tell what you can," he resumed, scarcely knowing which to bring uppermost, his anxiety for Hugh or his lofty, scornful anger. "Is the man a relative of yours?"

"No, not of mine. Oh, Joseph, please don't be angry with me! Not of mine, but of yours."

"Of mine!" cried proud Tod. "Thank you, Mrs. Todhetley."

"His name is Arne," she whispered.

"What!" shouted Tod.

"Joseph, indeed it is. Alfred Arne."

Had Tod been shot by a cannon-ball, he could hardly have been more completely struck into himself; doubled up, so to say. His mother had been an Arne; and he well remembered to have heard of an ill-doing mauvais sujet of a half-brother of hers, called Alfred, who brought nothing but trouble and disgrace on all connected with him. There ensued a silence, interrupted only by Mrs. Todhetley's tears. Tod was looking white in the moonlight.

"So it seems it is my affair!" he suddenly said; but though he drew up his head, all his fierce spirit seemed to have gone out of him. "You can have no objection to speak fully now."

And Mrs. Todhetley, partly because of her unresisting nature, partly in her fear for Hugh, obeyed him.

"I had seen Mr. Arne once before," she began. "It was the year that I first went home to Dyke Manor. He made his appearance there, not openly, but just as he has made it here now. His object was to get money from the Squire to go abroad with. And at length he did get it. But it put your father very much out; made him ill, in fact; and I believe he took a sort of vow, in his haste and vexation, to give Alfred Arne into custody if he ever came within reach of him again. I think—I fear—he always has something or other hanging over his head worse than debt; and for that reason can never show himself by daylight without danger."

"Go on," said Tod, quite calmly.

"One morning recently I suddenly met him. He stepped right into my path, here at this same spot, as I was about to descend the Ravine, and asked if I knew him again. I was afraid I did. I was afraid he had come on the same errand as before: and oh, Joseph, how thankful I felt that you and your father were away! He told me a long and pitiful tale, and I thought I ought to try and help him to the money he needed. He was impatient for it, and the same evening, supposing no one was at home but myself, he came to the dining-room window, wishing to ask if I had already procured the money. Johnny heard him knock."

"It might have been better that we had been here," repeated Tod. "Better that we should have dealt with him than you."

"Your father was so thankful that you were at school before, Joseph; so thankful! He said he would not have you know anything about Alfred Arne for the world. And so—I tried to keep it this time from both you and him, and, but for this fear about Hugh, I should have done it."

Tod did not answer. He looked at her keenly in the twilight of the summer's night, apparently waiting for more. She continued her explanation; not enlarging upon things, suffering, rather, inferences to be drawn. The following was its substance:—

Alfred Arne asked for fifty pounds. He had returned to England only a few months before, had got into some fresh danger, and had to leave it again, and to hide himself until he did so. The fifty pounds—to get him off, he said, and start him afresh in the colonies—he demanded not as a gift, but a matter of right: the Todhetleys, being his near relatives, must help him. Mrs. Todhetley knew but of one person she could borrow it from privately—Mrs. Coney—and she had gone from home just as she was about to be asked for it. Only this afternoon had Mrs. Todhetley received the money from her and paid it to Alfred Arne.

"I would not have told you this, but for being obliged, Joseph," she pleaded meekly, when the brief explanation was ended. "We can still keep it from your father; better, perhaps, that you should know it than he: you are young and he is not."

"A great deal better," assented Tod. "You have made yourself responsible to Mrs. Coney for the fifty pounds?"

"Don't think of that, Joseph. She is in no hurry for repayment, and will get it from me by degrees. I have a little trifle of my own, you know, that I get half-yearly, and I can economize in my dress. I did so hope to keep it from you as well as from your father."

I wondered if Tod saw all the patient, generous, self-sacrificing spirit. I wondered if he was growing to think that he had been always on the wrong tack in judging harshly of his stepmother. She turned away, thinking perhaps that time was being lost. I said something about Hugh.

"Hugh is all right, Johnny; he'll be found now," Tod answered in a dreamy tone, as he looked after her with a dreamy look. The next moment he strode forward, and was up with Mrs. Todhetley.

"I beg your pardon for the past, mother; I beg it with shame and contrition. Can you forgive me?"

"Oh, pray don't, dear Joseph! I have nothing to forgive," she answered, bursting into fresh tears as she took his offered hand. And that was the first time in all his life that Tod, prejudiced Tod, had allowed himself to call her "mother."

II

I never saw anything plainer in my life. It was not just opposite to where I stood, but lower down towards the end of the Ravine. Amongst the dark thick underwood of the rising bank it dodged about, just as if some one who was walking carried it in his hand lifted up in front of him. A round white light, exactly as the ghost's light was described to be. One might have fancied it the light of a wax-candle, only that a candle would flicker itself dim and bright by turns in the air, and this was steady and did not.

If a ghost was carrying it, he must have been pacing backwards and forwards; for the light confined itself to the range of a few yards. Beginning at the environs of the black old yew-tree, it would come on amidst the broom and shrubs to the group of alders, and then go back again Timberdale way, sometimes lost to sight for a minute, as if hidden behind a thicker mass of underwood, and then gleaming out afresh further on in its path. Now up, now down; backwards and forwards; here, there, everywhere; it was about as unaccountable a sight as any veritable ghost ever displayed, or I, Johnny Ludlow, had chanced to come upon.

The early part of the night had been bright. It was the same night, spoken of in the last chapter, when Hugh was being searched for. Up to eleven o'clock the moon had shone radiantly. Since then a curious sort of darkness had come creeping along the heavens, and now, close upon twelve, it overshadowed the earth like a pall. A dark, black canopy, which the slight wind, getting up, never stirred, though it sighed and moaned with a weird unpleasant sound down the Ravine. I did not mind the light myself; don't think I should much have minded the ghost: but Luke Mackintosh, standing by me, did. Considering that he was a good five-and-twenty years of age, and had led an out-of-door life, it may sound queer to say it, but he seemed timid as a hare.

"I don't like it, Master Johnny," he whispered, as he grasped the fence with an unsteady hand, and followed the light with his eyes. What with the trees around us, and the pall overhead, it was dark enough, but I could see his face, and knew it had turned white.

"I believe you are afraid, Luke!"

"Well, sir, so might you be if you knowed as much of that there light as I do. It never comes but it bodes trouble."

"Who brings the light?"

"It's more than I can say, sir. They call it here the ghost's light. And folks say, Master Johnny, that when it's seen, there's sure to be some trouble in the air."

"I think we have trouble enough just now without the light, Luke; and our trouble was with us before we saw that."

The Ravine lay beneath us, stretching out on either hand, weird, lonesome, dreary, the bottom hidden in gloom. The towering banks, whether we looked down the one we leaned over, or to the other opposite, presented nothing to the eye but darkness: we knew the masses of trees, bushes, underwood were there, but could not see them: and the spot favoured by the restless light was too wild and steep to be safe for the foot of man. Of course it was a curious speculation what it could be.

"Did you ever see the light before, Mackintosh?"

"Yes," he answered, "half-a-dozen times. Do you mind, Master Johnny, my getting that there bad cut in the leg with my reaping-hook awhile agone? Seven weeks I lay in Worcester Infirmary: they carried me there on a mattress shoved down in the cart."

"I remember hearing of it. We were at Dyke Manor."

Before Luke went on, he turned his face to me and dropped his voice to a deeper whisper.

"Master Ludlow, as true as us two be a-standing here, I saw the ghost's light the very night afore I got the hurt. I was working for Mr. Coney then, it was before I came into the Squire's service. Young Master Tom, he came out of the kitchen with a letter when we was at our seven-o'clock supper, and said I were to cut off to Timberdale with it and to look sharp, or the letter-box 'ud be shut. So I had to do it, sir, and I came through this here Ravine, a-whistling and a-holding my head down, though I'd rather ha' went ten mile round. When I got out of it on t'other side, on top of the zigzag, I chanced to look back over the stile, and there I see the light. It were opposite then, on this side, sir, and moving about in the same see-saw way it be now, for I stood and watched it."

"I wonder you plucked up the courage to stand and watch it, Luke?"

"I were took aback, sir, all in a maze like: and then I started off full pelt, as quick as my heels 'ud carry me. That was the very blessed night afore I got the hurt. When the doctors was a-talking round me at the infirmary, and I think they was arguing whether or not my leg must come off, I told 'em that I was afeared it wouldn't much matter neither way, for I'd seen the ghost's light the past night and knowed my fate. One of them, a young man he was, burst out laughing above my face as I lay, and t'other next him, a grave gentleman with white hair, turned round and hushed at him. Master Ludlow, it's all gospel true."

"But you got well, Luke."

"But I didn't think to," argued Luke. "And I see the light."

As he turned his face again, the old church clock at Timberdale struck twelve. It seemed to come booming over the Ravine with quite a warning sound, and Luke gave himself a shake. As for me, I could only wish one thing—that Hugh was found.

Tod came up the zigzag path, a lantern in his hand; I whistled to let him know I was near. He had been to look in the unused little shed-place nearly at the other end of the Ravine; not for Hugh, but for the man, Alfred Arne. Tod came up to us, and his face, as the lantern flashed upon it, was whiter and graver than that of Luke Mackintosh.

"Did you see that, sir?" asked Luke.

"See what?" cried Tod, turning sharply. He thought it might be some trace of Hugh.

"That there ghost light, sir. It's showing itself to-night."

Angry, perplexed, nearly out of his mind with remorse and fear, Tod gave Luke a word of a sort, ordering him to be silent for an idiot, and put the lantern down. He then saw the moving light, and let his eyes rest on it in momentary curiosity.

"It's the ghost light, sir," repeated Luke, for the man seemed as if he and all other interests were lost in that.

"The deuce take the ghost's light, and you with it," said Tod passionately. "Is this a time to be staring at ghosts' lights? Get you into Timberdale, Mackintosh, and see whether the police have news of the child."

"Sir, I'd not go through the Ravine to-night," was Luke's answer. "No, not though I knowed I was to be killed at to-morrow's dawn for disobeying the order."

"Man, what are you afraid of?"

"Of that," said Luke, nodding at the light. "But I don't like the Ravine in the night at no time."

"Why, that's nothing but a will-o'-the-wisp," returned Tod, condescending to reason with him.

Luke shook his head. There was the light; and neither his faith in it nor his fear could be shaken. Tod had his arms on the fence now, and was staring at the light as fixedly as Luke had done.

"Johnny."

"What?"

"That light is carried by some one. It's being lifted about."

"How could any one carry it there?" I returned. "He'd pitch head over heels down the Ravine. No fellow could get to the place, Tod, let alone keep his footing. It's where the bushes are thickest."

Tod caught up the lantern. As its light flashed on his face, I could see it working with new eagerness. He was taking up the notion that Hugh might have fallen on that very spot, and that some one was waving a light to attract attention. As to ghosts, Tod would have met an army of them without the smallest fear.

He went back down the Ravine, and we heard him go crashing through the underwood. Luke never spoke a word. Suddenly, long before Tod could get to it, the light disappeared. We waited and watched, but it did not come again.

"It have been like that always, Master Johnny," whispered Luke, taking his arms off the fence. "Folks may look as long as they will at that there light; but as soon as they go off, a-trying to get to see what it is, it takes itself away. It will be seen no more to-night, sir."

He turned off across the meadow for the high-road, to go and do Tod's bidding at Timberdale, walking at a sharp pace. Any amount of exertion would have been welcome to Mackintosh, as an alternative to passing through the Ravine.

It may be remembered that for some days we had been vaguely uneasy about Hugh, and the uneasiness had penetrated to Mrs. Todhetley. Tod had made private mockery of it to me, thinking she must be three parts a fool to entertain any such fear. "I should like to give madam a fright," he said to me one day—meaning that he would like to hide little Hugh for a time. But I never supposed he would really do it. And it was only to-night—hours and hours after Hugh disappeared, that Tod avowed to me the part he had taken in the loss. To make it clear to the reader, we must go back to the morning of this same day—Friday.

After breakfast I was shut up with my books, paying no attention to anything that might be going on, inside the house or out of it. Old Frost gave us a woeful lot to do in the holidays. The voices of the children, playing at the swing, came wafting in through the open window; but they died away to quietness as the morning went on. About twelve o'clock Mrs. Todhetley looked in.

"Are the children here, Johnny?"

She saw they were not, and went away without waiting for an answer. Lena ran up the passage, and I heard her say papa had taken Hugh out in the pony-gig. The interruption served as an excuse for putting up the books for the day, and I went out.

Of all young ragamuffins, the worst came running after me as I went through the fold-yard gate. Master Hugh! Whether he had been in the green pond again or over the house-roof, he was in a wonderful state; his blue eyes not to be seen for mud, his straw-hat bent, his brown holland blouse all tatters and slime, and the pretty fair curls that Hannah was proud of and wasted her time over, a regular mass of tangle.

"Take me with you, Johnny!"

"I should think I would, like that! What have you been doing with yourself?"

"Playing with the puppy. We fell down in the mud amongst the ducks. Joe says I am to stop in the barn and hide myself. I am afraid to go indoors."

"You'll catch it, and no mistake. Come, be off back again."

But he'd not go back, and kept running by my side under the high hedge. When we came to the gate at the end of the field, I stood and ordered him to go. He began to cry a little.

"Now, Hugh, you know you cannot go with me in that plight. Walk yourself straight off to Hannah and get her to change the things before your mamma sees you. There; you may have the biscuit: I don't much care for it."

It was a big captain's biscuit that I had caught up in going through the dining-room. He took that readily enough, the young cormorant, but he wouldn't stir any the more for it: and I might have had the small object with me till now, but for the appearance of the Squire's gig in the lane. The moment Hugh caught sight of his papa, he turned tail and scampered away like a young wild animal. Remembering Mrs. Todhetley's foolish fear, I mounted the gate and watched him turn safely in at the other.

"What are you looking at, Johnny?" asked the Squire, as he drove leisurely up.

"At Hugh, sir. I've sent him indoors."

"I'm going over to Massock's, Johnny, about the bricks for that cottage. You can get up, if you like to come with me."

I got into the gig at once, and we drove to South Crabb, to Massock's place. He was not to be seen; his people thought he had gone out for the day. Upon that, the Squire went on to see old Cartwright, and they made us stop there and put up the pony. When we reached home it was past dinner-time. Mrs. Todhetley came running out.

"Couldn't get here before: the Cartwrights kept us," called out the Squire. "We are going to catch it, Johnny," he whispered to me, with a laugh: "we've let the dinner spoil."

But it was not the dinner. "Where's Hugh?" asked Mrs. Todhetley.

"I've not seen Hugh," said the Squire, flinging the reins to Luke Mackintosh, who had come up. Luke did all kinds of odd jobs about the place, and sometimes helped the groom.

"But you took Hugh out with you," she said.

"Not I," answered the Squire.

Mrs. Todhetley's face turned white. She looked from one to the other of us in a helpless kind of manner. "Lena said you did," she returned, and her voice seemed to fear its own sound. The Squire talking with Mackintosh about the pony, noticed nothing particular.

"Lena did? Oh, ay, I remember. I let Hugh get up at the door and drove him round to the fold-yard gate. I dropped him there."

He went in as he spoke: Mrs. Todhetley seemed undecided whether to follow him. Tod had his back against the door-post, listening.

"What are you alarmed at?" he asked her, not even attempting to suppress his mocking tone.

"Oh, Johnny!" she said, "have you not seen him?"

"Yes; and a fine pickle he was in," I answered, telling her about it. "I dare say Hannah has put him to bed for punishment."

"But Hannah has not," said Mrs. Todhetley. "She came down at four o'clock to inquire if he had come in."

However, thinking that it might possibly turn out to be so, she ran in to ascertain. Tod put his hand on my shoulder, and walked me further off.

"Johnny, did Hugh really not go with you?"

"Why, of course he did not. Should I deny it if he did?"

"Where the dickens can the young idiot have got to?" mused Tod. "Jeffries vowed he saw him go off with you down the field, Johnny."

"But I sent him back. I watched him in at the fold-yard gate. You don't suppose I could take him further in that pickle!"

Tod laughed a little at the remembrance. Mrs. Todhetley returned, saying Hugh was not to be found anywhere. She looked ready to die. Tod was inwardly enjoying her fright beyond everything: it was better than a play to him. His particularly easy aspect struck her.

"Oh, Joseph!" she implored, "if you know where he is, pray tell me."

"How should I know?" returned Tod. "I protest on my honour I have not set eyes on him since before luncheon to-day."

"Do you know where he is, Tod?" I asked him, as she turned indoors.

"No; but I can guess. He's not far off. And I really did think he was with you, Johnny. I suppose I must go and bring him in, now; but I'd give every individual thing my pockets contain if madam had had a few hours' fright of it, instead of a few minutes'."

The dinner-bell was ringing, but Tod went off in an opposite direction. And I must explain here what he knew of it, though he did not tell me then. Walking through the fold-yard that morning, he had come upon Master Hugh, just emerging from the bed of green mud, crying his eyes out, and a piteous object. Hannah had promised Hugh that the next time he got into this state she would carry him to the Squire. Hugh knew she'd be sure to keep her word, and that the upshot would probably be a whipping. Tod, after gratifying his eyes with the choice spectacle, and listening to the fears of the whipping, calmly assured the young gentleman that he was "in for it," at which Hugh only howled the more. All in a moment it occurred to Tod to make use of this opportunity to frighten Mrs. Todhetley. He took Hugh off to the barn, and told him that if he'd hide himself there until the evening, he'd not only get him off his whipping, but give him all sorts of good things besides. Hugh was willing to promise, but said he wanted his dinner, upon which Tod went and brought him a plate of bread-and-butter, telling Molly, who cut it, that it was for himself. Tod left him devouring it in the dark corner behind the waggon, particularly impressing upon him the fact that he was to keep close and make no sign if his mamma, or Hannah, or anybody else, came to look for him. One of the men, Jeffries, was at work in the barn, and Tod, so to say, took him into confidence, ordering him to know nothing if Master Hugh were inquired for. As Hannah and Jeffries were at daggers drawn, and the man supposed this hiding was to spite her, he entered into it with interest.

There were two barns at Crabb Cot. One some way down the road in front of the house was the store barn, and you've heard of it before in connection with something seen by Maria Lease. It was called the yellow barn from the colour of its outer walls. The other, of red brick, was right at the back of the fold-yard, and it was in this last that Tod left Hugh, all safe and secure, as he thought, until told he might come out again.

But now, when Tod went into the dining-room to luncheon at half-past twelve—we country people breakfast early—at which meal he expected the hue and cry after Hugh to set in, for it was the children's dinner, he found there was a hitch in the programme. Mrs. Todhetley appeared perfectly easy on the score of Hugh's absence, and presently casually mentioned that he had gone out with his papa in the pony-gig. Tod's lips parted to say that Hugh was not in the pony-gig, but in a state of pickle instead. Prudence caused him to close them again. Hannah, standing behind Lena's chair, openly gave thanks that the child was got rid of for a bit, and said he was "getting a'most beyond her." Tod bit his lips with vexation: the gilt was taken off the gingerbread. He went to the barn again presently, and then found that Hugh had left it. Jeffries said he saw him going towards the lane with Master Ludlow, and supposed that the little lad had taken the opportunity to slip out of the barn when he (Jeffries) went to dinner, at twelve o'clock. And thus the whole afternoon had gone peaceably and unsuspiciously on; Mrs. Todhetley and Hannah supposing Hugh was with the Squire, Tod supposing he must be somewhere with me.

And when we both appeared at home without him, Tod took it for granted that Hugh had gone back to his hiding-place in the barn, and a qualm of conscience shot through him for leaving the lad there so many hours unlooked after. He rushed off to it at once, while the dinner-bell was ringing. But when he got there, Jeffries declared Hugh had not been back to it at all. Tod, in his hot way, retorted on Jeffries for saying so; but the man persisted that he could not be mistaken, as he had never been away from the barn since coming back from dinner.

And then arose the commotion. Tod came back with a stern face, almost as anxious as Mrs. Todhetley's. Hugh had not been seen, so far as could be ascertained, since I watched him in at the fold-yard gate soon after twelve. That was nearly seven hours ago. Tod felt himself responsible for the loss, and sent the men to look about. But the worst he thought then was, that the boy, whose fears of showing himself in his state of dilapidation Tod himself had mischievously augmented, had lain down somewhere or other and dropped asleep.

It had gone on, and on, and on, until late at night, and then had occurred that explanation between Tod and his step-mother told of in the other paper. Tod was all impulse, and pride, and heat, and passion; but his heart was made of sterling gold, just like the Squire's. Holding himself aloof from her in haughty condemnation, in the matter of the mysterious stranger, to find now that the stranger was a man called Alfred Arne, his relative, and that Mrs. Todhetley had been generously taking the trouble upon herself for the sake of sparing him and his father pain, completely turned Tod and his pride over.

He had grown desperately frightened as the hours went on. The moon-lit night had become dark, as I've already said, and the men could not pursue their search to much effect. Tod did not cease his. He got a lantern, and went rushing about as if he were crazy. You saw him come up with it from the Ravine, and now he had gone back on a wild-goose chase after the ghost light. Where was Hugh? Where could he be? It was not likely Alfred Arne had taken him, because he had that afternoon got from Mrs. Todhetley the fifty pounds he worried for, and she thought he had gone finally off with it. It stood to reason that the child would be an encumbrance to him. On the other hand, Tod's theory, that Hugh had dropped asleep somewhere, seemed, as the hours crept on, less and less likely to hold water, for he would have wakened up and come home long ago. As to the Ravine, in spite of Tod's suspicions that he might be there, I was sure the little fellow would not have ventured into it.

I stood on, in the dark night, waiting for Tod to come back again. It felt awfully desolate now Luke Mackintosh had gone. The ghost light did not show again. I rather wished it would, for company. He came at last—Tod, not the ghost. I had heard him shouting, and nothing answered but the echoes. A piece of his coat was torn, and some brambles were sticking to him, and the lantern was broken; what dangerous places he had pushed himself into could never be told.

"I wonder you've come out with whole limbs, Tod."

"Hold your peace, Johnny," was all the retort I got; and his voice rose nearly to a shout in its desperate sorrow.

Morning came, but no news with it, no Hugh. Tod had been about all night. With daylight, the fields, and all other seemingly possible places, were searched. Tom Coney went knocking at every house in North and South Crabb, and burst into cottages, and turned over, so to say, all the dwellings in that savoury locality, Crabb Lane, but with no result. The Squire was getting anxious; but none of us had ventured to tell him of our especial cause for anxiety, or to speak of Alfred Arne.

It appeared nearly certain now, to us, that he had gone with Alfred Arne, and, after a private consultation with Mrs. Todhetley, Tod and I set out in search of the man. She still wished to spare the knowledge of his visit to the Squire, if possible.

We had not far to go. Mrs. Todhetley's fears went ranging abroad to London, or Liverpool, or the Coral Islands beyond the sea, of which Arne had talked to Hugh: but Arne was found at Timberdale. In an obscure lodging in the further outskirts of the place, the landlord of which, a man named Cookum, was a bad character, and very shy of the police, Arne was found. We might have searched for him to the month's end, but for Luke Mackintosh. When Luke arrived at Timberdale in the middle of the night, ordered there by Tod to make inquiries at the police-station, he saw a tipsy man slink into Cookum's house, and recognized him for the one who had recently been exciting speculation at home. Luke happened to mention this to Tod, not connecting Hugh with it at all, simply as a bit of gossip: of course it was not known who Arne was, or his name, or what he had been waiting for.

We had a fight to get in. Cookum came leaping down the crazy stairs, and put himself in our way in the passage, swearing we should not go on. Tod lifted his strong arm.

"I mean to go on, Cookum," he said, in a slow, quiet voice that had determination in every tone of it. "I have come to see a man named Arne. I don't want to do him any ill, or you either; but, see him, I will. If you do not move out of my way I'll knock you down."

Cookum stood his ground. He was short, slight, and sickly, with a puffy face and red hair; a very reed beside Tod.

"There ain't no man here of that name. There ain't no man here at all."

"Very well. Then you can't object to letting me see that there is not."

"I swear that you shan't see, master. There!"

Tod flung him aside. Cookum, something like an eel, slipped under Tod's arm, and was in front of him again.

"I don't care to damage you, Cookum, as you must see I could do, and force my way in over your disabled body; you look too weak for it. But I'll either go in so, or the police shall clear an entrance for me."

The mention of the police scared the man; I saw it in his face. Tod kept pushing on and the man backing, just a little.

"I won't have no police here. What is it you want?"

"I have told you once. A man named Arne."

"I swear then that I never knowed a man o' that name; let alone having him in my place."

And he spoke with such passionate fervour that it struck me Arne did not go by his own name: which was more than probable. They were past the stairs now, and Cookum did not seem to care to guard them. The nasty passage, long and narrow, had a door at the end. Tod thought that must be the fortress.

"You are a great fool, Cookum. I've told you that I mean no harm to you or to any one in the place; so to make this fuss is needless. You may have a band of felons concealed here, or a cart-load of stolen goods; they are all safe for me. But if you force me to bring in the police it might be a different matter."

Perhaps the argument told on the man; perhaps the tone of reason it was spoken in; but he certainly seemed to hesitate.

"You can't prove that to me, sir: not that there's any felons or things in here. Show me that you don't mean harm, and you shall go on."

"Have you a stolen child here?"

Cookum's mouth opened with genuine surprise. "A stolen child!"

"We have lost a little boy. I have reason to think that a man who was seen to enter this passage in the middle of the night knows something of him, and I have come to ask and see. Now you know all. Let me go on."

The relief on the man's face was great. "Honour bright, sir."

"Don't stand quibbling, man," roared Tod passionately. "YES!"

"I've got but one man in all the place. He have no boy with him, he haven't."

"But he may know something of one. What's his name?"

"All the name he've given me is Jack."

"I dare say it's the same. Come! you are wasting time."

But Cookum, doubtful still, never moved. They were close to the door now, and he had his back against it. Tod turned his head.

"Go for the two policemen, Johnny. They are both in readiness, Cookum. I looked in at the station as I came by, to say I might want them."

Before I could get out, Cookum howled out to me not to go, as one in mortal fear. He took a latch-key from his pocket, and put it into the latch of the door, which had no other fastening outside, not even a handle. "You can open it yourself," said he to Tod, and slipped away.

It might have been a sort of kitchen but that it looked more like a den, with nothing to light it but a dirty sky-light above. The floor was of red brick; a tea-kettle boiled on the fire; there was a smell of coffee. Alfred Arne stood on the defensive against the opposite wall, a life-preserver in his hand, and his thin hair on end with fright.

"I am here on a peaceable errand, if you will allow it to be so," said Tod, shutting us in. "Is your name Arne?"

Arne dropped the life-preserver into the breast-pocket of his coat, and came forward with something of a gentleman's courtesy.

"Yes, my name is Arne, Joseph Todhetley. And your mother—as I make no doubt you know—was a very near relative of mine. If you damage me, you will bring her name unpleasantly before the public, as well as your own and your father's."

That he thought our errand was to demand back the fifty pounds, there could be no doubt: perhaps to hand him into custody if he refused to give it up.

"I have not come to damage you in any way," said Tod in answer. "Where's Hugh?"

Arne looked as surprised as the other man had. "Hugh!"

"Yes, Hugh: my little brother. Where is he?"

"How can I tell?"

Tod glanced round the place; there was not any nook or corner capable of affording concealment. Arne gazed at him. He stood on that side the dirty deal table, we on this.

"We have lost Hugh since mid-day yesterday. Do you know anything of him?"

"Certainly not," was the emphatic answer, and I at least saw that it was a true one. "Is it to ask that, that you have come here?"

"For that, and nothing else. We have been up all night searching for him."

"But why do you come after him here? I am not likely to know where he is."

"I think you are likely."

"Why?"

"You have been talking to the boy about carrying him off with you to see coral islands. You hinted, I believe, to Mrs. Todhetley that you might really take him, if your demands were not complied with."

Arne slightly laughed. "I talked to the boy about the Coral Islands because it pleased him. As to Mrs. Todhetley, if she has the sense of a goose, she must have known I meant nothing. Take off a child with me! Why, if he were made a present to me, I should only drop him at his own door at Crabb Cot, as they drop the foundlings at the gate of the Maison Dieu in Paris. Joseph Todhetley, I could not be encumbered with a child: the life of shifts and concealment I have to lead would debar it."

I think Tod saw he was in earnest. But he stood in indecision: this dashed out his great hope.

"I should have been away from here last night, but that I got a drop too much and must wait till dark again," resumed Arne. "The last time I saw Hugh was on Thursday afternoon. He was in the meadow with you."

"I did not see you," remarked Tod.

"I saw you, though. And that is the last time I saw him. Don't you believe me? You may. I like the little lad, and would find him for you if I could, rather than help to lose him. I'd say take my honour upon this, Joseph Todhetley, only you might retort that it has not been worth anything this many a year."

"And with justice," said Tod, boldly.

"True. The world has been against me and I against the world. But it has not come yet with me to stealing children. With the loan of the money now safe in my pocket, I shall make a fresh start in life. A precious long time your step-mother kept me waiting for it."

"She did her best. You ought not to have applied to her at all."

"I know that: it should have been to the other side of the house. She prevented me: wanting, she said, to spare you and your father."

"The knowledge of the disgrace. Yes."

"There's no need to have recourse to hard names, Joseph Todhetley. What I am, I am, but you have not much cause to grumble, for I don't trouble you often. As many thousand miles away as the seas can put between me and England, I'm going now: and it's nearly as many chances to one against your ever seeing me again."

Tod turned to depart: the intensely haughty look his face wore at odd moments had been upon it throughout the interview. Had he been a woman he might have stood with his skirts picked up, as if to save them contamination from some kind of reptile. He stayed for a final word.

"Then I may take your answer in good faith—that you know nothing of Hugh?"

"Take it, or not, as you please. If I knew that I was going to stand next minute in the presence of Heaven, I could not give it more truthfully. For the child's own sake, I hope he will be found. Why don't you ask the man who owns the rooms?—he can tell you I have had no boy here. If you choose to watch me away to-night, do so; you'll see I go alone. A child with me! I might about as well give myself up to the law at once, for I shouldn't long remain out of its clutches, Joseph Todhetley."

"Good-morning," said Tod shortly. I echoed the words, and we were civilly answered. As we went out, Arne shut the door behind us. In the middle of the passage stood Cookum.

"Have you found he was who you wanted, sir?"

"Yes," answered Tod, not vouchsafing to explain. "Another time when I say I do not wish to harm you, perhaps you'll take my word."

Mrs. Todhetley, pale and anxious, was standing under the mulberry-tree when we got back. She came across the grass.

"Any news?" cried Tod. As if the sight of her was not enough, that he need have asked!

"No, no, Joseph. Did you see him?"

"Yes, he had not left. He knows nothing of Hugh."

"I had no hope that he did," moaned poor Mrs. Todhetley. "All he wanted was the money."

We turned into the dining-room by the glass-doors, and it seemed to strike out a gloomy chill. On the wall near the window, there was a chalk drawing of Hugh in colours, hung up by a bit of common string. It was only a rough sketch that Jane Coney had done half in sport; but it was like him, especially in the blue eyes and the pretty light hair.

"Where's my father?" asked Tod.

"Gone riding over to the brick-fields again," she answered: "he cannot get it out of his mind that Hugh must be there. Joseph, as Mr. Arne has nothing to do with the loss, we can still spare your father the knowledge that he has been here. Spare it, I mean, for good."

"Yes. Thank you."

Hugh was uncommonly fond of old Massock's brick-fields; he would go there on any occasion that offered, had once or twice strayed there a truant; sending Hannah, for the time being, into a state of mortal fright. The Squire's opinion was that Hugh must have decamped there some time in the course of the Friday afternoon, perhaps followed the gig; and was staying there, afraid to come home.

"He might have hung on to the tail of the gig itself, and I and Johnny never have seen him, the 'cute Turk," argued the Squire.

Which I knew was just as likely as that he had, unseen, hung on to the moon. In the state he had brought his clothes to, he wouldn't have gone to the brick-fields at all. The Squire did not seem so uneasy as he might have been. Hugh would be sure to turn up, he said, and should get the soundest whipping any young rascal ever had.

But he came riding back from the brick-fields as before—without him. Tod, awfully impatient, met him in the road by the yellow barn. The Squire got off his horse there, for Luke Mackintosh was at hand to take it.

"Father, I cannot think of any other place he can have got to: we have searched everywhere. Can you?"

"Not I, Joe. Don't be down-hearted. He'll turn up; he'll turn up. Halloa!" broke off the Squire as an idea struck him, "has this barn been searched?"

"He can't be in there, sir; it's just a moral impossibility that he could be," spoke up Mackintosh. "The place was empty, which I can be upon my oath, when I locked it up yesterday afternoon, after getting some corn out; and the key have never been out o' my trousers' pocket since. Mr. Joseph, he was inside with me at the time, and knows it."

Tod nodded assent, and the Squire walked away. As there was no other accessible entrance to the front barn, and the windows were ever so many yards from the ground, they felt that it must be, as the man said, a "moral impossibility."

The day went on, it was Saturday, remember, and the miserable hours went on, and there came no trace of the child. The Ravine was again searched thoroughly: that is, as thoroughly as its overgrown state permitted. It was like waste of time; for Hugh would not have hidden himself in it; and if he had fallen over the fence he would have been found before from the traces that must have been left in the bushes. The searchers would come in, one after another, now a farm-servant, now one of the police, bringing no news, except of defeat, but hoping some one else had brought it. Every time that Tod looked at the poor mild face of Mrs. Todhetley, always meek and patient, striving ever to hide the anguish that each fresh disappointment brought, I know he felt ready to hang himself. It was getting dusk when Maria Lease came up with a piece of straw hat that she had found in the withy walk. But both Mrs. Todhetley and Hannah, upon looking at it, decided that the straw was of finer grain than Hugh's.

That afternoon they dragged the pond, but there was nothing found in it. We could get no traces anywhere. No one had seen him, no one heard of him. From the moment when I had watched him into the fold-yard gate, it seemed that he had altogether vanished from above ground. Since then all scent of him was missing. It was very strange: just as though the boy had been spirited away.

Sunday morning rose. As lovely a Sunday as ever this world saw, but all sad for us. Tod had flung himself back in the pater's easy-chair, pretty near done over. Two nights, and he had not been to bed. In spite of his faith in Alfred Arne's denial, he had chosen to watch him away in the night from Timberdale; and he saw the man steal off in the darkness on foot and alone. The incessant hunting about was bringing its reaction on Tod, and the fatigue of body and mind began to show itself. But as to giving in, he'd never do that, and would be as likely as not to walk and worry himself into a fever.

The day was warm and beautiful; the glass-doors stood open to the sweet summer air. Light fleecy clouds floated over the blue sky, the sun shone on the green grass of the lawn and sparkled amidst the leaves of the great mulberry-tree. Butterflies flitted past in pairs, chasing each other; bees sent forth their hum as they sipped the honey-dew from the flowers; the birds sang their love-songs on the boughs: all seemed happiness outside, as if to mock our care within.

Tod lay back with his eyes closed: I sat on the arm of the old red sofa. The bells of North Crabb Church rang out for morning service. It was rather a cracked old peal, but on great occasions the ringers assembled and did their best. The Bishop of Worcester was coming over to-day to preach a charity sermon: and North Crabb never had anything greater than that. Tod opened his eyes and listened in silence.

"Tod, do you know what it puts me in mind of?"

"Don't bother. It's because of the bishop, I suppose."

"I don't mean the bells. It's like the old fable, told of in 'The Mistletoe Bough,' enacted in real life. If there were any deep chest about the premises—"

"Hold your peace, Johnny!—unless you want to drive me mad. If we come upon the child like that, I'll—I'll—"

I think he was going to say shoot himself, or something of that sort, for he was given to random speech when put to it. But at that moment Lena ran in dressed for church, in her white frock and straw hat with blue ribbons. She threw her hands on Tod's knee and burst out crying.

"Joe, I don't want to go to church; I want Hugh."

Quite a spasm of pain shot across his face, but he was very tender with her. In all my life I had never seen Tod so gentle as he had been at moments during the last two days.

"Don't cry, pretty one," he said, pushing the fair curls from her face. "Go to church like a good little girl; perhaps we shall have found him by the time you come home."

"Hannah says he's lying dead somewhere."

"Hannah's nothing but a wicked woman," savagely answered Tod. "Don't you mind her."

But Lena would not be pacified, and kept on sobbing and crying, "I want Hugh; I want Hugh."

Mrs. Todhetley, who had come in then, drew her away and sat down with the child on her knee, talking to her in low, soothing tones.

"Lena, dear, you know I wish you to go with Hannah to church this morning. And you will put papa's money into the plate. See: it is a golden sovereign. Hannah must carry it, and you shall put it in."

"Oh, mamma! will Hugh never come home again? Will he die?"

"Hush, Lena," she said, as Tod bit his lip and gave his hair a dash backwards. "Shall I tell you something that sounds like a pretty story?"

Lena was always ready for a story, pretty or ugly, and her blue eyes were lifted to her mother's brightly through the tears. At that moment she looked wonderfully like the portrait on the wall.

"Just now, dear, I was in my room upstairs, feeling very, very unhappy; I'm not sure but I was sobbing nearly as much as you were just now. 'He will never come back,' I said to myself; 'he is lost to us for ever.' At that moment those sweet bells broke out, calling people to Heaven's service, and I don't know why, Lena, but they seemed to whisper a great comfort to me. They seemed to say that God was over us all, and saw our trouble, and would heal it in His good time."

Lena stared a little, digesting what she could of the words. The tears were nowhere.

"Will He send Hugh back?"

"I can't tell, darling. He can take care of Hugh, and bless him, and keep him, wherever he may be, and I know He will. If He should have taken him to heaven above the blue sky—oh then, Hugh must be very happy. He will be with the angels. He will see Jesus face to face; and you know how He loved little children. The bells seemed to say all this to me as I listened to them, Lena."

Lena went off contented: we saw her skipping along by Hannah's side, who had on a new purple gown and staring red and green trimmings to her bonnet. Children are as changeable as a chameleon, sobbing one minute, laughing the next. Tod was standing now with his back to the window, and Mrs. Todhetley sat by the table, her long thin fingers supporting her cheek; very meek, very, very patient. Tod was thinking so as he glanced at her.

"How you must hate me for this!" he said.

"Oh, Joseph! Hate you?"

"The thing is all my fault. A great deal has been my fault for a long while; all the unpleasantness and the misunderstanding."

She got up and took his hand timidly, as if she feared he might think it too great a liberty. "If you can only understand me for the future, Joseph; understand how I wish and try to make things pleasant to you, I shall be fully repaid: to you most especially in all the house, after your father. I have ever striven and prayed for it."

He answered nothing for the moment; his face was working a little, and he gave her fingers a grip that must have caused pain.

"If the worst comes of this, and Hugh never is amongst us again, I will go over the seas in the wake of the villain Arne," he said in a low, firm tone, "and spare you the sight of me."

Tears began to trickle down her face. "Joseph, my dear—if you will let me call you so—this shall draw us near to each other, as we never might have been drawn without it. You shall not hear a word of reproach from us, or any word but love; there shall never be a thought of reproach in my heart. I have had a great deal of sorrow in my life, Joseph, and have learnt patiently to bear, leaving all things to Heaven."

"And if Hugh is dead?"

"What I said to Lena, I meant," she softly whispered. "If God has taken him he is with the angels, far happier than he could be in this world of care, though his lot were of the brightest."

The tears were running down her cheeks as she went out of the room. Tod stood still as a stone.

"She is made of gold," I whispered.

"No, Johnny. Of something better."

The sound of the bells died away. None of us went to church; in the present excitement it would have been a farce. The Squire had gone riding about the roads, sending his groom the opposite way. He telegraphed to the police at Worcester; saying, in the message, that these country officers were no better than dummies; and openly lamented at home that it had not happened at Dyke Manor, within the range of old Jones the constable.

Tod disappeared with the last sound of the bells. Just as the pater's head was full of the brick-fields, his was of the Ravine; that he had gone off to beat it again I was sure. In a trouble such as this you want incessantly to be up and doing. Lena and Hannah came back from church, the child calling for Hugh: she wanted to tell him about the gentleman who had preached in big white sleeves and pretty frills on his wrists.

Two o'clock was the Sunday dinner-hour. Tod came in when it was striking. He looked dead-beat as he sat down to carve in his father's place. The sirloin of beef was as good as usual, but only Lena seemed to think so. The little gobbler ate two servings, and a heap of raspberry pie and cream.

How it happened, I don't know. I was just as anxious as any of them, and yet, in sitting under the mulberry-tree, I fell fast asleep, never waking till five. Mrs. Todhetley, always finding excuses for us, said it was worry and want of proper rest. She was sitting close to the window, her head leaning against it. The Squire had not come home. Tod was somewhere about, she did not know where.

I found him in the yard. Luke Mackintosh was harnessing the pony to the gig, Tod helping him in a state of excitement. Some man had come in with a tale that a tribe of gipsies was discovered, encamped beyond the brick-fields, who seemed to have been there for a week past. Tod jumped to the conclusion that Hugh was concealed with them, and was about to go off in search.

"Will you come with me, Johnny? Luke must remain in case the Squire rides in."

"Of course I will. I'll run and tell Mrs. Todhetley."

"Stay where you are, you stupid muff. To excite her hopes, in the uncertainty, would be cruel. Get up."

Tod need not have talked about excited hopes. He was just three parts mad. Fancy his great strong hands shaking as he took the reins! The pony dashed off in a fright with the cut he gave it, and brought us cleverly against the post of the gate, breaking the near shaft. Over that, but for the delay, Tod would have been cool as an orange.

"The phaeton now, single horse," he called out to Mackintosh.

"Yes, sir. Bob, or Blister?"

Tod stamped his foot in a passion. "As if it mattered! Blister; he is the more fiery of the two."

"I must get the harness," said Mackintosh. "It is in the yellow barn."

Mackintosh went round on the run to gain the front barn; the harness, least used, was kept there, hung on the walls. Tod unharnessed the pony, left me to lead him to the stable, and went after the man. In his state of impatience and his strength, he could have done the work of ten men. He met Mackintosh coming out of the barn, without the harness, but with a white face. Since he saw the ghost's light on Friday night the man had been scared at shadows.

"There's sum'at in there, master," said he, his teeth chattering.

"What?" roared Tod, in desperate anger.

"There is, master. It's like a faint tapping."

Tod dashed in, controlling his hands, lest they might take French leave and strike Luke for a coward. He was seeking the proper set of harness, when a knocking, faint and irregular, smote his ear. Tod turned to look, and thought it came from the staircase-door. He went forward and opened it.

Lying at the foot of the stairs was Hugh. Hugh! Low, and weak, and faint, there he lay, his blue eyes only half opened, and his pretty curls mingling with the dust.

"Hugh! is it you, my darling?"

Tod's gasp was like a great cry. Hugh put up his little feeble hand, and a smile parted his lips.

"Yes, it's me, Joe."

The riddle is easily solved. When sent back by me, Hugh saw Hannah in the fold-yard; she was, in point of fact, looking after him. In his fear, he stole round to hide in the shrubbery, and thence got to the front of the house, and ran away down the road. Seeing the front barn-door open, for it was when Luke Mackintosh was getting the corn, Hugh slipped in and hid behind the door. Luke went out with the first lot of corn, and the senseless child, hearing Tod's voice outside, got into the place leading to the stairs, and shut the door. Luke, talking to Tod, who had stepped inside the barn, saw the door was shut and slipped the big outside bolt, never remembering that it was not he who had shut it. Poor little Hugh, when their voices had died away, ran upstairs to get to the upper granary, and found its door fastened. And there the child was shut up beyond reach of call and hearing. The skylight in the roof, miles, as it seemed, above him, had its ventilator open. He had called and called; but his voice must have been lost amidst the space of the barn. It was too weak to disturb a rat now.

Tod took him up in his arms, tenderly as if he had been a new-born baby that he was hushing to the rest of death.

"Were you frightened, child?"

"I was till I heard the church-bells," whispered Hugh. "I don't know how long it was—oh, a great while—and I had ate the biscuit Johnny gave me and been asleep. I was not frightened then, Joe; I thought they'd come to me when church was over."

I met the procession. What the dirty object might be in Tod's arms was quite a mystery at first. Tod's eyes were dropping tears upon it, and his breath seemed laboured. Luke brought up the rear a few yards behind, looking as if he'd never find his senses again.

"Oh, Tod! will he get over it?"

"Yes. Please God."

"Is he injured?"

"No, no. Get out of my way, Johnny. Go to the mother now, if you like. Tell her he has only been shut up in the barn and I'm coming in with him. The dirt's nothing: it was on him before."

Just as meek and gentle she stood as ever, the tears rolling down her face, and a quiet joy in it. Tod brought him in, laying him across her knee as she sat on the sofa.

"There," he said. "He'll be all right when he has been washed and had something to eat."

"God bless you, Joseph!" she whispered.

Tod could say no more. He bent to kiss Hugh; lifted his face, and kissed the mother. And then he went rushing out with a burst of emotion.

CHAPTER III

OUR VISIT

I

We went down from Oxford together, I and Tod and William Whitney; accompanying Miss Deveen and Helen and Anna Whitney, who had been there for a few days. Miss Deveen's carriage was waiting at the Paddington Station; they got into it with Tod, and William and I followed in a cab with the luggage. Miss Deveen had invited us all to stay with her.

Miss Cattledon, the companion, with her tall, thin figure, her pinched-in waist and her creaking stays, stood ready to receive us when we reached the house. Miss Deveen held out her hand.

"How have you been, Jemima? Taking care of yourself, I hope?"

"Quite well, thank you, Miss Deveen; and very glad to see you at home again," returned Cattledon. "This is my niece, Janet Carey."

A slight, small girl, with smooth brown hair and a quiet face that looked as if it had just come out of some wasting illness, was hiding herself behind Cattledon. Miss Deveen said a few pleasant words of welcome, and took her hand. The girl looked as shy and frightened as though we had all been a pack of gorillas.

"Thank you, ma'am; you are very kind," she said in a tremble; and her voice, I noticed, was low and pleasant. I like nice voices, whether in man or woman.

"It wants but half-an-hour to dinner-time," said Miss Deveen, untying the strings of her bonnet. "Miss Cattledon, will you show these young friends of ours the rooms you have appropriated to them."

My room and Tod's—two beds in it—was on the second floor; Helen and Anna had the best company room below, near Miss Deveen's; Bill had a little one lower still, half-way up the first flight of stairs. Miss Cattledon's room, we found out, was next to ours, and her niece slept with her.

Tod threw himself full length on his counterpane—tired out, he said. Certain matters had not gone very smoothly for him at Oxford, and the smart remained.

"You'll be late, Tod," I said when I was ready.

"Plenty of time, Johnny. I don't suppose I shall keep dinner waiting."

Miss Deveen stood at the door of the blue room when I went down: that pretty sitting-room, exclusively hers, that I remembered so well. She had on a purple silk gown, with studs of pale yellow topaz in its white lace front, studs every whit as beautiful as the emeralds made free with by Sophie Chalk.

"Come in here, Johnny."

She was beginning to talk to me as we stood by the fire, when some one was heard to enter the inner room; Miss Deveen's bed-chamber, which opened from this room as well as from the landing. She crossed over into it, and I heard Cattledon's voice.

"It is so very kind of you, Miss Deveen, to have allowed me to bring my niece here! Under the circumstances—with such a cloud upon her—"

"She is quite welcome," interrupted Miss Deveen's voice.

"Yes, I know that; I know it: and I could not go down without thanking you. I have told Lettice to take some tea up to her while we dine. She can come to the drawing-room afterwards if you have no objection."

"Why can't she dine with us?" asked Miss Deveen.

"Better not," said Cattledon. "She does not expect it; and with so many at table—"

"Nonsense!" came Miss Deveen's quick, decisive interruption. "Many at table! There are sufficient servants to wait on us, and I suppose you have sufficient dinner. Go and bring her down."

Miss Deveen came back, holding out her hand to me as she crossed the room. The gong sounded as we went down to the drawing-room. They all came crowding in, Tod last; and we went in to dinner.

Miss Deveen, with her fresh, handsome face and her snow-white hair, took the head of the table. Cattledon, at the foot, a green velvet ribbon round her genteel throat, helped the soup. William Whitney sat on Miss Deveen's right, I on her left. Janet Carey sat next to him—and this brought her nearly opposite me.

She had an old black silk on, with a white frill at the throat—very poor and plain as contrasted with the light gleaming silks of Helen and Anna. But she had nice eyes; their colour a light hazel, their expression honest and sweet. It was a pity she could not get some colour into her wan face, and a little courage into her manner.

After coffee we sat down in the drawing-room to a round game at cards, and then had some music; Helen playing first. Janet Carey was at the table, looking at a view in an album. I went up to her.

Had I caught her staring at some native Indians tarred and feathered, she could not have given a worse jump. It might have been fancy, but I thought her face turned white.

"Did I startle you, Miss Carey? I am very sorry."

"Oh, thank you—no. Every one is very kind. The truth is"—pausing a moment and looking at the view—"I knew the place in early life, and was lost in old memories. Past times and events connected with it came back to me. I recognized the place at once, though I was only ten years old when I left it."

"Places do linger on the memory in a singularly vivid manner sometimes. Especially those we have known when young."

"I can recognize every spot in this," she said, gazing still at the album. "And I have not seen it for fifteen years."

"Fifteen. I—I understood you to say you were ten years old when you left it."

"So I was. I am twenty-five now."

So much as that! So much older than any of us! I could hardly believe it.

"I should not have taken you for more than seventeen, Miss Carey."

"At seventeen I went out to earn my own living," she said, in a sad tone, but with a candour that I liked. "That is eight years ago."

Helen's music ceased with a crash. Miss Deveen came up to Janet Carey.

"My dear, I hear you can sing: your aunt tells me so. Will you sing a song, to please me?"

She was like a startled fawn: looking here, looking there, and turning white and red. But she rose at once.

"I will sing if you wish it, madam. But my singing is only plain singing: just a few old songs. I have never learnt to sing."

"The old songs are the best," said Miss Deveen. "Can you sing that sweet song of all songs—'Blow, blow, thou wintry wind'?"

She went to the piano, struck the chords quietly, without any flourish or prelude, and began the first note.

Oh the soft, sweet, musical voice that broke upon us! Not a powerful voice, that astounds the nerves like an electric machine; but one of that intense, thrilling, plaintive harmony which brings a mist to the eye and a throb to the heart. Tod backed against the wall to look at her; Bill, who had taken up the cat, let it drop through his knees.

You might have heard a pin drop when the last words died away: "As friends remembering not." Miss Deveen broke the silence: praising her and telling her to go on again. The girl did not seem to have the least notion of refusing: she appeared to have lived under submission. I think Miss Deveen would have liked her to go on for ever.

"The wonder to me is that you can remember the accompaniment to so many songs without your notes," cried Helen Whitney.

"I do not know my notes. I cannot play."

"Not know your notes!"

"I never learnt them. I never learnt music. I just play some few chords by ear that will harmonize with the songs. That is why my singing is so poor, so different from other people's. Where I have been living they say it is not worth listening to."

She spoke in a meek, deprecating manner. I had heard of self-depreciation: this was an instance of it. Janet Carey was one of the humble ones.

The next day was Good Friday. We went to church under lowering clouds, and came home again to luncheon. Cattledon's face was all vinegar when we sat down to it.

"There's that woman downstairs again!—that Ness!" she exclaimed with acrimony. "Making herself at home with the servants!"

"I'm glad to hear it," smiled Miss Deveen. "She'll get some dinner, poor thing."

Cattledon sniffed. "It's not a month since she was here before."

"And I'm sure if she came every week she'd be welcome to a meal," spoke Miss Deveen. "Ah now, young ladies," she went on in a joking tone, "if you wanted your fortunes told, Mrs. Ness is the one to do it."

"Does she tell truth?" asked Helen eagerly.

"Oh, very true, of course," laughed Miss Deveen. "She'll promise you a rich husband apiece. Dame Ness is a good woman, and has had many misfortunes. I have known her through all of them."

"And helped her too," resentfully put in Cattledon.

"But does she really tell fortunes?" pursued Helen.

"She thinks she does," laughed Miss Deveen. "She told mine once—many a year ago."

"And did it come true?"

"Well, as far as I remember, she candidly confessed that there was not much to tell—that my life would be prosperous but uneventful."

"I don't think, begging your pardon, Miss Deveen, that it is quite a proper subject for young people," struck in Cattledon, drawing up her thin red neck.

"Dear me, no," replied Miss Deveen, still laughing a little. And the subject dropped, and we finished luncheon.

The rain had come on, a regular downpour. We went into the breakfast-room: though why it was called that, I don't know, since breakfast was never taken there. It was a fair-sized, square room, built out at the back, and gained by a few stairs down from the hall and a passage. Somehow people prefer plain rooms to grand ones for everyday use: perhaps that was why we all took a liking to this room, for it was plain enough. An old carpet on the floor, chairs covered with tumbled chintz, and always a good blazing fire in the grate. Miss Deveen would go in there to write her business letters—when she had any to write; or to cut out sewing with Cattledon for the housemaids. An old-fashioned secretary stood against the wall, in which receipts and other papers were kept. The French window opened to the garden.

"Pour, pour, pour! It's going to be wet for the rest of the day," said Tod gloomily.

Cattledon came in, equipped for church in a long brown cloak, a pair of clogs in her hand. Did none of us intend to go, she asked. Nobody answered. The weather outside was not tempting.

"You must come, Janet Carey," she said very tartly, angry with us all, I expect. "Go and put on your things."

"No," interposed Miss Deveen. "It would not be prudent for your niece to venture out in this rain, Jemima."

"The church is only over the way."

"But consider the illness she has only just recovered from. Let her stay indoors."

Cattledon went off without further opposition, Janet kneeling down unasked, to put on her clogs, and then opening her umbrella for her in the hall. Janet did not come in again. Miss Deveen went out to sit with a sick neighbour: so we were alone.

"What a cranky old thing that Cattledon is!" cried Bill, throwing down his newspaper. "She'd have walked that girl off in the wet, you see."

"How old is Cattledon?" asked Tod. "Sixty?"

"Oh, you stupid fellow!" exclaimed Helen, looking up from the stool on the hearthrug, where she was sitting, nursing her knees. "Cattledon sixty! Why, she can't be above forty-five."

It was disrespectful no doubt, but we all called her plain "Cattledon" behind her back.

"That's rather a queer girl, that niece," said Tod. "She won't speak to one: she's like a frightened hare."

"I like her," said Anna. "I feel very sorry for her. She gives one the idea of having been always put upon: and she looks dreadfully ill."

"I should say she has been kept in some Blue Beard's cupboard, amongst a lot of hanging wives that have permanently scared her," remarked Bill.

"It's Cattledon," said Tod; "it's not the wives. She puts upon the girl and frightens her senses out of her. Cattledon's a cross-grained, two-edged—"

He had to shut up: Janet Carey was coming in again. For about five minutes no one spoke. There seemed to be nothing to say. Bill played at ball with Miss Deveen's red penwiper: Anna began turning over the periodicals: Helen gave the cat a box when it would have jumped on her knee.

"Well, this is lively!" cried Tod. "Nothing on earth to do; I wonder why the rain couldn't have kept off till to-morrow?"

"I say," whispered Helen, treason sparkling from her bright eyes, "let us have up that old fortune-teller! I'll go and ask Lettice."

She whirled out of the room, shutting the tail of her black silk dress in the door, and called Lettice. A few minutes, and Mrs. Ness came in, curtsying. A stout old lady in a cotton shawl and broad-bordered cap with a big red bow tied in front.

"I say, Mrs. Ness, can you tell our fortunes?" cried Bill.

"Bless you, young gentlefolks, I've told a many in my time. I'll tell yours, if you like to bid me, sir."

"Do the cards tell true?"

"I believe they does, sir. I've knowed 'em to tell over true now and again—more's the pity!"

"Why do you say more's the pity?" asked Anna.

"When they've fortelled bad things, my sweet, pretty young lady. Death, and what not."

"But how it must frighten the people who are having them told!" cried Anna.

"Well, to speak the truth, young gentlefolks, when it's very bad, I generally softens it over to 'em—say the cards is cloudy, or some'at o' that," was the old woman's candid answer. "It don't do to make folks uneasy."

"Look here," said Helen, who had been to find the cards, "I should not like to hear it if it's anything bad."

"Ah, my dear young lady, I don't think you need fear any but a good fortune, with that handsome face and them bright eyes of yours," returned the old dame—who really seemed to speak, not in flattery, but from the bottom of her heart. "I don't know what the young lords 'ud be about, to pass you by."

Helen liked that; she was just as vain as a peacock, and thought no little of herself. "Who'll begin?" asked she.

"Begin yourself, Helen," said Tod. "It's sure to be something good."

So she shuffled and cut the cards as directed: and the old woman, sitting at the table, spread them out before her, talking a little bit to herself, and pointing with her finger here and there.

"You've been upon a journey lately," she said, "and you'll soon be going upon another." I give only the substance of what the old lady said, but it was interspersed freely with her own remarks. "You'll have a present before many days is gone; and you'll—stay, there's that black card—you'll hear of somebody that's sick. And—dear me! there's an offer for you—an offer of marriage,—but it won't come to anything. Well, now, shuffle and cut again, please."

Helen did so. This was repeated three times in all. But, so far as we could understand it, her future seemed to be very uneventful—to have nothing in it—something like Miss Deveen's.

"It's a brave fortune, as I thought, young lady," cried Mrs. Ness. "No trouble or care in store for you."

"But there's nothing," said Helen, too intently earnest to mind any of us. "When am I to be married?"

"Well, my dear, the cards haven't told so much this time. There'll be an offer, as I said—and I think a bit of trouble over it; but—"

"But you said it would not come to anything," interrupted Helen.

"Well, and no more it won't: leastways, it seemed so by the cards; and it seemed to bring a bother with it—old folks pulling one way maybe, and young 'uns the other. You'll have to wait a bit for the right gentleman, my pretty miss."

"What stupid cards they are!" cried Helen, in dudgeon. "I dare say it's all rubbish."

"Any ways, you've had nothing bad," said the old woman. "And that's a priceless consolation."

"It's your turn now, Anna."

"I won't have mine told," said Anna. "I'm afraid."

"Oh, you senseless donkey!" cried Bill. "Afraid of a pack of cards!" So Anna laughed, and began.

"Ah, there's more here," said the old woman as she laid them out. "You are going through some great ceremony not long first. See here—crowds of people—and show. Is it a great ball, I wonder?"

"It may be my presentation," said Anna.

"And here's the wedding-ring!—and there's the gentleman! See! he's turning towards you; a dark man it is; and he'll be very fond of you, too!—and—"

"Oh, don't go on," cried Anna, in terrible confusion as she heard all this, and caught Tod's eye, and saw Bill on the broad laugh. "Don't, pray don't; it must be all nonsense," she went on, blushing redder than a rose.

"But it's true," steadily urged the old lady. "There the wedding is. I don't say it'll be soon; perhaps not for some years; but come it will in its proper time. And you'll live in a fine big house; and—stay a bit—you'll—"

Anna, half laughing, half crying, pushed the cards together. "I won't be told any more," she said; "it must be all a pack of nonsense."

"Of course it is," added Helen decisively. "And why couldn't you have told me all that, Mrs. Ness?"

"Why, my dear, sweet young lady, it isn't me that tells; it's the cards."

"I don't believe it. But it does to while away a wet and wretched afternoon. Now, Miss Carey."

Miss Carey looked up from her book with a start. "Oh, not me! Please, not me!"

"Not you!—the idea!" cried Helen. "Why, of course you must. I and my sister have had our turn, and you must take yours."

As if further objection were out of the question, Miss Carey stood timidly up by the table and shuffled the cards that Dame Ness handed to her. When they were spread out, the old woman looked at the cards longer than she had looked for either Helen or Anna, then at the girl, then at the cards again.

"There has been sickness and trouble;—and distress," she said at length, "And—and—'tain't over yet. I see a dark lady and a fair man: they've been in it, somehow. Seems to ha' been a great trouble"—putting the tips of her forefingers upon two cards. "Here you are, you see, right among it,"—pointing to the Queen of Hearts. "I don't like the look of it. And there's money mixed up in the sorrow—"

A low, shuddering cry. I happened to be looking from the window at the moment, and turned to see Janet Carey with hands uplifted and a face of imploring terror. The cry came from her.

"Oh don't, don't! don't tell any more!" she implored. "I—was—not—guilty."

Down went her voice by little and little, down fell her hands; and down dropped she on the chair behind her. The next moment she was crying and sobbing. We stood round like so many helpless simpletons, quite put down by this unexpected interlude. Old Dame Ness stared, slowly shuffling the cards from hand to hand, and could not make it out.

"Here, I'll have my fortune told next, Mother Ness," said Bill Whitney, really out of good nature to the girl, that she might be left unobserved to recover herself. "Mind you promise me a good one."

"And so I will then, young gentleman, if the cards 'll let me," was the hearty answer. "Please shuffle 'em well, sir, and then cut 'em into three."

Bill was shuffling with all his might when we heard the front-door open, and Cattledon's voice in the hall. "Oh, by George, I say, what's to be done?" cried he. "She'll be fit to smother us. That old parson can't have given them a sermon."

Fortunately she stayed on the door-mat to take off her clogs. Dame Ness was smuggled down the kitchen stairs, and Bill hid the cards away in his pocket.

And until then it had not occurred to us that it might not be quite the right thing to go in for fortune-telling on Good Friday.

II

On Easter Tuesday William Whitney and Tod went off to Whitney Hall for a few days: Sir John wrote for them. In the afternoon Miss Deveen took Helen in the carriage to make calls; and the rest of us went to the Colosseum, in the Regent's Park. Cattledon rather fought against the expedition, but Miss Deveen did not listen to her. None of us—except herself—had seen it before: and I know that I, for one, was delighted with it.

The last scene of the performance was over. If I remember rightly, at this distance of time, it was the representation of the falling of an avalanche on a Swiss village, to bury it for ever in the snow; and we saw the little lighted church to which the terrified inhabitants were flying for succour, and heard the tinkling of its alarm bell. As we pushed out with the crowd, a policeman appeared in our way, facing us, a tall, big, fierce-looking man; not to impede the advance of the throng, but to direct its movements. Janet Carey seized my arm, and I turned to look at her. She stood something like a block of stone; her face white with terror, her eyes fixed on the policeman. I could not get her on, and we were stopping those behind. Naturally the man's eyes fell on her; and with evident recognition.

"Oh, it's you here, is it, Miss Carey!"

The tone was not exactly insolent: but it was cool and significant, wanting in respect. When I would have asked him how he dared so to address a young lady, the words were arrested by Janet. I thought she had gone mad.

"Oh, get me away, Mr. Ludlow, for Heaven's sake! Don't let him take me! Oh what shall I do? what shall I do?"

"What you've got to do is to get for'ard out o' this here passage and not block up the way," struck in the policeman. "I bain't after you now; so you've no call to be afeared this time. Pass on that way, sir."

I drew her onwards, and in half-a-minute we were in the open air, clear of the throng. Cattledon, who seemed to have understood nothing, except that we had stopped the way, shook Janet by the arm in anger, and asked what had come to her.

"It was the same man, aunt, that Mrs. Knox called in," she gasped. "I thought he had come to London to look for me."

Miss Cattledon's answer was to keep hold of her arm, and whirl her along towards the outer gates. Anna and I followed in wonder.

"What is it all, Johnny?" she whispered.

"Goodness knows, Anna. I—"

Cattledon turned her head, asking me to go on and secure a cab. Janet was helped into it and sat back with her eyes closed, a shiver taking her every now and then.

Janet appeared at dinner, and seemed as well as usual. In the evening Helen tore the skirt of her thin dress: and before she was aware, the girl was kneeling by the side of her chair with a needle and thread, beginning to mend it.

"You are very kind," said Helen heartily, when she saw what Janet was doing.

"Oh no," answered Janet, with an upward, humble glance from her nice eyes.

But soon after that, when we were describing to Helen and Miss Deveen the sights at the Colosseum, and the silence of the buried village after the avalanche had fallen, Janet was taken with an ague fit. The very chair shook; it seemed that she must fall out of it. Anna ran to hold her. Miss Deveen got up in consternation.

"That Colosseum has been too much for her: there's nothing so fatiguing as sightseeing. I did wrong in letting Janet go, as she is still weak from her illness. Perhaps she has taken cold."

Ringing the bell, Miss Deveen told George to make some hot wine and water. When it was brought in, she made Janet drink it, and sent her upstairs to bed, marshalled by Cattledon.

The next morning, Wednesday, I was dressing in the sunshine that streamed in at the bedroom windows, when a loud hulla-balloo was set up below, enough to startle the king and all his men.

"Thieves! robbers! murder!"

Dashing to the door, I looked over the balustrades. The shrieks and calls came from Lettice Lane, who was stumbling up the stairs from the hall. Cattledon opened her door in her night-cap, saw me, and shut it again with a bang.

"Murder! robbers! thieves!" shrieked Lettice.

"But what is it, Lettice?" I cried, leaping down.

"Oh, Mr. Johnny, the house is robbed!—and we might just as well all have been murdered in our beds!"

Every one was appearing on the scene. Miss Deveen came fully dressed—she was often up before other people; Cattledon arrived in a white petticoat and shawl. The servants were running up from the kitchen.

Thieves had broken in during the night. The (so-called) breakfast-room at the back presented a scene of indescribable confusion. Everything in it was turned topsy-turvy, the secretary had been ransacked; the glass-doors stood open to the garden.

It seemed that Lettice, in pursuance of her morning's duties, had gone to the room, and found it in this state. Lettice was of the excitable order, and went into shrieks. She stood now, sobbing and shaking, as she gave her explanation.

"When I opened the door and saw the room in this pickle, the window standing open, my very blood seemed to curdle within me. For all I knew the thieves might have done murder. Just look at the place, ma'am!—look at your secretary!"

It's what we were all looking at. The sight was as good as moving house. Chairs and footstools lay upside down, their chintz covers untied and flung off; the hearthrug was under the table; books were open, periodicals scattered about; two pictures had been taken from the wall and lay face downwards; every ornament was moved from the mantelpiece. The secretary stood open; all its papers had been taken out, opened, and lay in a heap on the floor; and Janet Carey's well-stocked work-box was turned bottom upwards, its contents having rolled anywhere.

"This must be your work, George," said Miss Cattledon, turning on the servant-man with a grim frown.

"Mine, ma'am!" he answered, amazed at the charge.

"Yes, yours," repeated Cattledon. "You could not have fastened the shutters last night; and that is how the thieves have got in."

"But I did, ma'am. I fastened them just as usual."

"Couldn't be," said Cattledon decisively, who had been making her way over the débris to examine the shutters. "They have not been forced in any way: they have simply been opened. The window also."

"And neither window nor shutters could be opened from the outside without force," remarked Miss Deveen. "I fear, George, you must have forgotten this room when you shut up last night."

"Indeed, ma'am, I did not forget it," was the respectful answer. "I assure you I bolted the window and barred the shutters as I always do."

Janet Carey, standing in mute wonder like the rest of us, testified to this. "When I came in here last night to get a needle and thread to mend Miss Whitney's dress, I am sure the shutters were shut: I noticed that they were."

Cattledon would not listen. She had taken up her own opinion of George's neglect, and sharply told Janet not to be so positive. Janet looked frightfully white and wan this morning, worse than a ghost.

"Oh, goodness!" cried Helen Whitney, appearing on the scene. "If ever I saw such a thing!"

"I never did—in all my life," cried Cattledon.

"Have you lost any valuables from the secretary, Miss Deveen?"

"My dear Helen, there were no valuables in the secretary to lose," was Miss Deveen's answer. "Sometimes I keep money in it—a little: but last night there happened to be none. Of course the thieves could not know that, and must have been greatly disappointed. If they did not come in through the window—why, they must have got in elsewhere."

Miss Deveen spoke in a dubious tone, that too plainly showed her own doubts on the point. George felt himself and his word reflected upon.

"If I had indeed forgotten this window last night, ma'am—though for me to do such a thing seems next door to impossible—I would confess to it at once. I can be upon my oath, ma'am, if put to it, that I made all secure here at dusk."

"Then, George, you had better look to your other doors and windows," was the reply of his mistress.

The other doors and windows were looked to: but no trace could be found of how the thieves got in. After breakfast, we succeeded in putting the room tolerably straight. The letters and bills took most time, for every one was lying open. And after it was all done, Miss Deveen came to the conclusion that nothing had been taken.

"Their object must have been money," she observed. "It is a good thing I happened to carry my cash-box upstairs yesterday. Sometimes I leave it here in the secretary."

"And was much in it?" one of us asked.

"Not very much. More, though, than one cares to lose: a little gold and a bank-note."

"A bank-note!" echoed Janet, repeating the words quickly. "Is it safe?—are you sure, ma'am, the note is safe?"

"Well, I conclude it is," answered Miss Deveen with composure. "I saw the cash-box before I came down this morning. I did not look inside it."

"Oh, but you had better look," urged Janet, betraying some excitement. "Suppose it should be gone! Can I look, ma'am?"

"What nonsense!" exclaimed Helen. "If the cash-box is safe, the money must be safe inside it. The thieves did not go into Miss Deveen's room, Janet Carey."

The servants wanted the police called in; but their mistress saw no necessity for it. Nothing had been carried off, she said, and therefore she should take no further trouble. Her private opinion was that George, in spite of his assertions, must have forgotten the window.

It seemed a curious thing that the thieves had not visited other rooms. Unless, indeed, the door of this one had been locked on the outside, and they were afraid to risk the noise of forcing it: and no one could tell whether the key had been turned, or not. George had the plate-basket in his bed-chamber; but on the sideboard in the dining-room stood a silver tea-caddy and a small silver waiter: how was it they had not walked off with these two articles? Or, as the cook said, why didn't they rifle her larder? She had various tempting things in it, including a fresh-boiled ham.

"Janet Carey has been ill all the afternoon," observed Anna, when I and Helen got home before dinner, for we had been out with Miss Deveen. "I think she feels frightened about the thieves, for one thing."

"Ill for nothing!" returned Helen slightingly. "Why should she be frightened any more than we are? The thieves did not hurt her. I might just as well say I am ill."

"But she has been really ill, Helen. She has a shivering-fit one minute and is sick the next. Cattledon says she must have caught cold yesterday, and is cross with her for catching it."

"Listen," said Helen, lowering her voice. "I can't get it out of my head that that old fortune-teller must have had to do with it. She must have seen the secretary and may have taken note of the window fastenings. I am in a state over it: as you both know, it was I who had her up."

Janet did not come down until after dinner. She was pale and quiet, but not less ready than ever to do what she could for every one. Helen had brought home some ferns to—transfer, I think she called it. Janet at once offered to help her. The process involved a large hand-basin full of water, and Miss Deveen sent the two girls into the breakfast-parlour, not to make a mess in the drawing-room.

"Well, my dears," said Miss Deveen, when she had read the chapter before bed-time, "I hope you will all sleep well to-night, and that we shall be undisturbed by thieves. Not that they disturbed us last night," she added, laughing. "Considering all things, I'm sure they were as polite and considerate thieves as we could wish to have to do with."

Whether the others slept well I cannot say: I know I did. So well that I never woke at all until the same cries from Lettice disturbed the house as on the previous morning. The thieves had been in again.

Downstairs we went, as quickly as some degree of dressing allowed, and found the breakfast-room all confusion, the servants all consternation: the window open as before; the furniture turned about, the ornaments and pictures moved from their places, the books scattered, the papers of the secretary lying unfolded in a heap on the carpet, and a pair of embroidered slippers of Helen Whitney's lying in the basin of water.

"What an extraordinary thing!" exclaimed Miss Deveen, while the rest of us stood in silent amazement.

Lettice's tale was the same as the previous one. Upon proceeding to the room to put it to rights, she found it thus, and its shutters and glass-doors wide open. There was no trace, except here, of the possible entrance or exit of thieves: all other fastenings were secure as they had been left over-night; other rooms had not been disturbed; and, more singular than all, nothing appeared to have been taken. What could the thieves be seeking?

"Shall you call in the police now, ma'am?" asked Cattledon, her tone implying that they ought to have been called in before.

"Yes, I shall," emphatically replied Miss Deveen.

"Oh!" shrieked Helen, darting in, after making a hasty and impromptu toilet, "look at my new slippers!"

After finishing the ferns last night they had neglected to send the basin away. The slippers were rose-coloured, worked with white flowers in floss silk; and the bits of loose green from the ferns floated over them like green weeds on a pond. Helen had bought them when we were out yesterday.

"My beautiful slippers!" lamented Helen. "I wish to goodness I had not forgotten to take them upstairs. What wicked thieves they must be! They ought to be hung."

"It's to know, mum, whether it was thieves," spoke the cook.

"Why, what else can it have been, cook?" asked Miss Deveen.

"Mum, I don't pretend to say. I've knowed cats do queer things. We've two on 'em—the old cat and her kitten."

"Did you ever know cats unlock a secretary and take out the papers, cook?" returned Miss Deveen.

"Well, no, mum. But, on the other hand, I never knowed thieves break into a house two nights running, and both times go away empty-handed."

The argument was unanswerable. Unless the thieves had been disturbed on each night, how was it they had taken nothing?

Miss Deveen locked the door upon the room just as it was; and after breakfast sent George to the nearest police-station. Whilst he was gone I was alone in the dining-room, stooping down to hunt for a book in the lowest shelf of the book-case, when Janet Carey came in followed by Cattledon. I suppose the table-cover hid me from them, for Cattledon began to blow her up.

"One would think you were a troubled ghost, shaking and shivering in that way, first upstairs and then down! The police coming!—what if they are? They are not coming after you this time. There's no money missing now."

Janet burst into tears. "Oh, aunt, why do you speak so to me? It is as though you believe me guilty!"

"Don't be a simpleton, Janet," rebuked Cattledon, in softer tones. "If I did not know you were not, and could not, be guilty, should I have brought you here under Miss Deveen's roof? What vexes me so much is to see you look as though you were guilty—with your white face, and your hysterics, and your trembling hands and lips. Get a little spirit into yourself, child: the police won't harm you."

Catching up the keys from the table, she went out again, leaving Janet sobbing. I stood forward. She started when she saw me, and tried to dry her eyes.

"I am sorry, Miss Carey, that all this bother is affecting you. Why are you so sad?"

"I—have gone through a great deal of trouble lately;—and been ill," she answered, with hesitation, arresting her tears.

"Can I do anything for you?—help you in any way?"

"You are very kind, Mr. Ludlow; you have been kind to me all along. There's nothing any one can do. Sometimes I wish I could die."

"Die!"

"There is so much unhappiness in the world!"

George's voice was heard in the hall with the policeman. Janet vanished. But whether it was through the floor or out at the door, I declare I did not see then, and don't quite know to this day.

I and Cattledon were allowed to assist at the conference between Miss Deveen and the policeman: a dark man with a double chin and stripes on his coat-sleeve. After hearing particulars, and examining the room and the mess it was in, he inquired how many servants were kept, and whether Miss Deveen had confidence in them. She told him the number, and said she had confidence in all.

He went into the kitchen, put what questions he pleased to the servants, looked at the fastenings of the doors generally, examined the outside of the window and walked about the garden. George called him Mr. Stone—which appeared to be his name. Mr. Stone had nothing of a report to bring Miss Deveen.

"It's one of two things, ma'am," he said. "Either this has been done by somebody in your own house; or else the neighbours are playing tricks upon you. I can't come to any other conclusion. The case is peculiar, you see, in-so-far as that nothing has been stolen."

"It is very peculiar indeed," returned Miss Deveen.

"I should have said—I should feel inclined to say—that the culprit is some one in the house—"

"It's the most unlikely thing in the world, that it should have been any one in the house," struck in Miss Deveen, not allowing him to go on. "To suspect any of the young people who are visiting me, would be simply an insult. And my servants would no more play the trick than I or Miss Cattledon would play it."

"Failing indoors then, we must look out," said Mr. Stone, after listening patiently. "And that brings up more difficulty, ma'am. For I confess I don't see how they could get the windows and shutters open from the outside, and leave no marks of damage."

"The fact of the window and shutters being wide open each morning, shows how they got out."

"Just so," said Mr. Stone; "but it does not show how they got in. Of course there's the possibility that they managed to secrete themselves in the house beforehand."

"Yesterday I thought that might have been the case," remarked Miss Deveen; "to-day I do not think so. It seems that, after what occurred, my servants were especially cautious to keep their doors and windows not only closed, but bolted all day yesterday, quite barring the possibility of any one's stealing in. Except, of course, down the chimneys."

Mr. Stone laughed. "They'd bring a lot of soot with 'em that way."

"And spoil my hearthrugs. No; that was not the way of entrance."

"Then we come to the question—did one of the servants get up and admit 'em?"

"But that would be doubting my servants still, you see. It really seems, Mr. Stone, as though you could not help me."

"Before saying whether I can or I can't, I should be glad, ma'am, to have a conversation with you alone," was the unexpected answer.

So we left him with Miss Deveen. Cattledon's stays appeared to resent it, for they creaked alarmingly in the hall, and her voice was tart.

"Perhaps the man wants to accuse you or me, Mr. Johnny!"

We knew later, after the upshot came, what it was he did want; and I may as well state it at once. Stone had made up his mind to watch that night in the garden; but he wished it kept secret from every one, except Miss Deveen herself, and he charged her strictly not to mention it. "How will it serve you, if, as you say, they do not come in that way?" she had asked. "But the probability is they come out that way," he answered. "At any rate, they fling the doors open, and I shall be there to drop upon them."

Janet Carey grew very ill as the day went on. Lettice offered to sit up with her, in case she wanted anything in the night. Janet had just the appearance of somebody worn out.

We went to bed at the usual time, quite unconscious that Mr. Stone had taken up his night watch in the summer-house at the end of the garden. The nights were very bright just then; the moon at about the full. Nothing came of it: neither the room nor the window was disturbed.

"They scented my watch," remarked the officer in private next morning to Miss Deveen. "However, ma'am, I don't think it likely you will be troubled again. Seeing you've put it into our hands, they'll not dare to risk further annoyance."

"I suppose not—if they know it," dubiously spoke Miss Deveen.

He shook his head. "They know as much as that, ma'am. Depend upon it their little game is over."

Mr. Stone was mistaken. On the following morning, the breakfast-room was found by Lettice in exactly the same state of confusion. The furniture dragged about, the ornaments moved from the mantelpiece, the bills and papers opened, as before. Miss Deveen was very silent over it, and said in the hearing of the servants that she should have to carry the grievance to Scotland Yard.

And I'm sure I thought she set out to do it. The carriage came to the door in the course of the morning. Miss Deveen, who was ready dressed, passed over the others, and asked me to go with her.

"Do you know what I'm going to do, Johnny?" she questioned, as George took his place on the box and the fat old coachman gave the word to his horses.

"I think I do, Miss Deveen. We are going to Scotland Yard."

"Not a bit of it, Johnny," she said. "My opinion has come round to Mr. Policeman Stone's—that we must look indoors for the disturber. I have brought you out with me to talk about it. It is a great mystery—for I thought I could have trusted the servants and all the rest of you with my life."

It was a mystery—and no mistake.

"A great mystery," repeated Miss Deveen; "a puzzle; and I want you to help me to unravel it, Johnny. I intend to sit up to-night in the breakfast-room. But not being assured of my nerves while watching in solitude for thieves, or ghosts, or what not, I wish you to sit up with me."

"Oh, I shall like it, Miss Deveen."

"I have heard of houses being disturbed before in a similar manner," she continued. "There was a story in the old days of the Cock-Lane ghost: I think that was something of the same kind, but my memory is rather cloudy on the point. Other cases I know have been traced to the sudden mania, solely mischievous or otherwise, of some female inmate. I hope it will not turn out to have been Lettice herself."

"Shall I watch without you, Miss Deveen?"

"No, no; you will bear me company. We will make our arrangements now, Johnny—for I do not intend that any soul shall know of this; not even Miss Cattledon. You will keep counsel, mind, like the true and loyal knight you are."

The house had gone to rest. In the dark breakfast-room sat Miss Deveen and I, side by side. The fire was dying away, and it gave scarcely any light. We sat back against the wall between the fireplace and the door, she in one armchair, I in another. The secretary was opposite the fire, the key in the lock as usual; the window, closed and barred, lay to the left, the door to the right, a table in the middle. An outline of the objects was just discernible in the fading light.

"Do you leave the key in the secretary as a rule, Miss Deveen?" I asked in a whisper.

"Yes. There's nothing in it that any one would care to look at," she replied in the same cautious tone. "My cash-box is generally there, but that is always locked. But I think we had better not talk, Johnny."

So we sat on in silence. The faint light of the fire died away, giving place to total darkness. It was weary watching there, hour after hour, each hour seeming an age. Twelve o'clock struck; one; two! I'd have given something to be able to fall asleep. Just to speak a word to Miss Deveen would be a relief, and I forgot her injunctions.

"Are you thinking of ghosts, Miss Deveen?"

"Just then I was thinking of God, Johnny. How good it is to know that He is with us in the dark as in the light."

Almost with the last word, my ears, younger and quicker than Miss Deveen's, caught the sound of a faint movement outside—as though steps were descending the stairs. I touched Miss Deveen's arm and breathed a caution.

"I hear something. I think it is coming now."

The door softly opened. Some white figure was standing there—as might be seen by the glimmer of light that came in through the passage window. Who or what it was, we could not gather. It closed the door behind it, and came slowly gliding along the room on the other side the table, evidently feeling its way as it went, and making for the window. We sat in breathless silence. Miss Deveen had caught my hand and was holding it in hers.

Next, the shutters were unfastened and slowly folded back; then the window was unbolted and its doors were flung wide. This let in a flood of moonlight: after the darkness the room seemed bright as day. And the white figure doing all this was—Janet Carey in her nightgown, her feet bare.

Whether Miss Deveen held my hand the tighter, or I hers, I dare say neither of us could tell. Janet's eyes turned on us, as we sat: and I fully expected her to go into a succession of shrieks.

But no. She took no manner of notice. It was just as though she did not see us. Steadily, methodically as it seemed, she proceeded to search the room, apparently looking for something. First, she took the chintz cover off the nearest chair, and shook it out; turned over the chair and felt it all over; a small round stand was served the same; a blotting-case that happened to lie on the table she carried to the window, knelt down, and examined it on the floor by the moonlight, passing her fingers over its few pages, unfolding a letter that was inside and shaking it out to the air. Then all that was left on the floor, and she turned over another chair, and so went on.

I felt as cold as charity. Was it her ghost that was doing this? How was it she did not see us sitting there? Her eyes were open enough to see anything!

Coming to the secretary, she turned the key, and began her search in it. Pulling out one drawer first, she opened every paper it contained, shook them one by one, and let them drop on the floor. As she was commencing at the next drawer, her back towards us, Miss Deveen whispered to me.

"We will get away, Johnny. You go on first. No noise, mind."

We got out without being seen or heard. At least, there was no outcry; no sign to tell we had been. Miss Deveen drew me into the dining-room; her face, as it caught the glimmer, entering by the fan-light over the hall-door, looked deadly pale.

"I understand it all, Johnny. She is doing it in her sleep."

"In her sleep?"

"Yes. She is unconscious. It was better to come away. As she came round to search our part of the room, she might have found us, and awoke. That would have been dangerous."

"But, Miss Deveen, what is she searching for?"

"I know. I see it all perfectly. It is for a bank-note."

"But—if she is really asleep, how can she go about the search in that systematic way? Her eyes are wide open: she seems to examine things as though she saw them."

"I cannot tell you how it is, Johnny. They do seem to see things, though they are asleep. What's more, when they awake there remains no consciousness of what they have done. This is not the first case of somnambulism I have been an eye-witness to. She throws the window and shutters open to admit the light."

"How can she have sense to know in her sleep that opening them will admit it?"

"Johnny, though these things are, I cannot explain them. Go up to your bed now and get to sleep. As I shall go to mine. You shall know about Janet in the morning. She will take no harm if left alone: she has taken none hitherto. Say nothing to any one."

It was the solution of the great puzzle. Janet Carey had done it all in her sleep. And what she had been searching for was a bank-note.

In the situation where Janet had been living as nursery-governess, a bank-note had disappeared. Janet was suspected and accused of taking it. Constitutionally timid and nervous, her spirits long depressed by circumstances, the accusation had a grave effect upon her. She searched the house for it incessantly, almost night and day, just as we had seen her searching the parlour at Miss Deveen's in her sleep, and then fell into a fever—which was only saved by great care from settling on the brain. When well enough, Miss Cattledon had her removed to London to Miss Deveen's; but the stigma still clung to her, and the incipient fever seemed still to hover about her. The day William Whitney left, she moved from Miss Cattledon's chamber to the one he had occupied: and that night, being unrestrained, she went down in her sleep to search. The situation of the room in which the note had been lost was precisely similar to this breakfast-room at Miss Deveen's—in her troubled sleep, poor girl, she must have taken it for the same room, and crept down, still asleep, to renew the endless search she had formerly made when awake. The night the policeman was watching in the summer-house, Lettice sat up with Janet; so that night nothing occurred. Lettice said afterwards that Miss Carey twice got out of bed in her sleep and seemed to be making for the door, but Lettice guided her back to bed again. And so there was the elucidation: and Janet was just as unconscious of what she had done as the bed-post.

Miss Deveen's medical man was called in, for brain-fever, escaped, appeared to be fastening on Janet in earnest now. He gave it as his opinion that she was no natural sleep-walker, but that the mind's disturbance had so acted on the brain and system, coupled with her fright at meeting the policeman at the Colosseum, as to have induced the result. At any rate, whatever may have caused it, and strange though it was, I have only given facts. And in the next paper we shall hear more about the bank-note.

CHAPTER IV

JANET CAREY

It was a summer's evening, some two years or so previous to the events told of in the last chapter, and the sun was setting in clouds of crimson and gold. On the green lawn at the back of Rose Villa—a pretty detached house, about twenty minutes' walk from the town of Lefford—sat a lady in a gay dress. She was dark and plain, with crinkled black hair, and a rough voice. A girl of twelve, fair, pretty, and not in the least like her, sat on the same bench. Three younger girls were scampering about at some noisy play; and a boy, the youngest of all, lay on the grass, whistling, and knotting a whip-cord. The sun's slanting rays tinted all with a warm hue.

"Get up, Dicky," said the lady to the boy.

Dicky, aged five, whistled on, without taking any notice.

"Did you hear mamma tell you to get up, Dicky?" spoke the fair girl by her mother's side. "Get up, sir."

"Shan't," said Dicky.

"You go in for me, Mina," said Mrs. Knox. "I want to know the time. Arnold took my watch into town this morning to have the spring mended."

Mina seemed in no more hurry to obey than Dicky was. Just then a low pony-chaise, driven by a boy-groom, rattled out from the stable-yard at the side of the house. Mina looked across at it.

"It must be about a quarter-past eight," she said. "You told James not to be later than that in going to the station."

"You might go and see," spoke Mrs. Knox: "James is not sure to be to time. How glad I shall be when that governess is here to take the trouble of you children off me!" she added, fretfully. Mina did not take the hint about going in: she made off to her sisters instead.

This house had once been a doctor's residence. Soon after Thomas Knox, surgeon and apothecary, set up in practice at Lefford, now five-and-twenty years ago, he married Mary Arnold. Rose Villa was hers, and some money besides, and they came to live at it, Mr. Knox keeping on his surgery in Lefford. They had one son, who was named Arnold. When Arnold was ten years old, his mother died. A year later his father married a second wife, Miss Amelia Carey: after which these five other young ones came to town. Arnold was to be a doctor like his father. His studies were in progress, when one morning a letter came to him in London—where he was walking Bartholomew's Hospital under that clever man, William Lawrence—saying that his father was alarmingly ill. Arnold reached Lefford just in time to see him die. The little one, Dicky, was a baby then in long-clothes. Arnold was only nineteen. No chance that he could set up in, and keep together the practice, which fell through. So he went back to London to study on, and pass, and what not; and by-and-by he came down again Dr. Knox: for he had followed the fashion just then getting common, of taking the M.D. degree. Arnold Knox had his share of good plain sense, and of earnestness too; but example is catching, and he only followed that of his fellow-students in going in thus early for the degree. He arrived at Lefford "Dr. Knox." Mr. Tamlyn laughed at him, before his face and behind his back, asking him what experience he had had that he should hasten to tack on M.D. to his name: why, not more experience than a country apothecary's apprentice. Arnold, feeling half ashamed of himself, for he was very modest, pleaded the new custom. Custom! returned old Tamlyn; in his days medical men had worked for their honours before taking them. Arnold engaged himself as assistant to Mr. Tamlyn, who had dropped into the best part of Dr. Knox's practice since that gentleman's death, in addition to his own.

Meanwhile, Mrs. Knox, the widow, had continued to live at Rose Villa. It belonged to Arnold, having descended to him in right of his mother. Mr. Knox had bequeathed by will five hundred pounds to Arnold for the completion of his studies; and all the rest of his money to his wife and second family. Lefford talked of it resentfully, saying it was an unjust will: for a good portion of the money had been Mary Arnold's and ought to have gone to her son. It was about three hundred and fifty pounds a-year in all; and Mrs. Knox bewailed and bemoaned her hard fate at having to bring up her children upon so little. She was one of those who must spend; and her extravagance had kept her husband poor, in spite of his good practice.

Never a hint did she offer her step-son of paying him rent for his house; never a word of thanks did she tender for the use of it.

Arnold said nothing: he was thoroughly warm-hearted and generous, considering every one before himself, and he would not have hurt her feelings or cramped her pocket for the world. As long as he did not want the house, she and his half-sisters and brother were welcome to it. When he came back from London he naturally went to it; it was his home; and Mrs. Knox did not at all like the addition he made to her housekeeping expenses: which could not be very much amongst the nine others to provide for. The very day after Arnold's bargain was made with Mr. Tamlyn, she asked him how much he was going to pay her for his board. Half his salary, Arnold promptly replied; seventy-five pounds a-year. And Mrs. Knox would have liked to say it was not enough.

"Seventy-five pounds a-year!" cackled Lefford, when it got hold of the news. "Why, it won't cost her half that. And she using his house and enjoying all the money that was his poor mother's! Well, she has a conscience, that Widow Knox!"

The arrangement had continued until now. Three years had elapsed since then, and Arnold was four-and-twenty. Mrs. Knox found herself often in money difficulties; when she would borrow from Arnold, and never think of repaying him. She was now going to increase expenses by taking a nursery-governess. Awfully tiresome those children were, and Mrs. Knox said they wore her out. She should have managed the little brats better: not indulged and neglected them by turns. One hour she'd let them run wild, the next hour was shrieking at them in words next door to swearing.

The governess engaged was a distant relative of her own, a Miss Janet Carey. She was an orphan, and had for a year or two been teacher in a boys' preparatory school, limited to thirty pupils. Mrs. Knox wrote to offer her twelve pounds a-year and a "very comfortable home at Rose Villa; to be as one of the family." It must have sounded tempting to Miss Carey after the thirty little boys, and she gratefully accepted it. Mrs. Knox had never seen her; she pictured to herself a tall, bony young woman with weak eyes, for that had been the portrait of her second cousin, Miss Carey's father.

"Crack! crack! Tally-ho! tally-ho!" shouted Dicky, who had completed his whip, and got up to stamp and smack it. "Yo-ho! Tally-ho, tally-ho!"

"Oh, do for goodness' sake be quiet, Dick!" screamed Mrs. Knox. "I can't have that noise now: I told you I had a headache. Do you hear me, then! Mina, come and take away this horrible whip."

Mina came running at the call. Master Dicky was so much given way to as a general rule, that to thwart him seemed to his sisters something delightful. Dicky dodged out of harm's way amongst the shrubs; and Mina was about to go after him, when some one came through the open glass-doors of what was called the garden-room.

"Here's Arnold," she cried.

Dr. Knox was a tall, strongly built, fair man, looking older than his four-and-twenty years. Nobody could help liking his thin face, for it was a good face, full of sense and thought, but it was not a handsome one. His complexion was sallow, and his light hair had a habit of standing up wild.

"You are home betimes," remarked Mrs. Knox.

"Yes; there was nothing more to do," he answered, sitting down in a rustic garden-chair. "I met James in the pony-chaise: where's he gone?"

"Why, Arnold, don't you know that the governess is coming this evening?" cried the second girl, Lotty, who was fanning her hot face with a cabbage-leaf. "James has gone to the station for her."

"I forgot all about the governess," said Dr. Knox. "Lotty, what a heat you are in!"

"We have been running races," said the child; "and the sun was blazing."

Dicky came tearing up. Something had happened to the whip.

"Look at it, Arnold," he said, throwing his arms and the whip on the doctor's knees. "The lash won't stay on."

"And you want me to mend it, I suppose."

"Yes. Do it now."

"Is that the way to ask?"

"Please do it now, Arnold."

"If I can. But I fear I can't, Dicky."

"No! You can mend arms and legs."

"Sometimes. Have you a strip of leather? Or some twine?"

Dicky pulled a piece of string out of some unfathomable pocket. He was not promoted to trousers yet, but wore white drawers reaching to the knee and a purple velvet tunic. Dr. Knox took out his penknife.

"What's the matter with that young Tamlyn again?" asked Mrs. Knox in a fretful tone.

"With Bertie?" returned Dr. Knox, rather carelessly, for he was intent on the whip. "It is one of the old attacks."

"Of course! I knew it was nothing more," spoke Mrs Knox in resentment. "There was to have been a party at Mrs. Green's this evening. Just as I was ready to start for it, her footman came to say it was put off on account of Miss Tamlyn, who could not come because Master Albert was ill."

"Miss Tamlyn would not leave Bertie when he is ill for all the parties in Christendom, mother."

"Miss Tamlyn is welcome to stay with him. But that's no reason why Mrs. Green should have put the rest of us off. Who's Bessy Tamlyn, that she should be considered before every one?—stupid old maid!"

Mrs. Knox pushed up her lace sleeves in wrath, and jingled her bracelets. Evening parties made the solace of her life.

The wheels of the returning chaise were heard, and the children went rushing round to the front of the house to look at the new governess. They brought Janet Carey back to the lawn. Mrs. Knox saw a small, slight young girl with a quiet, nice face and very simple manners. Dr. Knox rose. Mrs. Knox did not rise. Expecting to see a kind of dark strong giantess, she was struck with astonishment and remained sitting.

"You are surely not Matthew Carey's daughter?"

"Yes, madam, I am," was the young lady's answer, as a blush stole into the clear, meek face.

"Dear me! I should never have thought it. Mat Carey was as tall and big as a lamp-post. And—why!—you told me you were twenty-three!"

"I was twenty-three last March."

"Well, I trust you will be found competent to manage my children. I had no idea you were so young-looking."

The tone expressed a huge doubt of it. The ill-trained youngsters stood staring rudely into Miss Carey's face. Dr. Knox, pushing some of them aside, held out his hand with a smile of welcome.

"I hope you will be able to feel at home here, Miss Carey," he said: "the children must not be allowed to give you too much trouble. Have you had a pleasant journey?"

"Take Miss Carey to her room, Mina," sharply struck in Mrs. Knox, not at all pleased that her step-son should presume to say so much: as if the house were his. And Mina, followed by the shy and shrinking young governess, went indoors and up to the roof, and showed her a little comfortless chamber there.

(But the reader must understand that in writing this paper, I, Johnny Ludlow, am at a disadvantage. Not having been present myself at Lefford, I can only relate at second hand what happened at Mrs. Knox's.)

The time went on. Janet Carey proved herself equal to her work: although Mrs. Knox, judging by her young look and gentle manners, had been struck by a doubt of her capacity, and politely expressed it aloud. Janet's duties were something like the labours of Hercules: at least, as varied. Teaching was only one of them. She helped to dress and undress the children, or did it entirely if Sally the housemaid forgot to attend; she kept all the wardrobes and mended the clothes and the socks. She had to be in all places at once. Helping Mrs. Knox in the parlour, taking messages to the kitchen, hearing the girls' lessons, and rushing out to the field to see that Dicky was not worrying the pony or milking the cow on his own account. It was not an orderly household; two maids were kept and James. Mrs. Knox had no talent for management, and was frightfully lazy besides; and Janet, little foreseeing what additional labour she would bring on herself, took to remedy as far as she could the shortcomings and confusion. Mrs. Knox saw her value, and actually thanked her. As a reward, she made Janet her own attendant, her secretary, and partly her housekeeper. Mrs. Knox's hair, coarse and stiff, was rather difficult hair to manage; in the morning it was let go anyhow, and Janet dressed it in the afternoon. Janet wrote Mrs. Knox's letters; kept her accounts; paid the bills—paid them, that is, when she could get the money. Janet, you perceive, was made Jack-of-all-trades at Rose Villa. She was conscious that it was hardly fair, but she did it cheerfully; and, as Mrs. Knox would say, it was all in the day's work.

The only one who showed consideration for Miss Carey was Dr. Knox. He lectured the children about giving her so much unnecessary trouble: he bribed Dicky with lozenges and liquorice from the surgery drawers not to kick or spit at her; and he was, himself, ever kind and considerate to her. They only met at dinner and tea, for Dr. Knox snatched a scrambling breakfast (the servants never got it ready for him in time), and went off betimes to Lefford. Now and then he would come home tolerably early in the evening, but he had a great deal to do, and it did not happen often. Mr. Tamlyn was the parish doctor, and it gave Dr. Knox an incessant round of tramping: for the less pleasant division of the daily professional work was turned over to him.

They got to have a fellow-feeling for one another—Janet and Dr. Knox—a kind of mutual, inward sympathy. Both of them were overworked; in the lot of each was less of comfort than might have been. Dr. Knox compassionated Janet's hard place and the want of poetry in her life. Janet felt hurt to see him made so little of at home, and she knew about the house being his property, and the seventy-five pounds a-year he paid for the liberty of living in it,—and she knew that most of the income enjoyed by Mrs. Knox ought to have been Arnold's income. His breakfast was scanty; a cup of coffee, taken standing, and some bread-and-butter, hurriedly eaten. Or he would be off by cockcrow without chance of breakfast, unless he cut a slice of bread in the pantry: or perhaps would have to be out all night. Sometimes he would get home to dinner; one o'clock; more often it was two o-clock, or half-past, or three. In that case, Sally would bring in a plate of half-cold scraps for him—anything that happened to be left. Once, when Janet was carving a leg of mutton, she asked leave to cut off a slice or two that they might be kept warm for the doctor; but Mrs. Knox blew her up—a fine trouble that would be! As to tea, the chances were, if he came in to it at all, that the teapot would be drained: upon which, some lukewarm water would be dashed in, and the loaf and butter put before him. Dr. Knox took it all quietly: perhaps he saw how useless complaint would be.

Mr. Tamlyn's was a large, handsome, red-brick house, standing in a beautiful garden, in the best and widest street of Lefford. The surgery, built on the side of the house, consisted of two rooms: one containing the drugs and the scales, and so on; the other where the better class of patients waited. Mr. Tamlyn's wife was dead, and he had one son, who was a cripple. Poor Bertie was thrown down by his nurse when he was a child; he had hardly ever been out of pain since; sometimes the attacks were very bad. It made him more cross and fractious than a stranger would believe; rude, in fact, and self-willed. Mr. Tamlyn just worshipped Bertie. He only lived to one end—that of making money for Bertie, after he, himself, should be gone. Miss Bessy, Mr. Tamlyn's half-sister, kept his house, and she was the only one who tried to keep down Bertie's temper. Lefford thought it odd that Mr. Tamlyn did not raise Dr. Knox's salary: but it was known he wanted to put by what he could for Bertie.

The afternoon sun streamed full on the surgery-window, and Dr. Knox, who had just pelted back from dinner, stood behind the counter, making up bottles of physic. Mr. Tamlyn had an apprentice, a young fellow named Dockett, but he could not be trusted with the physic department yet, as he was apt to serve out calomel powder for camomile flowers. Of the three poor parish patients, waiting for their medicine, two sat and one stood, as there was not a third chair. The doctor spoke very kindly to them about their ailments; he always did that; but he did not seem well himself, and often put his hand to his throat and chest.

The physic and the parish patients done with, he went into the other room, and threw himself into the easy-chair. "I wonder what's the matter with me?" he said to himself: and then he got up again, for Mr. Tamlyn was coming in. He was a short man with a grey face, and iron grey hair.

"Arnold," said he, "I wish you'd take my round this afternoon. There are only three or four people who need be seen, and the carriage is at the door."

"Is Bertie worse than usual?" asked Arnold; who knew that every impediment in Mr. Tamlyn's way was caused by Bertie.

"He is in a great deal of pain. I really don't care to leave him."

"Oh, I'll go with pleasure," replied Arnold, passing into the surgery to get his hat.

Mr. Tamlyn walked with him across the flagged court to the gate, talking of the sick people he was going to see. Arnold got into the brougham and was driven away. When he returned, Mr. Tamlyn was upstairs in Bertie's sitting-room. Arnold went there.

"Anything more come in?" he asked. "Or can the brougham be put up?"

"Dear me, yes; here's a note from Mrs. Stephenson," said Mr. Tamlyn, replying to the first question. And he spoke testily: for Mrs. Stephenson was a lady of seventy, who always insisted on his own attendance, objecting to Dr. Knox on the score of his youth. "Well, you must go for once, Arnold. If she grumbles, tell her I was out."

On a sofa in the room lay Albert Tamlyn; a lad of sixteen with a fretful countenance and rumpled hair. Miss Tamlyn, a pleasant-looking lady of thirty-five, sat by the sofa at work. Arnold Knox went up to the boy, speaking with the utmost gentleness.

"Bertie, my boy, I am sorry you are in pain to-day."

"Who said I was in pain?" retorted Bertie, ungraciously, his voice as squeaky as a penny trumpet.

"Why, Bertie, you know you are in great pain: it was I who told Dr. Knox so," interposed the father.

"Then you had no business to tell him so," shrieked Bertie, with a hideous grin of resentment. "What is it to him?—or to you?—or to anybody?"

"Oh, Bertie, Bertie!" whispered Miss Tamlyn. "Oh, my boy, you should not give way like this."

"You just give your tongue a holiday, Aunt Bessy," fired Bertie. "I can't be bothered by you all in this way."

Dr. Knox, looking down at him, saw something wrong in the position he was lying in. He stooped, lifted him quietly in his strong arms, and altered it.

"There, Bertie, you will be better now."

"No, I'm not better, and why d'you interfere?" retorted Bertie in his temper, and burst out crying. It was weary work, waiting on that lad; the house had a daily benefit of it. He had always been given way to: his whims were studied, his tempers went unreproved, and no patience was taught him.

Dr. Knox drove to Mrs. Stephenson's. He dismissed the carriage when he came out; for he had some patients to see on his own score amongst the poor, and went on to them. They were at tea at Mr. Tamlyn's when he got back. He looked very ill, and sat down at once.

"Are you tired, Arnold?" asked the surgeon.

"Not very; but I feel out of sorts. My throat is rather painful."

"What's the matter with it?"

"Not much, I dare say. A little ulcerated perhaps."

"I'll have a look at it presently. Bessy, give Dr. Knox a cup of tea."

"Thank you, I shall be glad of it," interposed the doctor. It was not often he took a meal in the house, not liking to intrude on them. When he went up this evening he had thought tea was over.

"We are later than usual," said Miss Tamlyn, in answer to some remark he made. "Bertie dropped asleep."

Bertie was awake, and eating relays of bread-and-butter as he lay, speaking to no one. The handsome sitting-rooms downstairs were nearly deserted: Mr. Tamlyn could not bear even to take his meals away from Bertie.

It was growing dusk when Dr. Knox went home. Mr. Tamlyn told him to take a cooling draught and to go to bed early. Mrs. Knox was out for the evening. Janet Carey sat at the old piano in the schoolroom, singing songs to the children to keep them quiet. They were crowding round her, and no one saw him enter the room.

Janet happened to be singing the very song she sang later to us that night at Miss Deveen's—"Blow, blow, thou wintry wind." Although she had now been at Rose Villa nearly a twelvemonth, for early summer had come round again, Dr. Knox had never heard her sing. Mrs. Knox hated singing altogether, and especially despised Janet's: it was only when Janet was alone with the children that she ventured on it, hoping to keep them still. Arnold Knox sat in utter silence; entranced; just as we were at Miss Deveen's.

"You sing 'I've been roaming,' now," called out Dicky, before the song was well over.

"No, not that thing," dissented Mina. "Sing 'Pray, Goody,' Janet." They had long since called her by her Christian name.

The whole five (the other three taking sides), not being able to agree, plunged at once into a hot dispute. Janet in vain tried to make peace by saying she would sing both songs, one after the other: they did not listen to her. In the midst of the noise, Sally looked in to say James had caught a magpie; and the lot scampered off.

Janet Carey heaved a sad sigh, and passed her hand over her weary brow. She had had a tiring day: there were times when she thought her duties would get beyond her. Rising to follow the rebellious flock, she caught sight of Dr. Knox, seated back in the wide old cane chair.

"Oh! I—I beg your pardon. I had no idea any one was here."

He came forward smiling; Janet had sat down again in her surprise.

"And though I am here? Why should you beg my pardon, Miss Carey?"

"For singing before you. I did not know—I am very sorry."

"Perhaps you fancy I don't like singing?"

"Mine is such poor singing, sir. And the songs are so old. I can't play: I often only play to them with one hand."

"The singing is so poor—and the songs are so old, that I was going to ask of you—to beg of you—to sing one of them again for me."

She stood glancing up at him with her nice eyes, as shy as could be, uncertain whether he was mocking her.

"Do you know, Miss Carey, that I never ask a young lady for a song now. I don't care to hear the new songs, they are so poor and frivolous: the old ones are worth a king's ransom. Won't you oblige me?"

"What shall I sing?"

"The one you have just sung. 'Blow, blow, thou wintry wind.'"

He drew a chair close, and listened; and seemed lost in thought when it was over. Janet could not conveniently get up without pushing the stool against him, and so sat in silence.

"My mother used to sing that song," he said, looking up. "I can recall her every note as well as though I had heard her yesterday. 'As friends remembering not'! Ay: it's a harsh world—and it grows more harsh and selfish day by day. I don't think it treats you any too well, Miss Carey."

"Me, sir?"

"Who remembers you?"

"Not many people. But I have never had any friends to speak of."

"Will you give me another song? The one I heard Mina ask you for—'Pray, Goody.' My mother used to sing that also."

"I don't know whether I must stay. The children will be getting into mischief."

"Never mind the children. I'll take the responsibility."

Janet sang the song. Before it was finished the flock came in again. Dicky had tried to pull the magpie's feathers out, so James had let it fly.

After this evening, it somehow happened that Dr. Knox often came home early, although his throat was well again. He liked to make Miss Carey sing; and to talk to her; and to linger in the garden with her and the children in the twilight. Mrs. Knox was rarely at home, and had no idea how sociable her step-son was becoming. Lefford and its neighbourhood followed the unfashionable custom of giving early soirées: tea at six, supper at nine, at home by eleven. James used to go for his mistress; on dark nights he took a lighted lantern. Mrs. Knox would arrive at home, her gown well pinned up, and innocent of any treasonable lingerings out-of-doors or in. It was beyond Janet's power to get Mina and Lotty to bed one minute before they chose to go: though her orders from Mrs. Knox on the point were strict. As soon as their mother's step was heard they would make a rush for the stairs. Janet had to follow them, as that formed part of her duty: and by the time Mrs. Knox was indoors, the rooms were free, and Arnold was shut up in his study with his medical books and a skeleton.

For any treason that met the eye or the ear, Mrs. Knox might have assisted at all the interviews. The children might have repeated every word said to one another by the doctor and Janet, and welcome. The talk was all legitimate: of their own individual, ordinary interests, perhaps; of their lost parents; their past lives; the present daily doings; or, as the Vicar of Wakefield has it, of pictures, taste, Shakespeare, and the musical glasses. Dr. Knox never said such a thing to her as, miss, I am in love with you; Janet was the essence of respectful shyness, and called him sir.

One evening something or other caused one of the soirées to break up midway, and Mrs. Knox came home by twilight in her pink gauze gown. Instead of ringing at the front-door, she came round the garden to the lawn, knowing quite well the elder children were not gone to bed, and would probably be in the garden-room. Very softly went she, intending to surprise them. The moon shone full on the glass-doors.

The doors were shut. And she could see no children. Only Janet Carey sitting at the piano, and Dr. Knox sitting close by her, his eyes resting on her face, and an unmistakable look of—say friendship—in them. Mrs. Knox took in the whole scene by the light of the one candle standing on the table.

She let go the pink skirt and burst open the doors. Imagination is apt to conjure up skeletons of the future; a whole army of skeletons rushed into hers, any one of them ten times more ugly than that real skeleton in the doctor's study. A vision of his marrying Janet and taking possession of the house, and wanting all his money for himself instead of paying the family bills with it, was the worst.

Before a great and real dread, passion has to be silent. Mrs. Knox felt that she should very much like to buffet both of them with hands and tongue: but policy restrained her.

"Where are the children?" she began, as snappish as a fox; but that was only usual.

Janet had turned round on the music-stool; her meek hands dropping on her lap, her face turning all the colours of the rainbow. Dr. Knox just sat back in his chair and carelessly hummed to himself the tune Janet had been singing.

"Mina and Lotty are at Mrs. Hampshire's, ma'am," answered Janet. "She came to fetch them just after you left, and said I might send in for them at half-past nine. The little ones are in bed."

"Oh," said Mrs. Knox. "It's rather early for you to be at home; is it not, Arnold?"

"Not particularly, I think. My time for coming home is always uncertain, you know."

He rose, and went to his room as he spoke. Janet got out the basket of stockings; and Mrs. Knox sat buried in a brown study.

After this evening things grew bad for Miss Carey. Mrs. Knox watched. She noted her step-son's manner to Janet, and saw that he liked her ever so much more than was expedient. What to do, or how to stop it, she did not know, and was at her wits' end. To begin with, there was nothing to stop. Had she put together a whole week's looks and words of Arnold's, directed to Janet, she could not have squeezed one decent iota of complaint out of the whole. Neither dared she risk offending Arnold. What with the perpetual soirées out, and the general daily improvidence at home, Mrs. Knox was never in funds, and Arnold found oceans of household bills coming in to him. Tradesmen were beginning, as a rule now, to address their accounts to Dr. Knox. Arnold paid them; he was good-natured, and sensitively averse to complaining to his step-mother; but he thought it was hardly fair. What on earth she did with her income he could not imagine: rather than live in this chronic state of begging, she might have laid down the pony-carriage.

Not being able to attack the doctor, Mrs. Knox vented all her venom on Miss Carey. Janet was the dray horse of the family, and therefore could not be turned away: she was too useful to Mrs. Knox to be parted with. Real venom it was; and hard to be borne. Her work grew harder, and she was snubbed from morning till night. The children's insolence to her was not reproved; Mina took to ordering her about. Weary and heart-sick grew she: her life was no better than Cinderella's: the only ray of comfort in it being the rare snatches of intercourse with Dr. Knox. He was like a true friend to her, and ever kind. He might have been kinder had he known what sort of a life she really led. But Mrs. Knox was a diplomatist, and the young fry did not dare to worry people very much, or to call names before their big brother Arnold.

"Has Dr. Knox come in, Mr. Dockett?"

Mr. Dockett, lounging over the counter to tease the dog, brought himself straight with a jerk, and faced his master, Mr. Tamlyn.

"Not yet, sir."

"When he comes in, ask him if he'll be so kind as step to me in the dining-room."

Mr. Tamlyn shut the surgery-door, and the apprentice whistled to the dog, which had made its escape. Presently Dr. Knox came across the court-yard and received the message.

"Mr. Tamlyn wants you, sir, please. He is in the dining-room."

"Have you nothing to do, Dockett? Just set on and clean those scales."

The dining-room looked out on the garden and on the playing fountain. It was one of the prettiest rooms in Lefford; with white-and-gold papered walls, and mirrors, and a new carpet. Mr. Tamlyn liked to have things nice at home, and screwed the money out of the capital put by for Bertie. He sat at the table before some account-books.

"Sit down, Arnold," he said, taking off his spectacles. "I have some news for you: I hope it won't put you out too much."

It did put Dr. Knox out very considerably, and it surprised him even more. For some time past now he had been cherishing a private expectation that Mr. Tamlyn would be taking him into partnership, giving him probably a small share only at first. Of all things it seemed the most likely to Dr. Knox: and, wanting in self-assertion though he was, it seemed to him that it would be a right thing to do. Mr. Tamlyn had no one to succeed him: and all the best part of his practice was formerly Mr. Knox's. Had Arnold only been a little older when his father died, he should have succeeded to it himself: there would have been little chance of Mr. Tamlyn's getting any of it. In justice, then, if Mr. Tamlyn now, or later, took a partner at all, it ought to be Arnold. But for looking forward to this, Dr. Knox had never stayed on all this time at the paltry salary paid him, and worked himself nearly to a skeleton. As old Tamlyn talked, he listened as one in a dream, and he learnt that his own day-dream was over.

Old Tamlyn was about to take a partner: some gentleman from London, a Mr. Shuttleworth. Mr. Shuttleworth was seeking a country practice, and would bring in three thousand pounds. Arnold's services would only be required to the end of the year, as Mr. Shuttleworth would join on the first of January.

"There won't be room for three of us, Arnold—and Dockett will be coming on," said Mr. Tamlyn. "Besides, at your age, and with your talents, you ought to be doing something better for yourself. Don't you see that you ought?"

"I have seen it for some time. But—the truth is," added Arnold, "though I hardly like to own to it now, I have been cherishing a hope of this kind for myself. I thought, Mr. Tamlyn, you might some time offer it to me."

"And so I would, Arnold, and there's no one I should like to take as partner half so well as yourself, but you have not the necessary funds," said the surgeon with eagerness. "I see what you are thinking, Arnold—that I might have taken you without premium: but I must think of my poor boy. Shuttleworth brings in three thousand: I would have taken you with two."

"I could not bring in two hundred, let alone two thousand," said Dr. Knox.

"There's where it is. To tell you the truth, Arnold, I am getting tired of work; don't seem so much up to it as I was. Whoever comes in will have to do more even than you have done, and of course will expect to take at least a half-share of the yearly profits. I should not put by much then: I could not alter my style of living, you know, or put down the carriages and horses, or anything of that sort: and I must save for poor Bertie. A sum of three thousand pounds means three thousand to me."

"Are the arrangements fully made?" asked Dr. Knox.

"Yes. Mr. Shuttleworth came down to Lefford yesterday, and has been going into the books with me this morning. And, by the way, Arnold, I hope you will meet him here at dinner to-night. I should not a bit wonder, either, but he might tell you of some opening for yourself: he seems to know most of the chief medical men in London. He is selling a good practice of his own. It is his health that obliges him to come to the country."

"I hope you will suit one another," said Dr. Knox; for he knew that it was not every one who could get on with fidgety old Tamlyn.

"We are to give it a six months' trial," said Tamlyn. "He would not bind himself without that. At the end of the six months, if both parties are not satisfied, we cancel the agreement: he withdraws his money, and I am at liberty to take a fresh partner. For that half-year's services he will receive his half-share of profits: which of course is only fair. You see I tell you all, Arnold."

Dr. Knox dined with them, and found the new man a very pleasant fellow, but quite as old as Tamlyn. He could not help wondering how he would relish the parish work, and said so in a whisper to Mr. Tamlyn while Shuttleworth was talking to Bertie.

"Oh, he thinks it will be exercise for him," replied the surgeon. "And Dockett will be coming on, you know."

It was a dark night, the beginning of November, wet and splashy. Mrs. Knox had a soirée at Rose Villa; and when the doctor reached home he met the company coming forth with cloaks and lanterns and clogs.

"Oh, it's you, Arnold, is it!" cried Mrs. Knox. "Could you not have come home for my evening? Two of the whist-tables had to play dummy: we had some disappointments."

"I stayed to dine with Mr. Tamlyn," said Arnold.

Sitting together over the fire, he and she alone, Mrs. Knox asked him whether he would not give her a hundred pounds a-year for his board, instead of seventy-five. Which was uncommonly cool, considering what he paid for her besides in housekeeping bills. Upon which, Arnold told her he should not be with her beyond the close of the year: he was going to leave Lefford. For a minute, it struck her dumb.

"Good Heavens, Arnold, how am I to keep the house on without your help? I must say you have no consideration. Leave Lefford!"

"Mr. Tamlyn has given me notice," replied Arnold. "He is taking a partner."

"But—I just ask you—how am I to pay my way?"

"It seems to me that your income is quite sufficient for that, mother. If not—perhaps—if I may suggest it—you might put down the pony-chaise."

Mrs. Knox shrieked out that he was a cruel man. Arnold, who never cared to stand scenes, lighted his candle and went up to bed.

Shuttleworth had taken rather a fancy to Dr. Knox; perhaps he remembered, too, that he was turning him adrift. Anyway, he bestirred himself, and got him appointed to a medical post in London, where Arnold would receive two hundred a-year, and his board.

"I presume you know that I am about to run away, Miss Carey," said Dr. Knox, hastening up to join her one Sunday evening when they were coming out of church at Lefford.

"As if every one did not know that!" cried Mina. "Where's mamma, Arnold? and Lotty?"

"They are behind, talking to the Parkers."

The Parkers were great friends of Mina's, so she ran back. The doctor and Janet walked slowly on.

"You will be glad to leave, sir," said Janet, in her humble fashion. "Things have not been very comfortable for you at home—and I hear you are taking a much better post."

"I shall be sorry to leave for one thing—that is, because I fear things may be more uncomfortable for you," he spoke out bravely. "What Rose Villa will be when all restraint is taken from the children, and with other undesirable things, I don't like to imagine."

"I shall do very well," said Janet, meekly.

"I wonder you put up with it," he exclaimed. "You might be ten thousand times better and happier elsewhere."

"But I fear to change: I have no one to recommend me or to look out for me, you know."

"There's that lady I've heard you speak of—your aunt, Miss Cattledon."

"I could not think of troubling her. My mother's family do not care to take much notice of me. They thought my father was not my mother's equal in point of family, and when she married him, they turned her off, as it were. No, sir, I have only myself to look to."

"A great many of us are in the same case," he said. "Myself, for instance. I have been indulging I don't know what day-dreams for some time past: one of them that Mr. Tamlyn would give me a share in his practice: and—and there were others to follow in due course. Vain dreams all, and knocked on the head now."

"You will be sure to get on," said Janet.

"Do you think so?" he asked very softly, looking down into Janet's nice eyes by the gaslight in the road.

"At least, I hope you will."

"Well, I shall try for it."

"Arnold!—come back, Arnold; I want you to give me your arm up the hill," called out Mrs. Knox.

Dr. Knox had to enter on his new situation at quarter-day, the twenty-fifth of December; so he went up to London on Christmas-Eve. Which was no end of a blow to old Tamlyn, as it left all the work on his own shoulders for a week.

III

From two to three months passed on. One windy March day, Mrs. Knox sat alone in the garden-room, worrying over her money matters. The table, drawn near the fire, was strewed with bills and tradesmen's books; the sun shone on the closed glass-doors.

Mrs. Knox's affairs had been getting into an extremely hopeless condition. It seemed, by the accumulation of present debts, that Arnold's money must have paid for everything. Her own income, which came in quarterly, appeared to dwindle away, she knew not how or where. A piteous appeal had gone up a week ago to Arnold, saying she should be in prison unless he assisted her, for the creditors were threatening to take steps. Arnold's answer, delivered this morning, was a fifty-pound note enclosed in a very plain letter. It had inconvenienced him to send the money, he said, and he begged her fully to understand that it was the last he should ever send.

So there sat Mrs. Knox before the table in an old dressing-gown, and her black hair more dishevelled than a mop. The bills, oceans of them, and the fifty-pound note lay in a heap together. Master Dicky had been cutting animals out of a picture-book, leaving the scraps on the cloth and the old carpet. Lotty had distributed there a few sets of dolls' clothes. Gerty had been tearing up a newspaper for a kite-tail. The fifty pounds would pay about a third of the debts, and Mrs. Knox was trying to apportion a sum to each of them accordingly.

It bothered her finely, for she was no accountant. She could manage to add up without making very many mistakes; but when it came to subtraction, her brain went into a hopeless maze. Janet might have done it, but Mrs. Knox was furious with Janet and would not ask her. Ill-treated, over-worked, Janet had plucked up courage to give notice, and was looking out for a situation in Lefford. Just now, Janet was in the kitchen, ironing Dick's frilled collars.

"Take fifty-three from fourteen, and how much does remain?" groaned Mrs. Knox over the shillings. At that moment there was a sound of carriage-wheels, and a tremendous ring at the door. Sally darted in.

"Oh, ma'am, it's my Lady Jenkins! I knew her carriage at a distance. It have got red wheels!"

"Oh, my goodness!" cried Mrs. Knox, starting up. "Don't open the door yet, Sally: let me get upstairs first. Her ladyship's come to take me a drive, I suppose. Go and call Miss Carey—or stay, I'll go to her."

Mrs. Knox opened one of the glass-doors, and whisked round to the kitchen. She bade Janet leave the ironing and go to do her books and bills: hastily explaining that she wanted to know how far fifty pounds would go towards paying a fair proportion off each debt. Janet was to make it all out in figures.

"Be sure and take care of the note—I've left it somewhere," called back Mrs. Knox as she escaped to the stairs in hurry and confusion; for my Lady Jenkins's footman was working both bell and knocker alarmingly.

Janet only half comprehended. She went round to the garden-room, shut the glass-doors, and began upon the bills and books. But first of all, she looked out for the letters that were lying about, never supposing that the special charge had reference to anything else: at least, she said so afterwards: and put them inside Mrs. Knox's desk. From first to last, then and later, Janet Carey maintained that she did not see any bank-note.

Mrs. Knox dressed herself with Sally's help, and went out with my Lady Jenkins—the ex-Mayor of Lefford's wife. The bills and the calculations made a long job, and Janet's mind was buried in it, when a startling disturbance suddenly arose in the garden: Dicky had climbed into the mulberry-tree and fallen out of it. The girls came, dashing open the glass-doors, saying he was dead. Janet ran out, herself nearly frightened to death.

Very true. If Dicky was not dead, he looked like it. He lay white and cold under the tree, blood trickling down his face. James galloped off for Mr. Tamlyn. The two maids and Janet carried Dicky into the kitchen, and put him on the ironing-board, with his head on an old cushion. That revived him; and when Mr. Shuttleworth arrived, for Tamlyn was out, Dicky was demanding bread-and-treacle. Shuttleworth put some diachylon plaster on his head, ordered him to bed, and told him not to get into trees again.

Their fears relieved, the maids had time to remember common affairs. Sally found all the sitting-room fires out, and hastened to light them. As soon as Janet could leave Dicky, who had persisted in going to bed in his boots, she went back to the accounts. Mrs. Knox came in before they were done. She blew up Janet for not being quicker, and when she had recovered the shock of Dicky's accident, she blew her up for that.

"Where's the note?" she snapped.

"What note, ma'am?" asked Janet.

"The bank-note. The bank-note for fifty pounds that I told you to take care of."

"I have not seen any bank-note," said Janet.

Well, that began the trouble. The bank-note was searched for, and there was neither sign nor symptom of it to be found. Mrs. Knox accused Janet Carey of stealing it, and called in a policeman. Mrs. Knox made her tale good to the man, representing Janet as a very black girl indeed; but the man said he could not take her into custody unless Mrs. Knox would charge her formally with the theft.

And that, Mrs. Knox hesitated to do. She told the policeman she would take until the morrow to consider of it. The whole of that evening, the whole of the night, the whole of the next morning till midday, Janet spent searching the garden-room. At midday the policeman appeared again, and Janet went into a sort of fit.

When Mr. Shuttleworth was sent for to her, he said it was caused by fright, and that she had received a shock to the nervous system. For some days she was delirious, on and off; and when she could escape Sally's notice, who waited on her, they'd find her down in the garden-room, searching for the note, just as we afterwards saw her searching for it in her sleep at Miss Deveen's. It chanced that the two rooms resembled each other remarkably: in their situation in the houses, in their shape and size and building arrangements, and in their opening by glass-doors to the garden. Janet subsided into a sort of wasting fever; and Mrs. Knox thought it time to send for Miss Cattledon. The criminal proceedings might wait, she told Janet: like the heartless woman that she was! Not but that the loss of the money had thrown her flat on her beam-ends.

Miss Cattledon came. Janet solemnly declared, not only that she had not the bank-note, but that she had never seen the note: never at all. Mrs. Knox said no one but Janet could have taken it, and but for her illness, she would be already in prison. Miss Cattledon told Mrs. Knox she ought to be ashamed of herself for suspecting Janet Carey, and took Janet off by train to Miss Deveen's. Janet arrived there in a shivering-fit, fully persuaded that the Lefford policemen were following her by the orders of Mrs. Knox.

And for the result of it all we must go on to the next paper.

CHAPTER V

DR. KNOX

"MY DEAR ARNOLD,

"Come down to Lefford without delay if you can: I want to see you particularly. I am in a peck of trouble.

"Ever your friend,
"RICHARD TAMLYN."

The above letter reached Dr. Knox in London one morning in April. He made it right with the authorities to whom he was subject, and reached Lefford the same afternoon.

Leaving his bag at the station, he went straight to Mr. Tamlyn's house; every other person he met halting to shake hands with him. Entering the iron gates, he looked up at the windows, but saw no one. The sun shone on the pillared portico, the drawing-room blinds beside it were down. Dr. Knox crossed the flagged courtyard, and passed off to enter by the route most familiar to him, the surgery, trodden by him so often in the days not long gone by. Mr. Dockett stood behind the counter, compounding medicines, with his coat-cuffs and wristbands turned up.

"Well, I never!" exclaimed the young gentleman, dropping a bottle in his astonishment as he stared at Dr. Knox. "You are about the last person I should have expected to see, sir."

By which remark the doctor found that Mr. Tamlyn had not taken his apprentice into his confidence. "Are you all well here?" he asked, shaking hands.

"All as jolly as circumstances will let us be," said Mr. Dockett. "Young Bertie has taken a turn for the worse."

"Has he? I am sorry to hear that. Is Mr. Tamlyn at home? If so, I'll in and see him."

"Oh, he's at home," was the answer. "He has hardly stirred out-of-doors for a week, and Shuttleworth says he's done to death with the work."

Going in as readily as though he had not left the house for a day, Dr. Knox found Mr. Tamlyn in the dining-room: the pretty room that looked to the garden and the fountain. He was sitting by the fire, his hand rumpling his grey hair: a sure sign that he was in some bother or tribulation. In the not quite four months that had passed since Dr. Knox left him, he had changed considerably: his hair was greyer, his face thinner.

"Is it you, Arnold? I am glad. I thought you'd come if you could."

Dr. Knox drew a chair near the fire, and sat down. "Your letter gave me concern," he said. "And what do you mean by talking about a peck of trouble?"

"A peck of trouble!" echoed Mr. Tamlyn. "I might have said a bushel. I might have said a ton. There's trouble on all sides, Arnold."

"Can I help you out of it in any way?"

"With some of it, I hope you can: it's why I sent for you. But not with all: not with the worst. Bertie's dying, Arnold."

"I hope not!"

"As truly as that we are here talking to one another, I believe him to be literally dying," repeated the surgeon, solemnly, his eyes filling and his voice quivering with pain. "He has dropped asleep, and Bessy sent me out of the room: my sighs wake him, she says. I can't help sighing, Arnold: and sometimes the sigh ends with a groan, and I can't help that."

Dr. Knox didn't see his way clear to making much answer just here.

"I've detected the change in him for a month past; in my inward heart I felt sure he could not live. Do you know what your father used to say, Arnold? He always said that if Bertie lived over his sixteenth or seventeenth year, he'd do; but the battle would be just about that time. Heaven knows, I attached no importance to the opinion: I have hardly thought of it: but he was right, you see. Bertie would be seventeen next July, if he were to live."

"I'm sure I am very grieved to hear this—and to see your sorrow," spoke Arnold.

"He is so changed!" resumed Mr. Tamlyn, in a low voice. "You remember how irritable he was, poor fellow?—well, all that has gone, and he is like an angel. So afraid of giving trouble; so humble and considerate to every one! It was this change that first alarmed me."

"When did it come on?"

"Oh, weeks ago. Long before there was much change for the worse to be seen in him. Only this morning he held my hand, poor lad, and—and—" Mr. Tamlyn faltered, coughed, and then went on again more bravely. "He held my hand between his, Arnold, and said he thought God had forgiven him, and how happy it would all be when we met in heaven. For a long while now not a day has passed but he has asked us to forgive him for his wicked tempers—that's his word for it, wicked—the servants, and all."

"Is he in much pain?"

"Not much now. He has been in a great deal at times. But it made no difference, pain or no pain, to his sweetness of temper. He will lie resigned and quiet, the drops pouring down his face with the agony, never an impatient word escaping him. One day I heard him tell Bessy that angels were around him, helping him to bear it. We may be sure, Arnold, when so extraordinary a change as that takes place in the temperament, the close of life is not far off."

"Very true—as an ordinary rule," acquiesced Dr. Knox. "And now, how can I help you in this trouble?"

"In this trouble?—not at all," returned Mr. Tamlyn, rousing himself, and speaking energetically, as if he meant to put the thought behind him. "This trouble no earthly being can aid me in, Arnold; and I don't think there's any one but yourself I'd speak to of it: it lies too deep, you see; it wrings the soul. I could die of this trouble: I only fret at the other."

"And what is the other?"

"Shuttleworth won't stay."

"Won't he!"

"Shuttleworth says the kind of practice is not what he has been accustomed to, and the work's too hard, and he does not care how soon he leaves it. And yet Dockett has come on surprisingly, and takes his share now. The fact is, Arnold, Shuttleworth is just as lazy as he can hang together: he'd like to treat a dozen rose-water patients a-day, and go through life easily. My belief is, he means to do it."

"But that will scarcely bring grist to his mill, will it?" cried Dr. Knox.

"His mill doesn't want grist; there's the worst of it," said Tamlyn. "The man was not badly off when he came here: but since then his only brother must go and die, and Shuttleworth has come into all his money. A thousand a-year, if it's a penny."

"Then, I certainly don't wonder at his wanting to give up the practice," returned the doctor, with a smile.

"That's not all," grumbled old Tamlyn. "He wants to take away Bessy."

"To take away Bessy!"

"The two have determined to make themselves into one, I believe. Bessy only hesitated because of leaving poor Bertie. That impediment will not be in her way long."

He sighed as he spoke. Dr. Knox did not yet see what he was wanted for: and asked again.

"I've been leading up to it," said Mr. Tamlyn. "You must come back to me, Arnold."

"On the same terms as before?" inquired the doctor, after a pause.

"Nonsense. You'd say 'No,' off-hand, if I proposed them. In Shuttleworth's place."

"Of course, Mr. Tamlyn, I could not come—I would not come unless it were made worth my while. If it were, I should like it of all things."

"Yes, just so; that's what I mean. Don't you like your post in London?"

"I like it very well, indeed. And I have had no doubt that it will lead to something better. But, if I saw a fair prospect before me here, I should prefer to come back to Lefford."

"That shall be made fair enough. Things have changed with me, Arnold: and I shouldn't wonder but you will some time, perhaps not very far distant, have all my practice in your own hands. I feel to be getting old: spirits and health are alike broken."

"Nay, not old yet, Mr. Tamlyn. You may wait a good twenty years for that."

"Well, well, we'll talk further at another interview. My mind's at rest now, and that's a great thing. If you had refused, Arnold, I should have sold my practice for an old song, and gone clean away: I never could have stood being associated with another stranger. You are going up home, I conclude. Will you come in this evening?"

"Very well," said Dr. Knox, rising. "Can I go up and see Bertie?"

"Not now; I'd not have him awakened for the world; and I assure you the turning of a straw seems to do it. You shall see him this evening: he is always awake and restless then."

Calling for his bag at the station, Dr. Knox went on to Rose Villa. They were at tea. The children rose up with a shout: his step-mother looked as though she could not believe her eyesight.

"Why, Arnold! Have you come home to stay?"

"Only for a day or two," he answered. "I thought I should surprise you, but I had not time to write."

Shaking hands with her, kissing the children, he turned to some one else, who was seated at the tea-table and had not stirred. His hand was already out, when she turned her head, and he drew back his hand and himself together.

"Miss Mack, my new governess," spoke Mrs. Knox.

"I beg your pardon," said Dr. Knox to Miss Mack, who turned out to be a young person in green, with stout legs and slippers down at heel. "I thought it was Miss Carey," he added to his step-mother. "Where is Miss Carey?"

Which of the company, Miss Mack excepted, talked the fastest, and which the loudest, could not have been decided though a thousand-pound wager rested on it. It was a dreadful tale to tell. Janet Carey had turned out to be a thief; Janet Carey had gone out of her mind nearly with fever and fear when she knew she was to be taken to prison and tried: tried for stealing the money; and Janet's aunt had come down and carried her away out of the reach of the policemen. Dr. Knox gazed and listened, and felt his blood turning cold with righteous horror.

"Be silent," he sternly said. "There must have been some strange mistake. Miss Carey was good and upright as the day."

"She stole my fifty pounds," said Mrs. Knox.

"What?"

"She stole my fifty-pound note. It was the one you sent me, Arnold."

His face reddened a little. "That note? Well, I do not know the circumstances that led you to accuse Miss Carey; but I know they were mistaken ones. I will answer for Janet Carey with my life."

"She took that note; it could not have gone in any other manner," steadily persisted Mrs. Knox. "You'll say so yourself, Arnold, when you know all. The commotion it has caused in the place, and the worry it has caused me are beyond everything. Every day some tradesman or other comes here to ask whether the money has been replaced—for of course they know I can't pay them under such a loss, until it is; and I must say they have behaved very well. I never liked Janet Carey. Deceitful minx!"

With so many talking together, Dr. Knox did not gather a very clear account of the details. Mrs. Knox mixed up surmises with facts in a manner to render the whole incomprehensible. He said no more then. Later, Mrs. Knox saw that he was preparing to go out. She resented it.

"I think, Arnold, you might have passed this one evening at home: I want to have a talk with you about money matters. What I am to do is more than I know, unless Janet Carey or her friends can be made to return the money."

"I am going down to Tamlyn's, to see Bertie."

Dr. Knox let himself out at the street-door, and was walking down the garden-path, when he found somebody come flying past. It was Sally the housemaid, on her way to open the gate for him. Such an act of attention was unusual and quite unnecessary; the doctor thanked her, but told her she need not have taken the trouble.

"I—I thought I'd like to ask you, sir, how that—that poor Miss Carey is," said Sally, in a whisper, as she held the gate back, and her breath was so short as to hinder her words. "It was London she was took to, sir; and, as you live in the same town, I've wondered whether you might not have come across her."

"London is a large place," observed Dr. Knox. "I did not even know Miss Carey was there."

"It was a dreadful thing, sir, poor young lady. Everybody so harsh, too, over it. And I—I—I can't believe but she was innocent."

"It is simply an insult on Miss Carey to suppose otherwise," said Dr. Knox. "Are you well, Sally? What's the matter with your breath?"

"Oh, it's nothing but a stitch that takes me, thank you, sir," returned Sally, as she shut the gate after him and flew back again.

But Dr. Knox saw it was no "stitch" that had stopped Sally's breath and checked her utterance, but genuine agitation. It set him thinking.

No longer any sitting up for poor Bertie Tamlyn in this world! It was about eight o'clock when Dr. Knox entered the sick-chamber. Bertie lay in bed; his arms thrown outside the counterpane beside him, as though they were too warm. The fire gave out its heat; two lamps were burning, one on the mantelpiece, one on the drawers at the far end of the room. Bertie had always liked a great deal of light, and he liked it still. Miss Tamlyn met Dr. Knox at the door, and silently shook hands with him.

Bertie's wide-open eyes turned to look, and the doctor approached the bed; but he halted for one imperceptible moment in his course. When Mr. Tamlyn had said Bertie was dying, Arnold Knox had assumed it to mean, not that he was actually dying at that present time, but that he would not recover! But as he gazed at Bertie now in the bright light, he saw something in the face that his experienced medical eye could not mistake.

He took the wasted, fevered hand in his, and laid his soothing fingers on the damp brow. Miss Tamlyn went away for a minute's respite from the sick-room.

"Bertie, my boy!"

"Why didn't you come before, Arnold?" was the low, weak answer; and the breath was laboured and the voice down nowhere. "I have wanted you. Aunt Bessy would not write; and papa thought you would not care to come down from London, just for me."

"But I would, Bertie—had I known you were as ill as this."

Bertie's hands were restless. The white quilt had knots in it as big as peas, and he was picking at them. Dr. Knox sat down by the low bed.

"Do you think I am dying?" suddenly asked Bertie.

It took the doctor by surprise. One does not always know how to answer such home questions.

"I'll tell you more about it when I've seen you by daylight, Bertie. Are you in any pain?"

"Not a bit now: that's gone. But I'm weak, and I can't stir about in bed, and—and—they all look at me so. This morning papa and Shuttleworth brought in Dr. Green. Any way, you must know that I shall not get to be as well as I used to be."

"What with one ailment and another, with care, and pain, and sorrow, and wrong, it seems to me, Bertie, that very few of us are well for long together. There's always something in this world: it is only when we go to the next that we can hope for rest and peace."

Bertie lifted his restless hands and caught one of Dr. Knox's between them. He had a yearning, imploring look that quite pained the doctor.

"I want you to forgive me, Arnold," he said, the tears running down. "When I remember how wicked I was, my heart just faints with shame. Calling all of you hideous names!—returning bitter words for kind ones. When we are going to die the past comes back to us. Such a little while it seems to have been now, Arnold! Why, if I had endured ten times as much pain, it would be over now. You were all so gentle and patient with me, and I never cared what trouble I gave, or what ill words I returned. And now the time is gone! Arnold, I want you to forgive me."

"My dear boy, there's nothing to forgive. If you think there is, why then I forgive you with all my heart."

"Will God ever forgive me, do you think?"

"Oh, my boy, yes," said the doctor, in a husky tone. "If we, poor sinful mortals, can forgive one another, how much more readily will He forgive—the good Father in heaven of us all!"

Bertie sighed. "It would have been so easy for me to have tried for a little patience! Instead of that, I took pleasure in being cross and obstinate and wicked! If the time would but come over again! Arnold, do you think we shall be able to do one another good in the next world?—or will the opportunity be lost with this?"

"Ah, Bertie, I cannot tell," said Dr. Knox. "Sometimes I think that just because so few of us make use of our opportunities here, God will, perhaps, give us a chance once again. I have not been at very many death-beds yet, but of some of those the recollection of opportunities wasted has made the chief sting. It is only when life is closing that we see what we might have been, what we might have done."

"Perhaps He'll remember what my pain has been, Arnold, and how hard it was to bear. I was not like other boys. They can run, and climb, and leap, and ride on horseback, and do anything. When I've gone out, it has been in a hand-carriage, you know; and I've had to lie and lie on the sofa, and just look up at the blue sky, or on the street that tired me so: or else in bed, where it was worse, and always hot. I hope He will recollect how hard it was for me."

"He saw how hard it was for you at the time, Bertie; saw it always."

"And Jesus Christ forgave all who went to Him, you know, Arnold; every one; just for the asking."

"Why, yes, of course He did. As He does now."

Mr. Tamlyn came into the room presently: he had been out to a patient. Seeing that Bertie was half asleep, he and Dr. Knox stood talking together on the hearthrug.

"What's that?" cried the surgeon, suddenly catching sight of the movement of the restless fingers picking at the counterpane.

Dr. Knox did not answer.

"A trick he always had," said the surgeon, breaking the silence, and trying to make believe to cheat himself still. "The maids say he wears out all his quilts."

Bertie opened his eyes. "Is that you, papa? Is tea over?"

"Why, yes, my boy; two or three hours ago," said the father, going forward. "Why? Do you wish for some tea?"

"Oh, I—I thought Arnold would have liked some."

He closed his eyes again directly. Dr. Knox took leave in silence, promising to be there again in the morning. As he was passing the dining-room downstairs, he saw Mr. Shuttleworth, who had just looked in. They shook hands, began to chat, and Dr. Knox sat down.

"I hear you do not like Lefford," he said.

"I don't dislike Lefford: it's a pretty and healthy place," was Mr. Shuttleworth's answer. "What I dislike is my position in it as Tamlyn's partner. The practice won't do for me."

"A doubt lay on my mind whether it would suit you when you came down to make the engagement," said Dr. Knox. "Parish work is not to every one's taste. And there's a great deal of practice besides. But the returns from that must be good."

"I wouldn't stay in it if it were worth a million a-year," cried Mr. Shuttleworth. "Dockett takes the parish; I make him; but he is not up to much yet, and of course I feel that I am responsible. As to the town practice, why, I assure you nearly all of it has lain on me. Tamlyn, poor fellow, can think of nothing but his boy."

"He will not have him here long to think of, I fear."

"Not very long; no. I hear, doctor, he is going to offer a partnership to you."

"He has said something about it. I shall take it, if he does. Lefford is my native place, and I would rather live here than anywhere. Besides, I don't mind work," he added, with a smile.

"Ah, you are younger than I am. But I'd advise you, as I have advised Tamlyn, to give up the parish. For goodness' sake do, Knox. Tamlyn says that at one time he had not much else but the parish, but it's different now. Your father had all the better practice then."

"Shall you set up elsewhere?"

"Not at present," said Mr. Shuttleworth. "We—I—perhaps you have heard, though—that I and Bessy are going to make a match of it? We shall travel for a few months, or so, and then come home and pitch our tent in some pleasant sea-side place. If a little easy practice drops in to me there, well and good: if not, we can do without it. Stay and smoke a cigar with me?"

Arnold looked at his watch, and sat down again. He wanted to ask Mr. Shuttleworth about Miss Carey's illness.

"The cause of her illness was the loss of that bank-note," said the surgeon. "They accused her of stealing it, and wanted to give her into custody. A little more, and she'd have had brain-fever. She was a timid, inexperienced girl, and the fright gave her system a shock."

"Miss Carey would no more steal a bank-note than you or I would steal one, Shuttleworth."

"Not she. I told Mrs. Knox so: but she scoffed at me."

"That Miss Carey is innocent as the day, that she is an upright, gentle, Christian girl, I will stake my life upon," said Dr. Knox. "How the note can have gone is another matter."

"Are you at all interested in finding it out?" questioned Mr. Shuttleworth.

"Certainly I am. Every one ought to be, I think."

The surgeon took his cigar from his mouth. "I'll tell you my opinion, if you care to know it," he said. "The note was burnt."

"Burnt!"

"Well, it is the most likely solution of the matter that I can come to. Either burnt, or else was blown away."

"But why do you say this?" questioned Dr. Knox.

"It was a particularly windy day. The glass-doors of the room were left open while the house ran about in a fright, attending to the child, young Dick. A flimsy bit of bank-paper, lying on the table, would get blown about like a feather in a gale. Whether it got into the fire, caught by the current of the chimney, or whether it sailed out-of-doors and disappeared in the air, is a question I can't undertake to solve. Rely upon it, Knox, it was one of the two: and I should bet upon the fire."

It was just the clue Dr. Knox had been wishing for. But he did not think the whole fault lay with the wind: he had another idea.

Lefford had a shock in the morning. Bertie Tamlyn was dead. The news came to Dr. Knox in a note from Mr. Tamlyn, which was delivered whilst he was dressing. "You will stay for the funeral, Arnold," were the concluding words. And as Dr. Knox wanted to be at home a little longer on his own account, he wrote to London to say that business was temporarily detaining him. He then went to see what he could do for Mr. Tamlyn, and got back to Rose Villa for dinner.

Watching for an opportunity—which did not occur until late in the afternoon—Dr. Knox startled the servants by walking into the kitchen, and sitting down. Mrs. Knox had gone off in the pony-chaise; the children were out with the new governess. The kitchen and the servants were alike smartened-up for the rest of the day. Eliza, the cook, was making a new pudding-cloth; Sally was ironing.

"I wish to ask you both a few questions," said Dr. Knox, taking out his note-book and pencil. "It is not possible that Miss Carey can be allowed to lie under the disgraceful accusation that was brought against her, and I am about to try and discover what became of the bank-note. Mrs. Knox was not in the house at the time, and therefore cannot give me the details."

Eliza, who had risen and stood, work in hand, simply stared at the doctor in surprise. Sally dropped her iron on the blanket.

"We didn't take the note, sir," said Eliza, after a pause. "We'd not do such a thing."

"I'm sure I didn't; I'd burn my hands off first," broke in Sally, with a burst of tears.

"Of course you would not," returned Dr. Knox in a pleasant tone. "The children would not. Mrs. Knox would not. But as the note undoubtedly disappeared, and without hands, we must try and discover where the mystery lies and how it went. I dare say you would like Miss Carey to be cleared."

"Miss Carey was a downright nice young lady," pronounced the cook. "Quite another sort from this one we've got now."

"Well, give me all the particulars as correctly as you can remember," said the doctor. "We may get some notion or other out of them."

Eliza plunged into the narration. She was fond of talking. Sally stood over her ironing, sniffing and sighing. Dr. Knox listened.

"Mrs. Knox left the note on the table—which was much strewed with papers—when she went out with Lady Jenkins, and Miss Carey took her place at the accounts," repeated Dr. Knox, summing up the profuse history in a few concise words. "While—"

"And Miss Carey declared, sir, that she never saw the note; never noticed it lying there at all," came Eliza's interruption.

"Yes, just so. While Miss Carey was at the table, the alarm came that Master Dick had fallen out of the tree, and she ran to him—"

"And a fine fright that fall put us into, sir! We thought he was dead. Jim went galloping off for the doctor, and me and Sally and Miss Carey stayed bathing his head on that there very ironing-board, a-trying to find out what the damage was."

"And the children: where were they?"

"All round us here in the kitchen, sir, sobbing and staring."

"Meanwhile the garden-room was deserted. No one went into it, as far as you know."

"Nobody at all, sir. When Sally ran in to look at the fire, she found it had gone clean out. The doctor had been there then, and Master Richard was in bed. A fine pickle Sally found the room in, with the scraps of paper, and that, blown about the floor. The glass-doors was standing stark staring open to the wind."

"And, I presume, you gathered up some of these scraps of paper, and lighted the fire with them, Sally?"

Dr. Knox did not appear to look at Sally as he spoke, but he saw and noted every movement. He saw that her hand shook so that she could scarcely hold the iron.

"Has it never struck you, Sally, that you might have put the bank-note into the grate with these scraps of paper, and burnt it?" he continued. "Innocently, of course. That is how I think the note must have disappeared. Had the wind taken it into the garden, it would most probably have been found."

Sally flung her apron over her face and herself on to a chair, and burst into a howl. Eliza looked at her.

"If you think there is a probability that this was the case, Sally, you must say so," continued Dr. Knox. "You will never be blamed, except for not having spoken."

"'Twas only yesterday I asked Sally whether she didn't think this was the way it might have been," said the cook in a low tone to Dr. Knox. "She have seemed so put out, sir, for a week past."

"I vow to goodness that I never knew I did it," sobbed Sally. "All the while the bother was about, and Miss Carey, poor young lady, was off her head, it never once struck me. What Eliza and me thought was, that some tramps must have come round the side of the house and got in at the open glass-doors, and stole it. The night after Miss Carey left with her aunt, I was thinking about her as I lay in bed, and wondering whether the mistress would send the police after her or not, when all of a sudden the thought flashed across me that it might have gone into the fire with the other pieces of paper. Oh mercy, I wish I was somewhere!"

"What became of the ashes out of the grate?—the cinders?" asked Dr. Knox.

"They're all in the ash-place, sir, waiting till the garden's ready for them," sobbed Sally.

With as little delay as possible, Dr. Knox had the cinders carefully sifted and examined, when the traces of what had once undoubtedly been a bank-note were discovered. The greater portion of the note had been reduced to tinder, but a small part of it remained, enough to show what it had been, and—by singular good fortune—its number. It must have fallen out of the grate partly consumed, while the fire was lighting up, and been swept underneath by Sally with other remnants, where it had lain quietly until morning and been taken away with the ashes.

The traces gathered carefully into a small box and sealed up, Dr. Knox went into the presence of his step-mother.

"I think," he said, just showing the box as it lay in his hand, "that this proof will be accepted by the Bank of England; in that case they will make good the money to me. One question, mother, I wish to ask you: how could you possibly suspect Miss Carey?"

"There was no one else for me to suspect," replied Mrs. Knox in fretful tones; for she did not at all like this turn in the affair.

"Did you really suspect her?"

"Why, of course I did. How can you ask such foolish questions?"

"It was a great mistake in any case to take it up as you did. I am not alluding to the suspicion now; but to your harsh and cruel treatment."

"Just mind your own business, Arnold. It's nothing to you."

"For my own part, I regard it as a matter that we must ever look back upon with shame."

"There, that's enough," said Mrs. Knox. "The thing is done with, and it cannot be recalled. Janet Carey won't die of it."

Dr. Knox went about Lefford with the box in his hand, making things right. He called in at the police-station; he caused a minute account to be put in the Lefford News; he related the details to his private friends. Not once did he allude to Janet Carey, or mention her name: it was as though he would proudly ignore the stigma cast on her and assume that the world did the same. The world did: but it gave some hard words to Mrs. Knox.

Mr. Tamlyn had not much sympathy for wonders of any kind just then. Poor Bertie, lying cold and still in the chamber above, took up all his thoughts and his grief. Arnold spent a good deal of time with him, and took his round of patients.

It was the night before the funeral, and they were sitting together at twilight in the dining-room. Dr. Knox was looking through the large window at the fountain in the middle of the grass-plat: Mr. Tamlyn had his face buried; he had not looked up for the last half-hour.

"When is the very earliest time that you can come, Arnold?" he began abruptly.

"As soon as ever they will release me in London. Perhaps that will be in a month; perhaps not until the end of June, when the six months will be up."

Mr. Tamlyn groaned. "I want you at once, Arnold. You are all I have now."

"Shuttleworth must stay until I come."

"Shuttleworth's not you. You must live with me, Arnold?"

"Live with you?"

"Why, of course you must. What am I to do in this large house by myself now he is gone? Bessy will be gone too. I couldn't stand it."

"It would be much more convenient for me to be here, as far as the practice is concerned," remarked Dr. Knox, after reflection.

"And more sociable. Do you never think of marriage, Arnold?"

Dr. Knox turned a little red. "It has been of no use for me to think of it hitherto, you know, sir."

"I wish you would. Some nice, steady girl, who would make things pleasant here for us in Bessy's place. There's room for a wife as well as for you, Arnold. Think of these empty rooms: no one but you and me in them! And you know people like a married medical man better than a single one."

The doctor opened his lips to speak, but his courage failed him; he would leave it to the last thing before he left on the morrow, or else write from London. Tamlyn mistook his silence.

"You'll be well enough off to keep two wives, if the law allowed it, let alone one. From the day you join me, Arnold, half the profits shall be yours—I'll have the deed made out—and the whole practice at my death. I've no one to save for, now Bertie's gone."

"He is better off; he is in happiness," said Dr. Knox, his voice a little husky.

"Ay. I try to let it console me. But I've no one but you now, Arnold. And I don't suppose I shall forget you in my will. To confess the truth, turning you away to make room for Shuttleworth has lain on my conscience."

When Arnold reached home that night, Mrs. Knox and her eldest daughter were alone; she reading, Mina dressing a doll. Lefford was a place that went in for propriety, and no one gave soirées while Bertie Tamlyn lay dead. Arnold told Mrs. Knox of the new arrangement.

"Good gracious!" she exclaimed. "Coming back to Lefford! Well, I shall be glad to have you at home again," she added, thinking of the household bills.

"Mr. Tamlyn proposes that I shall live with him," said Dr. Knox.

"But you will never be so stupid as to do that!"

"I have promised to do it. It will be much more convenient."

Mrs. Knox looked sullen, and bit her lips. "How large a share are you to have?"

"I go in as full partner."

"Oh, I am so glad!" cried out Miss Mina—for they all liked their good-natured brother. "Arnold, perhaps you'll go and get married now!"

"Perhaps I may," he answered.

Mrs. Knox dropped her book in the sudden fright. If Arnold married, he might want his house—and turn her out of it! He read the fear in her face.

"We may make some arrangement," said he quietly. "You shall still occupy it and pay me a small nominal rent—five pounds a-year, say—which I shall probably return in toys for the children."

The thought of his marriage had always lain upon her with a dread. "Who is the lady?" she asked.

"The lady? Oh, I can't tell you, I'm sure. I have not asked any one yet."

"Is that all!"

"Quite all—at present."

"I think," said Mrs. Knox slowly, as if deliberating the point with herself, and in the most affectionate of tones, "that you would be happier in a single life, Arnold. One never knows what a wife is till she's tried."

"Do you think so? Well, we must leave it to the future. What will be, will be."

And now I am taking up the story for myself; I, Johnny Ludlow. Had I gone straight on with it after that last night of Janet's sleep-walking at Miss Deveen's, you would never have understood.

It was on the Saturday night that Janet was found out—as any one must remember who took the trouble to count up the nights and days. On the Sunday morning early, Miss Deveen's doctor was sent for. Dr. Galliard happened to be out of town, so Mr. Black attended for him. Cattledon was like vinegar. She looked upon Janet's proceedings as a regular scandal, and begged Miss Deveen's pardon for having brought her niece into the house. Upon which she was requested not to be silly.

Miss Deveen told the whole tale of the lost bank-note, to me and to Helen and Anna Whitney: at least, as much as she knew of it herself. Janet was innocent as a child; she felt sure of that, she said, and much to be pitied; and that Mrs. Knox, of Lefford, seemed to be a most undesirable sort of person. To us it sounded like a romance, or a story out of a newspaper police-report.

Monday came in; a warm, bright April day. I was returning to Oxford in the evening—and why I had not returned in the past week, as ought to have been the case, there's no space to tell here. Miss Deveen said we might go for a walk if we liked. But Helen and Anna did not seem to care about it; neither did I, to say the truth. A house with a marvel in it has attractions; and we would by far rather have gone upstairs to see Janet. Janet was better, quite composed, but weak, they said: she was up and dressed, and in Miss Deveen's own blue-room.

"Well, do you mean to go out, or not, you young people?" asked Miss Deveen. "Dear me, here are visitors!"

George came in bringing a card. "Dr. Knox."

"Why!—it must be some one from that woman at Lefford!" exclaimed Miss Deveen, in an undertone to me. "Oh no; I remember now, Johnny; Dr. Knox was the step-son; he was away, and had nothing to do with it. Show Dr. Knox in, George."

A tall man in black, whom one might have taken anywhere for a doctor, with a grave, nice face, came in. He said his visit was to Miss Carey, as he took the chair George placed near his mistress. Just a few words, and then we knew the whole, and saw a small sealed-up box in his hand, which contained the remains of the bank-note.

"I am more glad than if you brought Janet a purse of gold!" cried Miss Deveen, her eyes sparkling with pleasure. "Not that I think any one could have doubted her, Dr. Knox—not even your step-mother, in her heart,—but it is satisfactory to have it cleared up. It has made Miss Carey very ill; but this will set her at rest."

"Your servant told me Miss Carey was ill," he said. "It was for her I asked."

With a face of concern, he listened to what Miss Deveen had to say of the illness. When she spoke of Janet's fright at seeing the policeman at the Colosseum, his brow went red and he bit his lips. Next came the sleep-walking: she told it all.

"Her brain and nerves must have been overstrained to an alarming degree," he observed, after a short silence. "Mr. Shuttleworth, who attended her at the time, spoke to me of the shock to the system. But I hoped she had recovered."

"She would never have recovered, Dr. Knox, as long as the dread lay upon her that she was to be criminally prosecuted: at least, that is my opinion," said Miss Deveen. "I believe the chief thing that ails her is fright. Not a knock at the door, not the marching past the house of a policeman, not the sudden entrance of a servant into the room, but has brought to her a shock of agonizing fear. It is a mercy that she has escaped brain-fever. After all, she must possess a good constitution. The sight of that Lefford man at the Colosseum did great mischief."

"It was unfortunate that he should happen to be there," said Dr. Knox: "and that the man should have dared to accost her with his insolence! But I shall inquire into it."

"What you have in that box will be the best medicine for her," said Miss Deveen. "It will speedily effect a cure—or call me an untrue prophet. Dear me! how strangely things come out!"

"May I be allowed to see Miss Carey?" asked Dr. Knox. "And to—to tell her the story of her clearance in my own way?"

Miss Deveen made no reply. She looked at Dr. Knox, and seemed to hesitate.

"I think it may be better for Miss Carey that I should, madam. For more reasons than one."

"And really I don't see why you should not," said Miss Deveen, heartily. "I hesitated because Mr. Black forbade the admission of strangers. But—perhaps you are not a stranger to her?"

"Oh dear, no: I and Miss Carey are old friends," he answered, a curious smile lighting up his face. "And I should also wish to see her in my medical capacity."

But the one to put in her word against this, was Cattledon. She came down looking green, and protesting in Miss Deveen's ear that no male subject in her Majesty's dominions, save and except Mr. Black, ought to be admitted to the blue-room. Janet had no full dress on; nothing but skirts and a shawl.

"Oh, nonsense!" cried Miss Deveen. "Why, Dr. Knox might have seen her had she been in bed: he is a physician." And she took him up herself to the blue-room.

"Of all old maids that Cattledon's the worst!" nodded Helen Whitney.

Miss Deveen went in alone, leaving him outside the door. Janet sat in an armchair by the fire, muffled in an old brown shawl of Cattledon's.

"And how do you feel now, my dear?" said Miss Deveen, quietly. "Better, I see. And oh, I have such pleasant news for you: an old friend of yours has called to see you; and I think—I think—he will be able to cure you sooner than Mr. Black. It is Dr. Knox, my dear: not of Lefford now, you know: of London."

She called the doctor in, and Janet's pale cheeks took a tint of crimson. Janet's face had never been big: but as he stood looking at her, her hand in his, he was shocked to see how small it had become. Miss Deveen shut the door upon them. She hoped with all her heart he was not going to spare that woman at Lefford.

"Janet, my dear," he said in a fatherly kind of way as he drew a chair near her and kept her hand, "when that trouble happened at home, how was it you did not write to me?"

"Write to you! Oh, sir, I could not do such a thing," answered Janet, beginning to tremble.

"But you might have known I should be your friend. You might also have known that I should have been able to clear you."

"I did once think of writing to you, Dr. Knox: just to tell you that I had not indeed touched the bank-note," faltered Janet. "As the money came from you, I should have liked to write so much. But I did not dare."

"And you preferred to suffer all these weeks of pain, and the fright brought upon you by Mrs. Knox—for which," said he deliberately, "I shall never forgive her—rather than drop me a few lines! You must never be so foolish again, Janet. I should have gone to Lefford at once and searched out the mystery of the note—and found it."

Janet moved her lips and shook her head, as much as to say that he could never have done that.

"But I have done it," said he. "I have been down to Lefford and found it all out, and have brought the bank-note up with me—what remains of it. Sally was the culprit."

"Sally!" gasped Janet, going from red to white.

"Sally—but not intentionally. She lighted the fire that afternoon with the note and some more scraps. The note fell out, only partly burnt; and I am going to take it to the bank that they may exchange it for a whole one."

"And—will—they?" panted Janet.

"Of course they will; it is in the regular course of business that they should," affirmed Dr. Knox, deeming it best to be positive for her sake. "Now, Janet, if you are to tremble like this, I shall go away and send up Miss Cattledon—and she does not look as if she had a very amiable temper. Why, my dear child, you ought to be glad."

"Oh, so I am, so I am!" she said, breaking into sobs. "And—and does every one in Lefford know that I was innocent?"

"No one in Lefford believed you guilty. Of course, it is all known, and in the newspapers too—how Sally lighted the fire with a fifty-pound bank-note, and the remains were fished out of the ashes."

"Mrs. Knox—Mrs. Knox—" She could not go on for agitation.

"As to Mrs. Knox, I am not sure but we might prosecute her. Rely upon one thing, Janet: that she will not be very well welcomed at her beloved soirées for some long time to come."

Janet looked at the fire and thought. Dr. Knox kept silence, that she might recover herself after the news.

"I shall get well now," she said in a half-whisper. "I shall soon"—turning to him—"be able to take another situation. Do you think Mrs. Knox will give me a recommendation?"

"Yes, that she will—when it's wanted," said he, with a queer smile.

She sat in silence again, a tinge of colour in her face, and seeing fortunes in the fire. "Oh, the relief, the relief!" she murmured, slightly lifting her hands. "To feel that I may be at peace and fear nothing! I am very thankful to you, Dr. Knox, for all things."

"Do you know what I think would do you good?" said Dr. Knox suddenly. "A drive. The day is so fine, the air so balmy: I am sure it would strengthen you. Will you go?"

"If you please, sir. I do feel stronger, since you told me this."

He went down and spoke to Miss Deveen. She heartily agreed: anything that would benefit the poor girl, she said; and the carriage was coming round to the door, for she had been thinking of going out herself. Cattledon could not oppose them, for she had stepped over to the curate's.

"Would you very much mind—would you pardon me if I asked to be allowed to accompany her alone?" said Dr. Knox, hurriedly to Miss Deveen, as Janet was coming downstairs on Lettice's arm, dressed for the drive.

Miss Deveen was taken by surprise. He spoke as though he were flurried, and she saw the red look on his face.

"I can take care of her as perhaps no one else could," he added with a smile. "And I—I want to ask her a question, Miss Deveen."

"I—think—I—understand you," she said, smiling back at him. "Well, you shall go. Miss Cattledon will talk of propriety, though, when she comes home, and be ready to snap us all up."

And Cattledon was so. When she found Janet had been let go for a slow and easy drive, with no escort but Dr. Knox inside and the fat coachman on the box, she conjectured that Miss Deveen must have taken leave of her senses. Cattledon took up her station at the window to wait for their return, firing out words of temper every other second.

The air must have done Janet good. She came in from the carriage on Dr. Knox's arm, her cheeks bright, her pretty eyes cast down, and looking quite another girl.

"Have you put your question, Dr. Knox?" asked Miss Deveen, meeting him in the hall, while Janet came on.

"Yes, and had it answered," he said brightly. "Thank you, dear Miss Deveen; I see we have your sympathies."

She just took his hand in hers and squeezed it. It was the first day she had seen him, but she liked his face.

Cattledon began upon Janet at once. If she felt well enough to start off on promiscuous drives, she must be well enough to see about a situation.

"I have been speaking to her of one, Miss Cattledon," said Dr. Knox, catching the words as he came in. "I think she will accept it."

"Where is it?" asked Cattledon.

"At Lefford."

"She shall never go back to Rose Villa with my consent, sir. And I think you ought to know better than to propose it to her."

"To Rose Villa! Certainly not: at least at present. Rose Villa will be hers, though; the only little settlement that can be made upon her."

The words struck Cattledon silent. But she could see through a brick wall.

"Perhaps you want her, young man?"

"Yes, I do. I should have wanted her before this, but that I had no home to offer her. I have one now; and good prospects too. Janet has had it all explained to her. Perhaps you will allow me to explain it to you, Miss Cattledon."

"I'm sure it's more than Janet Carey could have expected," said Cattledon, growing pacified as she listened. "She's a poor thing. I hope she will make a good wife."

"I will risk it, Miss Cattledon."

"And she shall be married from my house," struck in Miss Deveen. "Johnny, if you young Oxford blades can get here for it, I will have you all to the wedding."

And we did get there for it: I, and Tod, and William Whitney, and saw the end, so far, of Janet Carey.

CHAPTER VI

HELEN WHITNEY'S WEDDING

I

"What a hot day it is going to be!" cried the Squire, flinging back his thin light coat, and catching the corner of the breakfast-cloth with it, so that he upset the salt-cellar. "Yesterday was about the hottest day I ever felt, but to-day will be worse."

"And all the jam-making about!" added Mrs. Todhetley.

"You need not go near the jam-making."

"I must to-day. Last year Molly made a mistake in the quantity of sugar: and never could be brought to acknowledge it."

"Molly— There's the letter-man," broke off the Squire. "Run, lad."

I went through the open glass-doors with all speed. Letters were not everyday events with us. In these fast and busy days a hundred letters are written where one used to be in those. It was one only that the man handed me now.

"That's all this morning, Mr. Johnny."

I put it beside the Squire's plate, telling him it was from Sir John Whitney. There was no mistaking Sir John's handwriting: the popular belief was that he used a skewer.

"From Whitney, is it," cried he. "Where are my spectacles? What's the postmark! Malvern? Oh, then, they are there still."

"Belle Vue Hotel, Malvern.

"DEAR TODHETLEY,

"Do take compassion upon a weary man, and come over for a day or two. A whole blessed week this day have I been here with never a friend to speak to, or to make up a rubber in the evening. Featherston's a bad player, as you know, but I wish I had him here. I and my wife might take double dummy, for all the players we can get. Helen is engaged to be married to Captain Foliott, Lord Riverside's nephew; and nobody has any time to think of me and my whist-table. Bring the boys with you: Bill is as moped as I am. We are at the Belle Vue, you see. The girls wanted to stand out for the Foley Arms: it's bigger and grander: but I like a place that I have been used to.

"From your old friend,
"JOHN WHITNEY."

The little Whitneys had caught scarlatina, all the fry of them. Recovered now, they had been sent to a cottage on the estate for change; and Sir John, his wife, William, Helen, and Anna went for a week to Malvern while the Hall was cleaned. This news, though, of Helen's engagement, took us by surprise.

"How very sudden!" cried the mater.

Tod was leaning back in his chair, laughing. "I told her I knew there was something up between her and that Captain Foliott!"

"Has she known him before?" asked the mater.

"Known him, yes," cried Tod. "She saw a good deal of him at Cheltenham. As if she would engage herself to any one after only a week's acquaintanceship!"

"As if Sir John would let her!" put in the Squire. "I can't answer for what Miss Helen would do." And Tod laughed again.

When the children were taken ill, Helen and Anna, though they had had the malady, were packed off to Sir John's sister, Miss Whitney, who lived at Cheltenham, and they stayed there for some weeks. After that, they came to us at Dyke Manor for three days, and then went with their father and mother to Malvern. Helen was then full of Captain Foliott, and talked of him to us in private from morning till night. She had met him at Cheltenham, and he had paid her no end of attention. Now, as it appeared, he had followed her to Malvern, and asked for her of Sir John.

"It seems to be a good match—a nephew of Lord Riverside's," observed the Squire. "Is he rich, I wonder?—and is the girl over head and ears in love with him?"

"Rich he may be: but in love with him she certainly is not," cried Tod. "She was too ready to talk of him for that."

The remark was amusing, coming from Tod. How had he learnt to be so worldly-wise?

"Shall you go to Malvern, father?"

"Shall I go!" repeated the Squire, astonished at the superfluous question. "Yes. And start as soon as ever I have finished my breakfast and changed my coat. You two may go also, as you are invited."

We reached Malvern in the afternoon. Sir John and Lady Whitney were alone, in one of the pleasant sitting-rooms of the Belle Vue Hotel, and welcomed us with outstretched hands.

"The girls and William?" cried Sir John, in answer to inquiries. "Oh, they are out somewhere—with Foliott, I conclude; for I'm sure he sticks to Helen like her shadow. Congratulate me, you say? Well, I don't know, Todhetley. It's the fashion, of course, to do it; but I'm not sure but we should rather be condoled with. No sooner do our girls grow up and become companionable, and learn not to revoke at whist when they can be tempted into taking a hand, than they want to leave us! Henceforth they must belong to others, not to us; and we, perhaps, see them no oftener than we see any other stranger. It's one of the crosses of life."

Sir John blew his old red nose, so like the Squire's, and my lady rubbed her eyes. Both felt keenly the prospect of parting with Helen.

"But you like him, don't you?" asked the Squire.

"As to liking him," cried Sir John, and I thought there was some hesitation in his tone; "I am not in love with him: I leave that to Helen. We don't all see with our children's eyes. He is well enough, I suppose, as Helen thinks so. But the fellow does not care for whist."

"I think we play too slow a game for him," put in Lady Whitney. "He chanced to say one evening that Lord Riverside is one of the first hands at whist; and I expect Captain Foliott has been in the habit of playing with him."

"Anyway, you are satisfied with the match, as a match, I take it?" observed the Squire.

"I don't say but that I am," said Sir John. "It might be better, of course; and at present their means will not be large. Foliott offers to settle an estate of his, worth about ten thousand pounds, upon Helen; and his allowance from his uncle Foliott is twelve hundred a-year. They will have to get along on that at present."

"And the captain proposes," added Lady Whitney, "that the three thousand pounds, which will come to Helen when she marries, shall be invested in a house: and we think it would be wise to do it. But he feels quite certain that Mr. Foliott will increase his allowance when he marries; probably double it."

"It's not Lord Riverside, then, who allows him the income?"

"Bless you, Todhetley, no!" spoke Sir John in a hurry. "He says Riverside's as poor as a church mouse, and vegetates from year's end to year's end at his place in Scotland. It is Foliott the mine-owner down in the North. Stay: which is it, Betsy?—mine-owner, or mill-owner?"

"Mill-owner, I think," said Lady Whitney. "He is wonderfully rich, whichever it is; and Captain Foliott will come into at least a hundred thousand pounds at his death."

Listening to all this as I stood on the balcony, looking at the beautiful panorama stretched out below and beyond, for they were talking at the open window, I dreamily thought what a good thing Helen was going to make of it. Later on, all this was confirmed, and we learnt a few additional particulars.

Mr. Foliott, mill-owner and millionaire, was a very great man in the North; employing thousands of hands. He was a good man, full of benevolence, always doing something or other to benefit his townspeople and his dependents. But his health had been failing of late, and he had now gone to the Cape, a sea-voyage having been advised by his doctors. He had never married, and Captain Foliott was his favourite nephew.

"It's not so bad, after all, is it, Johnny?"

The words were whispered over my shoulder, and I started back to see Helen's radiant face. She and Anna had come in unheard by me, and had caught the thread of conversation in the room.

"I call it very good, Helen. I hope he is good too."

"You shall see," she answered. "He is coming up with William."

Her dark brown eyes were sparkling, a bright colour glowed on her cheeks. Miss Helen Whitney was satisfied with her future bridegroom, and no mistake. She had forgotten all about her incipient liking for poor Slingsby Temple.

"What regiment is Captain Foliott in, Helen?"

"Not in any. He has sold out."

"Sold out!"

"His mother and his uncle made him do it. The detachment was ordered to India, and they would not let him go; would not part with him; begged and prayed of him to sell out. Nothing ever vexed him so much in his life, he says; but what could he do? His mother has only him: and on Mr. Foliott he is dependent for riches."

"Entirely dependent?"

"For riches, I said, Johnny. He has himself a small competence. Ten thousand pounds nearly comprises it. And that is to be settled on me."

A slight bustle in the room, and we both looked round. Bill Whitney was noisily greeting Tod. Some one else had followed Bill through the door.

A rather tall man, with reddish hair and drooping, reddish whiskers, bold handsome features, and a look I did not like in his red-brown eyes. Stepping over the window-sill from the balcony, they introduced me to him, Captain Richard Foliott.

"I have heard much of Johnny Ludlow," said he, holding out his hand with a cordial smile, "and I am glad to know him. I hope we shall soon be better acquainted."

I shook his hand and answered in kind. But I was not drawn to him; not a bit; rather repelled. The eyes were not nice: or the voice, either. It had not a true ring in it. Undeniably handsome he was, and I thought that was the best that could be said.

"Look here: we are going for a stroll," said Sir John; "you young people can come, or not, as you please. But if you go up the hill, remember that we dine at six o'clock. Once you get scampering about up there, you forget the time."

He went out with the Squire. Lady Whitney had a letter to write and sat down to do it; the rest of us stood, some on the balcony, some in the room. Helen, Tod, and Captain Foliott were apparently trying which could talk the fastest.

"Why do you look at me so earnestly?" suddenly demanded the latter.

It was to me he spoke. I laughed, and apologized; saying that his face put me in mind of some other face I had seen, but I could not remember whose. This was true. It was true also that I had been looking at him more fixedly than the strict rules of etiquette might require: but I had not an idea that he was observing me.

"I thought you might be wishing to take my portrait," said the captain, turning away to whisper to Helen.

"More likely to take your character," jestingly struck in Bill, with more zeal than discretion. "Johnny Ludlow sees through everybody; reads faces off like a book."

Captain Foliott wheeled sharply round at the words, and stood before me, his eyes gazing straight into mine.

"Can you read my face?" he asked. "What do you see there?"

"I see that you have been a soldier: your movements tell me that: right-about, face; quick march," answered I, turning the matter off with a jest. Tod opportunely struck in.

"How could you leave the army?" he asked with emphasis. "I only wish I had the chance of joining it." Though he knew that he had better not let the Squire hear him say so.

"It was a blow," acknowledged Foliott. "One does meet with raps in this world. But, you see, it was a case of—of the indulgence of my own gratification weighed in the scale against that of my mother: and I let my side go up. My uncle also came down upon me with his arguments and his opposition, and altogether I found myself nowhere. I believe he and she are equally persuaded that nobody ever comes out of India alive."

"Who will take my letter to the post?" called out Lady Whitney. All of us volunteered to do it, and went out together. We met Sir John and the Squire strolling about the village rubbing their red faces, and saying how intensely hot it was.

They left us to regale ourselves at the pastry-cook's, and sauntered on towards the dark trees shading that deep descent on which the hotel windows looked out. We found them sitting on one of the benches there.

"Well, Foliott!" cried Sir John. "You'd not have found it hotter than this in India."

"Not so hot, Sir John. But I like heat."

"How do-you-do?" struck in a big, portly gentleman, who was sitting on the same bench as the Squire and Sir John, and whose face was even redder than theirs. "Did not expect to meet you here."

Captain Foliott, who was the one addressed, wheeled round to the speaker in that sharp way of his, and was evidently taken by surprise. His manner was cold; never a smile sat on his face as he answered—

"Oh, is it you, Mr. Crane! Are you quite well? Staying at Malvern?"

"For an hour or two. I am passing a few days at Worcester, and my friends there would not let me go on without first bringing me to see Malvern."

The stranger spoke like a gentleman and looked like one, looked like a man of substance also (though Foliott did draw down his lips that same evening and speak of him as "nobody"); and Sir John, in his old-fashioned cordiality, begged of Captain Foliott to introduce his friend. Captain Foliott did it with a not very ready grace. "Mr. Crane, Sir John Whitney; Mr. Todhetley."

"A beautiful place this, sirs," cried he.

"Yes, only it's too hot to walk about to-day," answered they. "Have you been up the hill?"

"No, I can't manage that: but my friends are gone up. Have you heard lately from your uncle, Captain Foliott?" added Mr. Crane.

"Not very lately."

"I hear the outward voyage did him a world of good."

"I believe it did."

As if the questions of the stranger worried him, Captain Foliott strolled away towards the abbey: the two girls, Tod, and William following him. I stayed where I was: not liking the heat much more than the Squire did.

"You know Mr. Foliott of Milltown?" observed Sir John to the stranger.

"I know him very well indeed, sir. I am a mill-owner myself in the same place: but not as large a one as he is."

"He is uncommonly rich, we hear."

"Ay, he is. Could buy up pretty well half the world."

"And a good man into the bargain?"

"Downright good. Honest, upright, liberal; a true Christian. He does an immense deal for his fellow-men. Nobody ever asks him to put his hand in his pocket in vain."

"When is he expected home?"

"I am not sure when. That will depend, I expect, upon how he feels. But we hear the outward voyage has quite set him up."

"Captain Foliott often talks of his uncle. He seems to think there's nobody like him."

"He has cause to think it. Yes, I assure you, sirs, few men in the world can come up to George Foliott, the mill-owner, for probity and goodness."

How much more he might have said in Mr. Foliott's praise was cut short by the hasty appearance of two young men, evidently the friends of Mr. Crane. They laughed at the speed they had made down the hill, told him the carriage was ready, and that they ought to start at once to reach Worcester by dinner-time. So the portly old gentleman wished us good-day and departed. Running up the bank, I saw them drive off from the Crown in a handsome two-horse phæton.

It was on the day following this, that matters were finally settled with regard to Helen's marriage. Captain Foliott made good his wish—which, as it appeared, he had been harping upon ever since the proposal was first made: namely, that they should be married immediately, and not wait for the return of Mr. Foliott to England. Sir John had held out against it, asking where the hurry was. To this Captain Foliott had rejoined by inquiring what they had to wait for, and where was the need of waiting, and the chances were that his uncle would stay away for a year. So at last, Sir John, who was a simple-minded man, and as easily persuaded as a duck is to water, gave in; and the wedding was fixed to take place the next month, September, at Whitney.

We made the most of this, our one entire day at Malvern, for we should disperse the next. The Whitneys to Whitney Hall, the house now being in apple-pie order for them; ourselves back to Dyke Manor; Captain Foliott to get the marriage-settlement prepared. Helen's three thousand pounds, all she would have at present, was not to be settled at all, but invested in some snug little house that they would fix upon together after the marriage, so that Captain Foliott's lawyers took the preparation of the deeds of settlement on themselves, saving trouble to Sir John. Three parts of the day we spent roaming the hill: and I must say Foliott made himself as delightful as sun in harvest, and I told myself that I must have misjudged his eyes in thinking they were not nice ones.

But the next morning we received a shock. How swimmingly the world would go on without such things, I leave those who have experienced them to judge. It came when we were at the breakfast-table, in the shape of a letter to Lady Whitney. Scarlatina—which was supposed to have been cleaned and scrubbed out—had come into the Hall again, and the kitchen-maid was laid up with it.

Here was a pretty kettle of fish! Whether Sir John or my lady looked the most helplessly bewildered, might have puzzled a juror to decide. Back to the Hall they could not go; and what was to be done? The

Squire, open-handed and open-hearted, pressed them to accompany us and take up their quarters at Dyke Manor; and for a minute or two I thought they would have done it; but somebody, Helen, I think, suggested a furnished house in London, and that was finally decided upon. So to London they would go, hire the first suitable house that offered, and the marriage would take place there instead of at home. Captain Foliott, coming in after breakfast from his hotel, the Foley Arms, stared at the change of programme.

"I wouldn't go to London," said he, emphatically. "London at this season of the year is the most wretched wilderness on the face of the whole earth. Not a soul in it."

"The more room for us, Foliott," cried Sir John. "What will it matter to us whether the town is empty or full?"

"I would strongly advise you, Sir John, not to go. Lady Whitney will not like it, I am certain. As Mr. Todhetley has been good enough to offer you his hospitality—"

"Put, bless my heart," interrupted Sir John in a heat, "you don't suppose, do you, that I could trespass upon an old friend for weeks and weeks—a regular army of us! Were it a matter of a few days, I wouldn't say nay; but who is to foresee how long it may be before we can get into our own house? You've not a bit of thought, Foliott."

"Why not go to your sister's at Cheltenham, sir?" was all the captain said to this.

"Because I don't choose to go to my sister's at Cheltenham," retorted Sir John, who could be as obstinate as the Squire when he liked. "And why should we go to Cheltenham more than to London? Come?"

"I thought it would be less trouble for you, sir. Cheltenham is close at hand."

"And London is not far off. As to its being empty, I say that's so much the better: we shall more readily find a furnished house in it. To London we go to-day."

With Sir John in this resolute mood, there was no more to be said. And the notion became quite agreeable, now that they were growing reconciled to it.

"All things are directed for the best," concluded Lady Whitney in her simple faith. "I hardly see how we should have procured Helen's trousseau down at Whitney: there will be no difficulty in London."

"You are right, my dear lady, and I am wrong," conceded Captain Foliott, with a good-natured smile. "To us young men of fashion," he added, the smile deepening to a laugh, "London between August and April is looked upon as a nightmare. But circumstances alter cases; and I see that it will be the best and most convenient place for you."

Drawing Helen aside as he spoke, and taking a small morocco case from his pocket, he slipped upon her finger his first and parting gift: a magnificent hoop of diamonds.

"I should like you to wear it always, my love," he whispered. "As the pledge of your engagement now; later, as the guard of your wedding-ring."

"I shall go up in the smoking-carriage, Johnny."

"Shall you! You'll smell finely of smoke when we get there."

"Not I. I'll give my coat a shake at the end of the journey. By Jove! I shall be left behind, if I don't take care."

Tod was right. The train was already on the move. He dashed into the smoking-compartment; the porter closed the doors, and we were off.

Off to London. He and I were going up to Helen Whitney's wedding, to which we had been invited when staying at Malvern some weeks ago. The Squire declined for himself, though Sir John had wanted him also. This was Monday; the wedding was to be on Thursday; and on the Saturday Anna and William were to go back with us to Dyke Manor.

It was September weather, and a glorious day. Now, as the train steamed away on its windings and turnings, the Malvern Hills would glide into view; and now be lost again. But the beautiful landscape was always to be seen, with its woods and dales and fertile plains; and there was not a cloud in the deep blue sky to obscure the sun.

I had the carriage to myself; and pictured Tod one of a crowd of smokers. At Oxford he came back to the carriage, and got in.

"Had enough smoke, Tod?"

"Just for now, lad," he shortly answered; and began to whistle softly and pull at his whiskers. By which I knew he had something on his mind.

"I say, Johnny, I am in a dilemma," he began abruptly, when we were going on again, bending towards me from the opposite seat till his face nearly touched mine.

"What about? What is it?"

"Look here. When I got into the smoking-carriage it was full, all but one seat, which I took—and that was a corner one, which they had been polite enough to leave. The carriage was dark with smoke: pipes had been going, I expect, all the way from Worcester. I lighted mine, saying nothing, and nobody said anything to me. The man opposite to me and the one next me had a hot discussion on hand, touching a racehorse; not quarrelling, but talking loudly, so that they made a tolerable noise. At the other end of the carriage sat two men facing one another, just as you and I sit now; and one of them I'll vow was an Oxford man: I could tell him by his cut. They were talking together also, but rather in an undertone. All at once, when we were nearing Oxford, there was a lull at my end, and I heard a bit of what they were saying. The first word that particularly caught my ear was Foliott. 'What plant is Foliott up to now, I wonder?' cried one. 'Don't know,' said the other; 'nothing good, we may be sure of. A rumour reached me that he was going to be married.' 'What a chance for the girl!' cried the first. 'Poor thing! But it may not be true,' he went on, knocking the ashes out of his pipe: 'who would marry such a scamp as that?' Now, Johnny," broke off Tod, "the question is, were they speaking of this Foliott? This man that we are now on our way to see married to Helen?"

"Was that all you heard, Tod?"

"Every word. The train began to slacken speed then for the Oxford station, and the two men stood up to reach their overcoats and hand-bags, for they got out there. I had half a mind to stop them and ask what Foliott they had been speaking of; but I did not much like to, and while I hesitated they disappeared. They might just have told me to mind my own business if I had spoken; so perhaps it comes to the same."

"Foliott is not an absolutely uncommon name, Tod. There may be plenty of Foliotts about."

"Just so, lad. But, on the other hand, it may be the one we know of, Richard Foliott. One point coincides—he is going to be married."

I sat back on the seat, revolving probabilities, and thinking of many things. That instinctive dislike I had taken to Captain Foliott's eyes, or to himself, or to both, flashed over me with vivid force. The fine scenery we were just then whirling past, and on which my eyes seemed to be fixed, might have been a sandy desert, for all I saw of it.

"The worst is, the dilemma it puts one in," continued Tod. "To speak of this to the Whitneys, or not to speak?—that's the question. If it should turn out to be another Foliott, they might never forgive me. He never would."

"But then—Helen's whole future may be at stake. It may be in peril."

Tod pulled at his whiskers again. I read the name of the station we were flashing past.

"I hate a doubt of this sort," cried Tod impatiently, "where one can't see how one's duty lies. It bothers the mind. I think I'll let it go, Johnny."

"But, if it should turn out, when too late, that he is a scamp: and, for the want of a word, you have let him—let him make havoc of Helen's life!"

"What could I say?" he asked irritably. "That I overheard two fellows, in the smoking-compartment of a railway train, saying that one Foliott was a scamp. Sir John would naturally ask me what grounds I had for assuming that it was their Foliott. Well, I have no grounds. And how small I should look!"

"There are slight grounds, at any rate, Tod. The name is his, Foliott; and both are going to be married."

"All the same, I don't see that I can speak."

"Put it in this light, Tod," I said. "You don't speak; and they get married; and then something or other bad turns up about Foliott; and Sir John finds out that it was in your power to warn him in time, and you did not. What will he say then?"

"I'm sure I don't know," grunted Tod. "I wish I could see on which side land lies."

All the rest of the way to London we continued to discuss it by fits and starts, and at last hit upon a good thought—to tell the whole to William Whitney. It was the best thing to do, so far as we could see. It might all end in smoke, or—it might not.

The Whitneys had found a furnished house in Gloucester Place, near Portman Square. The maid who had taken the illness was soon well again, and the Hall was being regularly fumigated now, preparatory to their return. In Gloucester Place they were within a short drive of Miss Deveen's, a fact which had guided them to the locality. Indeed, it was only a walk for the younger of us.

Not until night did we get any chance of a private talk with William. Our bedrooms opened into one another; and after we went up for good, he sat down in our room.

"You won't be affronted, Bill, at something I am about to say?" struck in Tod, by way of prelude.

"Affronted!" cried Bill. "I! What on earth do you ask that stupid question for?"

"In coming up to-day, I heard a few words in the train," went on Tod. "Two fellows were talking, and they brought up a man's name in a disparaging manner. It is a friend of yours, Bill; and Johnny and I had a precious discussion, I can tell you, as to whether we should repeat it to you or not."

"Was it my name?" asked Bill. "What could they have to say against me?"

"No, no; they'd have got an answer from me had it been yours. First of all, we thought of mentioning it to Sir John; but I did not like to, and that's the truth. So we just concluded to put it before you, as one of ourselves, and you can tell him if you like."

"All right," said Bill. "Go ahead."

Tod told him all from beginning to end. Not that it was very much to tell: but he brought in our own conversation; the delicacy we felt in speaking at all, and the arguments for and against. Bill was not in the least put out; rather wondered, I thought, that we should be.

"It can't be Dick Foliott, you know," said he. "There's not anything against him; impossible that there should be."

"I am glad you say so," cried Tod, relieved. "It was only for Helen's sake we gave a thought to it."

"The name was the same, you see—Foliott," I put in. "And that man is going to be married as well as this one."

"True," answered Bill, slowly. "Still I feel sure it is quite impossible that it can be Foliott. If—if you think I had better mention it, I will. I'll mention it to himself."

"I should," said I eagerly, for somehow my doubts of the man were growing larger. "Better be on the safe side. You don't know much about him, after all, Bill."

"Not know much about him! What do you mean, Johnny? We know enough. He is Riverside's nephew, a very respectable old Scotch peer, and he is Foliott the mill-owner's nephew; and I'm sure he is to be respected, if it's only for the money he has made. And Dick has a very fair income of his own, and settles ten thousand pounds upon Helen, and will come into a hundred thousand by-and-by, or more. What would you have?"

I could not say what I would have; but the uneasiness lay on my mind. Tod spoke.

"The men alluded to conduct, I expect, Bill; not to means. They spoke of that Foliott as an out-and-out scamp, and called the girl he was going to marry 'Poor thing,' in a piteous tone. You wouldn't like that applied to Helen."

"By Jove, no. Better be on the safe side, as Johnny says. We'll say nothing to my father at present; but you and I, Tod, will quietly repeat to Foliott what you heard, and we'll put it to him, as man to man, to tell us in all honour whether the words could have related to himself. Of course the idea is altogether absurd; we will tell him that, and beg his pardon."

So that was resolved upon. And a great relief it was. To decide upon a course of action, in any unpleasant difficulty, takes away half its discomfort.

Captain Foliott had come to London but once since they met at Malvern. His stay was short; three days; and during those days he was so busy that Gloucester Place only saw him in the evenings. He had a great deal to do down in the North against his marriage, arranging his property preparatory to settling it on Helen, and seeing to other business matters. But the zeal he lacked in personal attention, he made up by letter. Helen had one every morning as regularly as the post came in.

He was expected in town on the morrow, Tuesday: indeed, Helen had thought he might perhaps have come to-day. Twelve o'clock on Wednesday, at Gloucester Place, was the hour fixed for signing the deeds of settlement: and by twelve o'clock on Thursday, the following day, all going well, he and Helen would be man and wife.

Amidst the letters waiting on the breakfast-table on Tuesday morning was one for Helen. Its red seal and crest told whence it came.

"Foliott always seals his letters to Helen," announced Bill for our information. "And what ill news has that one inside it?" continued he to his sister. "You look as cross as two sticks, Nelly."

"Just mind your own business," said Helen.

"What time will Captain Foliott be here to-day, my dear?" questioned her mother.

"He will not be here at all to-day," answered Helen, fractiously. "It's too bad. He says it is impossible for him to get away by any train, in time to see us to-night; but he will be here the first thing in the morning. His mother is worse, and he is anxious about her. People always fall ill at the wrong time."

"Is Mrs. Foliott coming up to the wedding?" I asked.

"No," said Lady Whitney. "I of course invited her, and she accepted the invitation; but a week ago she wrote me word she was not well enough to come. And now, children, what shall we set about first? Oh dear! there is such a great deal to do and to think of to-day!"

But we had another arrival that day, if we had not Captain Foliott. That was Mary Seabright, who was to act as bridesmaid with Anna. Brides did not have a string of maids in those days, as some have in these. Leaving them to get through their multiplicity of work—which must be connected, Bill thought, with bonnets and wedding-cake—we went up with Sir John in a boat to Richmond.

That evening we all dined at Miss Deveen's. It was to be one of the quietest of weddings; partly by Captain Foliott's express wish, chiefly because they were not at home at the Hall. Miss Deveen and Miss Cattledon were to be the only guests besides ourselves and Mary Seabright, and a Major White who would go to the church with Foliott. Just twelve of us, all told.

"But where's the bridegroom?" asked Miss Deveen, when we reached her house.

"He can't get up until late to-night; perhaps not until to-morrow morning," pouted Helen.

The dinner-table was a downright merry one, and we did not seem to miss Captain Foliott. Afterwards, when Sir John had made up his whist-table—with my lady, Miss Deveen, and the grey-haired curate, Mr. Lake, who had dropped in—we amused ourselves with music and games in the other room.

"What do you think of the bridegroom, Johnny Ludlow?" suddenly demanded Miss Cattledon, who had sat down by me. "I hear you saw him at Malvern."

"Think of him! Oh, he—he is a very fine man; good-looking, and all that."

"That I have seen for myself," retorted Cattledon, pinching her hands round her thin waist. "When he was staying in London, two or three weeks ago, we spent an evening in Gloucester Place. Do you like him?"

She put the "like" so very pointedly, staring into my face at the time, that I was rather taken aback. I did not like Captain Foliott: but there was no particular necessity for telling her so.

"I like him—pretty well, Miss Cattledon."

"Well, I do not, Johnny Ludlow. I fancy he has a temper; I'm sure he is not good-natured; and I—I don't think he'll make a very good husband."

"That will be a pity. Helen is fond of him."

Miss Cattledon coughed significantly. "Is she? Helen is fond of him in-so-far as that she is eager to be married—all girls are—and the match with Captain Foliott is an advantageous one. But if you think she cares for him in any other way, Johnny Ludlow, you are quite mistaken. Helen Whitney is no more in love with Captain Foliott than you are in love with me."

At which I laughed.

"Very few girls marry for love," she went on. "They fall in love, generally speaking, with the wrong person."

"Then what do they marry for?"

"For the sake of being married. With the fear of old-maidism staring them in the face, they are ready, silly things, to snap at almost any offer they receive. Go up to Helen Whitney now, tell her she is destined to live in single blessedness, and she would be ready to fret herself into a fever. Every girl would not be, mind you: but there are girls and girls."

Well, perhaps Miss Cattledon was not far wrong. I did not think as she did then, and laughed again in answer: but I have learned more of the world and its ways since.

In every corner of the house went Helen's eyes when we got back to Gloucester Place, but they could not see Captain Foliott. She had been hoping against hope.

III

Wednesday. Young women, bringing in huge band-boxes, were perpetually ringing at the door, and by-and-by we were treated to a sight of the finery. Sufficient gowns and bonnets to set up a shop were spread out in Helen's room. The wedding-dress lay on the bed: a glistening white silk, with a veil and wreath beside it. Near to it was the dress she would go away in to Dover, the first halting-place on their trip to Paris: a quiet shot-silk, Lady Whitney called it, blue one way, pink another. Shot, or not shot, it was uncommonly pretty. Straw bonnets were the mode in those days, and Helen's, perched above her travelling-dress, had white ribbons on it and a white veil—which was the mode for brides also. I am sure Helen, in her vanity, thought more of the things than of the bridegroom.

But she thought of him also. Especially when the morning went on and did not bring him. Twelve o'clock struck, and Sir John Whitney's solicitor, Mr. Hill, who had come up on purpose, was punctual to his appointment. Sir John had thought it right that his own solicitor should be present at the reading and signing of the settlements, to see that they were drawn up properly.

So there they sat in the back-parlour, which had been converted into a business room for the occasion, waiting for Captain Foliott and the deed with what patience they had. At one o'clock, when they came in to luncheon, Sir John was looking a little blue; and he remarked that Captain Foliott, however busy he might have been, should have stretched a point to get off in time. Appointments, especially important ones, ought to be kept.

For it was conclusively thought that the delay was caused by the captain's having been unable to leave the previous day, and that he was travelling up now.

So Mr. Hill waited, and Sir John waited, and the rest of us waited, Helen especially; and thus the afternoon passed in waiting. Helen was more fidgety than a hen with one chick: darting to the window every instant, peeping down the staircase at the sound of every ring.

Dinner-time; and no appearance of Captain Foliott. After dinner; and still the same. Mary Seabright, a merry girl, told Helen that her lover was like the knight in the old ballad—he loved and he rode away.

There was a good deal of laughing, and somebody called for the song, "The Mistletoe Bough." Of course it was all in jest: as each minute passed, we expected the next would bring Captain Foliott.

Not until ten o'clock did Mr. Hill leave, with the understanding that he should return the next morning at the same hour. The servants were beginning to lay the breakfast-table in the dining-room, for a lot of sweet dishes had been brought in from the pastry-cook's, and Lady Whitney thought they had better be put on the table at once. In the afternoon we had tied the cards together—"Mr. and Mrs. Richard Foliott"—with white satin ribbon, sealed them up in their envelopes with white wax, and directed them ready for the post on the morrow.

At twelve o'clock a move was made to go upstairs to bed; and until that hour we had still been expecting Captain Foliott.

"I feel positive some dreadful accident has happened," whispered Helen to me as she said good-night, her usually bright colour faded to paleness. "If I thought it was carelessness that is causing the delay, as they are cruelly saying, I—I should never forgive him."

"Wait a minute," said Bill to me aside, touching Tod also. "Let them go on."

"Are you not coming, William?" said Lady Whitney.

"In two minutes, mother."

"I don't like this," began Bill, speaking to us both over our bed-candles, for the other lights were out. "I'll be hanged if I think he means to turn up at all!"

"But why should he not?"

"Who is to know? Why has he not turned up already? I can tell you that it seems to me uncommonly strange. Half-a-dozen times to-night I had a great mind to call my father out and tell him about what you heard in the train, Tod. It is so extraordinary for a man, coming up to his wedding, not to appear: especially when he is bringing the settlements with him."

Neither of us spoke. What, indeed, could we say to so unpleasant a topic? Bill went on again.

"If he were a man in business, as his uncle, old Foliott, is, I could readily understand that interests connected with it might detain him till the last moment. But he is not; he has not an earthly thing to do."

"Perhaps his lawyers are in fault," cried Tod. "If they are backward with the deeds of settlement—"

"The deeds were ready a week ago. Foliott said so in writing to my father."

A silence ensued, rendering the street noises more audible. Suddenly there came a sound of a horse and cab dashing along, and it pulled up at our door. Foliott, of course.

Down we went, helter-skelter, out on the pavement. The servants, busy in the dining-room still, came running to the steps. A gentleman, getting out of the cab with a portmanteau, stared, first at us, then at the house.

"This is not right," said he to the driver, after looking about him. "It's next door but one."

"This is the number you told me, sir."

"Ah, yes. Made a mistake."

But so sure did it seem to us that this late and hurried traveller must be, at least, some one connected with Captain Foliott, if not himself, that it was only when he and his luggage had disappeared within the next house but one, and the door was shut, and the cab gone away, that we realized the disappointment, and the vague feeling of discomfort it left behind. The servants went in. We strolled to the opposite side of the street, unconsciously hoping that luck might bring another cab with the right man in it.

"Look there!" whispered Bill, pointing upwards.

The room over the drawing-room was Lady Whitney's; the room above that, the girls'. Leaning out at the window, gazing now up the street, now down, was Helen, her eyes restless, her face pale and woe-begone in the bright moonlight.

It was a sad night for Helen Whitney. She did not attempt to undress, as we knew later, but kept her post at that weary window. Every cab or carriage that rattled into view was watched by her with eager, feverish anxiety. But not one halted at the house, not one contained Captain Foliott. Helen Whitney will never forget that unhappy night of tumultuous feeling and its intolerable suspense.

But here was the wedding-morning come, and no bridegroom. The confectioners were rushing in with more dishes, and the dressmakers appearing to put the finishing touches to Helen. Lady Whitney was just off her head: doubtful whether to order all the paraphernalia away, or whether Captain Foliott might not come yet. In the midst of the confusion a little gentleman arrived at the house and asked for Sir John. Sir John and he had a long conference, shut in alone: and when they at length came out Sir John's nose was a dark purple. The visitor was George Foliott, the mill-owner: returned since some days from the Cape.

And the tale he unfolded would have struck dismay to the nose of many a wiser man than was poor Sir John. The scamp spoken of in the train was Richard Foliott; and a nice scamp he turned out to be. Upon Mr. Foliott's return to Milltown the prospective wedding had come to his ears, with all the villainy encompassing it; he had at once taken means to prevent Mr. Richard's carrying it out, and had now come up to enlighten Sir John Whitney.

Richard Foliott had been a scamp at heart from his boyhood; but he had contrived to keep well before the world. Over and over again had Mr. Foliott paid his debts and set him on his legs again. Captain Foliott had told the Whitneys that he quitted the army by the wish of his friends: he quitted it because he dared not stay in. Before Mr. Foliott departed for the Cape he had thrown Richard off; had been obliged to do it. His fond foolish mother had reduced herself to poverty for him. The estate, once worth ten thousand pounds, which he had made a pretence of settling upon Helen, belonged to his mother, and was mortgaged about a dozen deep. He dared not go much abroad for fear of arrest, especially in London. This, and a great deal more, was disclosed by Mr. Foliott to Sir John; who sat and gasped, and rubbed his face, and wished his old friend Todhetley was at hand, and thanked God for Helen's escape.

"He will never be any better," affirmed Mr. Foliott, "be very sure of that. He is innately bad, and the pain he has inflicted upon me for years has made me old before my time. But—forgive me, Sir John, for saying so—I cannot think you exercised discretion in accepting him so easily for your daughter."

"I had no suspicion, you see," returned poor Sir John. "How could I have any? Being your nephew, and Lord Riverside's nephew—"

"Riverside's nephew he called himself, did he! The old man is ninety, as I dare say you know, and never stirs from his home in the extreme north of Scotland. Some twenty years ago, he fell in with the sister of Richard's mother (she was a governess in a family up there), and married her; but she died within the year. That's how he comes to be Lord Riverside's 'nephew.' But they have never met in their lives."

"Oh dear!" bemoaned Sir John. "What a villain! and what a blessed escape! He made a great point of Helen's bit of money, three thousand pounds, not being tied up before the marriage. I suppose he wanted to get it into his own hands."

"Of course he did."

"And to pay his debts with it; as far as it would go."

"Pay his debts with it!" exclaimed Mr. Foliott. "Why, my good sir, it would take thirty thousand to pay them. He would just have squandered it away in Paris, at his gaming-tables, and what not; and then have asked you to keep him. Miss Whitney is well quit of him: and I'm thankful I came back in time to save her."

Great news to disclose to Helen! Deeply mortifying to have ordered a wedding-breakfast and wedding things in general when there was no wedding to be celebrated! The tears were running down Lady Whitney's homely cheeks, as Miss Deveen drove up.

Mr. Foliott asked to see Helen. All he said to her we never knew—but there's no doubt he was as kind as a father.

"He is a wicked, despicable man," sobbed Helen.

"He is all that, and more," assented Mr. Foliott. "You may be thankful your whole life long for having escaped him. And, my dear, if it will at all help you to bear the smart, I may tell you that you are not the first young lady by two or three he has served, or tried to serve, in precisely the same way. And to one of them he behaved more wickedly than I care to repeat to you."

"But," ruefully answered poor Helen, quietly sobbing, "I don't suppose it came so near with any of them as the very morning."

And that was the end of Helen Whitney's wedding.

CHAPTER VII

HELEN'S CURATE

I

A summons from Mr. Brandon meant a summons. And I don't think I should have dared to disobey one any more than I should those other summonses issued by the law courts. He was my guardian, and he let me know it.

But I was hardly pleased that the mandate should have come for me just this one particular day. We were at Crabb Cot: Helen, Anna, and William Whitney had come to it for a week's visit; and I did not care to lose a day with them. It had to be lost, however. Mr. Brandon had ordered me to be with him as early as possible in the morning: so that I must be off betimes to catch the first train.

It was a cold bleak day towards the end of February: sleet falling now and then, the east wind blowing like mad, and cutting me in two as I stood at the hall-door. Nobody else was down yet, and I had swallowed my breakfast standing.

Shutting the door after me, and making a rush down the walk between the evergreens for the gate, I ran against Lee, the Timberdale postman, who was coming in, with the letters, on his shaky legs. His face, shaded by its grey locks, straggling and scanty, had a queer kind of fear upon it.

"Mr. Johnny, I'm thankful to meet you; I was thinking what luck it would be if I could," said he, trembling. "Perhaps you will stand my friend, sir. Look here."

Of the two letters he handed to me, one was addressed to Mrs. Todhetley; the other to Helen Whitney. And this last had its envelope pretty nearly burnt off. The letter inside could be opened by anybody, and some of the scorched writing lay exposed.

"If the young lady would only forgive me—and hush it up, Mr. Johnny!" he pleaded, his poor worn face taking a piteous hue. "The Miss Whitneys are both very nice and kind young ladies; and perhaps she will."

"How was it done, Lee?"

"Well, sir, I was lighting my pipe. It is a smart journey here, all the way from Timberdale—and I had to take the long round to-day instead of the Ravine, because there was a newspaper for the Stone House. The east wind was blowing right through me, Mr. Johnny; and I thought if I had a bit of a smoke I might get along better. A spark must have fallen on the letter while I was lighting my pipe, and I did not see it till the letter was aflame in my hand. If—if you could but stand my friend, sir, and—and perhaps give the letter to the young lady yourself, so that the Squire does not see it—and ask her to forgive me."

One could only pity him, poor worn man. Lee had had pecks of trouble, and it had told upon him, making him old before his time. Now and then, when it was a bad winter's morning, and the Squire caught sight of him, he would tell him to go into the kitchen and get a cup of hot coffee. Taking the two letters from him to do what I could, I carried them indoors.

Putting Helen's with its tindered cover into an envelope, I wrote a line in pencil, and slipped it in also.

"DEAR HELEN,

"Poor old Lee has had a mishap and burnt your letter in lighting his pipe. He wants you to forgive it and not to tell the Squire. No real damage is done, so please be kind.

"J. L."

Directing this to her, I sent it to her room by Hannah, and made a final start for the train.

And this was what happened afterwards.

Hannah took the letter to Helen, who was in the last stage of dressing, just putting the finishing touches to her hair. Staring at the state her letter was in, she read the few words I had written, and then went into a passion at what Lee had done. Helen Whitney was as good-hearted a girl as ever lived, but hot and hasty in temper, saying anything that came uppermost when put out. She, by the help of time, had got over the smart left by the summary collapse of her marriage, and had ceased to abuse Mr. Richard Foliott. All that was now a thing of the past. And, not having had a spark of love for him, he was the more easily forgotten.

"The wicked old sinner!" she burst out: and with emphasis so startling, that Anna, reading by the window, dropped her Prayer-book.

"Helen! What is the matter?"

"That's the matter," flashed Helen, showing the half-burnt envelope and scorched letter, and flinging on the table the piece of paper I had slipped inside. Anna took the letter up and read it.

"Poor old man! It was only an accident, Helen; and, I suppose, as Johnny says, no real damage is done. You must not say anything about it."

"Must I not!" was Helen's tart retort.

"Who is the letter from?"

"Never you mind."

"But is it from home?"

"It is from Mr. Leafchild, if you must know."

"Oh," said Anna shortly. For that a flirtation, or something of the kind, had been going on between Helen and the curate, Leafchild, and that it would not be likely to find favour at Whitney Hall, she was quite aware of.

"Mr. Leafchild writes about the school," added Helen, after reading the letter; perhaps tendering the information as an apology for its having come at all. "Those two impudent girls, Kate and Judith Dill, have been setting Miss Barn at defiance, and creating no end of insubordination."

With the last word, she was leaving the room; the letter in her pocket, the burnt envelope in her hand. Anna stopped her.

"You are not going to show that, are you, Helen? Please don't."

"Mr. Todhetley ought to see it—and call Lee to account for his carelessness. Why, he might have altogether burnt the letter!"

"Yes; of course it was careless. But I dare say it will be a lesson to him. He is very poor and old, Helen. Pray don't tell the Squire; he might make so much commotion over it, and then you would be sorry. Johnny asks you not."

Helen knitted her brow, but put the envelope into her pocket with the letter: not conceding with at all a good grace, and went down nodding her head in semi-defiance. The cream of the sting lay no doubt in the fact that the letter was Mr. Leafchild's, and that other eyes than her own might have seen it.

She did not say anything at the breakfast-table, though Anna sat upon thorns lest she should: Helen was so apt to speak upon impulse. The Squire talked of riding out; Whitney said he would go with him: Tod seemed undecided what he should do. Mrs. Todhetley read to them the contents of her letter—which was from Mary Blair.

"I shall go for a walk," announced Helen, when the rest had dispersed. "Come and get your things on, Anna."

"But I don't care to go out," said Anna. "It is a very disagreeable day. And I meant to help Mrs. Todhetley with the frock she is making for Lena."

"You can help her when you come back. I am not going through that Crabb Ravine by myself."

"Through Crabb Ravine!"

"Yes. I want to go to Timberdale."

It never occurred to Anna that the errand to Timberdale could have any connection with the morning's mishap. She put her things on without more ado—Helen always domineered over her, just as Tod did over me—and the two girls went out together.

"Halloa!" cried Tod, who was standing by the pigeon-house. "Where are you off to?"

"Timberdale," replied Helen. And Tod turned and walked with them.

They were well through the Ravine, and close on to the entrance of Timberdale, before Helen said a word of what she had in her mind. Pulling the burnt envelope and the letter out then, she showed them to Tod.

"What do you think of that for a piece of carelessness!" she asked: and forthwith told him the whole story. Tod, hasty and impulsive, took the matter up as warmly as she had done.

"Lee ought to be reported for this—and punished. There might have been a bank-note in the letter."

"Of course there might," assented Helen. "And for Johnny Ludlow to want to excuse him, and ask me to hush it up!"

"Just like Johnny! In such things he is an out-and-out muff. How would the world go on, I wonder, if Johnny ruled it? You ought to have shown it to the Squire at once, Helen."

"So I should but for Johnny and Anna. As they had asked me not to, I did not quite like to fly in their faces. But I am going to show it to your postmaster at Timberdale."

"Oh, Helen!" involuntarily breathed Anna. And Tod looked up.

"Don't mind her," said Helen. "She and Johnny are just alike—making excuses for every one. Rymer the chemist is postmaster, is he not?"

"Rymer's dead—don't you remember that, Helen? Before he died, he gave up the post-office business. Salmon, the grocer opposite, took to it."

This Salmon was brother to the Salmon (grocer and draper) at South Crabb. Both were long-headed men, and flourishing tradesmen in their small way.

"Poor old Lee!" cried Tod, with a shade of pity. "He is too ailing and feeble; we have often said it. But of course he must be taught not to set fire to the letters."

Anna's eyelashes were wet. "Suppose, by your complaining, you should get him turned out of his post?" she suggested, with the timid deference she might have observed to a royal duke—but in the presence of those two she always lost her courage. Tod answered her gently. When he was gentle to any one, it was to her.

"No fear of that, Anna. Salmon will blow old Lee up, and there'll be an end of it. Whose letter was it, Helen?"

"It was from Mr. Leafchild—about our schools," answered Helen, turning her face away that he might not see its sudden rush of colour.

Well, they made their complaint to Salmon; who was properly indignant and said he would look into it, Tod putting in a word for the offender, Lee. "We don't want him reported to headquarters, or anything of that kind, you know, Salmon. Just give him a reprimand, and warn him to be cautious in future."

"I'll see to him, sir," nodded Salmon.

(The final result of the burning of this letter of Helen Whitney's, and of another person's letter that got burnt later, was recorded in the last Series, in a paper called "Lee the Letter-Man."

It may be as well to remind the reader that these stories told by "Johnny Ludlow" are not always placed consecutively as regards the time of their occurrence, but go backwards or forwards indiscriminately.)

Being so near, Helen and Anna thought they would call on Herbert Tanerton and Grace at the Rectory; next, they just looked in at Timberdale Court—Robert Ashton's. Altogether, what with one delay and another, they arrived at home when lunch was nearly over. And who should be sitting there, but Sir John Whitney! He had come over unexpectedly to pass an hour or two.

Helen Whitney was very clever in her way: but she was apt to be forgetful at times, as all the rest of us are. One thing she had totally and entirely forgotten to-day—and that was to ask Tod not to speak of the letter. So that when the Squire assailed them with reproaches for being late, Tod, unconscious that he was doing wrong, blurted out the truth. A letter from Mr. Leafchild to Helen had been partly burnt by old Lee, and they had been to Timberdale to complain to Salmon.

"A letter from Leafchild to Helen!" cried Sir John. "That must be a mistake. Leafchild would not presume to write to Helen."

She grew white as snow. Sir John had turned from the table to face her, and she dared not run away. The Squire was staring and frowning at the news of old Lee's sin, denouncing him hotly, and demanding to see the letter.

"Yes, where is this letter?" asked Sir John. "Let me see it, Helen."

"It—it was about the schools, papa."

"About the schools! Like his impudence! What have you to do with the schools? Give me the letter."

"My gracious me, burn a letter!" cried the Squire. "Lee must be in his dotage. The letter, my dear, the letter; we must see it."

Between them both, Helen was in a corner. She might have been capable of telling a white fib and saying she had not the letter, rather than let her father see it. Anna, who knew she had it in her pocket, went for nobody; but Tod knew it also. Tod suspecting no complications, was holding out his hand for her to produce it. With trembling lips, and fingers that shook in terror, she slowly drew it forth. Sir John took the letter from her, the Squire caught hold of the burnt envelope.

There was not a friendly hole in the floor for Helen to drop through. She escaped by the door to hide herself and her hot cheeks. For this was neither more nor less than a love-letter from the curate, and Sir John had taken it to the window to read it in the stronger light.

"Bless my heart and mind!" cried he when he had mastered its contents, just such an exclamation as the Squire would have made. "He—he—I believe the fellow means to make love to her! What a false-hearted parson he must be! Come here, Todhetley."

To see the two old heads poring over the letter together through their spectacles was something good, Tod said, when he told me all this later. It was just a love-letter and nothing less, but without a word of love in it. But not a bad love-letter of its kind; rather a sensible one. After telling Helen about the tracasserie in the parish school (which must have afforded him just the excuse for writing that he may have wanted), the curate went on to say a little bit about their mutual "friendship," and finished up by begging Helen to allow him to speak to Sir John and Lady Whitney, for he could not bear to think that by keeping silent they were deceiving them. "As honourable a letter in its way as you could wish to hear read," observed Tod; for Sir John and the Squire had read it aloud between them for the benefit of the dining-room.

"This comes of having grown-up daughters," bewailed poor Sir John. "Leafchild ought to be put in the pillory. And where's Helen got to? Where is that audacious girl?"

Poor Helen caught it hot and strong—Sir John demanding of her, for one thing, whether she had not had enough of encouraging disreputable young sparks with that Richard Foliott. Poor Helen sobbed and hid her head, and finally took courage to say that Mr. Leafchild was a saint on earth—not to be as much as named in the same sentence with Richard Foliott. And when I got home at night, everybody, from Helen downwards, was in the dumps, and Sir John had gone home to make mincemeat of the curate.

Buttermead was one of those straggling parishes that are often found in rural districts. Whitney Hall was situated in it, also the small village of Whitney, also that famous school of ours, Dr. Frost's, and there was a sprinkling of other good houses. Some farm homesteads lay scattered about; and the village boasted of a street and a half.

The incumbent of Buttermead, or Whitney, was the Reverend Matthew Singleton: his present curate was Charles Leafchild. Mr. Leafchild, though eight-and-twenty years of age, was only now ordained deacon, and this year was his first in the ministry. At eighteen he had gone out to the West Indies, a post having been found for him there. He did not go by choice. Being a steady-minded young fellow, religiously inclined, he had always wished to be a parson; but his father, Dr. Leafchild, a great light among Church dignitaries, and canon residentiary of a cathedral in the North, had set his face against the wish. The eldest son was a clergyman, and of his preferment Dr. Leafchild could take tolerable care, but he did not know that he could do much in that way for his younger sons, and so Charles's hopes had to go to the wall. Spiritual earnestness, however, at length made itself heard within him to some purpose; and he resolved, come what might, that he would quit money-making for piety. The West Indian climate did not agree with him; he had to leave it for home, and then it was that he made the change. "You would have been rich in time had you stuck to your post," remonstrated the Reverend Doctor to him: "now you may be nothing but a curate all your life." "True, father," was the answer, "but I shall hope to do my duty as one." So Charles Leafchild made himself into a parson, and here he was at Buttermead, reading through his first year, partially tabooed by his family, and especially by that flourishing divine, the head of it.

He was a good-looking young man, as men go. Rather tall than not, with a pale, calm face, brown hair that he wore long, and mild brown eyes that had no end of earnestness in their depths. A more self-denying man could not be found; though as a rule young men are not famous for great self-denial. The small stipend given by Mr. Singleton had to suffice for all his wants. Leafchild had never said what this stipend was; except that he admitted one day it was not more than seventy pounds: how much less than that, he did not state.

Just a few roods out of the village stood a small dwelling called Marigold Cottage. A tidy woman named Bean lived in it with her two daughters, one of whom was the paid mistress of the national girls'-school. Mr. Leafchild lodged here, as the late curate had before him, occupying the spare sitting-room and bedroom. And if Mrs. Bean was to be believed—and she had been a veracious woman all her life—three days out of the seven, at least, Mr. Leafchild went without meat at his dinner, having given it away to some sick or poor creature, who wanted it, he considered, more than he did. A self-denying, earnest, gentle-minded man; that's what he was: and perhaps it may be forgiven to Helen Whitney that she fell in love with him.

When Helen went home from London, carrying with her the mortification that came of her interrupted marriage and Captain Foliott's delinquency, she began to do what she had never done in her life before, busy herself a little in the parish: perhaps as a safety-valve to carry off her superfluous anger. The curate was a middle-aged man with a middle-aged wife and two babies, and Helen had no scruple in going about with him, here, there, and everywhere. To the schools, to the church, to practise the boys, to visit the poor, went she. But when in a few months that curate's heart was made glad by a living—two hundred a-year and a five-roomed Vicarage—and Mr. Leafchild came in his place, it was a little different. She did not run about with the new curate as she had with the old, but she did see a good deal of him, and he of her. The result was they fell in love with one another. For the first time in her life the uncertain god, Cupid, had pierced the somewhat invulnerable heart of Helen Whitney.

But now, could anything be so inappropriate, or look more hopeless? Charles Leafchild, B.A., curate of Buttermead, positively only yet reading for his full title, scantily paid, no prospect of anything better, lacking patronage; and Miss Helen Whitney, daughter of Sir John Whitney, baronet! Looking at it from a practical point of view, it seemed that he might just as well have expected to woo and wed one of the stars in the sky.

On the bleak February morning that followed Helen's expedition to Timberdale, Mr. Leafchild came down from his chamber and entered his sitting-room. The fire, a small one, for Mrs. Bean had received a general caution to be sparing of his coal, burnt brightly in the grate. He stood over it for a minute or two, rubbing his slender hands at the blaze: since he left the West Indies he had felt the cold more keenly than formerly. Then he turned to the breakfast-table, and saw upon it, a small portion of cold neck of mutton, an uncut loaf, and a pat of butter. His tea stood there, already made.

"If I leave the meat, it will do for dinner," he thought: and proceeded to make his meal of bread-and-butter. Letty Bean, who chiefly waited on him, came in.

"A letter for you, sir," she said, handing him a note.

He took it, looked at the handwriting, which was thick and sprawly and not familiar to him, and laid it beside his plate.

"Sir John Whitney's footman brought it, sir," continued Letty, volunteering the information: and a hot colour flushed the curate's face as he heard it. He opened it then. Short and peremptory, it merely requested the Reverend Charles Leafchild to call upon Sir John Whitney that morning at Whitney Hall.

"Is the man waiting for an answer, Letty?"

"No, sir. He went away as soon as he gave it me."

Mr. Leafchild half suspected what had occurred—that Sir John must, in some way, have become acquainted with the state of affairs. He judged so by the cold, haughty tone of the note: hitherto Sir John had always shown himself friendly. Far from being put out, Mr. Leafchild hoped it was so, and went on with his breakfast.

Another interruption. Mrs. Bean this time. She wore a mob cap and had lost her teeth.

"Here's that tipsy Jones come to the door, sir. He says you told him to come."

"Ah yes, I did; let him come in," said the curate. "Is he tipsy this morning?"

"No, sir, only shaky. And what shall I order you for dinner, sir, to-day? I may as well ask, as I am here."

"That will do," he answered, pointing to the cold meat. "And please mash the potatoes."

Jones came in. The man was not an incorrigibly bad doer, but weak and irresolute. If he worked two days, he idled and drank three, and his wife and children suffered. Mr. Leafchild, who felt more sorrow for him than anger, invited him to a seat by the fire, and talked to him long and persuasively, almost as one brother might talk to another, and gave him a hot cup of tea. Jones went away great in promises and penitence: and about eleven o'clock the curate betook himself to the Hall.

Of all men living, the Squire perhaps excepted, Sir John was about the worst to carry out any troublesome negotiation. He was good-hearted, irresolute, and quick-tempered.

When Mr. Leafchild was shown in, Sir John utterly forgot certain speeches he had conned over in his mind, broke down, went into a passion, and told the curate he was a designing, impudent villain.

Though his love for Helen, and that was intense, caused him to feel somewhat agitated in the presence of Helen's father, Mr. Leafchild's manner was quiet and calm, a very contrast to that of Sir John. After a little while, when the baronet had talked himself cool, Mr. Leafchild entered into a history of the affair: telling how he and Miss Whitney had met without any intention of any kind, except of that which might be connected with the parish interests, and how with as little intention, a mutual liking—nay, a love— had sprung up.

"Yes, that's all very fine," said Sir John, shuffling about his steel spectacles that were perched on his old red nose. "You knew she was my daughter; you knew well what you were about."

The young man reddened at the reproach.

"Sir, indeed you misjudge me. I never thought of such a thing as falling in love with Miss Whitney until the love had come. Had she been the most obscure of young women, it would have been all the same."

"Then you are an idiot for your pains," retorted Sir John. "Why, goodness gracious me! have you not one single atom of common sense? Can't you see how unfitting it is?"

"My family is a very good one; in point of fact, as good as yours, Sir John—if you will pardon me for saying so thus pointedly," urged the curate in his gentle voice. "And though—"

"Oh, bother!" interrupted Sir John, having no counter argument particularly at hand. "That goes for nothing. What are your prospects?"

"They are not great. Perhaps I ought to say that I have no prospects as yet. But, sir—"

"Now come! that's honest. No prospects! And yet you must go making love to my daughter."

"I have not done that, sir, in one sense—'made love.' Hardly a word, I think, has passed between myself and Miss Whitney that you might not have heard. But we have, notwithstanding, been fully aware of the state of each other's heart—"

"The state of each other's fiddlestick," spluttered Sir John. "A nice pair of you, I must say! And pray, what did you think it would come to?"

"What Miss Whitney may have thought I have not presumed to ask. For myself, I confess I am cherishing hopes for the future. It is some little time now since I have been wishing to speak to you, Sir John: and I intended, if you were so kind as not to entirely reject me, to write to my father, Dr. Leafchild, and lay the whole case before him. I think he can help me later if he will; and I certainly believe he will be only too glad to do it."

"Help you to what?"

"To a living."

"And, bless my heart and mind, how long do you suppose you might have to wait? A dozen years. Twenty years, for all you know. The curate who was here before you, poor Bell, had been waiting more than twenty years for one. It came to him last year, and he was forty-seven years old."

Mr. Leafchild could say nothing to this.

"And a fine living it is, now he has it!" went on Sir John. "No, no, sir: Helen Whitney cannot be dragged into that kind of fate."

"I should be the last to drag her, or wish to drag her into it. Believe that, Sir John. But, if I had a good living given to me, then I should like her to share it. And I think that my father would perhaps allow me some private means also, for Helen's sake. He has money, and could do it."

"But all those fancies and notions are just so many vapours, clouds up in the sky, and no better, don't you see! You young men are sanguine and foolish; you lose sight of facts in fallacies. We must look at what is, not at what might be. Why, you are not yet even a priest!"

"No. I shall be ordained to that in a few months' time."

"And then, I suppose, you will either remain here, or get a curacy elsewhere. And your income will be that of a curate—a hundred pounds a-year, all told. Some curates get but fifty."

"True. We are poorly paid."

"And that may go on till you are forty or fifty years of age! And yet, in the face of it, you ask me to let you have my daughter. Now, Mr. Leafchild, you are either a simpleton yourself, or you must think I am one," added Sir John, rising to end the interview, which had been to him one of thorough discomfort. "And I'm sure I hope you'll pick up a little common sense, young man, and I shall order Miss Helen to pick some up too. There, that's all."

"I trust you are not angry with me, sir," said the curate mildly, for Sir John was holding out his hand to be shaken.

"Well, yes, I am. Anything like this causes one such worry, you know. I'm sure I and my wife have had no sleep all night. You must not think any more of Helen. And now good-morning."

As Mr. Leafchild walked back to his lodgings at Dame Bean's, his hopes seemed to be about as dull as the wintry sky on which his nice brown eyes were fixed. His whole happiness, socially speaking, lay in Helen; hers lay with him; but only separation seemed to be looming in the air. Suddenly, when he was close to Marigold Cottage, a little rift broke in the leaden clouds, and a bit of pale blue sky shone forth.

"I will take that as an omen for good; pray God it may be so!" spoke the curate gladly and reverently, as he lifted his hat. "And—come what may, in storm and in tempest, God is over all."

Helen went home in the dumps and to sundry edifying lectures. An embargo was laid on her parish work, and she only saw the curate at church. One month, two months passed over thus, and she grew pale and thin. Sir John was cross, Lady Whitney uncomfortable; they were both simple-minded people, caring more for their children's happiness than for their grandeur. The former told the Squire in confidence that if the young fellow could get a decent living, he was not sure but he'd give in, and that he liked him ten thousand times better than he had ever liked that Foliott.

They met one day by accident. Helen was out moping in the long broad walk: which was beginning to be shady now, for May was all but in, and the trees were putting on their foliage. At the end of it she came to a standstill, leaning on the gate. The waters of the lake, out yonder, were blue as the unruffled sky. With a faint cry, she started aside, for Charles Leafchild stood before her.

Being a parson, and tacitly on honour to Sir John, he might have been expected to pass on his way without stopping; but Helen's hand was already stretched out over the gate. He could but shake it.

"You are not looking well," he said after a moment's silence. "I am sorry to see it."

What with his unexpected presence, and what with her mind's general discomfort, Helen burst into tears. Mr. Leafchild kept her hand in his.

"I have a bad headache to-day," said Helen, by way of excuse for her tears. "It has been gloomy weather lately."

"Gloomy within and without," he assented, giving a meaning to her words that she had not meant to imply. "But in every cloud, you know, however dark it may be, there is always a silver lining."

"We can't always see it," returned Helen, drying her tears.

"No; we very often cannot. But we may trust that it is there—and be patient."

"I think it sometimes happens that we never see it—that all is gloomy to the end, the end of life. What then?"

"Then we may be sure that it is best for us it should be so. God directs all things."

Helen sighed: she had not learnt the love and faith and submission that made up the sum of Mr. Leafchild's life, bringing into it so strange a peace.

"Is it true that you are going to leave?" she asked. "We heard it mentioned."

"Yes: when I shall be fully ordained. Mr. Singleton has to take his nephew. It was an old promise—that he should come to him for his first year, just as I have. I think I shall go to Worcester."

"To Worcester?"

"I have been offered a curacy there by one of the minor canons whose living is in the town, and I feel inclined to take it. The parish is large and has a good many of the very poor in it."

Helen made a face. "But would you like that? You might be frightfully overworked."

"It is what I should like. As to the work—it is done for our Master."

He shook hands with her again, and left, the cheery smile still on his face, the thoughtful light in his steadfast eyes. And never a word of love, you see, had passed.

It was, I take it, about a fortnight after this, that there went walking one afternoon to Whitney Hall, a tall, portly, defiant-looking gentleman in gold-rimmed spectacles and a laced-up clerical hat. By the way he turned his head here and there, and threw his shoulders about as he strode along, you might have taken him for a bishop at least, instead of a canon—but canons in those days were a great deal more self-important than bishops are in these. It was the Reverend Dr. Leafchild. A real canon was he, a great man in his own cathedral, and growing rich on his share of its substantial revenues: your honorary canons with their empty title and non-stipends had not sprung into fashion then. In his pompous manner, and he had been born pompous, Dr. Leafchild asked to see Sir John Whitney.

After Mr. Leafchild's interview with Sir John in February, he had written to his father and told him all about it, asking him whether he thought he could not help him later to a living, so that he might have a chance of winning Helen. But for Helen's being a baronet's daughter and the connection one that even the canon might be proud of, he would have turned a deaf ear: as it was, he listened. But Dr. Leafchild never did things in a hurry; and after some correspondence with his son (and a great deal of grumbling, meant for his good), he had now come into Worcestershire for the purpose of talking over the affair with Sir John.

The upshot was, that Sir John gave in, and sanctioned the engagement. There was an excellent living somewhere down in the North—eight hundred pounds a-year, a handsome house, and some land—the next presentation to which the canon could command. He had intended it for his eldest son; but he, by some lucky chance, had just obtained a better preferment, and the doctor could promise it to Charles. The present incumbent was old and ailing; therefore, in all probability, it would very speedily fall in. The canon added that he might settle on the young people a small sum at their marriage, say a hundred a-year, or so; and he also hinted that Charles might stand a chance of better preferment later—say a snug canonry. So Sir John shook hands heartily upon the bargain, invited the canon to stay dinner, and sent for Charles.

For the next six weeks who so happy as the curate and Helen? They came over to us at Dyke Manor (for we had gone back there) for a day or two, and we learnt to like him with our whole hearts. What a good, earnest, warm-natured man he was; and oh, how unselfish!

I remember one evening in particular when they were out together, pacing the field-path. Helen had his arm, and he was talking to her in what seemed an uncommonly solemn manner: for his hand was lifted now and then in earnestness, and both were gazing upwards. It was a beautiful sky: the sun had set in splendour, leaving crimson and gold clouds behind it, the evening star twinkled in the deepening canopy. Mrs. Todhetley sent me to them. A poor woman had come up for broth for her sick son, one of our labourers. She was in great distress: a change had taken place in him for the worse, he was calling for the clergyman to come to him before he died: but Mr. Holland was out that evening—gone to Evesham.

"Johnny, I—I think Mr. Leafchild would go," said the mater. "Do you mind asking him?"

Hardly any need to ask. At the first word he was hastening to the woman and walking away with her. Helen's eyes, gazing at the sky still, were wet with tears.

"Is it not beautiful, Johnny?"

"Very." It was a glorious sunset.

"But I never saw it as I see it now. He is teaching me many things. I cannot hope to be ever as he is, Johnny, not half as good; but I think in time he will make me a little like him."

"You have a happy life before you."

"Yes—I hope so," she said hesitatingly. "But sometimes a feeling makes itself heard within me—that one who is so entirely fitted for the next world may not long be left in this."

II

It was autumn weather—October. A lot of us were steaming over to Worcester in the train. Miss Whitney from Cheltenham, and a friend of hers—a maiden lady as ancient as herself, one Miss Conaway, of Devonshire—were staying at the Hall. Miss Conaway did not know Worcester, and was now being taken to see it—especially the cathedral. Lady Whitney, Helen, Anna, and I made up the party, and we filled the carriage. My being with them arose from chance: I had come over accidentally that morning to Whitney Hall. Of course Helen hoped to see something besides the cathedral her curate. For in June Mr. Leafchild, then in priest's orders, entered on his new curacy at Worcester, there to stay until the expected living should fall in.

"How is he?" I asked Helen, bending over the arm of the seat that divided us.

"Working himself to death," she whispered back to me, her tone a cross one.

"He said he was glad there would be plenty of work, you know. And it is a large parish."

"But he need not let it put everything else out of his head."

"Meaning you?"

"I have not heard from him for more than a week. Papa had a letter from Dr. Leafchild this morning. He said in it that Charles, when he last wrote, complained of being poorly."

"A great many curates do get very overtaxed."

"Oh, and what do you think?" went on Helen. "He is actually beginning to have scruples about taking that living, on the score that there'll be hardly any work to do."

"But—he will take it!"

"Yes, I suppose he will, because of me; but it will go against the grain, I fancy. I do think one may have too strict a conscience."

It was past one o'clock when we reached Worcester. Lady Whitney complained in the train of having started too late. First of all there was luncheon to be taken at the Star: that brought it to past two. Then various other things had to be done: see the cathedral, and stay the afternoon service, go over the china works at Diglis, and buy a bundle of articles at the linen-draper's. All these duties over, they meant to invade Mr. Leafchild's lodgings in Paradise Row.

They took the draper's to begin with, the whole of them trooping in, one after another, like sheep into a pen: and I vow that they only came out again when the bell was going for three-o'clock service. Helen was not in a genial mood: at this rate there would not be much time left for visiting the curate.

"It was Aunt Ann's fault," she grumbled to me—"and mamma's. They were a good half-hour looking at the stuff for the children's winter frocks. Aunt Ann maintained that cashmere was best, mamma held to merino. All the shelves they had taken down! I would not be a linen-draper's shopman for the world."

Just in time, were we, to get into our seats before the procession of clergy and choristers came in. The chanter that afternoon was Mr. Leafchild's rector: I knew him to speak to. But there's no space to linger upon details.

A small knot of people, ourselves and others, had collected in the transept after service, waiting for one of the old bedesmen to do the honours of the cathedral, when the chanter came down the steps of the south aisle, after disrobing in the vestry.

"Do you know who he is?" I said to Helen, who was standing with me a little apart.

"No—how should I know? Except that he must be one of the minor canons."

"He is Mr. Leafchild's rector."

"Is he?" she eagerly cried, the colour coming into her face. And just then he chanced to look our way, and nodded to me. I went up to him to speak.

"This is a terrible thing about Leafchild," he exclaimed in a minute or two.

"What is it?" I asked, my breath stopping.

Helen, who had slowly paced after me on the white flags, stood stock still and turned as pale as you please.

"Have you not heard of his illness? Perhaps not, though: it has been so sudden. A few days ago he was apparently as well as I am now. But it was only last night that the doctors began to apprehend danger."

"Is it fever?"

"Yes. A species of typhoid, I believe. Whether caught in his ministrations or not, I don't know. Though I suppose it must have been. He is lying at his lodgings in Paradise Row. Leafchild has not seemed in good condition lately," continued the clergyman. "He is most unremitting in his work, fags himself from morning till night, and lives anyhow: so perhaps he was not fortified to resist the attack of an enemy. He is very ill: and since last night he has been unconscious."

"He is dangerously ill, did you say?" spoke poor Helen, biting her lips to hide their tremor.

"Almost more than dangerous: I fear there is little hope left," he answered, never of course suspecting who Helen was. "Good-afternoon."

She followed him with her eyes as he turned to the cloister-door: and then moved away towards the north entrance, looking as one dazed.

"Helen, where are you going?"

"To see him."

"Oh, but it won't do. It won't, indeed, Helen."

"I am going to see him," she answered, in her most wilful tone. "Don't you hear that he is dying? I know he is; I feel it instinctively as a sure and certain fact. If you have a spark of goodness you'll come with me, Johnny Ludlow. It's all the same—whether you do or not."

I looked around for our party. They had disappeared up the other aisle under convoy of the bedesman, leaving Helen and myself to follow at our leisure; or perhaps not noticing our absence. Helen, marching away with quick steps, passed out at the grand entrance.

"It is not safe for you to go, Helen," I remonstrated, as we went round the graveyard and so up High Street. "You would catch the fever from him."

"I shall catch no fever."

"He caught it."

"I wish you'd be quiet. Can't you see what I am suffering?"

The sweetest sight to me just then would have been Lady Whitney, or any one else holding authority over Helen. I seemed responsible for any ill that might ensue: and yet, what could I do?

"Helen, pray listen to a word of reason! See the position you put me in. A fever is not a light thing to risk."

"I don't believe that typhoid fever is catching. He did not say typhus."

"Of course it's catching."

"Are you afraid of it?"

"I don't know that I am afraid. But I should not run into it by choice. And I'm sure you ought not to."

We were just then passing that large druggist's shop that the Squire always called Featherstonhaugh's—just because Mr. Featherstonhaugh once kept it. Helen darted across the street and into it.

"A pound of camphor," said she, to the young man behind the right-hand counter.

"A pound of camphor!" he echoed. "Did you say a pound, ma'am?"

"Is it too much?" asked Helen. "I want some to put about me: I am going to see some one who is ill."

It ended in his giving her two ounces. As we left the shop she handed part of it to me, stowing the rest about herself. And whether it was thanks to the camphor, I don't know, but neither of us took any harm.

"There. You can't grumble now, Johnny Ludlow."

Paradise Row, as every one knows, is right at the other end of the town, past the Tything. We had nearly reached the house when a gentleman, who looked like a doctor, came out of it.

"I beg your pardon," said Helen, accosting him as he met us, and coughing to hide her agitation, "but we think—seeing you come out of the house—that you may be attending Mr. Leafchild. Is he better?"

The doctor looked at us both, and shook his head as he answered—

"Better in one sense of the word, in so far as that he is now conscious; worse in another. He is sinking fast."

A tremor shook Helen from head to foot. She turned away to hide it. I spoke.

"Do you mean—dying?"

"I fear so."

"Are his friends with him?"

"Not any of them. His father was sent to yesterday, but he has not yet come. We did not write before, not having anticipated danger."

"Why don't they have Henry Carden to him?" cried Helen in passionate agitation as the doctor walked away. "He could have cured him."

"No, no, Helen; don't think that. Other men are just as clever as Henry Carden. They have only one treatment for fever."

A servant-girl answered the door, and asked us into the parlour. She took us for the relations from the north. Mr. Leafchild was lying in a room near—a comfortable bed-chamber. Three doctors were attending him, she said; but just now the nurse was alone with him. Would we like to go in? she added: we had been expected all day.

"Come with me, Johnny," whispered Helen.

He was lying in bed, white and still, his eyes wide open. The nurse, a stout old woman in light print gown and full white apron, stood at a round table in the corner, noiselessly washing a wine-glass. She turned her head, curtsied, and bustled out of the room.

But wasn't he weak, as his poor thin hands clasped Helen's! His voice was hollow as he tried to speak to her. The bitter tears, running down her checks, were dropping on to the bed-clothes.

"You should not have come", he managed to say. "My love, my love!"

"Is there no hope?" she sobbed. "Oh, Charles, is there no hope?"

"May God soothe it to you! May He have you always in His good keeping!"

"And is it no trouble to you to die?" she went on, reproach in her anguished tone. "Have you no regret for the world, and—and for those you leave behind?"

"It is God's will," he breathed. "To myself it is no trouble, for He has mercifully taken the trouble from me. I regret you, my Helen, I regret the world. Or, rather, I should regret it, but that I know I am going to one brighter and better. You will come to me there, my dear one, and we shall live together for ever."

Helen knelt down by the bed; he was lying close on the edge of it; and laid her wet face against his. He held her to him for a moment, kissed her fervently, and then motioned to me to take her away.

"For your own sake, my dear," he whispered. "You are in danger here. Give my dear love to them all."

Helen just waved her hand back at me, as much as to say, Don't you interfere. But at that moment the fat old nurse bustled in again, with the announcement that two of the doctors and Mr. Leafchild's rector were crossing the road. That aroused Helen.

One minute's close embrace, her tears bedewing his dying cheeks, one lingering hand-clasp of pain, and they parted. Parted for all time. But not for eternity.

"God be with you ever!" he breathed, giving her his solemn blessing. "Farewell, dear Johnny Ludlow!"

"I am so sorry! If you could but get well!" I cried, my eyes not much dryer than Helen's.

"I shall soon be well: soon," he answered with a sweet faint smile, his feeble clasp releasing my hand, which he had taken. "But not here. Fare you well."

Helen hid herself in a turn of the passage till the doctors had gone in, and then we walked down the street together, she crying softly. Just opposite Salt Lane, a fly passed at a gallop. Dr. Leafchild sat in it muffled in coats, a cloud of sorrow on his generally pompous face.

And that was the abrupt end of poor Charles Leafchild, for he died at midnight, full of peace. God's ways are not as our ways; or we might feel tempted to ask why so good and useful a servant should have been taken.

And so, you perceive, there was another marriage of Helen Whitney frustrated. Fortune seemed to be against her.

CHAPTER VIII

JELLICO'S PACK

I

The shop was not at all in a good part of Evesham. The street was narrow and dirty, the shop the same. Over the door might be seen written "Tobias Jellico, Linen-draper and Huckster." One Monday—which is market-day at Evesham, as the world knows—in going past it with Tod and little Hugh, the child trod on his bootlace and broke it, and we turned in to get another. It was a stuffy shop, filled with bundles as well as wares, and behind the counter stood Mr. Jellico himself, a good-looking, dark man of forty, with deep-set blue eyes, that seemed to meet at the nose, so close were they together.

The lace was a penny, he said, and Tod laid down sixpence. Jellico handed the sixpence to a younger man who was serving lower down, and began showing us all kinds of articles—neckties, handkerchiefs, fishing-lines, cigar-lights, for he seemed to deal in varieties. Hugh had put in his bootlace, but we could not get away.

"I tell you we don't want anything of this," said Tod, in his haughty way, for the persistent fellow had tired him out. "Give me my change."

The other man brought the change wrapped up in paper, and we went on to the inn. Tod had ordered the pony to be put in the chaise, and it stood ready in the yard. Just then a white-haired, feeble old man came into the yard, and begged. Tod opened the paper of half-pence.

"The miserable cheat," he called out. "If you'll believe me, Johnny, that fellow has only given me fourpence in change. If I had time I'd go back to him. Sam, do you know anything of one Jellico, who keeps a fancy shop?" asked he of the ostler.

"A fancy shop, sir?" echoed Sam, considering.

"Sells calico and lucifer-matches."

"Oh, I know Mr. Jellico!" broke forth Sam, his recollection coming to him. "He has got a cousin with him, sir."

"No doubt. It was the cousin that cheated me. Mistakes are mistakes, and the best of us are liable to them; but if that was a mistake, I'll eat the lot."

"It's as much of a leaving-shop as a draper's, sir. Leastways, it's said that women can take things in and borrow money on them."

"Oh!" said Tod. "Borrow a shilling on a Dutch oven to-day, and pay two shillings to-morrow to get it out."

"Anyway, Mr. Jellico does a fine trade, for he gives credit," concluded Sam.

But the wrong change might have been a mistake.

In driving home, Tod pulled up at George Reed's cottage. Every one must remember hearing where that was, and of Reed's being put into prison by Major Parrifer. "Get down, Johnny," said he, "and see if Reed's there. He must have left work."

I went up the path where Reed's children were playing, and opened the cottage door. Mrs. Reed and two neighbours stood holding out something that looked like a gown-piece. With a start and a grab, Mrs. Reed caught the stuff, and hid it under her apron, and the two others looked round at me with scared faces.

"Reed here? No, sir," she answered, in a sort of flurry. "He had to go over to Alcester after work. I don't expect him home much afore ten to-night."

I shut the door, thinking nothing. Reed was a handy man at many things, and Tod wanted him to help with some alteration in the pheasantry at the Manor. It was Tod who had set it up—a long, narrow place enclosed with green trellised work, and some gold and silver pheasants running about in it. The Squire had been against it at first, and told Tod he wouldn't have workmen bothering about the place. So Tod got Reed to come in of an evening after his day's work, and in a fortnight the thing was up. Now he wanted him again to alter it: he had found out it was too narrow. That was one of Tod's failings. If he took a thing into his head it must be done off-hand. The Squire railed at him for his hot-headed impatience: but in point of fact he was of just the same impatient turn himself. Tod had been over to Bill Whitney's and found their pheasantry was twice as wide as his.

"Confound Alcester," cried Tod in his vexation, as he drove on home. "If Reed could have come up now and seen what it is I want done, he might have begun upon it to-morrow evening."

"The pater says it is quite wide enough as it is, Tod."

"You shut up, Johnny. If I pay Reed out of my own pocket, it's nothing to anybody."

On Tuesday he sent me to Reed's again. It was a nice spring afternoon, but I'm not sure that I thanked him for giving me that walk. Especially when upon lifting the latch of the cottage door, I found it fastened. Down I sat on the low bench outside the open window to wait—where Cathy had sat many a time in the days gone by, making believe to nurse the children, and that foolish young Parrifer would be leaning against the pear-tree on the other side the path. I had to leave my message with Mrs. Reed; I supposed she had only stepped into a neighbour's, and might be back directly, for the two little girls were playing at "shop" in the garden.

Buzz, buzz: hum, hum. Why, those voices were in the kitchen! The lower part of the casement was level with the top of my head; I turned round and raised my eyes to look.

Well! surprises, it is said, are the lot of man. It was his face, unless my sight deceived itself. The same blue eyes that were in the shop at Evesham the day before, were inside Mrs. Reed's kitchen now: Mr. Tobias Jellico's. The place seemed to be crowded with women. He was smiling and talking to them in the most persuasive manner imaginable, his hands waving an accompaniment, on one of which glittered a ring with a yellow stone in it, a persuasive look on his rather well-featured face.

They were a great deal too agreeably engrossed to see me, and I looked on at leisure. A sort of pack, open, rested on the floor; the table was covered with all kinds of things for women's dress; silks, cottons, ribbons, mantles; which Mrs. Reed and the others were leaning over and fingering.

"Silks ain't for the like of us; I'd never have the cheek to put one on," cried a voice that I knew at once for shrill Peggy Dickon's. Next to her stood Ann Dovey, the blacksmith's wife; who was very pretty, and vain accordingly.

"What kind o' stuff d'ye call this, master?" Ann Dovey asked.

"That's called laine," answered Jellico. "It's all pure wool."

"It's a'most as shiny as silk. I say, Mrs. Reed, d'ye think this 'ud wear?"

"It would wear for ever," put in Jellico. "Ten yards of it would make as good a gown as ever went on a lady's back; and the cost is but two shillings a yard."

"Two shillings! Let's see—what 'ud that come to? Why, twenty, wouldn't it? My patience, I shouldn't never dare to run up that score for one gownd."

Jellico laughed pleasantly. "You take it, Mrs. Dovey. It just suits your bright cheeks. Pay me when you can, and how you can: sixpence a-week, or a shilling a-week, or two shillings, as you can make it easy. It's like getting a gown for nothing."

"So it is," cried Ann Dovey, in a glow of delight. And by the tone, Mr. Jellico no doubt knew that she had as good as yielded to the temptation. He got out his yard measure.

"Ten yards?" said he.

"I'm a'most afeard. Will you promise, sir, not to bother me for the money faster than I can pay it?"

"You needn't fear no bothering from me; only just keep up the trifle you've got to pay off weekly."

He measured off the necessary length. "You'll want some ribbon to trim it with, won't you?" said he.

"Ribbin—well, I dun know. Dovey might say ribbin were too smart for me."

"Not a bit on't, Ann Dovey," spoke up another woman—and she was our carter's wife, Susan Potter. "It wouldn't look nothing without some ribbin. That there narrer grass-green satin 'ud be nice upon't."

"And that grass-green ribbon's dirt cheap," said Jellico. "You'd get four or five yards of it for a shilling or two. Won't you be tempted now?" he added to Susan Potter. She laughed.

"Not with them things. I shouldn't never hear the last on't if Potter found out I went on tick for finery. He's rough, sir, and might beat me. I'd like a check apron, and a yard o' calico."

"Perhaps I might take a apron or two, sir, if you made it easy," said Mrs. Dickon.

"Of course I'll make it easy; and a gown too if you'll have it. Let me cut you off the fellow to this of Mrs. Dovey's."

Peggy Dickon shook her head. "It ain't o' no good asking me, Mr. Jellico. Ann Dovey can buy gownds; she haven't got no children; I've a bushel on 'em. No; I don't dare. I wish I might! Last year, up at Cookhill Wake, I see a sweet gownd, not unlike this, what had got green ribbins upon it," added the woman longingly.

Being (I suppose) a kind of Mephistopheles in his line, Mr. Tobias Jellico accomplished his wish and cut off a gown against her judgment. He sold other gowns, and "ribbins," and trumpery; the yard measure had nearly as little rest as the women's tongues. Mrs. Reed's turn to be served seemed to come last; after the manner of her betters, she yielded precedence to her guests.

"Now for me, sir," she said. "You've done a good stroke o' business here to-day, Mr. Jellico, and I hope you won't objec' to change that there gownd piece as I bought last Monday for some'at a trifle stronger. Me and some others have been a-looking at it, and we don't think it'll wear."

"Oh, I'll change it," readily answered Jellico. "You should put a few more shillings on, Mrs. Reed: better have a good thing when you're about it. It's always cheaper in the end."

"Well, I suppose it is," she said. "But I'm a'most frightened at the score that'll be running up."

"It's easily wiped off," answered the man, pleasantly. "Just a shilling or two weekly."

There was more chaffering and talking; and after that came the chink of money. The women had each a book, and Jellico had his book, and they were compared with his, and made straight. As he came out with the pack on his back, he saw me sitting on the bench, and looked hard at me: whether he knew me again, I can't say.

Just then Frank Stirling ran by, turning down Piefinch Lane. I went after him: the women's tongues inside were working like so many steam-engines, and it was as well to let them run down before speaking to Mrs. Reed.

Half-way down Piefinch Lane on the left, there was a turning, called Piefinch Cut. It had grown into a street. All kinds of shops had been opened, dealing in small wares: and two public-houses. A pawnbroker from Alcester had opened a branch establishment here—which had set the world gaping more than they would at a wild-beast show. It was managed by a Mr. Figg. The three gilt balls stood out in the middle of the Cut; and the blacksmith's forge, to which Stirling was bound, was next door. He wanted something done to a piece of iron. While we were standing amidst the sparks, who should go into the house the other side the way but Jellico and his pack!

"Yes, he should come into mine, he should, that fellow," ironically observed John Dovey: who was a good-natured, dark-eyed little man, with a tolerable share of sense. "I'd be after trundling him out again, feet foremost."

"Is he a travelling hawker?" asked Stirling.

"He's a sight worse, sir," answered Dovey. "If you buy wares off a hawker you must pay for 'em at the time: no money, no goods. But this fellow seduces the women to buy his things on tick, he does: Tuesday arter Tuesday he comes prowling into this here Cut, and does a roaring trade. His pack'll walk out o' that house a bit lighter nor it goes in. Stubbs's wife lives over there; Tanken's wife, she lives there; and there be others. If I hadn't learnt that nobody gets no good by interfering atween men and their wives, I'd ha' telled Stubbs and Tanken long ago what was going on."

It had been on the tip of my tongue to say where I had just seen Jellico, and the trade he was doing. Remembering in time that Mrs. Dovey had been one of the larger purchasers, I kept the news in.

"His name's Jellico," continued Dovey, as he hammered away at Stirling's iron. "He have got a fine shop somewhere over at Evesham. It's twelve or fifteen months now, Master Johnny, since he took to come here. When first I see him I wondered where the deuce the hawker's round could be, appearing in the Cut so quick and reg'lar; but I soon found he was no reg'lar hawker. Says I to my wife, 'Don't you go and have no dealings with that there pest, for I'll not stand it, and I might be tempted to stop it summary.' 'All right, Jack,' says she; 'when I want things I'll deal at the old shop at Alcester.' But there's other wives round about us doing strokes and strokes o' trade with him; 'tain't all of 'em, Master Ludlow, as is so sensible as our Ann."

Considering the stroke of trade I had just seen done by Ann Dovey, it was as well not to hear this.

"If he's not a hawker, what is he?" asked Stirling, swaying himself on a beam in the roof; and I'm sure I did not know either.

"It's a cursed system," hotly returned John Dovey; "and I say that afore your faces, young gents. It may do for the towns, if they chooses to have it—that's their business; but it don't do for us. What do our women here want o' fine shawls and gay gownds?—decking theirselves out as if they was so many

Jezebels? But 'tain't that. Let 'em deck, if they've got no sense to see how ill it looks on their sun-freckled faces and hands hard wi' work; it's the ruin it brings. Just you move on t'other side, Master Ludlow, sir; you be right in the way o' the sparks. There's a iron pot over there as does for sitting on."

"I'm all right, Dovey. Tell us about Jellico."

Jellico's system, to give Dovey's explanation in brief, was this: He brought over a huge pack of goods every Tuesday afternoon in a pony-gig from his shop at Evesham. He put up the pony, and carried the pack on his round, tempting the women right and left to buy. Husbands away at work, and children at school, the field was open. He asked for no ready money down. The purchases were entered in a book, to be paid off by weekly instalments. The payments had to be kept up; Jellico saw to that. However short the household had to run of the weekly necessaries, Jellico's money had to be ready for him. It was an awful tax, just as Dovey described it, and drifted into at first by the women without thought of ill. The debt in itself was bad enough; but the fear lest it should come to their husbands' ears was almost worse. As Dovey described all this in his homely, but rather flowery language, it put me in mind of those pleasure-seekers that sail too far over a sunny sea in thoughtlessness, and suspect no danger till their vessel is right upon the breakers.

"There haven't been no blow-ups yet to speak of," said the blacksmith. "But they be coming. I could just put my finger upon half-a-dozen women at this blessed minute what's wearing theirselves to shadders with the trouble. They come here to Figg's in the dusk o' evening wi' things hid under their aprons. The longer Jellico lets it go on, the worse it gets, for they will be tempted, the she-creatures, buying made flowers for their best bonnets to-day, and ribbuns for their Sunday caps to-morrow. If Jellico lets 'em, that is. He knows pretty sure where he may trust and where he mayn't. 'Tain't he as will let his pocket suffer in the long run. He knows another thing—that the further he staves off any big noise the profitabler it'll be for him. Once let that come, and Master Jellico might get hunted out o' the Cut, and his pack and its finery kicked to shreds."

"But why are the women such simpletons, Dovey?" asked Frank Stirling.

"You might as well ask why folks eats and drinks, sir," retorted Dovey, his begrimed eyes lighted with the flame. "A love o' their faces is just born with the women, and it goes with 'em to the grave. Set a parcel o' finery before 'em and the best'll find their eyes a-longing, and their mouths a-watering. It's said Eve used to do up her hair looking into a clear pool."

"Putting it in that light, Dovey, I wonder all the women here don't go in for Mr. Jellico's temptations."

"Some on 'em has better sense; and some has husbands what's up to the thing, and keeps the reins tight in their own hands," complacently answered the unconscious Dovey.

"Up to the thing!" repeated Stirling; "I should think all the men are up to it, if Jellico is here so constantly."

"No, sir, they're not. Most of 'em are at work when he comes. They may know some'at about him, but the women contrives to deceive 'em, and they suspects nothing. The fellow with the pack don't concern them or their folk at home, as they supposes, an' so they never bothers theirselves about him or his doings. I'd like to drop a hint to some of 'em to go home unexpected some Tuesday afternoon; but maybe it's best let alone."

"I suppose your wife is one of the sensible ones, Dovey?" And I kept my countenance as I said it.

"She daredn't be nothing else, Master Johnny. I be a trifle loud if I'm put out. Not she," emphatically added Dovey, his strong, bared arm dealing a heavy blow on the anvil, and sending up a whole cloud of sparks. "I'd never get put in jail for her, as she knows; I'd shave her hair off first. Run up a score with that there Jellico? No, she'd not be such a idiot as that. You should hear how she goes on again her neighbours that does run it, and the names she calls 'em."

Poor John Dovey! Where ignorance is bliss—

"Why, if I thought my wife could hoodwink me as some of 'em does their men, I'd never hold up my head of one while, for shame; no, not in my own forge," continued Dovey. "Ann's temper's a bit trying sometimes, and wants keeping in order; but she'd be above deceit o' that paltry sort. She don't need to act it, neither; I give her a whole ten shillings t'other day, and she went and laid it out at Alcester."

No doubt. Any amount of shillings would soon be sacrificed to Ann's vanity.

"How much longer is that thing going to take, Dovey?" interposed Stirling.

"Just about two minutes, sir. 'Twere a cranky— There he goes."

The break in Dovey's answer was caused by the appearance of Jellico. He came out, shouldering his pack. The blacksmith looked after him down the Cut, and saw him turn in elsewhere.

"I thought 'twas where he was going," said he; "'tain't often he passes that there dwelling. Other houses seem to have their days, turn and turn about; but that 'un gets him constant."

"It's where Bird's wife lives, is it not, Dovey?"

"It's where she lives, fast enough, sir. And Bird, he be safe at his over-looking work, five miles off, without fear of his popping in home to hinder the dealing and chaffering. But she'd better mind— though Bird do get a'most three pound a-week, he have got means for every sixpence of it, with his peck o' childern, six young 'uns of her'n, and six of his first wife's, and no more'n one on 'em yet able to earn a penny-piece. If Bird thought she was running up a score with Jellico, he'd give her two black eyes as soon as look at her."

"Bird's wife never seems to have any good clothes at all; she looks as if she hadn't a decent gown to her back," said Frank.

"What she buys is mostly things for the little 'uns: shimmys and pinafores, and that," replied Dovey. "Letty Bird's one o' them that's more improvidenter than a body of any sense 'ud believe, Master Stirling; she never has a coin by the Wednesday night, she hasn't. The little 'uns 'ud be a-rolling naked in the gutter, but for what she gets on tick off Jellico; and Bird, seeing 'em naked, might beat her for that. That don't mend the system; the score's a-being run up, and it'll bring trouble sometime as sure as a gun. Beside that, if there was no Jellico to serve her with his poison, she'd have to save enough for decent clothes. Don't you see how the thing works, sir?"

"Oh, I see," carelessly answered Stirling. "D'ye call the pack's wares poison, Dovey?"

"Yes, I do," said Dovey, stoutly, as he handed Frank his iron. "They'll poison the peace o' many a household in this here Cut. You two young gents just look out else, and see."

We came away with the iron. At the end of Piefinch Lane, Frank Stirling took the road to the Court, and I turned into Reed's. The wife was by herself then, giving the children their early tea.

"Reed shall come up to the Manor as soon as he gets home, sir," she said, in answer to Tod's message.

"I was here before this afternoon, Mrs. Reed, and couldn't get in. You were too busy to hear me at the door."

The knife halted in the bread she was cutting, and she glanced up for a moment; but seemed to think nothing, and finished the slice.

"I've been very busy, Master Ludlow. I'm sorry you've had to come twice, sir."

"Busy enough, I should say, with Jellico's pack emptied on the table, and you and the rest buying up at steam pace."

The words were out of my lips before I saw her startled gesture of caution, pointing to the children: it was plain they were not to know anything about Jellico. She had an honest face, but it turned scarlet.

"Do you think it is a good plan, Mrs. Reed, to get things upon trust, and have to make up money for them weekly?" I could not help saying to her as she came to the door.

"I'm beginning to doubt whether it is, sir."

"If Reed thought he had a debt hanging over him, that might fall at any moment—"

"For the love of mercy, sir, don't say nothing to Reed!" came the startled interruption. "You won't, will you, Master Johnny?"

"Not I. Don't fear. But if I were you, Mrs. Reed, for my own sake I should cut all connection with Jellico. Better deal at a fair shop."

She nodded her head as I went through the gate; but her face had now turned to a sickly whiteness that spoke of terror. Was the woman so deep in the dangerous books already?

Reed came up in the evening, and Tod showed him what he wanted done. As the man was measuring the trellis-work, Hannah happened to pass. She asked him how he was getting on.

"Amongst the middlings," answered Reed, shortly. "I was a bit put out just now."

"What by?" asked Hannah, who said anything she chose before me without the smallest ceremony: and Tod had gone away.

"As I was coming up here, Ingram stops me, and asks if I couldn't let him have the bit of money I owed him. I stared at the man: what money was I likely to owe him—"

"Ingram the cow-keeper?" interrupted Hannah.

"Ingram the cow-keeper. So, talking a bit, I found there was a matter of six shillings due to him for the children's milk: it was ever so long since my wife had paid. Back I went to her at once to know the reason why—and it was that made me late in coming up here, Master Johnny."

"I suppose he had sold her skim milk for new, and she thought she'd make him wait for his money," returned Hannah.

"All she said to me was that she didn't think it had been running so long; Ingram had said to me that she always told him she was short of money and couldn't pay," answered Reed. "Anyway, I don't think she'll let it run on again. It put me out, though. I'd rather go off into the workhouse, or die of starvation, than I'd let it be said in the place my wife didn't pay as she went on."

I saw through the difficulty, and should have liked to give Reed a hint touching Jellico.

Now it was rather strange that, all in two days, Jellico and the mischief he was working should be thus brought before me in three or four ways, considering that I had never in my life before heard of the man. But it chanced to be so. I don't want to say anything about the man personally, good or bad; the mischief lay in the system. That Jellico sold his goods at a nice rate for dearness, and used persuasion with the women to buy them, was as plain as the sun at noonday; but in these respects he was no worse than are many other people in trade. He went to the houses in turn, and the women met him; it might be several weeks before the meeting was held at Mrs. Reed's again. Ann Dovey could not enjoy the hospitality of receiving him at hers, as her husband's work lay at home. But she was a constant visitor to the other places.

And the time went on; and Mr. Jellico's trade flourished. But we heard nothing more about it at Dyke Manor, and I naturally forgot it.

II

"Just six shillings on it, Mr. Figg! That's all I want to-day, but I can't do without that."

That so well-conducted and tidy a woman as George Reed's wife should be in what the Cut called familiarly the "pawnshop," would have surprised every one not in the secret. But she was. Mr. Figg, a little man with weak eyes and a few scattered locks of light hair, turned over the offered loan with his finger and thumb. A grey gown of some kind of woollen stuff.

"How many times have this here gownd been brought here, Mrs. Reed?" asked he.

"I haven't counted 'em," she sighed. "Why? What's that got to do with it?"

"'Cause it's a proof as it must be getting the worse for wear," was the answer, given disparagingly.

"It's just as good as it was the day I had it out o' Jellico's pack," said Mrs. Reed, sadly subdued, as of late she had always seemed.

Mr. Figg held up the gown to the light, seeking for the parts in it most likely to be worn. "Look here," said he. "What d'ye call that?"

There was a little fraying certainly in places. Mrs. Reed had eyes and could see it. She did not answer.

"It don't stand to reason as a gownd will wear for ever and show no marks. You puts this here gownd in of a Wednesday morning, or so, and gets it out of a Saturday night to wear Sundays. Wear and tear is wear and tear."

Mrs. Reed could not deny the accusation. All the available articles her home contained; that is, the few her husband was not likely to observe the absence of; together with as much of her own wardrobe as she could by any shift do without, were already on a visit to Mr. Figg; which visit, according to the present look-out, promised to be permanent. This gown was obliged to be taken out periodically. Had she not appeared decent on Sundays, her husband would have demanded the reason why.

"You've gave me six shillings on it before," she argued.

"Can't again. Don't mind lending five; next week it'll be but four. It wasn't never worth more nor ten new," added Mr. Figg loudly, to drown remonstrances.

"Why, I gave Jellico double that for it! Where's the use of you running things down?"

As Jellico was in one sense a friend of Mr. Figg's—for he was certainly the cause of three parts of his pledges being brought to him—the pawnbroker let the question pass. Mrs. Reed went home with her five shillings, her eyes taking quite a wild look of distress and glancing cornerwise on all sides, as if she feared an ambush.

It had not been a favourable year; weather had been bad, strikes were prevalent, money was dear, labour scarce. Men were ready to snatch the work out of each other's hands; some were quite unemployed, others less than they used to be. Of course the homes in Piefinch Cut, and similar small homes not in the Cut, went on short-commons. And if the women had been scarcely able to get on before and stave off exposure, any one may see that that was a feat impracticable now. One of them, Hester Reed, thought the doubt and difficulty and remorse and dread would kill her.

Dread of her husband's discovering the truth, and dread of his being called upon to answer for the debt. Unable to keep up her weekly interest and payments to Mr. Jellico for some time now, the main debt had only accumulated. She owed him two pounds nineteen shillings. And two pounds nineteen shillings to a labourer's wife seems as a wide gulf that can never be bridged over while life shall last. Besides this, she had been obliged to go into debt at the general shop; that had added itself up now to eight-and-twenty shillings, and the shop was threatening procedure. There were other little odds and ends of liabilities less urgent, a few shillings in all. To those not acquainted with the simple living of a rural district, this may not sound so very overwhelming: those who are, know what it means, and how awful was the strait to which Mrs. Reed (with other wives) had reduced herself.

She had grown so thin as hardly to be able to keep her clothes upon her. Sleeping and waking, a dead wall crowded with figures, as a huge sum, seemed to be before her eyes. Lately she had taken to dreaming of hanging feet downwards over a precipice, held up only by the grasp of her hands on the edge. Nearly always she awoke with the horror: and it would seem to her that it was worse to wake up to life and its cares, than to fall down to death and be at rest from them. Her husband, perceiving that she appeared very ill, told her she had better speak to Dr. Duffham.

Carrying home the five shillings in her hand, Mrs. Reed sat down in her kitchen and wiped her face, damp with pallor. She had begun to ask—not so much what the ending would be, but how soon it would come. With the five shillings in her hand she must find food and necessaries until Saturday night; there was no more credit to be had. And this was only Wednesday morning. With credit stopped and supplies stopped, her husband would naturally make inquiries, and all must come out. Hester Reed wondered whether she should die of the shame—if she had to stay and face it. Three of the shillings must be paid that afternoon to Ingram the milkman; he would not be quiet any longer: and the woman cast her aching eyes round her room, and saw nothing that it was possible to take away and raise money on.

She had the potatoes on the fire when the children ran in, little toddling things, from school. Some rashers of bacon lay on the table ready to be toasted. Reed, earning pretty good wages, had been accustomed to live well: with careful management he knew they might do so still. Little did he suspect the state things had got into.

"Tatty dere, mov'er," began the eldest, who was extremely backward in speaking.

"Tatty dere" meant "Cathy's there;" and the mother looked up from the bacon. Cathy Parrifer (though nobody called her by her new name, but Cathy Reed still) stood at the outer gate, in tatters as usual, talking to some man who had a paper in his hand. Mrs. Reed's heart leaped into her mouth: she lived in dread of everything. A stranger approaching the place turned her sick. And now the terror, whose shadow had been so long looming, was come in reality. Catherine came bounding up the garden to tell the tale: the man, standing at the gate, was waiting to see her father come home to dinner to serve him with a summons for the county court. Mrs. Reed knew at once what it was for: the eight-and-twenty shillings owing at the general shop. Her face grew white as she sank into a chair.

"Couldn't you get him to leave the paper with me, Cathy?" she whispered, insane ideas of getting up the money somehow floating into her brain.

"He won't," answered Cathy. "He means to give that to father personally, he says, if he stays till night."

Just as many another has felt, in some apparently insurmountable obstacle, that seemed to be turning their hair grey in the little space of time that you can peel an apple, felt Mrs. Reed. Light seemed to be closing, shame and misery and blackness to be opening. Her hands seemed powerless to put the bacon into the Dutch oven.

But there ensued a respite. A very short one, but still a respite. While the summons-server was loitering outside, Reed came in through the back-garden, having got over the stile in Piefinch Lane. It was not often he chose that way; accident caused him to do it to-day. Mrs. Reed, really not knowing what she did or said, told Cathy there'd be a morsel of dinner for her if she liked to stop and eat it. As Cathy was not in the luck of such offers every day, she remained: and in her good-nature talked and laughed to divert any suspicion.

But the man at the gate began to smell a rat; perhaps the bacon as well. Dinner-hour almost over, and no George Reed had come home! He suddenly thought of the back-entrance, and walked up the front-path to see. Paper in hand, he gave a thump at the house-door. Reed was about to leave then: and he went down the path by the man's side, opening the paper. Mrs. Reed, more like a ghost than a woman, took a glance through the window.

"I can't face it, Catherine. When I'm gone, you'd better come home here and do what you can for the children. Tell him all; it's of no good trying to hide it any longer."

She took her worn old shawl from a press and put her bonnet on; and then stooped to kiss her children, saying good-bye with a burst of grief.

"But where are you going?" cried the wondering Cathy.

"Anywhere. If I am tempted to do anything desperate, Cathy, tell father not to think too bad of me, as he might if I was living."

She escaped by the back-door. Catherine let her go, uncertain what to be at for the best. Her father was striding back to the house up the garden-path, and the storm was coming. As a preliminary van-guard, Cathy snatched up the youngest girl and held her on her lap. The summons-server was calling after Reed, apparently giving some instructions, and that took up another minute or two; but he came in at last.

Cathy told as much of the truth as she dared; her father was too angry for her to venture on all. In his passion he said his wife might go and be hanged. Cathy answered that she had as good as said it was something of that she meant to go and do.

But talking and acting are two things; and when it came to be put to the test, Hester Reed found herself no more capable of entering upon any desperate course than the rest of us are. And, just as I had been brought in accidentally to see the beginning, so was I accidentally brought in at the ending.

We were at home again for the holidays, and I had been over for an afternoon to the Stirlings'. Events in this world happen very strangely. Upon setting out to walk back in the cool of the late summer's evening, I took the way by Dyke Brook instead of either of the two ordinary roads. Why I chose it I did not know then; I do not now; I never shall know. When fairly launched into the fields, I asked myself why on earth I had come that way, for it was the loneliest to be found in the two counties.

Turning sharp round the dark clump of trees by Dyke Brook (which just there is wide enough for a pond and as deep as one), I came upon somebody in a shabby grey straw bonnet, standing on its brink and looking down into the water.

"Halloa, Mrs. Reed! Is that you?"

Before I forget the woe-stricken face she turned upon me, the start she gave, I must lose memory. Down she sat on the stump of a tree, and burst into sobs.

"What is it?" I asked, standing before her.

"Master Johnny, I've been for hours round it, round and round, wanting the courage to throw myself in; and I haven't done it."

"Just tell me all about the trouble," I said, from the opposite stump, upon which I took my seat.

And she did tell me. Alone there for so many hours, battling with herself and Death (it's not wrong to say so), my coming seemed to unlock all the gates of reticence, and she disclosed to me what I've written above.

"God knows I never thought to bring it to such a pass as this," she sobbed. "I went into it without any sense of doing harm. One day, when I happened to be at Miles Dickon's, Jellico came in with his pack, and I was tempted to buy some ribbon. I said he might come and show me his things the next week, and he did, and I bought a gownd and a shawl. I know now how wrong and blind I was: but it seemed so easy, just to pay a shilling or two a-week; like having the things for nothing. And from that time it went on; a'most every Tuesday I took some trifle of him, maybe a bit o' print for the little ones, or holland for pinafores; and I gave Cathy a cotton gownd, for she hadn't one to her back. I didn't buy as some of 'em did, for the sake of show and bedeckings, but useful things, Master Johnny," she added, sobbing bitterly. "And this has come of it! and I wish I was at rest in that there blessed water."

"Now, Mrs. Reed! Do you suppose you would be at rest?"

"Heaven have mercy on me! It's the thought o' the sin, and of what might come after, that makes me hold back from it."

Looking at her, shading her eyes with her hand, her elbow on her lap, and her face one of the saddest for despair I ever saw, I thought of the strange contrasts there are in the world. For the want of about five pounds this woman was seeking to end her life; some have done as much for five-and-twenty thousand.

"I've not a friend in the whole world that could help me," she said. "But it's not that, Master Johnny; it's the shame on me for having brought things to such a pass. If the Lord would but be pleased to take me, and save me from the sin of lifting a hand against my own life!"

"Look here, Mrs. Reed. As to what you call the shame, I suppose we all have to go in for some sort or another of that kind of thing as we jog along. As you are not taken, and don't seem likely to be taken, I should look on that as an intimation that you must live and make the best of things."

"Live! how, sir? I can't never show myself at home. Reed, he'll have to go to jail; the law will put him there. I'd not face the world, sir, knowing it was all for my thoughtless debts."

Could I help her? Ought I to help her? If I went to old Brandon and begged to have five pounds, why, old Brandon in the end would give it me, after he had gone on rather hotly for an hour. If I did not help her, and any harm came to her, what should I—

"You promise me never to think about pools again, Mrs. Reed, except in the way of eels, and I'll promise to see you through this."

She looked up, more helpless than before. "There ain't nothing to be done for me, Master Johnny. There's the shame, and the talkin' o' the neighbours—"

"Yes, you need mind that. Why, the neighbours are all in the same boat!"

"And there's Reed, sir; he'd never forgive me. He'd—"

Of all cries, she interrupted herself with about the worst: something she saw behind me had frightened her. In another moment she had darted to the pond, and Reed was holding her back from it.

"Be thee a born fool?" roared Reed. "Dost think thee'st not done enough harm as it is, but thee must want to cap it by putting theeself in there? That would mend it, that would!"

She released herself from him, and slipped on the grass, Reed standing between her and the pond. But he seemed to think better of it, and stepped aside.

"Jump in, an' thee likes to," said he, continuing to speak in the familiar home manner. "I once see a woman ducked in the Severn for pocket-picking, at Worcester races, and she came out all the cooler and better for't."

"I never thought to bring trouble on you or anybody, George," she sobbed. "It seems to have come on and on, like a great monster growing bigger and bigger as you look at him, till I couldn't get away from it."

"Couldn't or wouldn't, which d'ye mean?" retorted Reed. "Why you women were ever created to bother us, hangs me. I hope you'll find you can keep the children when I and a dozen more of us are in jail. 'Twon't be my first visit there."

"Look here, Reed; I've promised to set it right for her. Don't worry over it."

"I'll not accept help from anybody; not even from you, Master Johnny. What she has done she must abide by."

"The bargain's made, Reed; you can't break it if you would. Perhaps a great trouble may come to me some time in my life that I may be glad to be helped out of. Mrs. Reed will get the money to-morrow, only she need not tell the parish where she found it."

"Oh, George, let it be so!" she implored through her tears. "If Master Johnny's good enough to do this, let him. I might save up by little and little to repay him in time. If you went to jail through me!—I'd rather die!"

"Will you let it be a lesson to you—and keep out of Jellico's clutches in future?" he asked, sternly.

"It's a lesson that'll last me to the end of my days," she said, with a shiver. "Please God, you let Master Johnny get me out o' this trouble, I'll not fall into another like it."

"Then come along home to the children," said he, his voice softening a little. "And leave that pond and your folly behind you."

I was, of course, obliged to tell the whole to Mr. Brandon and the Squire, and they both pitched into me as fiercely as tongues could pitch. But neither of them was really angry; I saw that. As to the five pounds, I only wish as much relief could be oftener given with as little money.

CHAPTER IX

CAROMEL'S FARM

I

You will be slow to believe what I am about to write, and say it savours of romance instead of reality. Every word of it is true. Here truth was stranger than fiction.

Lying midway between our house, Dyke Manor, and Church Dykely, was a substantial farm belonging to the Caromels. It stood well back from the road a quarter-of-a-mile or so, and was nearly hidden by the trees that surrounded it. An avenue led to the house; which was a rambling, spacious, very old-fashioned building, so full of queer angles inside, nooks and corners and passages, that you might lose your way in them and never find it again. The Caromels were gentlemen by descent; but their means had dwindled with years, so that they had little left besides this property. The last Caromel who died, generally distinguished as "Old Caromel" by all the parish, left two sons, Miles and Nash. The property was willed to the elder, Miles: but Nash continued to have his home with him. As to the house, it had no particular name, but was familiarly called "Caromel's Farm."

Squire Todhetley had been always intimate with them; more like a brother than anything else. Not but that he was considerably their senior. I think he liked Nash the best: Nash was so yielding and easy. Some said Nash was not very steady in private life, and that his brother, Miles, stern and moral, read him a lecture twice a-week. But whether it was so no one knew; people don't go prying into their neighbours' closets to look up their skeletons.

At the time I am beginning to tell of, old Caromel had been dead about ten years; Nash was now five-and-thirty, Miles forty. Miles had married a lady with a good fortune, which was settled upon herself and her children; the four of them were girls, and there was no son.

At the other end of Church Dykely, ever so far past Chavasse Grange, lived a widow lady named Tinkle. And when the world had quite done wondering whether Nash Caromel meant to marry (though, indeed, what had he to marry upon?), it was suddenly found out that he wanted Mrs. Tinkle's daughter, Charlotte. The Tinkles were respectable people, but not equal to the Caromels. Mrs. Tinkle and her son farmed a little land, she had also a small private income. The son had married well. Just now he was away; having gone abroad with his wife, whose health was failing.

Charlotte Tinkle was getting on towards thirty. You would not have thought it, to look at her. She had a gentle face, a gentle voice, and a young, slender figure; her light brown hair was always neat; and she possessed one of those inoffensive natures that would like to be at peace with the whole world. It was natural that Mrs. Tinkle should wish her daughter to marry, if a suitable person presented himself—all mothers do, I suppose—but to find it was Nash Caromel took her aback.

"You think it will not do," observed the Squire, when Mrs. Tinkle was enlarging on the grievance to him one day that they met in a two-acre field.

"How can it do?" returned poor Mrs. Tinkle, in a tone between wailing and crying. "Nash Caromel has nothing to keep her on, sir, and no prospects."

"That's true," said the pater. "At present he has thoughts of taking a farm."

"But he has no money to stock a farm. And look at that tale, sir, that was talked of—about that Jenny Lake. Other things have been said also."

"Oh, one must not believe all one hears. For myself, I assure you, Mrs. Tinkle, I know no harm of Nash. As to the money to stock a farm, I expect his brother could help him to it, if he chose."

"But, sir, you would surely not advise them to marry upon an uncertainty!"

"I don't advise them to marry at all; understand that, my good lady; I think it would be the height of imprudence. But I can't prevent it."

"Mr. Todhetley," she answered, a tear rolling down her thin cheeks, on which there was a chronic redness, "I am unable to describe to you how much my mind is set against the match: I seem to foresee, by some subtle instinct, that no good would ever come of it; nothing but misery for Charlotte. And she has had so peaceful a home all her life."

"Tell Charlotte she can't have him—if you think so strongly about it."

"She won't listen—at least to any purpose," groaned Mrs. Tinkle. "When I talk to her she says, 'Yes, dear mother; no, dear mother,' in her dutiful way: and the same evening she'll be listening to Nash Caromel's courting words. Her uncle, Ralph Tinkle, rode over from Inkberrow to talk to her, for I wrote to him: but it seems to have made no permanent impression on her. What I am afraid of is that Nash Caromel will marry her in spite of us."

"I should like to see my children marry in spite of me!" cried the Squire, giving way to one of his hot fits. "I'd 'marry' them! Nash can't take her against her will, my dear friend: it takes two people, you know, to complete a bargain of that sort. Promise Charlotte to shake her unless she listens to reason. Why should she not listen! She is meek and tractable."

"She always has been. But, once let a girl be enthralled by a sweetheart, there's no answering for her. Duty to parents is often forgotten then."

"If— Why, mercy upon us, there is Charlotte!" broke off the Squire, happening to lift his eyes to the stile. "And Nash too."

Yes, there they were: standing on the other side the stile in the cross-way path. "Halloa!" called out Mr. Todhetley.

"I can't stay a moment," answered Nash Caromel, turning his good-looking face to speak: and it cannot be denied it was a good-looking face, or that he was an attractive man. "Miles has sent me to that cattle sale up yonder, and I am full late."

With a smile and a nod, he stepped lightly onwards, his slender supple figure, of middle height, upright as a dart; his fair hair waving in the breeze. Charlotte Tinkle glanced shyly after him, her cheeks blushing like a peony.

"What's this I hear, young lady?—that you and Mr. Nash yonder want to make a match of it, in spite of pastors and masters?" began the Squire. "Is it true?"

Charlotte stood like a goose, making marks on the dusty path with the end of her large grass-green parasol. Parasols were made for use then, not show.

"Nash has nothing, you know," went on the Squire. "No money, no house, no anything. There wouldn't be common sense in it, Charlotte."

"I tell him so, sir," answered Charlotte, lifting her shy brown eyes for a moment.

"To be sure; that's right. Here's your mother fretting herself into fiddlestrings for fear of—of—I hardly know what."

"Lest you should be tempted to forget your duty to me, Lottie," struck in the mother. "Ah, my dear! you young people little think what trouble and anxiety you bring upon us."

Charlotte Tinkle suddenly burst into tears, to the surprise of her beholders. Drying them up as soon as she could, she spoke with a sigh.

"I hope I shall never bring trouble upon you, mother, never; I wouldn't do it willingly for the world. But—"

"But what, child?" cried the mother, for Charlotte had come to a standstill.

"I—I am afraid that parents and children see with different eyes—just as though things were for each a totally opposite aspect," she went on timidly. "The difficulty is how to reconcile that view and this."

"And do you know what my father used to say to me in my young days?" put in the Squire. "'Young folks think old folks fools, but old folks know the young ones to be so.' There was never a truer saying than that, Miss Charlotte."

Miss Charlotte only sighed in answer. The wind, high that day, was taking her muslin petticoats, and she had some trouble to keep them down. Mrs. Tinkle got over the stile, and the Squire turned back towards home.

A fortnight or so had passed by after this, when Church Dykely woke one morning to an electric shock; Nash Caromel and Charlotte had gone and got married. They did it without the consent of (as the Squire had put it) pastors and masters. Nash had none to consult, for he could not be expected to yield obedience to his brother; and Charlotte had asked Mrs. Tinkle, and Mrs. Tinkle had refused to countenance the ceremony, though she did not actually walk into the church to forbid it.

Taking a three weeks' trip by way of honeymoon, the bride and bridegroom came back to Church Dykely. Caromel's Farm refused to take them in; and Miles Caromel, indignant to a degree, told his brother that "as he had made his bed, so must he lie upon it," which is a very convenient reproach, and often used.

"Nash is worse than a child," grumbled Miles to the Squire, his tones harder than usual, and his manner colder. "He has gone and married this young woman—who is not his equal—and now he has no home to give her. Did he suppose that we should receive him back here?—and take her in as well? He has acted like an idiot."

"Mrs. Tinkle will not have anything to do with them, I hear," returned the Squire: "and Tinkle, of Inkberrow, is furious."

"Tinkle of Inkberrow's no fool. Being a man of substance, he thinks they may be falling back upon him."

Which was the precise fear that lay upon Miles himself. Meanwhile Nash engaged sumptuous lodgings (if such a word could be justly applied to any rooms at Church Dykely), and drove his wife out daily in the pony-gig that was always looked upon as his at Caromel's Farm.

Nash was flush of money now, for he had saved some; but he could not go on living upon it for ever. After sundry interviews with his brother, Miles agreed to hand him over a thousand pounds: not at all too large a sum, considering that Nash had given him his services, such as they were, for a number of years for just his keep as a gentleman and a bonus for pocket-money. A thousand pounds would not go far with such a farm as Nash had been used to and would like to take, and he resolved to emigrate to America.

Mrs. Tinkle (the Squire called her simple at times) was nearly wild when she heard of it. It brought her out of her temper with a leap. Condoning the rebellious marriage, she went off to remonstrate with Nash.

"But now, why need you put yourself into this unhappy state?" asked Nash, when he had heard what she had to say. "Dear Mrs. Tinkle, do admit some common sense into your mind. I am not taking Charlotte to the 'other end of the world,' as you put it, but to America. It is only a few days' passage. Outlandish foreigners! Not a bit of it. The people are, so to speak, our own countrymen. Their language is ours; their laws are, I believe, much as ours are."

"You may as well be millions of miles away, practically speaking," bewailed Mrs. Tinkle. "Charlotte will be as much lost to me there as she would be at the North Pole. She is my only daughter, Nash Caromel, she has never been away from me: to part with her will be like parting with life."

"I am very sorry," said poor Nash, who was just a woman when any appeal was made to his feelings. "Live with you? No, that would not do: but, thank you all the same for offering it. Nothing would induce me to spunge upon you in that way: and, were I capable of it, your son Henry would speedily turn us out when he returned. I must get a home of my own, for Charlotte's sake as well as for mine: and I know I can do that in America. Land, there, may be had for an old song; fortunes are made in no time. The probability is that before half-a-dozen years have gone over our heads, I shall bring you Charlotte home a rich woman, and we shall settle down here for life."

There isn't space to pursue the arguments—which lasted for a week or two. But they brought forth no result. Nash might have turned a post sooner than the opinions of Mrs. Tinkle, and she might as well have tried to turn the sun as to stop his emigrating. The parish looked upon it as not at all a bad scheme. Nash might get on well over there if he would put off his besetting sin, indolence, and not allow the Yankees to take him in.

So Nash Caromel and Charlotte his wife set sail for New York; Mrs. Tinkle bitterly resenting the step, and wholly refusing to be reconciled.

II

About five years went by. Henry Tinkle's wife had died, leaving him a little girl, and he was back with the child at his mother's: but that has nothing to do with us. A letter came from the travellers now and then, but not often, during the first three years. Nash wrote to Caromel's Farm; Charlotte to the parson's wife, Mrs. Holland, with whom she had been very friendly. But none of the letters gave much information as to personal matters; they were chiefly filled with descriptions of the new country, its manners and customs, and especially its mosquitoes, which at first nearly drove Mrs. Nash Caromel mad. It was gathered that Nash did not prosper. They seemed to move about from place to place, making New York a sort of standing point to return to occasionally. For the past two years no letters at all had come, and it was questioned whether poor Nash and his wife had not dropped out of the world.

In the midst of this uncertainty, Miles Caromel, who had been seriously ailing for some months, died. And to Nash, if he were still in existence, lapsed the Caromel property.

Old Mr. Caromel's will had been a curious one. He bequeathed Caromel Farm, with all its belongings, the live stock, the standing ricks, the crops, the furniture, and all else that might be in or upon it, to his son Miles, and to Miles's eldest son after him. If Miles left no son, then it was to go to Nash (with all that might then be upon it, just as before), and so on to Nash's son. But if neither of them had a son, and Nash died during Miles's lifetime—in short, if there was no male inheritor living, then Miles could dispose of the property as he pleased. As could Nash also under similar circumstances.

The result of this odd will was, that Nash, if living, came into the farm and all that was upon it. If Nash had, or should have, a son, it must descend to said son; if he had not, the property was his absolutely. But it was not known whether Nash was living; and, in the uncertainty, Miles made a will conditionally, bequeathing it to his wife and daughters. It was said that possessing no son had long been a thorn in the shoes of Miles Caromel; that he had prayed for one, summer and winter.

But now, who was to find Nash? How could the executors let him know of his good luck? The Squire, who was one of them, talked of nothing else. A letter was despatched to Nash's agents in New York, Abraham B. Whitter and Co., and no more could be done.

In a shorter time than you would have supposed possible, Nash arrived at Church Dykely. He chanced to be at these same agents' house in New York, when the letter got there, and he came off at full speed. So the will made by Miles went for nothing.

Nash Caromel was a good bit altered—looked thinner and older: but he was evidently just as easy and persuadable as he used to be: people often wondered whether Nash had ever said No in his whole life. He did not tell us much about himself, only that he had roamed over the world, hither and thither, from country to country, and had been lately for some time in California. Charlotte was at San Francisco. When Nash took ship from thence for New York, she was not well enough to undertake the voyage, and had to stay behind. Mrs. Tinkle, who had had time, and to spare, to get over her anger, went into a way at this last item of news; and caught up the notion that Charlotte was dead. For which she had no grounds whatever.

Charlotte had no children; had not had any; consequently there was every probability that Caromel's Farm would be Nash's absolutely, to will away as he should please. He found Mrs. Caromel (his brother's widow) and her daughters in it; they had not bestirred themselves to look out for another residence. Being very well off, Mrs. Caromel having had several substantial windfalls in the shape of legacies from rich uncles and aunts, they professed to be glad that Nash should have the property—whatever they might have privately felt. Nash, out of a good-natured wish not to disturb them too soon, bade them choose their own time for moving, and took up his abode at Nave, the lawyer's.

There are lawyers and lawyers. I am a great deal older now than I was when these events were enacted, and have gained my share of worldly wisdom; and I, Johnny Ludlow, say that there are good and honest lawyers as well as bad and dishonest. My experience has lain more amidst the former class than the latter. Though I have, to my cost, been brought into contact with one or two bad ones in my time; fearful rogues.

One of these was Andrew Nave: who had recently, so to say, come, a stranger, to settle at Church Dykely. His name might have had a "K" prefixed, and been all the better for it. Of fair outward show, indeed rather a good-looking man, he was not fair within. He managed to hold his own in the parish estimation, as a rule: it was only when some crafty deed or other struggled to the surface that people would say, "What a sharper that man is!"

The family lawyer of the Caromels, Crow, of Evesham, chanced to be ill at this time, and gone away for change of air, and Nave rushed up to greet Nash on his return, and to offer his services. And the fellow was so warm and hearty, so fair-speaking, so much the gentleman, that easy Nash, to whom the man was an entire stranger, and who knew nothing of him, bad or good, clasped the hand held out to him, and promised Knave his patronage forthwith. If I've made a mistake in spelling the name, it can go.

To begin with, Nave took him home. He lived a door or two past Duffham's: a nice house, well kept up in paint. Some five years before, the sleepy old lawyer, Wilkinson, died in that house, and Nave came down from London and took to the concern. Nave thought that he was doing a first-rate stroke of business now by securing Nash Caromel as an inmate, the solicitorship to the Caromel property being worth trying for: though he might not have been so eager to admit Nash had he foreseen all that was to come of it.

Not caring to trouble Mrs. Caromel with his company, Nash accepted Nave's hospitality; but, liking to be independent, he insisted upon paying for it, and mentioned a handsome weekly sum. Nave made a show of resistance—which was all put on, for he was as fond of shillings as he was of pounds—and then gave in. So Nash, feeling free, stayed on at his ease.

When Nave had first come to settle at Church Dykely with his daughter Charlotte, he was taken for a widower. It turned out, however, that there was a Mrs. Nave living somewhere with the rest of the children, she and her husband having agreed to what was called an amicable separation, for their tempers did not agree. This eldest daughter, Charlotte, a gay, dashing girl of two-and-twenty then, was the only creature in the world, it was said, for whom Nave cared.

Mrs. Caromel did not appear readily to find a place to her liking. People are particular when about to purchase a residence. She made repeated apologies to Nash for keeping him out of his home, but he assured her that he was in no hurry to leave his present quarters.

And that was true. For Charlotte Nave was casting her glamour over him. She liked to cast that over men; and tales had gone about respecting her. Nothing very tangible: and perhaps they would not have held water. She was a little, fair, dashing woman, swaying about her flounces as she walked, with a great heap of beautiful hair, bright as gold. Her blue eyes had a way of looking into yours rather too freely, and her voice was soft as a summer wind. A dangerous companion was Miss Nave.

Well, they fell in love with one another, as was said; she and Nash. Nash forgot his wife, and she her old lovers. Being now on the road to her twenty-eighth year, she had had her share of them. Once she had been mysteriously absent from home for two weeks, and Church Dykely somehow took up the idea that she and one of her lovers (a young gentleman who was reading law with Nave) were taking a fraternal tour together as far as London to see the lions. But it turned out to be a mistake, and no one laughed at the notion more than Charlotte when she returned. She wished she had been on a tour—and seeing lions, she said, instead of moping away the whole two weeks at her aunt's, who had a perpetual asthma, and lived in a damp old house at Chelsea.

But that is of the past, and Nash is back again. The weeks went on. Autumn weather came in. Mrs. Caromel found a place to suit her at Kempsey—one of the prettiest of the villages that lie under the wing of Worcester. She bought it; and removed to it with her private goods and chattels. Nash, even now, made no haste to quit the lawyer's house for his own. Some said it was he who could not tear himself away from Charlotte; others said Miss Charlotte would not let him go; that she held him fast by a silken cord. Anyhow, they were always together, out-of-doors and in; she seemed to like to parade their friendship before the world, as some girls like to lead about a pet monkey. Perhaps Nash first took to her from her name being the same as his wife's.

One day in September, Nash walked over to the Manor and had a long talk in private with the Squire. He wanted to borrow twelve hundred pounds. No ready money had come to him from his brother, and it was not a favourable time for selling produce. The Squire cheerfully agreed to lend it him: there was no risk.

"But I'd counsel you to remember one thing, Nash Caromel—that you have a wife," said he, as they came out of the room when Nash was going away. "It's time you left off dallying with that other young woman."

Nash laughed a laugh that had an uneasy sound in it. "It is nothing, Todhetley."

"Glad to hear you say so," said the pater. "She has the reputation of being a dangerous flirt. You are not the first man she has entangled, if all tales be true. Get out of Nave's house and into your own."

"I will," acquiesced Nash.

Perhaps that was easier said than done. It happened that the same evening I overheard a few words between the lawyer and Nash. They were not obliged to apply to Miss Nave: but, the chances were that they did.

The Squire sent me to Nave's when dinner was over, to take a note to Nash. Nave's smart waiting-maid, in a muslin apron and cherry cap-strings, was standing at the door talking and laughing with some young man, under cover of the twilight. She was as fond of finery as her mistress; perhaps as fond of sweethearts.

"Mr. Caromel? Yes, sir, he is at home. Please to walk in."

Showing me to a sitting-room on the left of the passage—the lawyer's offices were on the right—she shut me in, and went, as I supposed, to tell Caromel. At the back of this room was the dining-room. I heard the rattle of glasses on the table through the unlatched folding-doors, and, next, the buzz of voices. The lawyer and Nash were sitting over their wine.

"You must marry her," said Nave, concisely.

"I wish I could," returned Nash; and his wavering, irresolute tone was just a contrast to the other's keen one. "I want to. But how can I? I'm heartily sorry."

"And as soon as may be. You must. Attentions paid to young ladies cannot be allowed to end in smoke. And you will find her thousand pounds useful."

"But how can I, I say?" cried Nash ruefully. "You know how impracticable it is—the impediment that exists."

"Stuff and nonsense, Caromel! Where there's a will there's a way. Impediments only exist to be got over."

"It would take a cunning man to get over the one that lies between me and her. I assure you, and you may know I say it in all good faith, that I should ask nothing better than to be a free man to-morrow—for this one sole cause."

"Leave things to me. For all you know, you are free now."

The opening of their door by the maid, who had taken her own time to do it, and the announcement that I waited to see Mr. Caromel, stopped the rest. Nash came in, and I gave him the note.

"Wants to see me before twelve to-morrow, does he?—something he forgot to say," cried he, running his eyes over it. "Tell the Squire I will be there, Johnny."

Caromel was very busy after that, getting into his house—for he took the Squire's advice, and did not linger much longer at Nave's. And I think two or three weeks only had passed, after he was in it, when news reached him of his wife's death.

It came from his agent in New York, Abraham B. Whitter, who had received the information from San Francisco. Mr. Whitter enclosed the San Francisco letters. They were written by a Mr. Munn: one letter to himself, the other (which was not as yet unsealed) to Nash Caromel.

We read them both: Nash brought them to the Squire before sending them to Mrs. Tinkle—considerate as ever, he would not let her see them until she had been prepared. The letters did not say much. Mrs. Nash Caromel had grown weaker and weaker after Nash departed from San Francisco for New York, and she finally sank under low fever. A diary, which she had kept the last few weeks of her life, meant only for her husband's own eye, together with a few letters and sundry other personal trifles, would be forwarded the first opportunity to Abraham B. Whitter and Co., who would hold the box at Mr. Caromel's disposal.

"Who is he, this Francis Munn, who writes to you?" asked the Squire. "A friend of your wife's?—she appears to have died at his house."

"A true friend of hers and of mine," answered Nash. "It was with Mr. and Mrs. Munn that I left Charlotte, when I was obliged to go to New York. She was not well enough to travel with me."

"Well—look here, Caromel—don't go and marry that other Charlotte," advised the Squire. "She is as different from your wife as chalk is from cheese. Poor thing! it was a hard fate—dying over there away from everybody!"

But now—would any one believe it?—instead of taking the Squire's advice and not marrying her at all, instead even of allowing a decent time to elapse, in less than a week Nash went to church with Charlotte the Second. Shame, said Parson Holland under his breath; shame, said the parish aloud; but Nash Caromel heeded them not.

We only knew it on the day before the wedding was to be. On Wednesday morning, a fine, crisp, October day, a shooting party was to meet at old Appleton's, who lived over beyond Church Dykely. The Squire and Tod started for it after an early breakfast, and they let me go part of the way with them. Just after passing Caromel's Farm, we met Pettipher the postman.

"Anything for the Manor?" asked the pater.

"Yes, sir," answered the man; and, diving into his bundle, he handed a letter.

"This is not mine," said the Squire, looking at the address; "this is for Mr. Caromel."

"Oh! I beg your pardon, sir; I took out the wrong letter. This is yours."

"What a thin letter!—come from foreign parts," remarked the pater, reading the address, "Nash Caromel, Esq." "I seem to know the handwriting: fancy I've seen it before. Here, take it, Pettipher."

In passing the letter to Pettipher, which was a ship's letter, I looked at the said writing. Very small poor writing indeed, with long angular tails to the letters up and down, especially the capitals. The Squire handed me his gun and was turning to walk on, opening his letter as he did so; when Pettipher spoke and arrested him.

"Have you heard what's coming off yonder, to-morrow, sir?" asked he, pointing with his thumb to Caromel's Farm.

"Why no," said the Squire, wondering what Pettipher meant to be at. "What should be coming off!"

"Mr. Caromel's going to bring a wife home. Leastways, going to get married."

"I don't believe it," burst forth the pater, after staring angrily at the man. "You'd better take care what you say, Pettipher."

"But it's true, sir," reasoned Pettipher, "though it's not generally known. My niece is apprentice to Mrs. King the dressmaker, as perhaps you know, sir, and they are making Miss Nave's wedding-dress and bonnet. They are to be married quite early, sir, nine o'clock, before folks are about. Well yes, sir, it is not seemly, seeing he has but now heard of his wife's death, poor Miss Charlotte Tinkle, that grew up among us—but you'll find it's true."

Whether the Squire gave more hot words to Nash Caromel, or to Charlotte the Second, or to Pettipher for telling it, I can't say now. Pettipher touched his hat, said good-morning, and turned up the avenue to Caromel's Farm to leave the letter for Nash.

And, married they were on the following morning, amidst a score or two of spectators. What was agate had slipped out to others as well as ourselves. Old Clerk Bumford looked more fierce than a raven when he saw us flocking into the church, after Nash had fee'd him to keep it quiet.

As the clock struck nine, the party came up. The bride and one of her sisters, both in white silk; Nave and some strange gentleman, who might be a friend of his; and Caromel, pale as a ghost. Charlotte the Second was pale too, but uncommonly pretty, her mass of beautiful hair shining like threads of gold.

The ceremony over, they filed out into the porch; Nash leading his bride, and Nave bringing up the rear alone; when an anxious-looking little woman with a chronic redness of face was seen coming across the churchyard. It was Mrs. Tinkle, wearing the deep mourning she had put on for Charlotte. Some one had carried her the tidings, and she had come running forth to see whether they could be true.

And, to watch her, poor thing, with her scared face raised to Nash, and her poor hands clasped in pain, as he and his bride passed her on the pathway, was something sad. Nash Caromel's face had grown white again; but he never looked at her; never turned his eyes, fixed straight out before him, a hair's point to the right or left.

"May Heaven have mercy upon them—for surely they'll need it!" cried the poor woman. "No luck can come of such a wedding as this."

III

The months went on. Mrs. Nash was ruling the roast at Caromel's Farm, being unquestionably both mistress and master. Nash Caromel's old easy indolence had grown now to apathy. It almost seemed as though the farm might go as it liked for him; but his wife was energetic, and she kept servants of all kinds to their work.

Nash excused himself for his hasty wedding when people reproached him—and a few had done that on his return from the honeymoon. His first wife had been dead for some months, he said, and the farm wanted a mistress. She had only been dead to him a week, was the answer he received to this: and, as to the farm, he was quite as competent to manage that himself without a mistress as with one. After all, where was the use of bothering about it when the thing was done?—and the offence concerned himself, not his neighbours. So the matter was condoned at length; Nash was taken into favour again, and the past was dropped.

But Nash, as I have told you, grew apathetic. His spirits were low; the Squire remarked one day that he was like a man who had some inward care upon him. Mrs. Nash, on the contrary, was cheerful as a summer's day; she filled the farm with visitors, and made the money fly.

All too soon, a baby arrived. It was in May, and he must have travelled at railroad speed. Nurse Picker, called in hastily on the occasion, could not find anything the matter with him. A beautiful boy, she said, as like his father, Master Nash (she had known Nash as a boy), as one pea was like another. Mrs. Nash told a tale of having been run after by a cow; Duffham, when attacked by the parish on the point, shut his lips, and would say never a word, good or bad. Anyway, here he was; a fine little boy and the son and heir: and if he had mistaken the proper time to appear, why, clearly it must be his own fault or the cow's: other people were not to be blamed for it. Mrs. Nash Caromel, frantic with delight at its being a boy, sent an order to old Bumford to set the bells a-ringing.

But now, it was a singular thing that the Squire should chance to be present at the delivery of another of those letters that bore the handwriting with the angular tails. Not but that very singular coincidences do take place in this life, and I often think it would not hurt us if we paid more heed to them. Caromel's Farm was getting rather behind-hand with its payments. Whether through its master's apathy or its mistress's extravagance, ready money grew inconveniently short, and the Squire could not get his interest paid on the twelve hundred pounds.

"I'll go over and jog his memory," said he one morning, as we got up from breakfast. "Put on your cap, Johnny."

There was a pathway to Caromel's across the fields, and that was the way we took. It was a hot, lovely day, early in July. Some wheat on the Caromel land was already down.

"Splendid weather it has been for the corn," cried the Squire, turning himself about, "and we shall have a splendid harvest. Somehow I always fancy the crops ripen on this land sooner than on any other about here, Johnny."

"So they do, sir."

"Fine rich land it is; shouldn't grumble if it were mine. We'll go in at this gate, lad."

"This gate" was the side-gate. It opened on a path that led direct to the sitting-room with glass-doors. Nash was standing just inside the room, and of all the uncomfortable expressions that can sit on a man's face, the worst sat on his. The Squire noticed it, and spoke in a whisper.

"Johnny, lad, he looks just as though he had seen a ghost."

It's just what he did look like—a ghost that frightened him. We were close up before he noticed us. Giving a great start, he smoothed his face, smiled, and held out his hand.

"You don't look well," said the Squire, as he sat down. "What's amiss?"

"Nothing at all," answered Nash. "The heat pothers me, as usual: can't sleep at night for it. Why, here's the postman! What makes him so late, I wonder?"

Pettipher was coming straight down to the window, letters in hand. Something in his free, onward step seemed to say that he must be in the habit of delivering the letters to Nash at that same window.

"Two, sir, this morning," said Pettipher, handing them in.

As Nash was taking the letters, one of them fell, either by his own awkwardness or by Pettipher's. I picked it up and gave it to him, address upwards. The Squire saw it.

"Why, that's the same handwriting that puzzled me," cried he, speaking on the impulse of the moment. "It seemed familiar to me, but I could not remember where I had seen it. It's a ship letter, as was the other."

Nash laughed—a lame kind of laugh—and put both letters into his pocket. "It comes from a chum of mine that I picked up over yonder," said he to the Squire, nodding his head towards where the sea might be supposed to lie. "I don't think you could ever have been familiar with it."

They went away to talk of business, leaving me alone. Mrs. Nash Caromel came in with her baby. She wore a white dress and light green ribbons, a lace cap half shading her bright hair. Uncommonly pretty she looked—but I did not like her.

"Is it you, Johnny Ludlow?" said she, pausing a moment at the door, and then holding out her hand. "I thought my husband was here alone."

"He is gone into the library with the Squire."

"Sit down. Have you seen my baby before? Is he not a beauty?"

It was a nice little fellow, with fat arms and blue knitted shoes, a good deal like Nash. They had named him Duncan, after some relative of hers, and the result was that he was never called anything but "Dun." Mrs. Caromel was telling me that she had "short-coated" him early, as it was hot weather, when the others appeared, and the Squire marched me off.

"Johnny," said he, thoughtfully, as we went along, "how curiously Nash Caromel is altered!"

"He seems rather—down, sir," I answered, hesitating for a word.

"Down!" echoed the Squire, slightingly; "it's more than that. He seems lost."

"Lost, sir?"

"His mind does. When I told him what I had come about: that it was time, and long ago, too, that my interest was paid, he stared at me more like a lunatic than a farmer—as if he had forgotten all about it, interest, and money, and all. When his wits came to him, he said it ought to have been paid, and he'd see Nave about it. Nave's his father-in-law, Johnny, and I suppose will take care of his interests; but I know I'd as soon entrust my affairs to Old Scratch as to him."

The Squire had his interest paid. The next news we heard was that Caromel's Farm was about to give an entertainment on a grand scale; an afternoon fête out-of-doors, with a sumptuous cold collation that you might call by what name you liked—dinner, tea, or supper—in the evening. An invitation printed on a square card came to us, which we all crowded round Mrs. Todhetley to look at. Cards had not come much into fashion then, except for public ceremonies, such as the Mayor's Feast at Worcester. In our part of the world we were still content to write our invitations on note-paper.

The mother would not go. She did not care for fêtes, she said to us. In point of fact she did not like Mrs. Nash Caromel any better than she had liked Charlotte Nave, and she had never believed in the cow. So she sent a civil note of excuse for herself. The Squire accepted, after some hesitation. He and the Caromels had been friends for so many years that he did not care to put the slight of a refusal upon Nash; besides, he liked parties, if they were jolly.

But now, would any rational being believe that Mrs. Nash had the cheek to send an invitation to Mrs. Tinkle and her son Henry? It was what Harry Tinkle called it—cheek. When poor Mrs. Tinkle broke the red seal of the huge envelope, and read the card of invitation, from Mr. and Mrs. Caromel, her eyes were dim.

"I think they must have sent it as a cruel joke," remarked Mrs. Tinkle, meeting the Squire a day or two before the fête. "She has never spoken to me in her life. When we pass each other she picks up her skirts as if they were too good to touch mine. Once she laughed at me, rudely."

"Don't believe she knows any better," cried the Squire in his hot partisanship. "Her skirts were not fit to touch your own Charlotte's."

"Oh, Charlotte! poor Charlotte!" cried Mrs. Tinkle, losing her equanimity. "I wish I could hear the particulars of her last moments," she went on, brushing away the tears. "If Mr. Caromel has had details—and that letter, telling of her death, promised them, you know—he does not disclose them to me."

"Why don't you write a note and ask him, Mrs. Tinkle?"

"I hardly know why," she answered. "I think he cannot have heard, or he would surely tell me; he is not bad-hearted."

"No, only too easy; swayed by anybody that may be at his elbow for the time being," concluded the Squire. "Nash Caromel is one of those people who need to be kept in leading-strings all their lives. Good-morning."

It was a fête worth going to. The afternoon as sunny a one as ever August turned out, and the company gay, if not numerous. Only a sprinkling of ladies could be seen; but amongst them was Miles Caromel's widow, with her four daughters. Being women of consideration, deserving the respect of the world, their presence went for much, and Mrs. Nash had reason to thank them. They scorned and despised her in their hearts, but they countenanced her for the sake of the honour of the Caromels.

Archery, dancing, promenading, and talking took up the afternoon, and then came the banquet. Altogether it must have cost Caromel's Farm a tidy sum.

"It is well for you to be able to afford this," cried the Squire confidentially to Nash, as they stood together in one of the shady paths beyond the light of the coloured lanterns, when the evening was drawing to an end. "Miles would never have done it."

"Oh, I don't know—it's no harm once in a way," answered Nash, who had exerted himself wonderfully, and finished up by drinking his share of wine. "Miles had his ways, and I have mine."

"All right: it is your own affair. But I wouldn't have done one thing, my good friend—sent an invitation to your mother-in-law."

"What mother-in-law?" asked Nash, staring.

"Your ex-mother-in-law, I ought to have said—Mrs. Tinkle. I wouldn't have done it, Caromel, under the circumstances. It pained her."

"But who did send her an invitation? Is it likely? I don't know what you are talking about, Squire."

"Oh, that's it, is it?" returned the Squire, perceiving that the act was madam's and not his. "Have you ever had those particulars of Charlotte's death?"

Nash Caromel's face changed from red to a deadly pallor: the question unnerved him—took his wits out of him.

"The particulars of Charlotte's death," he stammered, looking all abroad. "What particulars?"

"Why, those promised you by the man who wrote from San Francisco—Munn, was his name? Charlotte's diary, and letters, and things, that he was sending off to New York."

"Oh—ay—I remember," answered Nash, pulling his senses together. "No, they have not come."

"Been lost on the way, do you suppose? What a pity!"

"They may have been. I have not had them."

Nash Caromel walked straight away with the last words. Either to get rid of the subject, or to join some people who had just then crossed the top of the path.

"Caromel does not like talking of her: I can see that, Johnny," remarked the Squire to me later. "I don't believe he'd have done as he did, but for this second Charlotte throwing her wiles across his path. He fell into the snare and his conscience pricks him."

"I dare say, sir, it will come right with time. She is very pretty."

"Yes, most crooked things come straight with time," assented the Squire. "Perhaps this one will."

Would it, though!

The weeks and the months went on. Caromel's Farm seemed to prosper, its mistress being a most active manager, ruling with an apparently soft will, but one firm as iron; and little Dun grew to be about fifteen months old. The cow might have behaved ungenteelly to him, as Miss Bailey's ghost says to Captain Smith, but it had not hurt the little fellow, or his stout legs either, which began now to be running him into all kinds of mischief. And so the time came round again to August—just a year after the fête, and nearly twenty-two months after Nash's second marriage.

One evening, Tod being out and Mrs. Todhetley in the nursery, I was alone with the Squire in the twilight. The great harvest moon was rising behind the trees; and the Squire, talking of some parish grievance that he had heard of from old Jones the constable, let it rise: while I was wishing he would call for lights that I might get on with "The Old English Baron," which I was reading for about the seventeenth time.

"And you see, Johnny, if Jones had been firm, as I told him this afternoon, and taken the fellow up, instead of letting him slope off and be lost, the poachers— Who's this coming in, lad?"

The Squire had caught sight of some one turning to the door from the covered path. I saw the fag-end of a petticoat.

"I think it must be Mrs. Scott, sir. The mother said she had promised to come over one of these first evenings."

"Ay," said the Squire. "Open the door for her, Johnny."

I had the front-door open in a twinkling, and saw a lady with a travelling-cloak on her arm. But she bore no resemblance to Mrs. Scott.

"Is Mr. Todhetley at home?"

The soft voice gave me a thrill and a shock, though years had elapsed since I heard it. A confused doubt came rushing over me; a perplexing question well-nigh passed my lips: "Is it a living woman or a dead one?" For there, before me, stood Nash Caromel's dead wife, Charlotte the First.

CHAPTER X

CHARLOTTE AND CHARLOTTE

I

People are apt to say, when telling of a surprise, that a feather would have knocked them down. I nearly fell without the feather and without the touch. To see a dead woman standing straight up before me, and to hear her say "How are you, and is the Squire at home?" might have upset the balance of a giant.

But I could not be mistaken. There, waiting at the front-door to come in, her face within an inch of mine, was Nash Caromel's first wife, Charlotte Tinkle; who for some two years now had been looked upon as dead and buried over in California.

"Is Mr. Todhetley at home!" she repeated. "And can I see him?"

"Yes," I answered, coming partially out of my bewilderment. "Do you mind staying here just a minute, while I tell him?"

For, to hand in a dead woman, might take him aback, as it had taken me. The pater stood bolt upright, waiting for Mrs. Scott (as he had supposed it to be) to enter.

"It is not Mrs. Scott," I whispered, shutting the door and going close up to him. "It—it is some one else. I hardly like to tell you, sir; she may give you a fright."

"Why, what does the lad mean?—what are you making a mystery of now, Johnny?" cried he, staring at me. "Give me a fright! I should like to see any woman give me that. Is it Mrs. Scott, or is it not?"

"It is some one we thought dead, sir."

"Now, Johnny, don't be a muff. Somebody you thought dead! What on earth's come to you, lad? Speak out!"

"It is Nash Caromel's first wife, sir: Charlotte Tinkle."

The pater gazed at me as a man bereft of reason. I don't believe he knew whether he stood on his head or his heels. "Charlotte Tinkle!" he exclaimed, backing against the curtain. "What, come to life, Johnny?"

"Yes, sir, and she wants to see you. Perhaps she has never been dead."

"Bless my heart and mind! Bring her in."

The first thing Charlotte the First did when she came in and the Squire clasped her by her two hands, was to burst into a fit of sobbing. Some wine stood on the sideboard; the Squire poured her out a glass, and she untied the strings of her bonnet as she sat down.

"If I might take it off for a minute?" she said. "I have had it on all the way from Liverpool."

"Do so, my dear. Goodness me! I think I must be in a dream. And so you are not dead!"

"Yes, I knew it was what you must have all been thinking," she answered, stifling her sobs. "Poor Nash!—what a dreadful thing it is! I cannot imagine how the misconception can have arisen."

"What misconception?" asked the pater, whose wits, once gone a wool-gathering, rarely came back in a hurry.

"That I had died."

"Why, that friend of yours with whom you were staying—Bunn—Munn—which was it, Johnny?—wrote to tell your husband so."

Mrs. Nash Caromel, sitting there in the twilight, her brown hair as smooth as ever and her eyes as meek, looked at the Squire in surprise.

"Oh no, that could not have been; Mr. Munn would not be likely to write anything of the sort. Impossible."

"But, my dear lady, I read the letter. Your husband brought it to me as soon as it reached him. You remained at San Francisco, very ill after Nash's departure, and you got no better, and died at last of low fever."

She shook her head. "I was very poorly indeed when Nash left, but I grew better shortly. I had no low fever, and I certainly did not die."

"Then why did Munn write it?"

"He did not write it. He could not have written it. I am quite certain of that. He and his wife are my very good and dear friends, and most estimable people."

"The letter certainly came to your husband," persisted the Squire. "I read it with my own eyes. It was dated San Francisco, and signed Francis Munn."

"Then it was a forgery. But why any one should have written it, or troubled themselves about me and my husband at all, I cannot imagine."

"And then, Nash—Nash— Good gracious, what a complication!" cried the Squire, breaking off what he meant to say, as the thought of Charlotte Nave crossed his mind.

"I know," she quietly put in: "Nash has married again."

It was a complication, and no mistake, all things considered. The Squire rubbed up his hair and deliberated, and then bethought himself that it might be as well to keep the servants out of the room. So I went to tell old Thomas that the master was particularly engaged with a friend, and no one was to come in unless rung for. Then I ran upstairs to whisper the news to the mother—and it pretty nearly sent her into a fit of hysterics.

Charlotte Caromel was entering on her history to the Squire when I got back. "Yes," she said, "I and my husband went to California, having found little luck in America. Nash made one or two ventures there also, but nothing seemed to succeed; not as well even as it did in America, and he resolved to go back there, and try at something or other again. He sailed for New York, leaving me in San Francisco with

Francis Munn and his wife; for I had been ill, and was not strong enough for the tedious voyage. The Munns kept a dry-goods store at San Francisco, and—"

"A dry-goods store!" interrupted the Squire.

"Yes. You cannot afford to be fastidious over there; and to be in trade is looked upon as an honour, rather than the contrary. Francis Munn was the youngest son of a country gentleman in England; he went to California to make his fortune at anything that might turn up; and it ended in his marrying and keeping a store. They made plenty of money, and were very kind to me and Nash. Well, Nash started for New York, leaving me with them, and he wrote to me soon after his arrival there. Things were looking gloomy in the States, he said, and he felt inclined to take a run over to England, and ask his brother Miles to help him with some money. I wrote back a letter in duplicate, addressing one to the agents' in New York, the other to Caromel's Farm—not knowing, you perceive, in which place he might be. No answer reached me—but people think little of the safety of letters out there, so many seem to miscarry. We fancied Nash might be coming back to San Francisco and did not trouble himself to write: like me, he is not much of a scribe. But the months went on, and he did not come; he neither came nor wrote."

"What did you think hindered him?"

"We did not know what to think—except, as I say, that the letters had miscarried. One day Mr. Munn brought in a file of English newspapers for me and his wife to read: and in one of them I saw an announcement that puzzled me greatly—the marriage of one Nash Caromel, of Caromel's Farm, to Charlotte Nave. Just at first it startled me; I own that; but I felt so sure it could not be my Nash, my husband, that I remained only puzzled to know what Nash Caromel it could be."

"There is only one Nash Caromel," growled the Squire, half inclined to tell her she was a simpleton—taking things in this equable way.

"I only knew of him; but I thought he must have some relative, a cousin perhaps, of the same name, of whom I had not heard. However," continued Charlotte, "I wrote then to Caromel's Farm, telling Nash what we had read, and asking him what it meant, and where he was. But that letter shared the fate of the former one, and obtained no reply. In the course of time we saw another announcement—The wife of Nash Caromel of a son. Still I did not believe it could be my Nash, but I could see that Mr. Munn did believe it was. At least he thought there was something strange about it all, especially our not hearing from Nash: and at length I determined to come home and see about it."

"You must have been a long time coming," remarked the Squire. "The child is fifteen months old."

"But you must remember that often we did not get news until six months after its date. And I chose a most unfortunate route—overland from California to New York."

"What on earth— Why, people are sometimes a twelvemonth or so doing that!" cried the Squire. "There are rocky mountains to scale, as I've heard and read, and Red Indians to encounter, and all sorts of horrors. Those who undertake it travel in bands, do they not? and are called pilgrims, and some of them don't get to the end of the journey alive."

"True," she sighed. "I would never have attempted it had I known what it would be: but I did so dread the sea. Several of us were laid up midway, and had to be left behind at a small settlement: one or two died. It was a long, long time, and only after surmounting great discomforts and difficulties, we reached New York."

"Well?" said the Squire. It must be remembered that they were speaking of days now gone by, when the journey was just what she described it.

"I could hear nothing of my husband in New York," she resumed, "except that Abraham Whitter believed him to be at home here. I took the steamer for Liverpool, landed at dawn this morning, and came on by rail. And I find it is my husband who is married. And what am I to do?"

She melted away into tears again. The Squire told her that she must present herself at the farm; she was its legal mistress, and Nash Caromel's true wife. But she shook her head at this: she wouldn't bring any such trouble upon Nash for the world, as to show him suddenly that she was living. What he had done he must have done unwittingly, she said, believing her to be dead, and he ought not to suffer for it more than could be helped. Which was a lenient way of reasoning that put the Squire's temper up.

"He deserves no quarter, ma'am, and I will not give it him if you do. Within a week of the time he heard of your death he went and took that Charlotte Nave. Though I expect it was she who took him—brazen hussy! And I am glad you have come to put her out!"

But, nothing would induce Charlotte the First to assume this view, or to admit that blame could attach to Nash. Once he had lost her by death, he had a right to marry again, she contended. As to the haste— well, she had been dead (as he supposed) a great many months when he heard of it, and that should be considered. The Squire exploded, and walked about the room, and rubbed his hair the wrong way, and thought her no better than an imbecile.

Mrs. Todhetley came in, and there was a little scene. Charlotte declined our offer of a bed and refreshment, saying she would like to go to her mother's for the night: she felt that she should be received gladly, though they had parted in anger and had held no communication with one another since.

Gladly? ay, joyfully. Little doubt of that. So the Squire put on his hat, and she her bonnet, and away they started, and I with them.

We took the lonely path across the fields: her appearance might have raised a stir in the highway. Charlotte was but little altered, and would have been recognized at once. And I have no space to tell of the scene at Mrs. Tinkle's, which was as good as a play, or of the way they rushed into one another's arms.

"Johnny, there's something on my mind," said the Squire in a low tone as we were going back towards home: and he was looking grave and silent as a judge. "Do you remember those two foreign letters we chanced to see of Nash Caromel's, with the odd handwriting, all quavers and tails?"

"Yes, I do, sir. They were ship letters."

"Well, lad, a very ugly suspicion has come into my head, and I can't drive it away. I believe those two letters were from Charlotte—the two she speaks of—I believe the handwriting which puzzled me was hers. Now, if so, Nash went to the altar with that other Charlotte, knowing this one was alive: for the first letter came the day before the marriage."

I did not answer. But I remembered what I had overheard Nave the lawyer say to Nash Caromel: "You must marry her: where there's a will there's a way"—or words to that effect. Had Nave concocted the letters which pretended to tell of Mrs. Nash Caromel's death, and got them posted to Nash from New York?

With the morning, the Squire was at Caromel's Farm. The old-fashioned low house, the sun shining on its quaint windows, looked still and quiet as he walked up to the front-door across the grass-plat, in the middle of which grew a fine mulberry-tree. The news of Charlotte's return, as he was soon to find, had travelled to it already; had spread to the village. For she had been recognized the night before on her arrival; and her boxes, left in charge of a porter, bore her full name, Mrs. Nash Caromel.

Nash stood in that little library of his in a state of agitation not to be described; he as good as confessed, when the Squire tackled him, that he had known his wife might have been alive, and that it was all Nave's doings. At least he suspected that the letter, telling of her death, might be a forgery.

"Anyway, you had a letter from her the day before you married, so you must have known it by that," cried the Squire; who had so much to do always with the Caromel family that he deemed it his duty to interfere. "What on earth could have possessed you?"

"I—was driven into a corner," gasped Nash.

"I'd be driven into fifty corners before I'd marry two wives," retorted the Squire. "And now, sir, what do you mean to do?"

"I can't tell," answered Nash.

"A pretty kettle of fish this is! What do you suppose your father would have said to it?"

"I'm sure I can't tell," repeated Nash helplessly, biting his lips to get some life into them.

"And what's the matter with your hands that they are so hot and white?"

Nash glanced at his hands, and hid them away in his pockets. He looked like a man consumed by inward fever.

"I have not been over well for some time past," said he.

"No wonder—with the consciousness of this discovery hanging over your head! It might have sent some men into their graves."

Nash drummed upon the window pane. What in the world to do, what to say, evidently he knew not.

"You must put away this Jez—this lady," went on the Squire. "It was she who bewitched you; ay, and set herself out to do it, as all the parish saw. Let her go back to her father: you might make some provision for her: and instal your wife here in her proper place. Poor thing! she is so meek and patient! She won't hear a word said against you; thinks you are a saint. I think you a scoundrel, Nash: and I tell you so to your face."

The door had slowly opened; somebody, who had been outside, listening, put in her head. A very pretty head, and that's the truth, surmounting a fashionable morning costume of rose-coloured muslin, all flounces and furbelows. It was Charlotte the Second. The Squire had called her a brazen hussy behind her back; he had much ado this morning not to call her so to her face.

"What's that I hear you saying to my husband, Mr. Todhetley—that he should discard me and admit that creature here! How dare you bring your pernicious counsels into this house?"

"Why, bless my heart, he is her husband, madam; he is not yours. You'd not stay here yourself, surely!"

"This is my home, and he is my husband, and my child is his heir; and that woman may go back over the seas whence she came. Is it not so, Nash? Tell him."

She put her hand on Nash's shoulder, and he tried to get out something or other in obedience to her. He was as much under her finger and thumb as Punch in the street is under the showman's. The Squire went into a purple heat.

"You married him by craft, madam—as I believe from my very soul: you married him, knowing, you and your father also, that his wife was alive. He knew it, too. The motive must have been one of urgency, I should say, but I've nothing to do with that—"

"Nor with any other business of ours," she answered with a brazen face.

"This business is mine, and all Church Dykely's," flashed the Squire. "It is public property. And now, I ask you both, what you mean to do in this dilemma you have brought upon yourselves? His wife is waiting to come in, and you cannot keep her out."

"She shall never come in; I tell you that," flashed Charlotte the Second. "She sent word to him that she was dead, and she must abide by it; from that time she was dead to him, dead for ever. Mr. Caromel married me equally in the eyes of the world: and here I shall stay with him, his true and lawful wife."

The Squire rubbed his face; the torrent of words and the heat made it glisten.

"Stay here, would you, madam! What luck do you suppose would come of that?"

"Luck! I have quite as much luck as I require. Nash, why do you not request this—this gentleman to leave us?"

"Why, he dare not keep you here," cried the Squire, passing over the last compliment. "He would be prosecuted for—you know what."

"Let him be prosecuted! Let the wicked woman do her worst. Let her bring an action, and we'll defend it. I have more right to him than she has. Mr. Caromel, do you wish to keep up this interview until night?"

"Perhaps you had better go now, Squire," put in the man pleadingly. "I—I will consult Nave, and see what's to be done. She may like to go back to California, to the Munns; the climate suited her: and—and an income might be arranged."

This put the finishing stroke to the Squire's temper. He flung out of the room with a few unorthodox words, and came home in a tantrum.

We had had times of commotion at Church Dykely before, but this affair capped all. The one Mrs. Nash Caromel waiting to go into her house, and the other Mrs. Nash Caromel refusing to go out of it to make room for her. The Squire was right when saying it was public property: the public made it theirs. Tongues pitched into Nash Caromel in the fields and in the road: but some few of us pitied him, thinking what on earth we could do ourselves in a like position. While old Jones the constable stalked briskly about, expecting to get a warrant for taking up the master of Caromel's Farm.

But the great drawback to instituting legal proceedings lay with Mrs. Nash Caromel the First. She declined to prosecute. Her husband might refuse to receive her; might hold himself aloof from her; might keep his second wife by his side; but she would never hurt a hair of his head. Heaven might bring things round in its own good time, she said; meanwhile she would submit—and bear.

And she held to this, driving indignant men distracted. They argued, they persuaded, they remonstrated; it was said that one or two strong-minded ones swore. All the same. She stayed on at her mother's, and would neither injure her husband herself, nor let her family injure him. Henry Tinkle, her brother, chanced to be from home (as he was when she had run away to be married), or he might have acted in spite of her. And, when this state of things had continued for two or three weeks, the world began to call it a "crying scandal." As to Nash Caromel, he did not show his face abroad.

"Not a day longer shall the fellow retain my money," said the pater, speaking of the twelve hundred pounds he had lent to Nash: and in fact the term it had been lent for was already up. But it is easier to make such a threat than to enforce it; and it is not everybody who can extract twelve hundred pounds at will from uncertain coffers. Any way the Squire found he could not. He wrote to Nash, demanding its return; and he wrote to Nave.

Nash did not answer him at all. Nave's clerk sent a semi-insolent letter, saying Mr. Caromel should be communicated with when occasion offered. The Squire wrote in a rage to his lawyer at Worcester, bidding him enforce the repayment.

"You two lads can take the letter to the post," said he.

But we had not got many yards from home when we heard the Squire coming after us. We all walked into Church Dykely together; and close to the post-office, which was at Dame Chad's shop, we met Duffham. Of course the Squire, who could not keep anything in had he been bribed to do it, told Duffham what steps he was about to take.

"Going to enforce payment," nodded Duffham. "The man deserves no quarter. But he is ill."

"Serve him right. What's the matter with him?"

"Nervous fever. Has fretted or frightened himself into it. Report says that he is very ill indeed."

"Don't you attend him?"

"Not I. I did not please madam at the time the boy was born—would not give in to some of her whims and fancies. They have called in that new doctor who has settled in the next parish, young Bluck."

"Why, he is no better than an apothecary's boy, that young Bluck! Caromel can't be very ill, if they have him."

"So ill, that, as I have just heard, he is in great danger—likely to die," replied Duffham, tapping his cane against the ledge of Dame Chad's window. "Bluck's young, but he is clever."

"Bless my heart! Likely to die! What, Nash Caromel! Here, you lads, if that's it, I won't annoy him just now about the money, so don't post the letter."

"It is posted," said Tod. "I have just put it in."

"Go in and explain to Dame Chad, and get it out again. Or, stay; the letter can go, and I'll write and say it's not to be acted on until he is well again. Nervous fever! I'm afraid his conscience has been pricking him."

"I hope it has," said Duffham.

II

A few days went on. Nash Caromel lay in the greatest danger. Nave was at the farm day and night. A physician was called in from a distance to aid young Bluck; but it was understood that there remained very little hope of recovery. We began to feel sorry for Nash and to excuse his offences, the Squire especially. It was all that strong-minded young woman's doings, said he; she had drawn him into her toils, and he had not had the pluck, first or last, to escape from them.

But a change for the better took place; Nash passed the crisis, and would probably, with care, recover. I think every one felt glad; one does not wish a fellow quite to die, though he has misinterpreted the laws on the ticklish subject of matrimony. And the Squire felt vexed later when he learned that his lawyer had disregarded his countermanding letter and sent a peremptory threat to Nash of enforcing instant proceedings, unless the money was repaid forthwith. That was not the only threat conveyed to Caromel's Farm. Harry Tinkle returned; and, despite his sister's protestations, took the matter into his own hands, and applied for the warrant that had been so much talked about. As soon as Nash Caromel could leave his bed, he would be taken before the magistrates.

Soon a morning came that we did not forget in a hurry. While dressing with the window open to the white flowers of the trailing jessamine and the sweet perfume of the roses, blooming in the warm September air, Tod came in, fastening his braces.

"I say, Johnny, here's the jolliest lark! The pater—"

And what the lark was, I don't know to this day. At that moment the passing-bell tolled out—three times three; its succession of quick strokes following it. The wind blew in our direction from the church, and it sounded almost as though it were in the room.

"Who can be dead?" cried Tod, stretching his neck out at the window to listen. "Was any one ill, Jenkins?" he called to the head-gardener, then coming up the path with a barrow; "do you know who that bell's tolling for?"

"It's for Mr. Caromel," answered Jenkins.

"What?" shouted Tod.

"It's tolling for Mr. Caromel, sir. He died in the night."

It was a shock to us all. The Squire, pocketing his indignation against madam and the Nave family in general, went over to the farm after breakfast, and saw Miss Gwendolen Nave, who was staying with her sister. They called her Gwinny.

"We heard that he was better—going on so well," gasped the Squire.

"So he was until a day or two ago," said Miss Gwinny, holding her handkerchief to her eyes. "Very well indeed until then—when it turned to typhus."

"Goodness bless me!" cried the Squire, an unpleasant feeling running through him. "Typhus!"

"Yes, I am sorry to say."

"Is it safe to be here? Safe for you all?"

"Of course it is a risk. We try not to be afraid, and have sent as many out of the house as we could. I and the old servant Grizzel alone remain with Mrs. Caromel. The baby has gone to papa's."

"Dear me, dear me! I was intending to ask to look at poor Nash; we have known each other always, you see. But, perhaps it would not be prudent."

"It would be very imprudent, Mr. Todhetley. The sickness was of the worst type; it might involve not only your own death, but that of others to whom you might in turn carry it. You have a wife and children, sir."

"Yes, yes, quite right," rejoined the Squire. "Poor Nash! How is—your sister?" He would not, even at that trying moment for them, call her Mrs. Caromel.

"Oh, she is very ill; shocked and grieved almost to death. For all we know, she has taken the fever and may follow her husband; she attended upon him to the last. I hope that woman, who came here to disturb the peace of a happy family, that Charlotte Tinkle, will reap the fruit of what she has sown, for it is all owing to her."

"People do mostly reap the fruit of their own actions, whether they are good or bad," observed the Squire to this, as he got up to leave. But he would not add what he thought—that it was another Charlotte who ought to reap what she had sown. And who appeared to be doing it.

"Did the poor fellow suffer much?"

"Not at the last," said Miss Gwinny. "His strength was gone, and he lay for many hours insensible. Up to yesterday evening we thought he might recover. Oh, it is a dreadful calamity!"

Indeed it was. The Squire came away echoing the words in his heart.

Three days later the funeral took place: it would not do to delay it longer. The Squire went to it: when a man was dead, he thought animosity should cease. Harry Tinkle would not go. Caromel, he said, had escaped him and the law, to which he had rendered himself amenable, and nobody might grumble at it, for it was the good pleasure of Heaven, but he would not show Caromel respect, dead or living.

All the parish seemed to have been bidden to the funeral. Some went, some did not go. It looked a regular crowd, winding down the lawn and down the avenue. Few ventured indoors; they preferred to assemble outside: for an exaggerated fear of Caromel's Farm and what might be caught in it, ran through the community. So, when the men came out of the house, staggering under the black velvet pall with its deep white border, followed by Lawyer Nave, the company fell up into line behind.

Little Dun would have been the legal heir to the property had there been no Charlotte the First. That complication stood in his way, and he could no more inherit it than I could. Under the peculiar circumstances there was no male heir living, and Nash Caromel, the last of his name, had the power to make a will. Whether he had done so, or not, was not known; but the question was set at rest after the return from the funeral. Nave had gone strutting next the coffin as chief mourner, and he now produced the will. Half-a-dozen gentlemen had entered, the Squire one of them.

It was executed, the will, all in due form, having been drawn up by a lawyer from a distance; not by Nave, who may have thought it as well to keep his fingers out of the pie. A few days after the return of Charlotte the First, when Nash first became ill, the strange lawyer was called in, and the will was made.

Caromel's Farm and every stick and stone upon it, and all other properties possessed by Nash, were bequeathed to the little boy, Duncan Nave (as it was worded), otherwise Duncan Nave Caromel. Not to him unconditionally, but to be placed in the hands of trustees for his ultimate benefit. The child's mother (called in the will Charlotte Nave, otherwise Charlotte Caromel) was to remain at the farm if she pleased, and to receive the yearly income derived from it for the mutual maintenance of herself and child. When the child should be twenty-one, he was to assume full possession, but his mother was at liberty to continue to have her home with him. In short, they took all; Charlotte Tinkle, nothing.

"It is a wicked will," cried one of the hearers when they came out from listening to it.

"And it won't prosper them; you see if it does," added the Squire. "She stands in the place of Charlotte Tinkle. The least Caromel could have done, was to divide the property between them."

So that was the apparent ending of the Caromel business, which had caused the scandal in our quiet place, and a very unjust ending it was. Charlotte Tinkle, who had not a sixpence of her own in the world, remained on with her mother. She would come to church in her widow's mourning, a grievous look of sorrow upon her meek face; people said she would never get over the cruelty of not having been sent for to say farewell to her husband when he was dying.

As for Charlotte Nave, she stayed on at the farm without let or hindrance, calling herself, as before, Mrs. Nash Caromel. She appeared at church once in a way; not often. Her widow's veil was deeper than the other widow's, and her goffered cap larger. Nobody took the fever: and Nave the lawyer sent back the Squire's twelve hundred pounds within a month of Nash's death. And that, I say, was the ending, as we all supposed, of the affair at Caromel's Farm.

But curious complications were destined to crop up yet.

III

Nash Caromel died in September. And in how short, or long, a time it was afterwards that a very startling report grew to be whispered, I cannot remember; but I think it must have been at the turn of winter. The two widows were deep in weeds as ever, but over Charlotte Nave a change had come. And I really think I had better call them in future Charlotte Tinkle and Charlotte Nave, or we may get in a fog between the two.

Charlotte Nave grew pale and thin. She ruled the farm, as before, with the deft hand of a capable woman, but her nature appeared to be changing, her high spirits to have flown for ever. Instead of filling the house with company, she secluded herself in it like a hermit, being scarcely ever seen abroad. Ill-natured people, quoting Shakespeare, said the thorns, which in her bosom lay, did prick and sting her.

It was reported that the fear of the fever had taken a haunting hold upon her. She could not get rid of it. Which was on-reasonable, as Nurse Picker phrased it; for if she'd ha' been to catch it, she'd ha' caught it at the time. It was not for herself alone she feared it, but for others, though she did fear it for herself still, very much indeed. An impression lay on her mind that the fever was not yet out of the house, and never would be out of it, and that any fresh person, coming in to reside, would be liable to take it. More than once she was heard to say she would give a great deal not to be tied to the place—but the farm could not get on without a head. Before Nash died, when it was known the disorder had turned to typhus, she had sent all the servants (except Grizzel) and little Dun out of the house. She would not let them come back to it. Dun stayed at the lawyer's; the servants in time got other situations. The gardener's wife went in by day to help old Grizzel with the work, and some of the out-door men lived in the bailiff's house. Nave let out one day that he had remonstrated with his daughter in vain. Some women are cowards in these matters; they can't help being so; and the inward fear, perpetually tormenting them, makes a havoc of their daily lives. But in this case the fear had grown to an exaggerated height. In short, not to mince the matter, it was suspected her brain, on that one point, was unhinged.

Miss Gwinny could not leave her. Another sister, Harriet Nave, had come to her father's house, to keep it and take care of little Dun. Dun was allowed to go into the grounds of the farm and to play under the mulberry-tree on the lawn; and once or twice on a wet day, it was said, his mother had taken him into the parlour that opened with glass-doors, but she never let him run the risk of going in farther. At last old Nave, as was reported, consulted a mad doctor about her, going all the way to Droitwich to do it.

But all this had nothing to do with the startling rumour I spoke of. Things were in this condition when it first arose. It was said that Nash Caromel "came again."

At first the whisper was not listened to, was ridiculed, laughed at: but when one or two credible witnesses protested they had seen him, people began to talk, and then to say there must be something in it.

A little matter that had occurred soon after the funeral, was remembered then. Nash Caromel had used to wear on his watch-chain a small gold locket with his own and his wife's hair in it. I mean his real wife. Mrs. Tinkle wrote a civil note to the mistress of Caromel's Farm asking that the locket might be restored to her daughter—whose property it in fact was. She did not receive any answer, and wrote again. The second letter was returned to Mrs. Tinkle in a blank envelope with a wide black border.

Upon this, Harry Tinkle took up the matter. Stretching a point for his sister, who was pining for the locket and Nash's bit of hair in it, for she possessed no memento at all of her husband, he called at the farm and saw the lady. Some hard words passed between them: she was contemptuously haughty; and he was full of inward indignation, not only at the general treatment accorded to his sister, but also at the unjust will. At last, stung by some sneering contumely she openly cast upon his sister, he retorted in her own coin—answering certain words of hers—

"I hope his ghost will haunt you, you false woman!" Meaning, you know, the ghost of the dead man.

People recalled these words of Harry Tinkle's now, and began to look upon them (spoken by one of the injured Tinkles) in the light of prophecy. What with this, and what with their private belief that Nash Caromel's conscience would hardly allow him to rest quietly in his grave, they thought it very likely that his ghost was haunting her, and only hoped it would not haunt the parish.

Was this the cause of the change apparent in her? Could it be that Nash Caromel's spirit returned to the house in which he died, and that she could not rest for it? Was this the true reason, and not the fever, why she kept the child and the servants out of the house?—lest they should be scared by the sight? Gossips shivered as they whispered to one another of these unearthly doubts, which soon grew into a belief. But you must understand that never a syllable had been heard from herself, or a hint given, that Caromel's Farm was troubled by anything of the kind; neither did she know, or was likely to hear, that it was talked of abroad. Meanwhile, as the time slipped on, every now and then something would occur to renew the report—that Nash Caromel had been seen.

One afternoon, during a ride, the Squire's horse fell lame. On his return he sent for Dobbs, the blacksmith and farrier. Dobbs promised to be over about six o'clock; he was obliged to go elsewhere first. When six o'clock struck, the Squire, naturally impatient, began to look out for Dobbs. And if he sent Thomas out of the room once during dinner, to see whether the man had arrived, he sent him half-a-dozen times.

Seven o'clock, and no Dobbs. The pater was in a fume; he did nothing but walk to and fro between the house and the stables, and call Dobbs names as he looked out for him. At last, there came a rush across the fold-yard, and Dobbs appeared, his face looking very peculiar, and his hair standing up in affright, like a porcupine's quills.

"Why, what on earth has taken you?" began the Squire, surprised out of the reproach that had been upon his tongue.

"I don't know what has taken me," gasped Dobbs. "Except that I've seen Mr. Nash Caromel."

"What?" roared the Squire, his surprise changing to anger.

"As true as I'm a living man, I've seen him, sir," persisted Dobbs, wiping his face with a blue cotton handkerchief. "I've seen his shadow."

"Seen the Dickens!" retorted the Squire, slightingly. "One would think he was after you, by the way you flew up here. I wonder you are not ashamed of yourself, Dobbs."

"Being later than I thought to be, sir, I took the field way; it's a bit shorter," went on Dobbs, attempting to explain. "In passing through that little copse at the back of Caromel's Farm, I met a curious-looking shadow of a figure that somehow startled me. May I never stir from this spot, sir, if it was not Caromel himself."

"You have been drinking, Dobbs."

"A strapping pace I was going at, knowing I was being waited for here," continued Dobbs, too much absorbed in his story to heed the sarcasm. "I never saw Mr. Nash Caromel plainer in his lifetime than I saw him then, sir. Drinking? No, that I had not been, Squire; the place where I went to is teetotal. It was up at the Glebe, and they don't have nothing stronger in their house than tea. They gave me two good cups of that."

"Tea plays some people worse tricks than drink, especially if it is green," observed the Squire: and I am bound to confess that Dobbs, apart from his state of fright, seemed as sober as we were. "I wouldn't confess myself a fool, Dobbs, if I were you."

Dobbs put out his brawny right arm. "Master," said he, with quite a solemn emphasis, "as true as that there moon's a-shining down upon us, I this night saw Nash Caromel. I should know him among a thousand. And I thought my heart would just ha' leaped out of me."

To hear this strong, matter-of-fact man assert this, with his sturdy frame and his practical common sense, sounded remarkable. Any one accustomed to seeing him in his forge, working away at his anvil, would never have believed it of him. Tod laughed. The Squire marched off to the stables with an impatient word. I followed with Dobbs.

"The idea of your believing in ghosts and shadows, Dobbs!"

"Me believe in 'em, Master Johnny! No more I did; I'd have scorned it. Why, do you remember that there stir, sir, about the ghost that was said to haunt Oxlip Dell? Lots of people went into fits over that, a'most lost their heads; but I laughed at it. Now, I never put credit in nothing of the kind; but I have seen Mr. Caromel's ghost to-night."

"Was it in white?"

"Bless your heart, sir, no. He was in a sort o' long-skirted dark cloak that seemed to wrap him well round; and his head was in something black. It might ha' been a cap; I don't know. And here we are at the stable, so I'll say no more: but I can't ever speak anything truer in my life than I've spoke this, sir."

All this passed. In spite of the blacksmith's superstitious assertion, made in the impulse of terror, there lay on his mind a feeling of shame that he should have betrayed fear to us (or what bordered upon it) in an unguarded moment; and this caused him to be silent to others. So the matter passed off without spreading further.

Several weeks later, it cropped up again. Francis Radcliffe (if the reader has not forgotten him, and who had not long before been delivered out of his brother's hands at Sandstone Torr) was passing along at the back of Caromel's Farm, when he saw a figure that bore an extraordinary resemblance to Nash Caromel. The Squire laughed well when told of it, and Radcliffe laughed too. "But," said he, "had Nash Caromel not been dead, I could have sworn it was he, or his shadow, before any justice of the peace."

His shadow! The same word that Dobbs had used. Francis Radcliffe told this story everywhere, and it caused no little excitement.

"What does this silly rumour mean—about Nash Caromel being seen?" demanded the Squire one day when he met Nave, and condescended to stop to speak to him.

And Nave, hearing the question, turned quite blue: the pater told us so when he came home. Just as though Nave saw the apparition before him then, and was frightened at it.

"The rumour is infamous," he answered, biting his cold lips to keep down his passion. "Infamous and ridiculous both. Emanating from idle fools. I think, sir, as a magistrate, you might order these people before you and punish them."

"Punish people for thinking they see Caromel's ghost!" retorted the Squire. "Bless my heart! What an ignorant man (for a lawyer) you must be! No act has been passed against seeing ghosts. But I'd like to know what gives rise to the fancy about Caromel."

The rumour did not die away. How could it, when from time to time the thing continued to be seen? It frightened Mary Standish into a fit. Going to Caromel's Farm one night to beg grace for something or other that her ill-doing husband, Jim, then working on the farm, had done or left undone, she came upon a wonderfully thin man standing in the nook by the dairy window, and took him to be the bailiff, who was himself no better than a walking lamp-post. "If you please, sir," she was beginning, thinking to have it out with him instead of Mrs. Caromel, "if you please, sir—"

When, upon looking into his pale, stony face, she saw the late master. He vanished into air or into the wall, and down fell Mary Standish in a fainting-fit. The parish grew uneasy at all this—and wondered what had been done to Nash, or what he had done, that he could not rest.

One night I was coming, with Tod, across from Mrs. Scott's, who lived beyond Hyde Stockhausem's. We took the field way from Church Dykely, as being the shortest route, and that led us through the copse at the back of Caromel's Farm. It was a very light night, though not moonlight; and we walked on at a good rate, talking of a frightful scrape Sam Scott had got into, and which he was afraid to tell his mother of. All in a moment, just in the middle of the copse, we came upon a man standing amongst the trees, his face towards us. Tod turned and I turned; and we both saw Nash Caromel. Now, of course, you will laugh. As the Squire did when we got home (in a white heat) and told him: and he called us a couple of poltroons. But, if ever I saw the face of Nash Caromel, I saw it then; and if ever I saw a figure that might be called a shadow, it was his.

"Fine gentlemen, both of you!" scoffed the Squire. "Clear and sensible! Seen a ghost, have you, and confess to it! Ho, ho! Running through the back copse, you come upon somebody that you must take for an apparition! Ha, ha! Nice young cowards! I'd write an account of it to the Worcester papers if I were you. A ghost, with glaring eyes and a white face! Death's head upon a mopstick, lads! I shouldn't have wondered at Johnny; but I do wonder at you, Joe," concluded the Squire, smoothing down.

"I am no more afraid of ghosts than you are, father," quietly answered Joe. "I was not afraid when we saw—what we did see; I can't answer for Johnny. But I do declare, with all my senses (which you are pleased to disparage) about me, that it was the form and face of Nash Caromel, and that 'it' (whatever it might be) seemed to vanish from our sight as we looked."

"Johnny calls it a shadow," mocked the Squire, amiably.

"It looked shadowy," said Tod.

"A tree-trunk, I dare be bound, lads, nothing else," nodded the Squire. And you might as well have tried to make an impression on a post.

IV

September came in: which made it a year since Nash died. And on one of its bright days, when the sun was high, and the blue sky cloudless, Church Dykely had a stir given it in the sight of the mistress of Caromel's Farm. She and her father were in a gig together, driving off on the Worcester road: and it was so very rare a thing to see her abroad now, that folks ran to their windows and doors to stare. Her golden hair, what could be seen of it for her smart blue parasol, shone in the sunlight; but her face looked white and thin through the black crape veil.

"Just like a woman who gets disturbed o' nights," pronounced Sam Rimmer, thinking of the ghostly presence that was believed to haunt the house.

Before that day's beautiful sun had gone down to light the inhabitants of the other hemisphere, ill-omened news reached Church Dykely. An accident had happened to the horse and gig. It was said that both Nave and his daughter were dreadfully injured; one of them nearly killed. Miss Gwinny, left at home to take care of Caromel's Farm, posted off to the scene of damage.

Holding Caromel's Farm in small respect now, the Squire yet chose to show himself neighbourly; and he rose up from his dinner to go there and inquire particulars. "You may come with me, lads, if you like," said he. Tod laughed.

"He's afraid of seeing Caromel," whispered he in my ear, as we took down our hats.

And, whether the Squire was afraid of it or not, he did see him. It was a lovely moonlight night, bright and clear as the day had been. Old Grizzel could not tell us much more of the accident than we had heard before; except that it was quite true there had been one, and that Miss Gwinny had gone. And, by the way Grizzel inwardly shook and shivered while she spoke, and turned her eyes to all corners in some desperate fear, one might have thought she had been pitched out of a gig herself.

We had left the door—it was the side-entrance—when the Squire turned back to put some last query to her. Tod and I went on. The path was narrow, the overhanging trees on either side obscured the moonlight, making it dark. Chancing to glance round, I noticed the Squire, at the other end of the path, come soberly after us. Suddenly he seemed to halt, to look sideways at the trees, and then he came on with a bound.

"Boys! Boys!" cried he, in a half-whisper, "come on. There's Caromel yonder."

And to see the pater's face in its steaming consternation, and to watch him rush on to the gate, was better than a play. Seen Caromel! It was not so long since he had mocked at us for saying it.

Through the gate went he, bolt into the arms of some unexpected figure, standing there. We peered at it in the uncertain lights cast by the trees, and made it out to be Dobbs, the blacksmith.

Dobbs, with a big coat on, hiding his shirt-sleeves and his leather apron: Dobbs standing as silent as the grave: arms folded, head bent: Dobbs in stockinged feet, without his shoes.

"Dobbs, my good fellow, what on earth do you put yourself in people's way for, standing stock-still like a Chinese image?" gasped the Squire. "Dobbs—why, you have no boots on."

"Hush!" breathed Dobbs, hardly above his breath. "I ask your pardon, Squire. Hush, please! There's something uncanny in this place; some ugly mystery. I mean to find it out if I can, sirs, and this is the third night I've come here on the watch. Hark!"

Sounds, as of a woman's voice weeping and wailing, reached us faintly from somewhere—down beyond the garden trees. The pater looked regularly flustered.

"Listen!" repeated Dobbs, raising his big hand to entreat for silence. "Yes, Squire; I don't know what the mystery is; but there is something wrong about the place, and I can't sleep o' nights for it. Please hearken, sirs."

The blacksmith was right. Wrong and mystery, such as the world does not often hear of, lay within Caromel's Farm. Curious mystery; wicked wrong. Leaning our arms on the gate, watching the moonlight flickering on the trees, we listened to Dobbs's whispered revelation. It made the Squire's hair stand on end.

CHAPTER XI

THE LAST OF THE CAROMELS

When a house is popularly allowed to be haunted, and its inmates grow thin and white and restless, it is not the best place in the world for children: and this was supposed by Church Dykely to be the reason why Mrs. Nash Caromel the Second had never allowed her child to come home since the death of its father. At first it was said that she would not risk having him lest he should catch the fever Nash had died of: but, when the weeks went on, and the months went on, and years (so far as could be seen) were likely to go on, and still the child was kept away, people put it down to the other disagreeable fact.

Any way, Mrs. Nash Caromel—or Charlotte Nave, as you please—did not have the boy home. Little Dun was kept at his grandfather's, Lawyer Nave; and Miss Harriet Nave took care of him: the other sister, Gwinny, remaining at Caromel's Farm. Towards the close of spring, the spring which followed the death of Nash, when Dun was about two years old, he caught whooping-cough and had it badly. In August he was sent for change of air to a farm called the Rill, on the other side of Pershore, Miss Harriet Nave taking the opportunity to go jaunting off elsewhere. The change of air did the child good, and he was growing strong quickly, when one night early in September croup attacked him, and he lay in great danger. News of it was sent to his mother in the morning. It drove her nearly wild with fear, and she set off for the Rill in a gig, her father driving it: as already spoken of. So rare was the sight of her now, for she kept indoors at Caromel's Farm as a snail keeps to its shell, that no wonder Church Dykely thought it an event, and talked of it all the day.

Mr. Nave and his daughter reached the Rill—which lay across country, somewhere between Pershore and Wyre—in the course of the morning, and found little Dun gasping with croup, and inhaling steam from a kettle. Moore told us there was nothing half so sweet in life as love's young dream; but to Charlotte Nave, otherwise Caromel, there was nothing sweet at all except this little Dun. He was the light of her existence; the apple of her eye, to put it poetically. She sat down by the bed-side, her pale face (so pale and thin to what it used to be) bent lovingly upon him, and wiping away the tears by stealth that came into her eyes. In the afternoon Dun was better; but the doctor would not say he was out of danger.

"If I could but stay here for the night! I can't bear to leave him," Charlotte snatched an opportunity to say to her father, when their friends, the farmer and his wife, were momentarily occupied.

"But you can't, you know," returned Lawyer Nave. "You must be home by sunset."

"By sunset? Nay, an hour after that would do."

"No, it will not do. Better be on the safe side."

"It seems cruel that I should have to leave him," she exclaimed, with a sob.

"Nonsense, Charlotte! The child will do as well without you as with you. You may see for yourself how much better he is. The farm cannot be left to itself at night: remember that. We must start in half-an-hour."

No more was said. Nave went to see about getting ready the gig; Charlotte, all down in the dumps, stayed with the little lad, and let him pull about as he would her golden hair, and drank her tea by his side. Mr. and Mrs. Smith (good hospitable people, who had stood by Charlotte Nave through good report and ill report, believing no ill of her) pressed her to stay all night, promising, however, that every care should be taken of Duncan, if she did not.

"My little darling must be a good child and keep warm in bed, and when mamma comes in the morning he will be nearly well," breathed Charlotte, showering tears and kisses upon him when the last moment had come. And, with that, she tore herself away.

"Such a pity that you should have to go!" said Mrs. Smith, stepping to the door with her. "I think Gwendolen and old Grizzel might have been left for one night: they'd not have run away, nor the house neither. Come over as soon as you can in the morning, my dear; and see if you can't make arrangements to stay a day or two."

They were starting from the back-door, as being the nearest and handiest; Nave, already in the gig, seemed in a rare hurry to be off. Mr. Smith helped Charlotte up: and away the lawyer drove, across the fold-yard, one of the farm-boys holding the outer gate open for them. The sun, getting down in the west, shone right in their eyes.

"Oh dear, I have left my parasol!" cried Charlotte, just as they reached the gate. "I must have it: my blue parasol!" And Nave, giving an angry growl to parasols in general, pulled the horse up.

"You need not get out, hindering time!" growled he. "Call out for it. Here, Smith! Mrs. Caromel has forgotten her blue parasol." But the farmer, then nearing the house, did not hear.

"I'll run for it, ma'am," said the lad. And he set off to do so, leaving the gate to itself. Charlotte, who had been rising to get out, looked back to watch him; the lawyer looked back to shout again, in his impatience, to Mr. Smith. Their faces were both turned from the side where the gate was, and they did not see what was about to happen.

The gate, swinging slowly and noiselessly forward, touched the horse, which had been standing sideways, his head turned to see what the stoppage might be about.

Touched him, and startled him. Bounding upwards, he tore forward down the narrow lane on which the gate opened; tried to scale a bank, and pitched the lawyer and Charlotte out of the gig.

The farmer, and as many of his people as could be gathered at the moment, came running down, some of them armed with pitchforks. Nave was groaning as he lay; Charlotte was insensible. Just at first they thought her dead. Both were carried back to the Rill on hurdles, and the doctor was sent for. After which, Mr. Smith started off a man on horseback to tell the ill-news of the accident at Caromel Farm.

Ill-news. No doubt a bad and distressing accident. But now, see how curiously the "power that shapes our ends" brings things about. But for that accident, the mystery and the wrong being played out at Caromel's Farm might never have had daylight thrown upon it. The accident, like a great many other accidents, must have been sent to this wise and good end. At least, so far as we, poor blind mortals that we all are, down here, might presume to judge.

The horseman, clattering in at a hard pace to Caromel's Farm, delivered to Miss Gwendolen Nave, and to Grizzel, the old family servant, the tidings he was charged with—improving upon them as a thing of course.

Lawyer Nave, he were groaning awful, all a-bleeding, and unable to move a limb. The young lady, she were dead; leastways, looked like it.

With a scream and a cry, Gwendolen gave orders for her own departure. Seeking the bailiff, she bade him drive her over in the tax-cart, there being no second gig.

"Now mind, Grizzel," she said, laying hold of the old woman's arm after flinging on her bonnet and shawl anyhow, "you will lock all the doors as soon as I am gone, and take out the keys. Do you hear?"

"I hear, Miss Gwinny. My will's good to do it: you know that."

"Take care that you do do it."

Fine tidings to go flying about Church Dykely in the twilight! Lawyer Nave half killed, his daughter quite. The news reached us at Dyke Manor; and Squire Todhetley, though holding Caromel's Farm in little estimation, thought it only neighbourly to walk over there and inquire how much was true, how much not. You remember what happened. That in leaving the farm after interviewing Grizzel, we found ourselves in contact with Dobbs the blacksmith. Dobbs standing stock-still, like a marble pillar, outside the gate under the dark, overhanging trees; Dobbs standing on the watch, in a stealthy, mysterious manner, without his boots.

"But what on earth are you here for, Dobbs?" reiterated the Squire. "Where are your boots?"

And all Dobbs did for answer, was to lay his hand respectfully on the Squire's coat-sleeve to begin with, so as to prevent his running away. Then he entered upon his whispered tale. Leaning our arms upon the low gate, we listened to it, and to the curious sound of weeping and wailing that stole faintly on our ears from amongst the garden trees. The scene altogether looked weird enough in the moonlight, flickering through the rustling leaves.

Dobbs, naturally an unbeliever in ghosts, had grown to think that this ghost, so long talked of, was no ghost at all, but some one got up to resemble one by Caromel's Farm, for some mysterious purpose of its own. Remembering his attack of fright, and resenting it excessively, Dobbs determined if possible to unearth the secret: and this was the third night he had come upon the watch.

"But why stand without your boots?" whispered the Squire, who could not get over the shoeless feet.

"That I may make no noise in running to pounce upon him, sir," Dobbs whispered back. "I take 'em off and hide 'em in the copse behind here. They be just at your back, Master Johnny."

"Pounce upon whom?" demanded the Squire. "Can't you speak plainly?"

"That's what I'd like to know," breathed Dobbs. "I feel nearly sure, Squire, that the—the thing looking like Nash Caromel is not Nash Caromel. Nor his ghost, either."

"I never saw two faces more alike, and I have just seen it now," put in the Squire. "At least, as much as a shadow can look like a face."

"Ay," assented Dobbs. "I'm as sure, sir, as I am of my own forge, that it is a likeness got up by Nave to scare us. And I'll eat the forge," added Dobbs with emphasis, "if there's not something worse than ghosts at Caromel's Farm—though I can't guess what it is."

"What a villain he must be: and Nave, too!" cried the Squire, rubbing his red nose, while Tod simply stared at the man. "But, look here, Dobbs—how could any man put on the face of Nash Caromel?"

"I don't know how he does it, Squire, or what he does, but I'm good to find out," returned the blacksmith. "And if—just hark there again, sirs!"

The same faint sounds of wailing, of entreaty in a woman's voice, rose again upon the air. Dobbs, with a gesture to ask for silence, went noiselessly down the dark path in his brown woollen stockings, that looked thick enough for boots. Tod, eager for any adventure, stole after him, and I brought up the rear. The Squire remained where he was, and held the gate open, expecting perhaps that we might want to make a rush through it as he had just done.

Two minutes more, and the mystery was solved. Near the house, under the shade of the closely intersecting trees, stood old Grizzel and the figure people had taken to be the ghost of Nash Caromel. It was Grizzel's voice we heard, full of piteous entreaty to him not to do something.

"Just for this night, master, for the love of Heaven! Don't do it, just this night that I'm left in charge! They've trusted me, you see!"

The words seemed to make no impression. Pushing her hands back, the figure was turning impatiently away, when Dobbs seized upon it.

But, in sheer astonishment, or perhaps in terror, Dobbs let go again to step backwards; and the prize might have escaped but for the strong arms of Tod. It was indeed Nash Caromel. Not his ghost, but himself.

Nash Caromel worn to the veriest shadow mortal eyes ever gazed upon. The Squire came up; we all went into the house together, and explanation ensued.

Nash had not died. When the fever, of which it was feared he would die, reached its crisis, he awoke to life, not to death. But, terrified at his position—the warrant, applied for by Henry Tinkle, being out against him—overwhelmed with a sense of shame, he had feigned death as the only chance of escaping disgrace and punishment. The first thought perhaps was Nave's; indeed there was no doubt of it—or his and his daughter's combined. They wanted to keep the income, you see. Any way, they carried the thought out, and had successfully contrived to deceive doctors, undertakers, and the world. Nash, weak as a rat, had got out of bed to watch his own funeral procession wind down the avenue.

And there, in the upper rooms of the house, he had since lived until now, old Grizzel sharing the secret. But a grievous complaint, partly brought on by uneasiness of mind, partly inherited from his father, who had died of it, had speedily attacked Nash, one for which there was no cure. It had worn him to a shadow.

He had walked in the garden sometimes. He had come out in the twilight of the evening or at night; he had now and then passed through the gate and crossed over to the copse; simply because to live entirely without fresh air, to remain inactive indoors, was intolerable to him. His wife and her sister did their best to prevent it. Nave came in the daytime and would blow him up by the hour together; but they could not always keep him in. At last they grew alarmed. For, when they attempted to use force, by locking the doors, he told them that unless he was allowed his way in this, he would declare himself to the world. Life could not have been a bed of roses for any of them.

To look at him, as he sat there to-night by the kitchen fire, his cheeks white and hollow, his sunken eyes encased in dark rims, and his thin lips on the shiver, you'd hardly have given him a week of life. A great pity sat in the blacksmith's face.

"Don't reproach yourself, Dobbs: it's the best thing that could have happened to me," spoke Nash Caromel, kindly. "I am not sure but I should have gone out this very night and declared myself. Grizzel thought it, and put herself into a paroxysm of fear. Nobody but myself knows the yearning to do it that has been upon me. You won't go and tell it out in the market-place, will you, Dobbs?"

"I'll not tell on't to a single soul, sir," said Dobbs, earnestly, standing straight in his brown stockings. "Nobody shall know on't from me. And I'm as glad as glad can be that you be alive and did not die in that fever."

"We are all safe and sure, Caromel; not a hint shall escape us," spoke the Squire from the midst of his astonishment.

"The first thing must be to get Duffham here."

"Duffham can't do any good; things have gone too far with me," said poor Nash. "Once this disorder lays regular hold of a man, there's no hope for him: you know that, Todhetley."

"Stuff!" said the pater. "I don't believe it has gone too far, only you've got moped here and think so. We'll have Duffham here at once. You boys can go for him."

"No," dissented Caromel. "Duffham may tell the tale abroad. I'd rather die in peace, if I can."

"Not he. Duffham! Why, you ought to know him better. Duffham will be as secret as ourselves. Do you suppose that he, a family doctor, has not many a weighty secret to keep? Come, be off, lads: and, mind, we trust you."

Nash Caromel sighed, and said no more. He had been wanting badly enough to see a friend or two, but not to be shown up to the parish. We went out with Dobbs, who rushed into the copse to find his shoes.

This discovery might never have ensued, I take it, had Charlotte Nave and the lawyer not been upset in the gig. They would have stood persistently in his light—perhaps have succeeded in locking him in by force! As it was, we had it all our own way.

"How could you lend yourself to so infamous a deception?" cried the Squire to old Grizzel, following her into the pantry to ask it, when she returned from bolting the door after us. "I'm not at all sure that you could not be punished for it. It's—it's a conspiracy. And you, of all people, old Grizzel, to forget the honour of the Caromels! Why, you lived with his father!—and with his brother. All these years!"

"And how could I tell again him when I was asked not to?" contended Grizzel, the tears dropping on to a tin saucepan she was rubbing out. "Master Nash was as dear to me as the others were. Could it be me to speak up and say he was not in the coffin, but only old things to make up weight! Could it be me to tell he was alive and hiding up aloft here, and so get him put in prison? No, sir; the good name of the Caromels was much to me, but Master Nash was more."

"Now, come, old woman, where's the use of crying like that? Well, yes; you have been faithful, and it's a great virtue. And—and there's a shilling or two for you."

"Have you been blowing her up?" asked Nash, as the Squire went back to him, and sat down on the other side the wide kitchen hearth, the fire throwing its glow upon the bricks, square and red and shining, and upon Nash Caromel's wan face, in which it was not very difficult to read death. He had put his out-of-door coat off, a long brown garment, and sat in a grey suit. Tho Squire's belief was that he wouldn't have minded getting into the fire itself; he sat there shivering and shaking, and seeming to have no warmth left in him. The room was well guarded from outer observation. The shutters were up, and there was not a chink in them.

"I have," said the Squire, in answer. "Told her she did not show much regard for the honour of the family—lending herself to such a deception!"

"Poor old Grizzel!" sighed Nash, with a half-smile. "She has lived upon thorns, fearing I should be discovered. As to the family honour, Todhetley, the less said about that the better."

"How could you do it, Caromel?"

"I don't know," answered Nash, with apathy, bringing his face closer to the blaze. "I let it be done, more than did it. All I did, or could do, was just to lie still in my bed. The fever had left me weaker than a child—"

"Did it really turn to typhus?" interrupted the Squire.

"No, it didn't. They said so to scare people away. I was weaker than a child," continued Nash, "both in mind and body. And when I grew stronger—what was done could not be undone. Not that I seek to defend or excuse myself. Don't think that."

"And, in the name of all that's marvellous, what could have put so monstrous an idea into their heads?" demanded the Squire, getting up to face the kitchen.

"Well, I have always fancied that business at Sandstone Torr did," replied Nash, who had no idea of reticence now, but spoke out as freely as you please. "It had come to light, you know, not long before. Stephen Radcliffe had hidden his brother in the old tower, passing him off to the world as dead; and so, I suppose, it was thought that I could be hidden and passed off as dead."

"But Stephen Radcliffe never got up a mock funeral. His tale was that Frank had died in London. You were bold people. What will Parson Holland say, when he comes to learn that he read the burial-service over a box of rubbish?"

"I don't know," was the helpless reiteration of poor Nash. "The trouble and worry of it altogether, the discomforts of my position, the constant, never-ceasing dread of discovery have—have been to me what you cannot realize. But for going out of the house at night and striding about in the fresh, free air, I should have become mad. It was a taste of freedom. Neither could I always confine myself to the walks in the garden; whether I would nor not, my feet would carry me beyond it and into the shaded copse."

"Frightening people who met you!"

"When I heard footsteps approach I hid myself—though not always quite in time. I was more put out at meeting people than they were at meeting me."

"I wonder your keepers here ever let you get out!" cried the Squire, musingly.

"They tried hard to keep me in: and generally succeeded. It was only by fits and starts I gained my way. They were afraid, you see, that I should carry out my threat of disclosing myself but for being yielded to now and then."

But the Squire did not get over the discovery. He strode about the large kitchen, rubbing his face, giving out sundry Bless my hearts! at intervals. The return to life of Charlotte Tinkle had been marvellous enough, but it was nothing to this.

Meanwhile we were on our road to Duffham's. Leaving Dobbs at his own forge, we rushed on, and found the doctor in his little parlour at supper; pickled eels and bread-and-cheese: the eels in the wide stone jar they were baked in—which was Nomy's way of serving pickled fish.

"Will you sit down and take some?" asked Duffham, pointing to the jar: out of which he took the pieces with a fork as he wanted them.

"I should like to, but there's no time for it," answered Tod, eyeing the jar wistfully.

Pickled eels are a favourite dish in our parts: and you don't often eat anything as good.

"Look here, Duffham," he went on: "we want you to go with us and see—see somebody: and to undertake not to tell tales out of school. The Squire has answered for it that you will not."

"See who?" asked Duffham, going on with his supper.

"A ghost," said Tod, grimly. "A dead man."

"What good can I do them?"

"Well, the man has come to life again. Not for long, though, I should say, judging by his looks. You are not to go and tell about it, mind."

"Tell what?"

"That he is alive, instead of being, as is supposed, under a gravestone in yonder churchyard. I am not sure but that you went to his funeral."

Tod's significant tone, half serious, half mocking, attracted Duffham's curiosity more even than the words. But he still went on with his eels.

"Who is it?"

"Nash Caromel. There. Don't fall off in a faint. Caromel has come to life."

Down went Duffham's fork. "Why—what on earth do you mean?"

"It is not a joke," said Tod. "Nash Caromel has been alive all this time, concealed in his house—just as Francis Radcliffe was concealed in the tower. The Squire is with him now—and he is very ill."

Duffham appealed to me. "Is this true, Johnny Ludlow?"

"Yes, sir, it is. We found him out to-night. He looks as if he were dying. Dobbs is sure he is. You never saw anything so like a ghost."

Leaving his eels now, calling out to old Nomy that she might take away the supper, Duffham came off with us at once. Dobbs ran up as we passed his forge, and went with us to the turning, talking eagerly.

"If you can cure him, Mr. Duffham, sir, I should take it as a great favour, like, showed to myself," spoke the blacksmith. "I'd not have pounced upon him for all the world, to give him pain, in the state he's in. He looks as if he were dying."

They were in the kitchen still, when Grizzel opened the door to us, the fire bigger and hotter than ever. The first thing Duffham did was to order Caromel to bed, and to have a good fire lighted in his room.

But there was no hope for Nash Caromel. The Squire told us so going home that night. Duffham thought about ten days more would see the end of him.

II

"And how have things gone during my short absence, Grizzel?" demanded Miss Gwinny Nave, alighting from the tax-cart the following morning, upon her return to Caromel's Farm.

"Oh, pretty well," answered Grizzel, who in her heart detested Miss Gwinny and all the Naves. "The master seems weaker. He have took to his bed, and got a fire in his room."

"When did he do that?"

"He came down last night after you went, Miss Gwinny, and sat over this here kitchen fire for ever so long. Then he went up to bed, and I lighted him a fire and took him up some hot arrowroot with a wine glass o' brandy in it. Shivering with cold, he was."

"And he has not got up this morning?"

"No; and he says he does not mean to get up. 'I've taken to my bed for good, Grizzel,' he says to me this morning when I went in to light the fire again and see what he'd eat for breakfast. And I think he has, Miss Gwinny."

Which information considerably lightened the doubt which was tormenting Miss Nave's mind. She wanted, oh how badly, and was wanted, to remain at the Rill, being sorely needed there; but she had not seen her way clear to do it. If Nash was indeed confined to his bed, she might perhaps venture to leave him for a day or two to Grizzel.

But, please don't think old Grizzel mean for keeping in what had taken place: she was only obeying orders. Duffham and the Squire had laid their heads together and then talked to Caromel; and it was agreed that for the present nothing should be disclosed. They gave their orders to Grizzel, and her master confirmed them.

"And what news have you brought from the Rill, ma'am?" questioned Grizzel, who was making a custard pudding at the kitchen table. "I hope you found things better than you feared."

"They could not well be worse," sighed Miss Gwinny, untying her bonnet. She had not the beauty of Charlotte. Her light complexion was like brick-dust, and her hair was straw-coloured. Not but that she was proud of her hair, wearing it in twists, with one ringlet trailing over the left shoulder. "Your mistress lies unconscious still; it is feared the brain is injured; and papa's leg is broken in two places."

"Alack a-day?" cried Grizzel, lifting her hands in consternation. "Oh, but I am sorry to hear it, Miss Gwendolen! And the pretty little boy?"

Miss Gwendolen shook her head. "The croup came on again last night worse than ever," she said, with a rising sob. "They don't know whether they will save him."

Grizzel brushed away some tears as she began to beat up her eggs. She was a tender-hearted old thing, and loved little Dun. Miss Nave put aside her bonnet and shawl, and turned to the staircase to pay a visit to Nash. But she looked back to ask a question.

"Then, I am to understand that you had no trouble with the master last night, Grizzel? He did not want to force himself out?"

"The time for that has gone by, ma'am, I think," answered Grizzel, evasively; not daring and not wishing to confess that he had forced himself out, and what the consequences were. "He seems a deal weaker to-day, Miss Gwinny, than I've ever seen him."

And when Miss Gwinny got into Nash's room she found the words true. Weak, inert, fading, there lay poor Nash. With the discovery, all struggle had ceased; and it is well known that to resign one's self to weakness quietly, makes weakness ten times more apparent. One thing struck her greatly: the hollow sound in the voice. Had it come on suddenly? If not, how was it she had never noticed it before? It struck her with a sort of unpleasant chill: for she believed that peculiar hollowness is generally the precursor of death.

"You are feeling worse, Nash, Grizzel says," she observed; and she thought she had never seen him looking half so ill.

"Oh, I am all right, Gwendolen," answered he. "What of Charlotte and the child?"

Sitting down on the edge of the large bed, Gwendolen told him all there was to tell. Her papa would get well in time, though he could not be moved yet awhile; but Charlotte and the child were lying in extreme danger.

"Dear me! dear me!" he said, and began to cry, as Grizzel had begun. When a man is reduced, as Nash was, faint in mind and in body, the tears are apt to lie near the eyes.

"And there's nobody to attend upon them but Mrs. Smith and her maids—two of the stupidest country wenches you ever saw," said Gwendolen. "I did not know how to come away this morning. The child is more than one person's work."

"Why did you come?"

"Because I could not trust you; you know that, Nash. You want to be up to your tricks too often."

"My tricks!"

"Yes. Going out of doors at night. I'm sure it is a dreadful responsibility that's thrown upon me. And all for your own sake!"

"You need no longer fear that—if you call my going out the responsibility. I shall never get out of this bed again, Gwinny."

"What makes you think so?"

"Look at me," answered Nash. "See if you think it likely. I do not."

She shook her head doubtingly. He certainly did look too ill to stir—but she remembered the trouble there had been with him; the fierce, wild yearning for exit, that could not be controlled.

"Are you not satisfied? Listen, then: I give you my solemn word of honour not to go out of doors; not to attempt to do so. You must go back to Charlotte and the boy."

"I'll see later," decided Gwinny. "I shall stay here till the afternoon, at any rate."

And when the afternoon came she took her departure for the Rill. Convinced by Nash's state that he could not quit his bed, and satisfied at length by his own solemn and repeated assurances that he would not, Gwinny Nave consigned him to the care of Grizzel, and quitted Caromel's Farm.

Which left the field open again, you perceive. And the Squire and Duffham were there that evening as they had been the previous one.

It was a curious time—the few days that ensued. Gwendolen Nave came over for an hour or two every other day, but otherwise Caromel's Farm was a free house. Her doubts and fears were gone, for Nash grew worse very rapidly; and, though he sat up in his room sometimes, he could hardly have got downstairs though the house were burning—as Grizzel put it. And he seemed so calm, so tranquil, so entirely passive under his affliction, so resigned to his enfeebled state, so averse to making exertion of any kind, that Miss Gwinny could not have felt much easier had he been in the burial-ground where Church Dykely supposed him to be.

What with his past incarceration, which had endured twelve months, and what with the approach of death, which he had seen looming for pretty nearly half that time, Nash Caromel's conscience had come back to him. It was pricking him in more corners than one. As his love for Charlotte Nave weakened— and it had been going down a long time, for he saw what the Naves were now, and what they had done for him—his love for Charlotte Tinkle came back, and he began to wish he could set wrongs to rights. That never could be done; he had put it out of his power; but he meant to make some little reparation, opportunity being allowed him.

"I want to make a will, Todhetley," he said one evening to the Squire, as he sat by the fire, dressed, a huge carriage-rug thrown on his knees for warmth. "I wonder if my lawyer could be induced to come to me?"

"Do you mean Nave?" retorted the Squire, who could not for the life of him help having a fling at Caromel once in a way. "He has been your lawyer of late years."

"You know I don't mean Nave; and if I did mean him he could not come," said poor Nash. "I mean our family lawyer, Crow. Since I discarded him for Nave he has turned the cold shoulder upon me. When I've met him in the street at Evesham, he has either passed me with a curt nod or looked another way. I would rather have Crow than anybody, for he'd be true, I know, if he could be induced to come."

"I'll see about it," said the Squire.

"And you'll be executor, won't you, Todhetley? you and Duffham."

"No," said the Squire. "And what sort of a will are you going to make?"

"I should like to be just," sighed Nash. "As just as I know how. As just as I can be under the unfortunate circumstances I am placed in."

"That you have placed yourself in, Caromel."

"True. I think of it night and day. But she ought to be provided for. And there's the boy!"

"Who ought to be?"

"My second wife."

"I don't say to the contrary. But there is somebody else, who has a greater and prior claim upon you."

"I know. My heart would be good to leave her all. But that would hardly be just. Poor Charlotte, how patient she has been!"

"Ah, you threw off a good woman when you threw her off. And when you made that other infamous will, leaving her name out of it—"

"It was Nave made it," interrupted Nash, as hotly as his wasted condition allowed him to speak. "He got another lawyer to draw it up, for look's sake—but he virtually made it. And, Todhetley, I must—I must get another one made," he added, getting more and more excited; "and there's no time to be lost. If I die to-night that will would have to stand."

With the morning light the Squire went off to Evesham, driving Bob and Blister, and saw the lawyer, Crow—an old gentleman with a bald head. The two shut themselves up in a private room, and it seemed as if they never meant to come out again.

First of all, old Crow had to recover his astonishment at hearing Nash Caromel was living, and that took him some time; next, he had to get over his disinclination and refusal—to act again for Nash, and that took him longer.

"Mind," said he at last, "if I do consent to act—to see the man and make his will—it will be done out of the respect I bore his father and his brother, and because I don't like to stand in the way of an act of justice. Mrs. Nash Caromel was here yesterday—"

"Mrs. Nash Caromel!" interrupted the Squire, in a puzzle, for his thoughts had run over to Charlotte Nave. Which must have been very foolish, seeing she was in bed with a damaged head.

"I speak of his wife," said the old gentleman, loftily. "I have never called any other woman Mrs. Nash Caromel. Her uncle, Tinkle, of Inkberrow, called about the transfer of some of his funded property, and she was with him. I respect that young woman, Squire Todhetley."

"Ay, to be sure. So do I. Well, now, you will let me drive you back this afternoon, and you'll take dinner with me, and we'll go to Caromel's Farm afterwards. We never venture there before night; that Miss Gwinny Nave makes her appearance sometimes in the daytime."

"It must be late in the afternoon then," said the lawyer, rather crossly—for he did not enter into the business with a good grace yet.

"All the same to me," acquiesced the pater, pleased at having got his consent on any terms.

And when the Squire drove in that evening just at the dinner-hour and brought Lawyer Crow with him, we wondered what was agate. Old Jacobson, who had called in, and been invited to stay by the mater, was as curious as anything over it, and asked the Squire aside, what he was up to, that he must employ Crow instead of his own man.

The will Nash Caromel wished to make was accomplished, signed and sealed, himself and this said Evesham lawyer being alone privy to its contents. Dobbs the blacksmith was fetched in, and he and Grizzel witnessed it.

And, as if Nash Caromel had only lived to make the will, he went galloping on to death at railroad speed directly it was done. A change took place in him the same night. His bell rang for Grizzel, and the old woman thought him dying.

But he rallied a bit the next day: and when the Squire got there in the evening, he was sitting up by the fire dressed. And terribly uneasy.

"I want to see her," he began, before the Squire had time to say, How are you, or How are you not. "I can't die in peace unless I see her. And it will not be long first now. I am a bit better, but I thought I was dying in the night: has Grizzel told you?"

The Squire nodded in silence. He was struck with the change in Nash.

"Who is it you want to see? Charlotte Tinkle?"

"Ay, you've guessed it. 'Twasn't hard to guess, was it? I want to see her, Todhetley. I know she'd come."

Little doubt of that. Had Nash wanted her to visit him in the midst of a fiery furnace, she'd have rushed into it headlong.

But there were difficulties in the way. Charlotte Tinkle was not one of your strong-minded women who are born without nerves; and to tell her that Nash Caromel was living, and not dead, might send her into hysterics for a week. Besides that, Harry Tinkle was Nash Caromel's bitter enemy: if he learnt the truth he might be for handing him over, dying or living, to old Jones the constable.

"I don't see how she is to be got here, and that's the truth, Caromel," spoke the Squire, awaking from his reverie. "It's not a thing I should like to undertake. Here comes Duffham."

"I know what you are thinking of—Harry Tinkle," returned Nash, as Duffham felt his pulse. "When I was supposed to have died, balking him of his revenge, he grew mad with rage. For a month afterwards he abused me to everybody in the most atrocious terms: in public rooms, in—"

"Who told you that?" interrupted the Squire. "Nave?"

"Nave. I saw no one else to tell me." Duffham laughed.

"Then it was just as false as Nave is. You might have known Harry Tinkle better."

Nash looked up. "False!—was it?"

"Why, of course it was," repeated the Squire. "I say you might have known Harry Tinkle better."

Nash sighed. "Well, I suppose you think he might give me trouble now. But he would hardly care to apprehend a dying man."

"We'll see about it," they said. Duffham undertook this expedition—if you can call it one. He found it easier than he anticipated. That same evening, upon quitting Caromel's Farm, Duffham went mooning along, deep in thought, as to how he should make the disclosure to Charlotte, when he overtook her near his home. Her crape veil was thrown back; her face looked pale and quiet in the starlight.

"You are abroad late," said Duffham.

"I went to see old Miss Pinner this afternoon, and stayed tea with her," answered Charlotte. "And now I am going to run home."

"Would you mind coming in for a few minutes, Mrs. Caromel?" he asked, as they reached his door. "I have something to say to you."

"Can you say it another time? It is nine o'clock, and my mother will be wondering."

"No; another time may not do," said Duffham. "Come in. I won't detain you long."

And being just one of those yielding people that never assert a will of their own, in she went.

Shut up in Duffham's surgery, which was more remote from Nomy's ears than the parlour, Duffham disclosed to her by degrees the truth. Whether he had to get out his sal-volatile over it, or to recover her from fits, we did not hear. One thing was certain: that when Mrs. Nash Caromel recommenced her walk homewards, she was too bewildered to know whether she went on her feet or her head. By that time on the following evening she would have seen her husband.

At least, such was the programme Duffham carved out. But to that bargain, as he found the next day, there might be two words.

Eleven was striking in the morning by the kitchen clock at Caromel's Farm, when Grizzel saw Miss Gwinny driving in. The damaged gig had been mended, and she now drove backwards and forwards herself.

"How's the master?" asked she, when she entered the kitchen.

"Very ill," answered Grizzel. "He won't be with us long, now, ma'am."

And when Miss Gwinny saw Nash, and saw how greatly he was altered in the last two days, she thought as Grizzel did—that death was close at hand. Under these circumstances, she sat down to reflect on what she ought to do: whether to remain herself in the house, or whether to go back to the Rill and report to her father and sister. For the latter had come out of her insensibility; the doctors said there was no permanent injury, and she could soon be removed home if she wished to be.

"What do you think, Grizzel?" she inquired, condescending to ask counsel. "It does not seem right to leave him—and you won't like to be left alone, either, at the last. And I don't see that any end will be gained by my hastening back to tell them. They'll know it soon enough: and they cannot come to him."

"As you please, Miss Gwinny," replied Grizzel, trembling lest she should remain and complicate matters, but not daring to urge her departure; Gwinny Nave being given, as a great many more ladies are, to act by the rules of contrary in the matter of advice. "It seems hardly right, though, not to let the mistress know he is dying. And I am glad the child's well: dear little thing!"

Gwinny Nave sat pulling at her one straw ringlet, her brow knitted in abstraction. Various reflections, suggesting certain unpleasant facts, passed rapidly through her mind. That Nash would not be here many days longer, perhaps not many hours, was a grave fact: and then, what of the after-necessities that would arise? A sham funeral had gone out of that house not very long ago: but how was the real funeral to go out, and who was to make the arrangements for it? The truth of Nash Caromel's being alive, and of the trick which had been played, would have to be disclosed then. And Mr. Nave was incapacitated; he could do nothing, and her sister could do as little; and it seemed to be all falling upon herself, Gwinny; and who was to know but she might be punished for letting Nash lie and die without calling in a doctor to him?

With every fresh moment of thought, some darker complication presented itself. Miss Gwinny began to see that she had better get away, and leave old Grizzel to it. The case must be laid before her father. He might invent some scheme to avoid exposure: for though Lawyer Nave was deprived for the present of action, his mind was not less keen and fertile than usual.

"I think, Grizzel, that the mistress ought to be told how ill he is," said she, at length. "I shall go back to the Rill. Do all you can for the master: I dare say he will rally."

"That he never will," spoke Grizzel, on impulse.

"Now don't you be obstinate," returned Miss Gwinny.

Gwendolen Nave drove back to the Rill. Leaving, as she thought, all responsibility upon old Grizzel. And, that evening, the coast being clear again, Charlotte Tinkle, piloted by Duffham, came to Caromel's Farm and had an interview with her once recreant husband. It lasted longer than Duffham had bargained for; every five minutes he felt inclined to go and knock at the door. Her sobs and his dying voice, which seemed to be sobbing too, might be heard by all who chose to listen. At last Duffham went in and said that it must end: the emotion was bad for Nash. She was kneeling before the sofa on which he lay, her tears dropping.

"Good-bye, good-bye, Charlotte," he whispered. "I have never cared for any one as I cared for you. Believe that. God bless you, my dear—and forgive me!"

And the next to go in was Harry Tinkle—to clasp Caromel's hand, and to say how little he had needed to fear him. And the next was the Reverend Mr. Holland; Nash had asked for the parson to be sent for.

Grizzel had a surprise the next day. She had just taken some beef-tea up to the master, which Duffham had called out for—for the end was now so near that the doctor had not chosen to defer his visit till dark—when a closed fly drove up, out of which stepped Miss Gwinny and her sister. Old Grizzel dropped the waiter, thinking it must be her mistress's ghost.

But it was Charlotte herself. Upon hearing Gwinny's report she had insisted upon coming home—and Nave supported her views. That stupid old Grizzel, left to her own devices, might be for getting frightened and call in half the parish. The doctor in attendance at the Rill had said Mrs. Caromel might go home if she had any urgent reason for wishing it—and here she was. And really she seemed tolerably well again; quite herself.

Passing Grizzel with a nod, she went straight upstairs, opened Nash's door, and then—drew back with a scream. For there she saw two strangers. Mr. Duffham was leaning over the bed, trying to feed Nash with spoonfuls of beef-tea; Parson Holland (who had stayed with Nash all night) sat by the fire. Poor Nash himself lay without motion: the hours were very limited now.

Well, there ensued a commotion. Charlotte Nave went down to blow up Grizzel; and she did it well, in spite of her recent illness. Grizzel answered that she was not to blame; it was not she who had betrayed him: Dobbs the blacksmith and Squire Todhetley had found him out, and the Squire had called in Duffham. Charlotte the Second had to make the best of a bad case; but she did not suspect half the treachery that had been at work.

There is no space to enlarge upon the day. Nash died that night; without having been able to speak a word to Charlotte the Second; he was past that when she came; though he shook hands with her.

And the other funeral, which Miss Nave had foreseen a difficulty over, took place without any difficulty. Unless it might be said that the crowd made one. Nash Caromel dead a second time! Church Dykely had never been astounded like this.

But the one dire act of treachery had to come out yet. Nash Caromel had made a fresh will. Crow the lawyer brought it in his pocket when he came from Evesham to attend the funeral, and he read it aloud afterwards. Mrs. Nash the Second sat biting her lips as she listened.

Caromel's Farm and everything upon it, every stick and stone possessed by Nash, was directed to be sold without delay. Of the money this should realize, the one half was devised to "my dear wife Charlotte, formerly Charlotte Tinkle;" the other half was to be invested by trustees and settled upon "my child, Duncan Nave." His mother, Charlotte Nave, was to receive a stated portion of the interest for life, or until she should marry again; and that was all the will said about Charlotte the Second.

There's not much more to tell. As soon as might be, the changes were carried out. Before Lawyer Nave's leg was fit to go again, Caromel's Farm had been purchased by the Squire, and Harry Tinkle had taken it from him on a long lease. Just after Harry got into it with his little girl, Mrs. Tinkle died; and Charlotte, well off now, came to live in it with him. The other Charlotte proclaimed herself to be in bad health, and went off to stay at the sea-side. And Nave, when he came out again to rejoice the eyes of Church Dykely (walking lame), was fit to swallow us up with rage. He considered ladies' parasols an infamous institution, and wished they were all sunk in the sea; especially that particular blue one of Charlotte's which had led to the accident that unlucky afternoon.

It seemed strange that, after all the chances and changes, it should be a Mrs. Nash Caromel (she was always given her true name now) to inhabit Caromel's Farm. She, forgiving and loving, made friends with little Dun for poor Nash's sake, inviting him often to spend the day with her, and picking him choice fruit off the trees.

CHAPTER XII

A DAY IN BRIAR WOOD

That day, and its events, can never go out of my memory. There are epochs in life that lie upon the heart for ever, marking the past like stones placed for retrospect. They may be of pleasure, or they may be of pain; but there they are, in that great store-field locked up within us, to be recalled at will as long as life shall last.

It was in August, and one of the hottest days of that hot month. A brilliant day: the sun shining with never a cloud to soften it, the sky intensely blue. Just the day for a picnic, provided you had shade.

Shade we had. Briar Wood abounds in it. For the towering trees are dark, and their foliage thick. Here and there the wood opens, and you come upon the sweetest little bits of meadow-land scenery that a painter's eye could desire. Patches of green glade, smooth enough for fairy revels; undulating banks, draped with ferns and fragrant with sweet wild-flowers; dells dark, and dim, to roam in and fancy yourself out of the world.

Briar Wood belonged to Sir John Whitney. It was of a good length but narrow, terminating at one end in the tangled coppice which we had dashed through that long-past day when we played at hare and hounds, and poor Charles Van Rheyn had died, in that same coppice, of the running. The other and best end, up where these lonely glades lie sheltered, extends itself nearly to the lands belonging to Vale Farm—if you have not forgotten that place. The wood was a rare resort for poachers and gipsies, as well as picnic parties, and every now and again Sir John would declare that it should be rooted up.

We were staying at Whitney Hall. Miss Deveen was there on a visit (Cattledon included, of course), and Sir John wrote over to invite us for a few days to meet her: the Squire and Mrs. Todhetley, I and Tod. And, there we were, enjoying ourselves like anything.

It was Sir John himself who proposed the picnic. He called it a gipsy-party: indeed, the word "picnic" had hardly come in then, for this happened many a year ago. The weather was so hot indoors that Sir John thought it might be an agreeable change to live a day in the open air; and lie in the shade and look up at the blue sky through the flickering trees. So the cook was told to provide fowls and ham and pigeon pies, with apple puffs, salads, and creams.

"The large carriage and the four-wheeled chaise shall take the ladies," observed Sir John, "and I dare say they can make room for me and the Squire amongst them; it's a short distance, and we shan't mind a little crowding. You young men can walk."

So it was ordained. The carriages started, and we after them, William and Henry Whitney disputing as to which was the best route to take: Bill holding out for that by Goose Brook, Harry for that by the river. It ended in our dividing: I went with Bill his way; the rest of the young Whitneys and Tod the other, with Featherston's nephew; an overgrown young giant of seventeen, about six feet high, who had been told he might come.

Barring the heat, it was a glorious walk: just as it was a glorious day. Passing Goose Brook (a little stream meandering through the trees, with a rustic bridge across it: though why it should bear that name I never knew), we soon came to the coppice end of the wood.

"Now," said Bill to me, "shall we plunge into the wood at once, and so onwards right through it; or skirt round by the Granary?"

"The wood will be the shadiest," I answered.

"And pleasantest. I'm not at all sure, though, Johnny, that I shan't lose my way in it. It has all kinds of bewildering tricks and turnings."

"Never mind if you do. We can find it again."

"We should have been safe to meet some of those Leonards had we gone by the Granary," observed Bill, as we turned into the wood, where just at present the trees were thin, "and they might have been wanting to join us, pushing fellows that they are! I don't like them."

"Who are those Leonards, I wonder? Who were they before they came here?"

"Old Leonard made a mint of money in India, and his sons are spending it for him as fast as they can. One day when he was talking to my father, he hinted that he had taken this remote place, the Granary, and brought them down here, to get them out of the fast lives they were leading in London. He got afraid, he said."

"Haven't the sons any professions, Bill?"

"Don't seem to have. Or anything else that's good—money excepted?"

"What do they do with their time?"

"Anything. Idle it away. Keep dogs; and shoot, and fish, and lounge, and smoke, and— Halloa! look yonder, Johnny!"

Briar Wood had no straight and direct road through it; but plenty of small paths and byways and turnings and windings, that might bring you, by good luck, to landing at last; or might take you unconsciously back whence you came. Emerging from a part, where the trees grew dark and dense and thick, upon one of those delightful glades I spoke of before, we saw what I took to be a small gipsy encampment. A fire of sticks, with a kettle upon it, smoked upon the ground; beside it sat a young woman and child; a few tin wares, tied together, lay in a corner, and some rabbits' skins were stretched out to dry on the branches of trees.

Up started the woman, and came swiftly towards us. A regular gipsy, with the purple-black hair, the yellow skin, and the large soft gleaming eyes. It was a beautiful young face, but worn and thin and anxious.

"Do you want your fortunes told, my good young gentlemen? I can—"

"Not a bit of it," interrupted Bill. "Go back to your fire. We are only passing through."

"I can read the lines of your hands unerringly, my pretty sirs. I can forewarn you of evil, and prepare you for good."

"Now, look you here," cried Bill, turning upon her good-humouredly, as she followed up with a lot of the like stuff, "I can forewarn you of it, unless you are content to leave us alone. This wood belongs to Sir John Whitney, as I dare say all your fraternity know, and his keepers wage war against you when they find you are encamped here, and that I am sure you know. Mind your own affairs, and you may stay here in peace, for me: keep on bothering us, and I go straight to Rednal and give him a hint. I am Sir John's son."

He threw her a sixpence, and the woman's face changed as she caught it. The persuasive smile vanished as if by magic, giving place to a look of anxious pain.

"What's the matter?" said he.

"Do you know my husband, sir?" she asked. "It's more than likely that you do."

"And what if I do?" cried Whitney.

The woman took the words as an affirmative answer. She drew near, and laid her small brown finger on his coat-sleeve.

"Then, if you chance to meet him, sir, persuade him to come back to me, for the love of Heaven. I can read the future: and for some days past, since we first halted here, I have foreseen that evil is in store for him. He won't believe me; he is not one of us; but I scent it in the air, and it comes nearer and nearer; it is drawing very close now. He may listen to you, sir, for we respect Sir John, who is never hard on us as some great owners of the land are; and oh, send him back here to me and the child! Better that it should fall on him when by our side than when away from us."

"Why—what do you mean?" cried Whitney, surprised out of the question, and hardly understanding her words or their purport. And he might have laughed outright, as he told me later, but for the dreadful trouble that shone forth from her sad, wild eyes.

"I don't know what I mean: it's hidden from me," she answered, taking the words in a somewhat different light from what he meant to imply. "I think it may be sudden sickness; or it may be trouble: whatever it is, it will end badly."

Whitney nodded to her, and we pursued our way. I had been looking at the little girl, who had drawn shyly up to gaze at us. She was fair as a lily, with a sweet face and eyes blue as the sky.

"What humbugs they are!" exclaimed Whitney, alluding to gipsies and tramps in general. "As to this young woman, I should say she's going off her head!"

"Do you know her husband?"

"Don't know him from Adam. Johnny, I hope that's not a stolen child! Fair as she is, she can't be the woman's: there's nothing of the gipsy in her composition."

"How well the gipsy appears to speak! With quite a refined accent."

"Gipsies often do, I've heard. Let us get on."

What with this adventure, and dawdling, and taking a wrong turn or two, it was past one o'clock when we got in, and they were laying the cloth for dinner. The green, mossy glade, with the sheltering trees around, the banks and the dells, the ferns and wild-flowers, made a picture of a retreat on a broiling day. The table (some boards, brought from the Hall, and laid on trestles) stood in the middle of the grass; and Helen and Anna Whitney, in their green-and-white muslins, were just as busy as bees placing the dishes upon it. Lady Whitney (with a face redder than beetroot) helped them: she liked to be always doing something. Miss Cattledon and the mater were pacing the dell below, and Miss Deveen sat talking with the Squire and Sir John.

"Have they not got here?" exclaimed William.

"Have who not got here?" retorted Helen.

"Todhetley and the boys."

"Ages ago. They surmised that you two must be lost, stolen, or strayed."

"Then where are they?"

"Making themselves useful. Johnny Ludlow, I wish you'd go after them, and tell them of all things to bring a corkscrew. No one can find ours, and we think it is left behind."

"Why, here's the corkscrew, in my pocket," called out Sir John. "Whatever brings it there? And— What's that great thing, moving down to us?"

It was Tod with a wooden stool upon his head, legs upwards. Rednal the gamekeeper lived close by, and it was arranged that we should borrow chairs, and things, from his cottage.

We sat down to dinner at last—and a downright jolly dinner it was. Plenty of good things to eat; cider, lemonade, and champagne to drink: and every one talking together, and bursts of laughter.

"Look at Cattledon!" cried Bill in my ear. "She is as merry as the rest of us."

So she was. A whole sea of smiles on her thin face. She wore a grey gown as genteel as herself, bands of black velvet round her pinched-in waist and long throat. Cattledon looked like vinegar in general, it's true; but I don't say she was bad at heart. Even she could be genial to-day, and the rest of us were off our head with jollity, the Squire's face and Sir John's beaming back at one another.

If we had only foreseen how pitifully the day was to end! It makes me think of some verses I once learnt out of a journal—Chambers's, I believe. They were written by Mrs. Plarr.

"There are twin Genii, who, strong and mighty,
Under their guidance mankind retain;
And the name of the lovely one is Pleasure,
And the name of the loathly one is Pain.
Never divided, where one can enter
Ever the other comes close behind;
And he who in Pleasure his thoughts would centre
Surely Pain in the search shall find!

"Alike they are, though in much they differ—
Strong resemblance is 'twixt the twain;
So that sometimes you may question whether

It can be Pleasure you feel, or Pain.
Thus 'tis, that whatever of deep emotion
Stirreth the heart—be it grave or gay
Tears are the Symbol—from feeling's ocean
These are the fountains that rise to-day.

"Should not this teach us calmly to welcome
Pleasure when smiling our hearths beside?
If she be the substance, how dark the shadow;
Close doth it follow, the near allied.
Or if Pain long o'er our threshold hover,
Let us not question but Pleasure nigh
Bideth her time her face to discover,
Rainbow of Hope in a clouded sky."

Yes, it was a good time. To look at us round that dinner-table, you'd have said there was nothing but pleasure in the world. Not but that ever and anon the poor young gipsy woman's troubled face and her sad wild eyes, and the warning some subtle instinct seemed to be whispering to her about her husband, would rise between me and the light.

The afternoon was wearing on when I got back to the glade with William Whitney (for we had all gone strolling about after dinner) and found some of the ladies there. Mrs. Todhetley had gone into Rednal's cottage to talk to his wife, Jessy; Anna was below in the dell; all the rest were in the glade. A clean-looking, stout old lady, in a light cotton gown and white apron, a mob cap with a big border and bow of ribbon in front of it, turned round from talking to them, smiled, and made me a curtsy.

The face seemed familiar to me: but where had I seen it before? Helen Whitney, seeing my puzzled look, spoke up in her free manner.

"Have you no memory, Johnny Ludlow? Don't you remember Mrs. Ness!—and the fortune she told us on the cards?"

It came upon me with a rush. That drizzling Good Friday afternoon at Miss Deveen's, long ago, and Helen smuggling up the old lady from downstairs to tell her fortune. But what brought her here? There seemed to be no connection between Miss Deveen's house in town and Briar Wood in Worcestershire. I could not have been more at sea had I seen a Chinese lady from Pekin. Miss Deveen laughed.

"And yet it is so easy of explanation, Johnny, so simple and straightforward," she said. "Mrs. Ness chances to be aunt to Rednal's wife, and she is staying down here with them."

Simple it was—as are most other puzzles when you have the clue. The old woman was a great protégée of Miss Deveen's, who had known her through her life of misfortune: but Miss Deveen did not before know of her relationship to Rednal's wife or that she was staying at their cottage. They had been talking of that past afternoon and the fortune-telling in it, when I and Bill came up.

"And what I told you, miss, came true—now didn't it?" cried Mrs. Ness to Helen.

"True! Why, you told me nothing!" retorted Helen. "There was nothing in the fortune. You said there was nothing in the cards."

"I remember it," said Mother Ness; "remember it well. The cards showed no husband for you then, young lady; they might tell different now. But they showed some trouble about it, I recollect."

Helen's face fell. There had indeed been trouble. Trouble again and again. Richard Foliott, the false, had brought trouble to her; and so had Charles Leafchild, now lying in his grave at Worcester: not to speak of poor Slingsby Temple. Helen had got over all those crosses now, and was looking up again. She was of a nature to look up again from any evil that might befall her, short of losing her head off her shoulders. All dinner-time she had been flirting with Featherston's nephew.

This suggestion of Mrs. Ness, "the cards might tell different now," caught hold of her mind. Her colour slightly deepened, her eyes sparkled.

"Have you the cards with you now, Mrs. Ness?"

"Ay, to be sure, young lady. I never come away from home without my cards. They be in the cottage yonder."

"Then I should like my fortune told again."

"Oh, Helen, how can you be so silly!" cried Lady Whitney.

"Silly! Why, mamma, it is good fun. You go and fetch the cards, Mrs. Ness."

"I and Johnny nearly had our fortune told to-day," put in Bill, while Mrs. Ness stood where she was, hardly knowing what to be at. "We came upon a young gipsy woman in the wood, and she wanted to promise us a wife apiece. A little girl was with her that may have been stolen: she was too fair to be that brown woman's child."

"It must have been the Norths," exclaimed Mrs. Ness. "Was there some tinware by 'em, sir; and some rabbit skins?"

"Yes. Both. The rabbit skins were hanging out to dry."

"Ay, it's the Norths," repeated Mrs. Ness. "Rednal said he saw North yesterday; he guessed they'd lighted their campfire not far off."

"Who are the Norths? Gipsies?"

"The wife is a gipsy, sir; born and bred. He is a native of these parts, and superior; but he took to an idle, wandering life, and married the gipsy girl for her beauty. She was Bertha Lee then."

"Why, it is quite a romance," said Miss Deveen, amused.

"And so it is, ma'am. Rednal told me all on't. They tramp the country, selling their tins, and collecting rabbit skins."

"And is the child theirs?" asked Bill.

"Ay, sir, it be. But she don't take after her mother; she's like him, her skin fair as alabaster. You'd not think, Rednal says, that she'd a drop o' gipsy blood in her veins. North might ha' done well had he only turned out steady; been just the odds o' what he is—a poor tramp."

"Oh, come, never mind the gipsies," cried Helen, impatiently. "You go and bring the cards, Mrs. Ness."

One can't go in for stilts at a picnic, or for wisdom either; and when Mrs. Ness brought her cards (which might have been cleaner) none of them made any objection. Even Cattledon looked on, grimly tolerant.

"But you can't think there's anything in it—that the cards tell true," cried Lady Whitney to the old woman.

"Ma'am, be sure they do. I believe in 'em from my very heart. And so, I make bold to say, would everybody here believe, if they had read the things upon 'em that I've read, and seen how surely they've come to pass."

They would not contradict her openly; only smiled a little among themselves. Mother Ness was busy with the cards, laying them out for Helen's fortune. I drew near to listen.

"You look just as though you put faith in it," whispered Bill to me.

"I don't put faith in it. I should not like to be so foolish. But, William, what she told Helen before did come true."

Well, Helen's "fortune" was told again. It sounded just as uneventful as the one told that rainy afternoon long ago—for we were now some years older than we were then. Helen Whitney's future, according to the cards, or to Dame Ness's reading of them, would be all plain sailing; smooth and easy, and unmarked alike by events and by care. A most desirable career, some people would think, but Helen looked the picture of desolation.

"And you say I am not to be married!" she exclaimed.

Dame Ness had her head bent over the cards. She shook it without looking up.

"I don't see a ring nowhere, young lady, and that's the blessed truth. There ain't one, that's more. There ain't a sign o' one. Neither was there the other time, I remember: that time in London. And so—I take it that there won't never be."

"Then I think you are a very disagreeable story-telling old woman!" flashed Helen, all candour in her mortification. "Not be married, indeed!"

"Why, my dear, I'd be only too glad to promise you a husband if the cards foretelled it," said Dame Ness, pityingly. "Yours is the best fortune of all, though, if you could but bring your mind to see it. Husbands is more plague nor profit. I'm sure I had cause to say so by the one that fell to my share, as that there dear good lady knows," pointing to Miss Deveen.

In high dudgeon, Helen pushed the cards together. Mrs. Ness, getting some kind words from the rest of us, curtsied as she went off to the cottage to see about the kettles for our tea.

"You are a nice young lady!" exclaimed Bill. "Showing your temper because the cards don't give you a sweetheart!"

Helen threw her fan at him. "Mind your own business," returned she. And he went away laughing.

"And, my dear, I say the same as William," added Lady Whitney. "One really might think that you were—were anxious to be married."

"All cock-a-hoop for it," struck in Cattledon: "as the housemaids are."

"And no such great crime, either," returned Helen, defiantly. "Fancy that absurd old thing telling me I never shall be!"

"Helen, my dear, I think the chances are that you will not be married," quietly spoke Miss Deveen.

"Oh, do you!"

"Don't be cross, Helen," said her mother. "Our destinies are not in our own hands."

Helen bit her lip, laughed, and recovered her temper. She was like her father; apt to flash out a hot word, but never angry long.

"Now—please, Miss Deveen, why do you think I shall not be?" she asked playfully.

"Because, my dear, you have had three chances, so to say, of marriage, and each time it has been frustrated. In two of the instances by—if we may dare to say it—the interposition of Heaven. The young men died beforehand in an unexpected and unforeseen manner: Charles Leafchild and Mr. Temple—"

"I was never engaged to Mr. Temple," interrupted Helen.

"No; but, by all I hear, you shortly would have been."

Helen gave no answer. She knew perfectly well that she had expected an offer from Slingsby Temple; that his death, as she believed, alone prevented its being made. She would have said Yes to it, too. Miss Deveen went on.

"We will not give more than an allusion to Captain Foliott; he does not deserve it; but your marriage with him came nearest of all. It may be said, Helen, without exaggeration, that you have been on the point of marriage twice, and very nearly so a third time. Now, what does this prove?"

"That luck was against me," said Helen, lightly.

"Ay, child: luck, as we call it in this world. I would rather say, Destiny. God knows best. Do you wonder that I have never married?" continued Miss Deveen in a less serious tone.

"I never thought about it," answered Helen.

"I know that some people have wondered at it; for I was a girl likely to marry—or it may be better to say, likely to be sought in marriage. I had good looks, good temper, good birth, and a good fortune: and I dare say I was just as willing to be chosen as all young girls are. Yes, I say that all girls possess an innate wish to marry; it is implanted in their nature, comes with their mother's milk. Let their station be high or low, a royal princess, if you will, or the housemaid Jemima Cattledon suggested just now, the same natural instinct lies within each—a wish to be a wife. And no reason, either, why they should not wish it; it's nothing to be ashamed of; and Helen, my dear, I would rather hear a girl avow it openly, as you do, than pretend to be shocked at its very mention."

Some gleams of sunlight flickered on Miss Deveen's white hair and fine features as she sat under the trees, her bronze-coloured silk gown falling around her in rich folds, and a big amethyst brooch fastening her collar. I began to think how good-looking she must have been when young, and where the eyes of the young men of those days could have been. Lady Whitney, looking like a bundle in her light dress that ill became her, sat near, fanning herself.

"Yes, I do wonder, now I think of it, that you never married," said Helen.

"To tell you the truth, I wonder myself sometimes," replied Miss Deveen, smiling. "I think—I believe—that, putting other advantages aside, I was well calculated to be a wife, and should have made a good one. Not that that has anything to do with it; for you see the most incapable women marry, and remain incapable to their dying day. I could mention wives at this moment, within the circle of my acquaintance, who are no more fitted to be wives than is that three-legged stool Johnny is balancing himself upon; and who in consequence unwittingly keep their husbands and their homes in a state of perpetual turmoil. I was not one of these, I am sure; but here I am, unmarried still."

"Would you marry now?" asked Helen briskly: and we all burst into a laugh at the question, Miss Deveen's the merriest.

"Marry at sixty! Not if I know it. I have at least twenty years too many for that; some might say thirty. But I don't believe many women give up the idea of marriage before they are forty; and I do not see why they should. No, nor then, either."

"But—why did you not marry, Miss Deveen?"

"Ah, my dear, if you wish for an answer to that question, you must ask it of Heaven. I cannot give one. All I can tell you is, that I did hope to be married, and expected to be married, waited to be married; but here you see me in my old age—Miss Deveen."

"Did you—never have a chance of it—an opportunity?" questioned Helen with hesitation.

"I had more than one chance: I had two or three chances, just as you have had. During the time that each 'chance' was passing, if we may give it the term, I thought assuredly I should soon be a wife. But each chance melted away from this cause or that cause, ending in nothing. And the conclusion I have come to, Helen, for many a year past, is, that God, for some wise purpose of His own, decreed that I should not marry. What we know not here, we shall know hereafter."

Her tone had changed to one of deep reverence. She did not say more for a little time.

"When I look around the world," she at length went on, "and note how many admirable women see their chances of marriage dwindle down one after another, from unexpected and apparently trifling causes, it is impossible not to feel that the finger of God is at work. That—"

"But now, Miss Deveen, we could marry if we would—all of us," interrupted Helen. "If we did not have to regard suitability and propriety, and all that, there's not a girl but could go off to church and marry somebody."

"If it's only a broomstick," acquiesced Miss Deveen, "or a man no better than one. Yes, Helen, you are right: and it has occasionally been done. But when we fly wilfully in the teeth of circumstances, bent on following our own resolute path, we take ourselves out of God's hands—and must reap the consequences."

"I—do not—quite understand," slowly spoke Helen.

"Suppose I give you an instance of what I mean, my dear. Some years ago I knew a young lady—"

"Is it true? What was her name?"

"Certainly it is true, every detail of it. As to her name—well, I do not see any reason why I should not tell it: her name was Eliza Lake. I knew her family very well indeed, was intimate with her mother. Eliza was the third daughter, and desperately eager to be married. Her chances came. The first offer was eligible; but the two families could not agree about money matters, and it dropped through. The next offer Eliza would not accept—it was from a widower with children, and she sent him to the right-about. The third went on smoothly nearly to the wedding-day, and a good and suitable match it would have been, but something occurred then very unpleasant though I never knew the precise particulars. The bridegroom-elect fell into some trouble or difficulty, he had to quit his country hastily, and the marriage was broken off—was at an end. That was the last offer she had, so far as I knew; and the years went on, Eliza gadding out to parties, and flirting and coquetting, all in the hope to get a husband. When she was in her thirtieth year, her mother came to me one day in much distress and perplexity. Eliza, she said, was taking the reins into her own hands, purposing to be married in spite of her father, mother, and friends. Mrs. Lake wanted me to talk to Eliza; she thought I might influence her, though they could not; and I took an opportunity of doing so—freely. It is of no use to mince matters when you want to save a girl from ruin. I recalled the past to her memory, saying that I believed, judging by that past, that Heaven did not intend her to marry. I told her all the ill I had heard of the man she was now choosing; also that she had absolutely thrown herself at him, and he had responded for the sake of the little money she possessed; and that if she persisted in marrying him she would assuredly rue it. In language as earnest as I knew how to choose, I laid all this before her."

"And what was her answer to you?" Helen spoke as if her breath was short.

"Just like the reckless answer that a blinded, foolish girl would make. 'Though Heaven and earth were against me, I should marry him, Miss Deveen. I am beyond the control of parents, brothers, sisters, friends; and I will not die an old maid to please any of you.' Those were the wilful words she used; I have never forgotten them; and the next week she betook herself to church."

"Did the marriage turn out badly?"

"Ay, it did. Could you expect anything else? Poor Eliza supped the cup of sorrow to its dregs: and she brought bitter sorrow and trouble also on her family. That, Helen, is what I call taking one's self out of God's hands, and flying determinedly in the face of what is right and seemly, and evidently appointed."

"You say yourself it is hard not to be married," quoth Helen.

"No, I do not," laughed Miss Deveen. "I say that it appears hard to us when our days of youth are passing, and when we see our companions chosen and ourselves left: but, rely upon it, Helen, as we advance in years, we acquiesce in the decree; many of us learning to be thankful for it."

"And you young people little think what great cause you have to be thankful for it," cried Lady Whitney, all in a heat. "Marriage brings a bushel of cares: and no one knows what anxiety boys and girls entail until they come."

Miss Deveen nodded emphatically. "It is very true. I would not exchange my present lot with that of the best wife in England; believe that, or not, as you will, Helen. Of all the different states this busy earth can produce, a lot such as mine is assuredly the most exempt from trouble. And, my dear, if you are destined never to marry, you have a great deal more cause to be thankful than rebellious."

"The other day, when you were preaching to us, you told us that trouble came for our benefit," grumbled Helen, passing into rebellion forthwith.

"I remember it," assented Miss Deveen, "and very true it is. My heart has sickened before now at witnessing the troubles, apparently unmerited, that some people, whether married or single, have to undergo; and I might have been almost tempted to question the loving-kindness of Heaven, but for remembering that we must through much tribulation enter into the Kingdom."

Anna interrupted the silence that ensued. She came running up with a handful of wild roses and sweetbriar, gathered in the hedge below. Miss Deveen took them when offered to her, saying she thought of all flowers the wild rose was the sweetest.

"How solemn you all look!" cried Anna.

"Don't we!" said Helen. "I have been having a lecture read to me."

"By whom?"

"Every one here—except Johnny Ludlow. And I am sure I hope he was edified. I wonder when tea is going to be ready!"

"Directly, I should say," said Anna: "for here comes Mrs. Ness with the cups and saucers."

I ran forward to help her bring the things. Rednal's trim wife, a neat, active woman with green eyes and a baby in her arms, was following with plates of bread-and-butter and cake, and the news that the kettle was "on the boil." Presently the table was spread; and William, who had come back to us, took up the baby's whistle and blew a blast, prolonged and shrill.

The stragglers heard it, understood it was the signal for their return, and came flocking in. The Squire and Sir John said they had been sitting under the trees and talking: our impression was, they had been sleeping. The young Whitneys appeared in various stages of heat; Tod and Featherston's nephew smelt of smoke. The first cups of tea had gone round, and Tod was making for Rednal's cottage with a notice that the bread-and-butter had come to an end, when I saw a delicate little fair-haired face peering at us from amid the trees.

"Halloa!" cried the Squire, catching sight of the face at the same moment. "Who on earth's that?"

"It's the child we saw this morning—the gipsy's child," exclaimed William Whitney. "Here, you little one! Stop! Come here."

He only meant to give her a piece of cake: but the child ran off with a scared look and fleet step, and was lost in the trees.

"Senseless little thing!" cried Bill: and sat down to his tea again.

"But what a pretty child it was!" observed the mater. "She put me in mind of Lena."

"Why, Lena's oceans of years older," said Helen, free with her remarks as usual. "That child, from the glimpse I caught of her, can't be more than five or six."

"She is about seven, miss," struck in Rednal's wife, who had just come up with a fresh supply of tea. "It is nigh upon eight years since young Walter North went off and got married."

"Walter North!" repeated Sir John. "Who's Walter North? Let me see? The name seems familiar to me."

"Old Walter North was the parish schoolmaster over at Easton, sir. The son turned out wild and unsteady; and at the time his father died he went off and joined the gipsies. They had used to encamp about here more than they do now, as Rednal could tell you, Sir John; and it was said young North was in love with a girl belonging to the tribe—Bertha Lee. Any way, they got married. Right-down beautiful she was—for a gipsy; and so young."

"Then I suppose North and his wife are here now—if that's their child?" remarked Sir John.

"They are here sure enough, sir; somewhere in the wood. Rednal has seen him about this day or two past. Two or three times they'll be here, pestering, during the summer, and stop ten or twelve days. Maybe young North has a hankering after the old spots he was brought up in, and comes to see 'em," suggestively added Rednal's wife; whose tongue ran faster than any other two women's put together. And that's saying something.

"And how does this young North get a living?" asked Sir John. "By poaching?—and rifling the poultry-yards?"

"Like enough he do, Sir John. Them tramps have mostly light fingers."

"They sell tins—and collect rabbit skins," struck in William. "Johnny Ludlow and I charged the encampment this morning, and nearly got our fortunes told."

Jessy Rednal's chin went up. "They'd better let Rednal catch 'em at their fortune-telling!—it was the wife, I know, sir, did that. When she was but a slip of a girl she'd go up as bold as brass to any gentleman or lady passing, and ask them to cross her hand with silver."

With this parting fling at the gipsies, Rednal's wife ran off to the cottage for another basin of sugar. The heat made us thirsty, and we wanted about a dozen cups of tea apiece.

But now, I don't know why it was, I had rather taken a fancy to this young woman, Bertha North, and did not believe the words "as bold as brass" could be properly applied to her. Gipsy though she was, her face, for good feeling and refinement, was worth ten of Jessy Rednal's. It's true she had followed us, wanting to tell our fortunes, but she might have been hard up for money.

When we had swallowed as much tea as the kettles would produce, and cleared the plates of the eatables, Sir John suggested that it would soon be time to move homewards, as the evening would be coming on. This had the effect of scattering some of us at once. If they did not get us, they could not take us. "Home, indeed! as early as this!" cried Helen, wrathfully—and rushed off with her brother Harry and Featherston's nephew.

I was ever so far down one of the wood paths, looking about, for somehow I had missed them all, when sounds of wailing and crying from a young voice struck my ear. In a minute, that same fair little child came running into view, as if she were flying for her life from some pursuing foe, her sobs wild with terror, her face white as death.

What she said I could not make out, though she made straight up to me and caught my arm; the language seemed strange, the breath gone. But there was no mistaking the motions: she pulled me along with her across the wood, her little arms and eyes frantically imploring.

Something must be amiss, I thought. What was it? "Is there a mad bull in the way, little one? And are you making off with me to do battle with him?"

No elucidation from the child: only the sobs, and the words I did not catch. But we were close to the outskirts of the wood now (it was but narrow), and there, beyond the hedge that bordered it, crouched down against the bank, was a man. A fair-faced, good-looking young man, small and slight, and groaning with pain.

No need to wonder who he was: the likeness between him and the child betrayed it. How like they were! even to the expression in the large blue eyes, and the colour of the soft fair hair. The child's face was his own in miniature.

"You are Walter North," I said. "And what's to do?"

His imploring eyes in their pitiful pain looked up to mine, as if he would question how I needed to ask it. Then he pulled his fustian coat aside and pointed to his side. It made me start a step back. The side was steeped in blood.

"Oh dear, what is it?—what has caused it? An accident?"

"I have been shot," he answered—and I thought his voice sounded ominously weak. "Shot from over yonder."

Looking across the field in front of us, towards which he pointed, I could see nothing. I mean, nothing likely to have shot him. No men, no guns. Off to the left, partly buried amidst its grounds, lay the old house called the Granary; to the right in the distance, Vale Farm. The little child was stretched on the ground, quiet now, her head resting on his right shoulder; it was the left side that was injured. Suddenly he whispered a few words to her; she sprang up with a sob and darted into the wood. The child, as we heard later, had been sent out by her mother to look for her father: it was in seeking for him that she had come upon our tea-party and peeped at us. Later, she found him, fallen where he was now, just after the shot which struck him was fired. In her terror she was flying off for assistance, and met me. The man's hat lay near him, also an old drab-coloured bag, some tin basins, and a Dutch-oven.

"Can I move you, to put you easier?" I asked between his groans. "Can I do anything in the world to help you?"

"No, no, don't touch me," he said, in a hopeless tone. "I am bleeding to death."

And I thought he was. His cheeks and lips were growing paler with every minute. The man's diction was as good as mine; and, tramp though he was, many a gentleman has not half as nice a face as his.

"If you don't mind being left, I will run for a doctor—old Featherston."

Before he could answer yes or no, Harry Vale, who must have espied us from their land, came running up.

"Why—what in the world—" he began. "Is it you, North? What? Shot, you say?"

"From over yonder, sir; and I've got my death-blow: I think I have. Perhaps if Featherston—"

"I'll fetch him," cried Harry Vale. "You stay here with him, Johnny." And he darted away like a lamplighter, his long legs skimming the grass.

I am nothing but a muff; you know that of old. And never did I feel my own deficiencies come home to me as they did then. Any one else might have known how to stop the bleeding—for of course it ought to be stopped—if only by stuffing a handkerchief into the wound. I did not dare attempt it; I was worse at any kind of surgery than a born imbecile. All in a moment, as I stood there, the young gipsy-woman's words of the morning flashed into my mind. She had foreseen some ill for him, she said; had scented it in the air. How strange it seemed!

The next to come upon the scene was the Squire, crushing through the brambles when he heard our voices. He and Sir John, in dire wrath at our flight, had come out to look for us and to marshal us back for the start home. I gave him a few whispered words of explanation.

"What!" cried he. "Dying?" and his face went as pale as the man's. "Oh, my poor fellow, I am sorry for this!"

Stooping over him, the Squire pulled the coat aside. The stains were larger now, the flow was greater. North bent his head forward to look, and somehow got his hand wet in the process. Wet and red. He snatched it away with a kind of horror. The sight seemed to bring upon him the conviction that his minutes were numbered. His minutes. Which is the last and greatest terror that can seize upon man.

"I'm going before God now, and I'm not fit for it," he cried, a shrieking note, born of emotion, in his weakening voice. "Can there be any mercy for me?"

The Squire seemed to feel it—he has said so since—as one of the most solemn moments of his life. He took off his spectacles—a habit of his when much excited—dropped them into his pocket, and clasped his hands together.

"There's mercy with God through the Lord Jesus always," he said, bending over the troubled face. "He pardoned the thief on the Cross. He pardoned all who came to Him. If you are Walter North, as they tell me, you must know all this as well as I do. Lord God have mercy upon this poor dying man, for Christ's sake!"

And perhaps the good lessons that North had learnt in childhood from his mother, for she was a good woman, came back to him then to comfort him. He lifted his own hands towards the skies, and half the terror went out of his face.

Some one once said, I believe, that by standing stock still in the Strand, and staring at any given point, he could collect a crowd about him in no time. In the thronged thoroughfares of London that's not to be surprised at; but what I should like to know is this—how is it that people collect in deserts? They do, and you must have seen it often. Before many minutes were over we had quite a levee: Sir John Whitney, William, and Featherston's nephew; three or four labourers from Vale Farm; Harry Vale, who had met Featherston, and outrun him; and one of the tall sons of Colonel Leonard. The latter, a young fellow with lazy limbs, a lazy voice, and supercilious manner, strolled up, smacking a dog-whip.

"What's the row here?" cried he: and William Whitney told him. The man had been shot: by whom or by what means, whether wilfully or accidentally, remained to be discovered.

"Did you do it—or your brothers?" asked Harry Vale of him in a low tone. And Herbert Leonard whirled round to face Vale with a haughty stare.

"What the devil do you mean? What should we want to shoot a tramp for?"

"Any way, you were practising with pistols at your target over yonder this afternoon."

Leonard did not condescend to reply. The words had angered him. By no possibility could a shot, aimed at their target, come in this direction. The dog-whip shook, as if he felt inclined to use it on Harry Vale for his insolent suggestion.

"Such a fuss over a tramp!" cried Leonard to Sir John, not caring who heard him. "I dare say the fellow was caught thieving, and got served out for his pains."

But he did not well know Sir John—who turned upon him like lightning.

"How dare you say that, young man! Are you not ashamed to give utterance to such sentiments?"

"Look here!" coolly retorted Leonard.

Catching hold of the bag to shake it, out tumbled a dead hen with ruffled feathers. Sir John looked grave. Leonard held it up.

"I thought so. It is still warm. He has stolen it from some poultry-yard."

I chanced to be standing close to North as Leonard said it, and felt a feeble twitch at my trousers. Poor North was trying to attract my attention; gazing up at me with the most anxious face.

"No," said he, but he was almost too faint to speak now. "No. Tell them, sir, No."

But Harry Vale was already taking up the defence. "You are wrong, Mr. Herbert Leonard. I gave that hen myself to North half-an-hour ago. Some little lads, my cousins, are at the farm to-day, and one of them accidentally killed the hen. Knowing our people would not care to use it, I called to North, who chanced to be passing at the time, and told him he might take it if he liked."

A gleam of a smile, checked by a sob, passed over the poor man's face. Things wear a different aspect to us in the hour of death from what they do in lusty life. It may be that North saw then that theft, even of a fowl, was theft, and felt glad to be released from the suspicion. Sir John looked as pleased as Punch: one does not like to hear wrong brought home to a dying man.

Herbert Leonard turned off indifferently, strolling back across the field and cracking his whip; and Featherston came pelting up.

The first thing the doctor did, when he had seen North's face, was to take a phial and small glass out of his pocket, and give him something to drink. Next, he made a clear sweep of us all round, and knelt down to examine the wound, just as the poor gipsy wife, fetched by the child, appeared in sight.

"Is there any hope?" whispered the Squire.

"Hope!" whispered back Featherston. "In half-an-hour it will be over."

"God help him!" prayed the Squire. "God pardon and take him!"

Well, well—that is about all there is to tell. Poor North died, there as he lay, in the twilight; his wife's arm round his neck, and his little girl feebly clasped to him.

What an end to the bright and pleasant day! Sir John thanked Heaven openly that it was not we who had caused the calamity.

"For somebody must have shot him, lads," he observed, "though I dare say it was accidental. And it might have chanced to be one of you—there's no telling: you are not too cautious with your guns."

The "somebody" turned out to be George Leonard. Harry Vale (who had strong suspicions) was right. When they dispersed after their target practising, one of them, George, went towards Briar Wood, his pistol loaded. The thick trees afforded a promising mark, he thought, and he carelessly let off the pistol at them. Whether he saw that he had shot a man was never known; he denied it out and out: didn't know one was there, he protested. A waggoner, passing homewards with his team, had seen him fire the pistol, and came forward to say so; or it might have been a mystery to the end. "Accidental Death," decided the jury at the inquest; but they recommended the supercilious young man (just as indifferent as his brothers) to take care what he fired at for the future. Mr. George did not take the rebuke kindly.

For these sons had hard, bad natures; and were doing their best to bring down their father's grey hairs with sorrow to the grave.

But how strange it seemed altogether! The poor young gipsy-wife's subtle instinct that evil was near!—and that the shot should just have struck him instead of spending itself harmlessly upon one of the hundreds of trees! Verily there are things in this world not to be grasped by our limited understandings.

CHAPTER XIII

THE STORY OF DOROTHY GRAPE

DISAPPEARANCE

I

According to Mrs. Todhetley's belief, some people are born to be unlucky. Not only individuals, but whole families. "I have noticed it times and again, Johnny, in going through life," she has said to me: "ill-luck in some way lies upon them, and upon all they do; they cannot prosper, from their cradle to their grave." That there will be some compensating happiness for these people hereafter—for they do exist—is a belief we all like to cherish.

I am now going to tell of people in rather humble life whom this ill-luck seemed to attend. That might never have brought the family into notice, ups and downs being so common in the world: but two mysterious disappearances occurred in it, which caused them to be talked about; and those occurrences I must relate before coming to Dorothy's proper history. They took place before my time; in fact when Squire Todhetley was a young man, and it is from him that I repeat it.

At this end of the village of Islip, going into it from Crabb, there stood on the right-hand side of the road a superior cottage residence, with lovely yellow roses intertwining themselves about its porch. Robert Grape and his wife lived in it, and were well enough to do. He was in the "post-horse duty," the Squire said—whatever that might mean; and she had money on her own account. The cottage was hers absolutely, and nearly one hundred pounds a-year income. The latter, however, was only an annuity, and would die with her.

There were two children living: Dorothy, softened by her friends into Dolly; and Thomas. Two others, who came between them, went off in what Mrs. Grape used to call a "galloping consumption." Dolly's cheeks were bright and her eyes were blue, and her soft brown hair fell back in curls from her dimpled face. All the young men about, including the Squire, admired the little girl; more than their mothers did, who said she was growing up vain and light-headed. Perhaps she might be; but she was a modest, well-behaved little maiden. She went to school by day, as did her brother.

Mr. Grape's occupation, connected with the "post-horse duty," appeared to consist in driving about the country in a gig. The length of these journeys varied, but he would generally be absent about three weeks. Then he would come home for a short interval, and go off again. He was a well-conducted man and was respected.

One Monday morning in summer, when the sun was shining on the yellow roses and the dew glittered on the grass, Robert Grape was about to start on one of these journeys. Passing out to his gig, which waited at the gate, after kissing his wife and daughter, he stopped to pluck a rose. Dolly followed him out. She was sixteen now and had left school.

"Take care your old horse does not fall this time, father," said she, gaily and lightly.

"I'll take care, lass, if I can," he answered.

"The truth is, Robert, you want a new horse," said Mrs. Grape, speaking from the open door.

"I know I do, Mary Ann. Old Jack's no longer to be trusted."

"Shall you be at Bridgenorth to-morrow?"

"No; on Wednesday evening. Good-bye once more. You may expect me home at the time I've said." And, with those last words he mounted his gig and drove away.

From that day, from that hour, Robert Grape was never more seen by his family. Neither did they hear from him: but he did not, as a rule, write to them when on his journeys. They said to one another what delightful weather he was having this time, and the days passed pleasantly until the Saturday of his expected return.

But he did not come. Mrs. Grape had prepared a favourite dinner of his for the Sunday, lamb and peas, and a lemon cheese-cake. They had to take it without him. Three or four more days passed, and still they saw nothing of him. Mrs. Grape was not at all uneasy.

"I think, children, he must have been mistaken in a week," she said to Dolly and Tom. "It must be next Saturday that he meant. I shall expect him then."

He did not come. The Saturday came, but he did not. And the following week Mrs. Grape wrote a letter to the inn at Bridgenorth, where he was in the habit of putting-up, asking when he had left it, and for what town.

Startling tidings came back in answer. Mr. Grape had quitted the place nearly four weeks ago, leaving his horse and gig at the inn. He had not yet returned for them. Mrs. Grape could not make it out; she went off to Worcester to take the stage-coach for Bridgenorth, and there made inquiries. The following was the substance of what she learned:—

On Wednesday evening, the next day but one after leaving his home, Mr. Grape approached Bridgenorth. Upon entering the town, the horse started and fell: his master was thrown out of the gig, but not hurt; the shafts were broken and the horse lamed. "A pretty kettle of fish, this is," cried Mr. Grape in his good-humoured way to the ostler, when the damaged cavalcade reached the inn: "I shall have to take a week's holiday now, I suppose." The man's answer was to the effect that the old horse was no longer of much good; Mr. Grape nodded assent, and remarked that he must be upon the look-out for another.

In the morning, he quitted the inn on foot, leaving the horse to the care of the veterinary surgeon, who said it would be four or five days before he would be fit to travel, and the gig to have its shafts repaired. Mr. Grape observed to the landlord that he should use the opportunity to go on a little expedition which otherwise he could not have found time for, and should be back before the horse was well. But he never had come back. This was recounted to Mrs. Grape.

"He did not give any clue as to where he was going," added the landlord; "he started away with nothing but his umbrella and what he might have put in his pockets, saying he should walk the first stage of his journey. His portmanteau is up in his bedroom now."

All this sounded very curious to Mrs. Grape. It was unlike her open, out-speaking husband. She inquired whether it was likely that he had been injured in the fall from the gig and could be lying ill somewhere.

The landlord shook his head in dissent. "He said he was not hurt a bit," replied he, "and he did not seem to be. He ate a good supper that night and made a famous breakfast in the morning."

An idea flashed across Mrs. Grape's mind as she listened. "I think he must have gone off for a ramble about the Welsh mountains," spoke she. "He was there once when a boy, and often said how much he should like to go there again. In fact he said he should go when he could spare the time."

"May be so," assented the landlord. "Them Welsh mountains be pleasant to look upon; but if a mist comes on, or one meets with an awkward pass, or anything of that sort—well, ma'am, let's hope we shall see him back yet."

After bringing all the inquiries to an end that she was able to make, Mrs. Grape went home in miserable uncertainty. She did not give up hope; she thought he must be lying ill amongst the Welsh hills, perhaps had caught a fever and lost his senses. As the days and the weeks passed on, a sort of nervous expectancy set in. Tidings of him might come to her any day, living or dead. A sudden knock at the door made her jump; if the postman by some rare chance paid them a visit—for letters were not written in those days by the bushel—it set her trembling. More than once she had hastily risen in the middle of the night, believing she heard a voice calling to her outside the cottage. But tidings of Robert Grape never came.

That was disappearance the first.

In the spring of the following year Mrs. Grape sold her pretty homestead and removed to Worcester. Circumstances had changed with her. Beyond what little means had been, or could be, saved, the children would have nothing to help them on in the world. Tom, thirteen years old now, must have a twelvemonth's good schooling before being placed at some business. Dolly must learn a trade by which to get her living. In past times, young people who were not specially educated for it, or were of humble birth, did not dream of making themselves into governesses.

"You had better go to the mantua-making, Dolly," said Mrs. Grape. "It's nice genteel work."

Dolly drew a wry face. "I should not make much hand at that, mother."

"But what else is there? You wouldn't like the stay-making—"

"Oh dear, no."

"Or to serve in a pastry-cook's shop, or anything of that sort. I should not like to see you in a shop, myself; you are too—too giddy," added Mrs. Grape, pulling herself up from saying too pretty. "I think it must be the mantua-making, Dolly: you'll make a good enough hand at it, once you've learnt it. Why not?"

II

The house rented by Mrs. Grape at Worcester was near the London Road. It was semi-detached, and built, like its fellow in rather a peculiar way, as though the architect had found himself cramped for space in width but had plenty of it in depth. It was close to the road, about a yard only of garden ground lying between. The front-door opened into the sitting-room; not a very uncommon case then with houses of its class. It was a fair-sized room, light and pretty, the window being beside the door. Another door, opposite the window, led to the rest of the house: a small back-parlour, a kitchen, three rooms above, with a yard and a strip of garden at the back. It was a comfortable house, at a small rent; and, once Mrs. Grape had disposed her tasty furniture about it to advantage, she tried to feel at home and to put aside her longing to be back under the old roof at Islip.

In the adjoining house dwelt two Quaker ladies named Deavor, an aunt and niece, the latter a year or two older than Dolly. They showed themselves very friendly to the new-comers, as did their respectable old servant-maid, and the two families became intimate neighbours.

Dolly, seventeen now, was placed with Miss Pedley, one of the first dressmakers in the city, as out-door apprentice. She was bound to her for three years, and went to and fro daily. Tom was day-scholar at a gentleman's school in the neighbourhood.

One Saturday evening in summer, when they had been about three months in their new abode, Mrs. Grape was sitting at the table in the front-room, making up a smart cap for herself. She had never put on mourning for her husband, always cherishing the delusive hope that he would some day return. Tom sat by her, doing his lessons; Dolly was near the open window, nursing a grey kitten. Tom looked as hot as the evening, as he turned over the books before him with a puzzled face. He was a good-looking boy, with soft brown eyes, and a complexion as brilliant as his sister's.

"I say, mother," cried he, "I don't think this Latin will be of much good to me. I shan't make any hand at it."

"You will be like me then, Tom, for I'm sure I shall never make much of a hand at dressmaking," spoke up Dolly. "Miss Pedley sees it too."

"Be quiet, Dolly; don't talk nonsense," said Mrs. Grape. "Let Tom finish his tasks."

Thus reprimanded, silence ensued again. It grew dusk; candles were lighted and the window was shut down, as the breeze blew them about; but the bright moonlight still streamed in. Presently Dolly left the room to give the kitten its supper. Suddenly, Tom shut up his books with a bang.

"Finished, Tom?"

"Yes, mother."

He was putting them away when a knock came to the front-door. Tom opened it.

"Halloa, Bill!" said he.

"Halloa, Tom!" responded a boy's voice. "I've come up to ask if you'll go fishing with me to-morrow."

"To-morrow!" echoed Tom in surprise. "Why, to-morrow's Sunday!"

"Bother! I mean Monday. I'm going up to the Weir at Powick: there's first-rate fishing there. Will you come, Tom?"

Mrs. Grape wondered who the boy was; she knew the voices of some of Tom's schoolfellows, but did not recognize this one. Tom, standing on the low step outside, had partly closed the door behind him, and she could not see out; but she heard every word as plainly as though the speakers had been in the room.

"I should like to go, but I'm sure I could never get leave from school," said Tom. "Why, the Midsummer examination comes on the end of next week; our masters just do keep us to it!"

"Stingy old misers! You might take French leave, Tom."

"Mother would never let me do that," returned Tom; and he probably made a sign to indicate that his mother was within hearing, as both voices dropped to a lower key; but Mrs. Grape still heard distinctly. "Are you going to take French leave yourself, Bill?" added young Grape. "How else shall you manage to get off?"

"Oh, Monday will be holiday with us; it's a Saint's Day. Look here, Tom; you may as well come. Fishing, up at Powick, is rare fun; and I've some prime bait."

"I can't," pleaded Tom: "no good thinking about it. You must get one of your own fellows instead."

"Suppose I must. Well, good-night."

"Good-night, Bill."

"I touched you last," added the strange voice. There was a shout of laughter, the door flew back, Tom's hand came in to snatch up his cap, which lay on a table near, and he went flying after the other boy.

They had entered upon the fascinating game of "Titch-touch-last." Mrs. Grape got up, laid her finished cap upon the table, shook the odds and ends of threads from her black gown, and began to put her needles and cotton in the little work-box. While she was doing this, Dolly came in from the kitchen. She looked round the room.

"Why, where's Tom, mother?"

"Some boy called to speak to him, and they are running about the road at Titch-touch-last. The cap looks nice, does it not, Dolly?"

"Oh, very," assented Dolly. It was one she had netted for her mother; and the border was spread out in the shape of a fan—the fashion then—and trimmed with yellow gauze ribbon.

The voices of the boys were still heard, but at a distance. Dolly went to the door, and looked out.

"Yes, there the two are," she cried. "What boy is it, mother?"

"I don't know," replied Mrs. Grape. "I did not see him, or recognize his voice. Tom called him 'Bill.'"

She went also to the door as she spoke, and stood by her daughter on the low broad step. The voices were fainter now, for the lads, in their play, were drawing further off and nearer to the town. Mrs. Grape could see them dodging around each other, now on this side the road, now on that. It was a remarkably light night, the moon, in the cloudless sky, almost dazzlingly bright.

"They'll make themselves very hot," she remarked, as she and Dolly withdrew indoors. "What silly things boys are!"

Carrying her cap upstairs, Mrs. Grape then attended to two or three household matters. Half-an-hour had elapsed when she returned to the parlour. Tom had not come in. "How very thoughtless of him!" she cried; "he must know it is his bed-time."

But neither she nor Dolly felt any uneasiness until the clock struck ten. A shade of it crept over Mrs. Grape then. What could have become of the boy?

Standing once more upon the door-step, they gazed up and down the road. A few stragglers were passing up from the town: more people would be out on a Saturday night than on any other.

"How dost thee this evening, friend Grape?" called out Rachel Deavor, now sitting with her niece at their open parlour window in the moonlight. Mrs. Grape turned to them, and told of Tom's delinquency. Elizabeth Deavor, a merry girl, came out laughing, and linked her arm within Dolly's.

"He has run away from thee to take a moonlight ramble," she said jestingly. "Thee had been treating him to a scolding, maybe."

"No, I had not," replied Dolly. "I have such a pretty grey kitten, Elizabeth. One of the girls at Miss Pedley's gave it to me."

They stood on, talking in the warm summer night, Mrs. Grape at the window with the elder Quakeress, Dolly at the gate, with the younger, and the time went on. The retiring hour of the two ladies had long passed, but they did not like to leave Mrs. Grape to her uncertainty: she was growing more anxious with every minute. At length the clocks struck half-past eleven, and Mrs. Grape, to the general surprise, burst into tears.

"Nay, nay, now, do not give way," said Rachel Deavor kindly. "Doubtless he has but gone to the other lad's home, and is letting the time pass unthinkingly. Boys will be boys."

"That unaccountable disappearance of my husband makes me more nervous than I should otherwise be," spoke Mrs. Grape in apology. "It is just a year ago. Am I going to have a second edition of that, in the person of my son?"

"Hush thee now, thee art fanciful; thee should not anticipate evil. It is a pity but thee had recognized the boy who came for thy son; some of us might go to the lad's house."

"I wish I had," sighed Mrs. Grape. "I meant to ask Tom who it was when he came in. Tom called him 'Bill;' that is all I know."

"Here he comes!" exclaimed Dolly, who was now standing outside the gate with Elizabeth Deavor. "He is rushing round the corner, at full speed, mother."

"Won't I punish him!" cried Mrs. Grape, in her relieved feelings: and she too went to the gate.

Dolly's hopeful eagerness had misled her. It was not Tom. But it was one of Tom's schoolfellows, young Thorn, whom they all knew. He halted to explain that he had been to a boys' party in the Bath Road, and expected to "catch it" at home for staying so late. Dolly interrupted him to speak of Tom.

"What an odd thing!" cried the lad. "Oh, he'll come home presently, safe enough. Which of our fellows are named Bill, you ask, Miss Grape? Let's see. There's Bill Stroud; and Bill Hardwick—that is, William—"

"It was neither Stroud nor Hardwick; I should have known the voices of both," interrupted Mrs. Grape. "This lad cannot, I think, be in your school at all, Thorn: he said his school was to have holiday on Monday because it would be a Saint's Day."

"Holiday, because it was a Saint's Day!" echoed Thorn. "Oh then, he must have been one of the college boys. No other school goes in for holidays on the Saints' Days but that. The boys have to attend service at college, morning and afternoon, so it's not a complete holiday: they can get it easily, though, by asking leave."

"I don't think Tom knows any of the college boys," debated Dolly.

"Yes, he does; our school knows some of them," replied Thorn. "Good-night: I can't stay. He is sure to turn up presently."

But Tom Grape did not turn up. At midnight his mother put on her bonnet and shawl and started out to look for him in the now deserted streets of the town. Now and again she would inquire of some late wayfarer whether he had met a boy that night, or perhaps two boys, and described Tom's appearance; but she could learn nothing. The most feasible idea she could call up, and the most hopeful, was that Tom had really gone home with the other lad and that something must have happened to keep him there; perhaps an accident. Dolly felt sure it must be so. Elizabeth Deavor, running in at breakfast-time next morning to ask for news, laughingly said Tom deserved to be shaken.

But when the morning hours passed and did not bring the truant or any tidings of him, this hope died away. The first thing to be done was to find out who the other boy was, and to question him. Perhaps he had also disappeared!

Getting from young Thorn the address of those of the college boys—three—who, as he chanced to know, bore the Christian name of William, Mrs. Grape went to make inquiries at their houses. She could learn nothing. Each of the three boys disclaimed all knowledge of the affair; their friends corroborating their assertion that they had not been out on the Saturday night. Four more of the King's scholars were named William, they told her; two of them boarding in the house of the head-master, the Reverend Allen Wheeler.

To this gentleman's residence, in the College Green, Mrs. Grape next proceeded. It was then evening. The head-master listened courteously to her tale, and became, in his awakened interest, as anxious as she was to find the right boy. Mrs. Grape said she should not know him, but should know his voice. Not one of the three boys, already seen, possessed the voice she had heard.

The two boarders were called into the room, as a mere matter of form; for the master was able to state positively that they were in bed at the hour in question. Neither of them had the voice of the boy who had called for Tom. It was a very clear voice, Mrs. Grape said; she should recognize it instantly.

"Let me see," said the master, going over mentally the list of the forty King's scholars: "how many more of you boys are named William, beyond those this lady has seen?"

The boys considered, and said there were two others; William Smith and William Singleton; both called familiarly "Bill" in the school. Each of these boys had a clear, pleasant voice, the master observed; but neither of them had applied for leave for Monday, nor had he heard of any projected fishing expedition to Powick.

To the house of the Singletons next went Mrs. Grape: but the boy's voice there did not answer to the one she had heard. The Smith family she could not see; they had gone out for the evening: and she dragged herself home, utterly beaten down both in body and spirit.

Another night of anxiety was passed, and then Mrs. Grape returned to Mr. Smith's and saw "Bill." But Bill was hoarse as a raven; it was not at all the clear voice she had heard; though he looked desperately frightened at being questioned.

So there it was. Tom Grape was lost. Lost! and no clue remained as to the why and wherefore. He must have gone after his father, said the sympathizing townspeople, full of wonder; and a superstitious feeling crept over Mrs. Grape.

But ere the week was quite over, news came to the desolate home: not of Tom himself; not of the manner of his disappearance; only of the night it happened. On the Friday evening Mrs. Grape and Dolly were sitting together, when a big boy of sixteen appeared at their door, Master Fred Smith, lugging in his brother Bill.

"He is come to confess, ma'am," said the elder. "He blurted it all out to me just now, too miserable to keep it in any longer, and I've brought him off to you."

"Oh, tell me, tell me where he is!" implored Mrs. Grape from her fevered lips; as she rose and clasped the boy, Bill, by the arm.

"I don't know where he is," answered the boy in trembling earnestness. "I can't think where; I wish I could. I know no more than the dead."

"For what have you come here then?"

"To confess that it was I who was with him. You didn't know my voice on the Monday because I had such a cold," continued he, laying hold of a chair-back to steady his shaking hands. "I must have caught it playing with Tom that night; we got so hot, both of us. When I heard he had never been home since, couldn't be found anywhere, I felt frightened to death and didn't like to say it was me who had been with him."

"Where did you leave him? Where did you miss him?" questioned the mother, her heart sinking with despair.

"We kept on playing at titch-touch-last; neither of us would give in, each wanted to have the last touch; and we got down past the Bath Road, and on up Sidbury near to the canal bridge. Tom gave me a touch; it was the last; and he rushed through the Commandery gates. I was getting tired then, and a thought came to me that instead of going after him I'd play him a trick and make off home; and I did so, tearing over the bridge as hard as I could tear. And that's all the truth," concluded the boy, bursting into tears, "and I never saw Tom again, and have no more to tell though the head-master hoists me for it to-morrow."

"It is just what he said to me, Mrs. Grape," put in the brother quietly, "and I am sure it is the truth."

"Through the Commandery gates," repeated Mrs. Grape, pressing her aching brow. "And you did not see him come out again?"

"No, ma'am, I made off as hard as I could go. While he was rushing down there—I heard his boots clattering on the flags—I rushed over the bridge homewards."

The boy had told all he knew. Now that the confession was made, he would be too glad to add more had he been able. It left the mystery just as it was before; no better and no worse. There was no outlet to the Commandery, except these iron gates, and nothing within it that could have swallowed up Tom. It was a cul-de-sac, and he must have come out again by these self-same gates. Whither had he then gone?

It was proved that he did come out. When Mr. Bill Smith's confession was made public, an assistant to a doctor in the town remembered to have seen Tom Grape, whom he knew by sight, as he was passing the Commandery about that same time to visit a patient in Wyld's Lane. Tom came flying out of the gates, laughing, and looking up and down the street. "Where are you, Bill?" he called out. The young doctor, whose name was Seton, looked back at Tom, as he went on his way.

But the young man added something more, which nobody else had thought to speak of, and which afforded a small loop-hole of conjecture as to what poor Tom's fate might have been. Just about that hour a small barge on the canal, after passing under Sidbury bridge, came in contact with another barge. Very little damage was done, but there was a great deal of shouting and confusion. As Mr. Seton walked over the bridge, not a second before he saw Tom, he heard the noise and saw people making for the spot. Had Tom Grape made for it? He could easily have reached it. And if so, had he, amidst the general pushing and confusion on the canal bank, fallen into the canal? It was hardly to be imagined that any accident of this kind could happen to him unseen; though it might be just possible, for the scene for some minutes was one of tumult; but nothing transpired to confirm it. The missing lad did not reappear, either dead or alive.

And so poor Tom Grape had passed out of life mysteriously as his father had done. Many months elapsed before his mother gave up her search for him; she was always thinking he would come home again, always hoping it. The loss affected her more than her husband's had, for Tom vanished under her very eye, so to say; all the terror of it was palpably enacted before her, all the suspense had to be borne and lived through; whereas the other loss took place at a distance and she only grew to realize it by degrees; which of course softened the blow. And the time went on by years, but nothing was seen of Tom Grape.

That was disappearance the second.

Dolly left her place of business at the end of the three years for which she had been apprenticed, and set up for herself; a brass plate on her mothers door—"Miss Grape, Mantua-maker"—proclaiming the fact to the world. She was only twenty then, with as sweet a face, the Squire says, as Worcester, renowned though it is for its pretty faces, ever saw. She had never in her heart taken kindly to her business, so would not be likely to set the world on fire with her skill; but she had tried to do her best and would continue to do it. A little work began to come in now and then; a gown to be turned or a spencer to be made, though not so many of them as Dolly hoped for: but, as her mother said, Rome was not built in a day.

III

"Mother, I think I shall go to college this morning."

So spoke Dolly at the breakfast-table one Sunday in July. The sun was shining in at the open window, the birds were singing.

"It's my belief, Dolly, you would go off to college every Sunday of your life, if you had your way," said Mrs. Grape.

Dolly laughed. "And so I would, mother."

For the beautiful cathedral service had charms for Dolly. Islip Church was a very primitive church, the good old clergyman was toothless, the singing of the two psalms was led off by the clerk in a cracked bass voice; there was no organ. Accustomed to nothing better than this, the first time Dolly found herself at the cathedral, after their removal to Worcester, and the magnificent services burst upon her astonished senses, she thought she must have ascended to some celestial sphere. The fine edifice, the musical chanting of the prayers by the minor canons, the singing of the numerous choir, men and boys in their white surplices, the deep tones of the swelling organ, the array of white-robed prebendaries, the dignified and venerable bishop—Cornwall—in his wig and lawn sleeves, the state, the ceremony of the whole, and the glittering colours of the famed east window in the distance; all this laid hold of Dolly's senses for ever. She and her mother attended St. Martin's Church generally, but Dolly would now and then lure her mother to the cathedral. Latterly Mrs. Grape had been ailing and did not go anywhere.

"If you could but go to college to-day, mother!" went on Dolly.

"Why!"

"Mr. Benson preaches. I met Miss Stafford yesterday afternoon, and she told me Mr. Benson had come into residence. The Herald said so too."

"Then you must go betimes if you would secure a seat," remarked Mrs. Grape. "And mind you don't get your new muslin skirt torn."

So Dolly put on her new muslin, and her bonnet, and started.

When the Reverend Christopher Benson, Master of the Temple, became one of the prebendaries of Worcester, his fame as a preacher flew to all parts of the town. You should hear the Squire's account of the crush in getting into the cathedral on the Sundays that he was in residence: four Sundays in the year; or five, as the case might be; all told. Members of other churches, Dissenters of different sects, Quakers, Roman Catholics, and people who never went anywhere at other times, scrupled not to run to hear Mr. Benson. For reading like unto his, or preaching like unto his, had rarely been heard in that cathedral or in any other. Though it might be only the Gospel that fell to his share in the communion service, the crowd listened, enraptured, to his sweet, melodious tones. The college doors were besieged before the hour for opening them; it was like going into a theatre.

Dolly, on this day, made one in the crowd at the cloister entrance; she was pushed here and there; and although she hurried well with the rest as soon as the doors were unlocked, every seat was taken when she reached the chancel. She found standing room opposite the pulpit, near King John's tomb, and felt very hot in the crush.

"Is it always like this, here?"

The whispered words came from a voice at her side. Dolly turned, and saw a tall, fine-looking, well-dressed man about thirty, with a green silk umbrella in his hand.

"No," she whispered back again. "Only for four or five Sundays, at this time of the year, when Mr. Benson preaches."

"Indeed," said the stranger. "His preaching ought to be something extraordinary to attract such a crowd as this."

"And so it is," breathed Dolly. "And his reading—oh, you never heard any reading like it."

"Very eloquent, I suppose?"

"I don't know whether it may be called eloquence," debated Dolly, remembering that a chance preacher she once heard, who thumped the cushions with his hands and shook the air with his voice, was said to be eloquent. "Mr. Benson is the quietest preacher and reader I ever listened to."

The stranger seemed to be a kind sort of man. During the stir made by the clergy, preceded by the six black-robed, bowing bedesmen, going up to the communion-table, he found an inch of room on a bench, and secured it for Dolly. She thanked him gratefully.

Mr. Benson's sermon came to an end, the bishop gave the blessing from his throne, and the crowd poured out. Dolly, by way of a change, made her exit from the great north entrance. The brightness of the day had changed; a sharp shower was falling.

"Oh dear! My new muslin will be wet through!" thought Dolly. "This parasol's of no use."

"Will you allow me to offer you my umbrella—or permit me to hold it over you?" spoke the stranger, who must have followed her out. And Dolly hesitated and flushed, and did not know whether she ought to say yes or no.

He held the umbrella over Dolly, letting his own coat get wet. The shower ceased presently; but he walked on by her side to her mother's door, and then departed with a bow fit for an emperor.

"What a polite man!" thought Dolly. "Quite a gentleman." And she mentioned the occurrence to her mother; who seemed to-day more poorly than usual.

They sat at the open window in the afternoon, and Dolly read aloud the evening psalms. It was the fifth day of the month. As Dolly finished the last verse and closed the book, Mrs. Grape, after a moment's silence, repeated the words:—

"The Lord shall give strength unto His people: the Lord shall give His people the blessing of peace."

"What a beautiful promise that is, Dolly!" she said in hushed tones. "Peace! Ah, my dear, no one can know what that word means until they have been sorely tried. Peace everlasting!"

Mrs. Grape leaned back in her chair, gazing upwards. The sky was of a deep blue; a brilliant gold cloud, of peculiar shape, was moving slowly across it just overhead.

"One could almost fancy it to be God's golden throne in the brighter land," she murmured. "My child, do you know, the thought comes across me at times that it may not be long before I am there. And I am getting to long for it."

"Don't say that, mother," cried the startled girl.

"Well, well, dear, I don't want to frighten you. It is all as God pleases."

"I shall send to ask Mr. Nash to come to see you to-morrow, mother. Do you feel worse?"

Mrs. Grape slightly shook her head. Presently she spoke.

"Is it not almost teatime, Dolly?—whoever is that?"

A gentleman, passing, with a red rose in his button-hole and silk umbrella in his hand, was taking off his hat to Dolly. Dolly's face turned red as the rose as she returned the bow, and whispered to her mother that it was the polite stranger. He halted to express a hope that the young lady had not taken cold from the morning shower.

He turned out to be a Mr. Mapping, a traveller in the wine trade for some London house. But, when he was stating this to Mrs. Grape during the first visit paid her (for he contrived to make good his entrance to the house), he added in a careless, off-hand manner, that he was thankful to say he had good private means and was not dependent upon his occupation. He lingered on in Worcester, and became intimate with the Grapes.

Events thickened. Before the next month, August, came in, Mrs. Grape died. Dolly was stunned; but she would have felt the blow even more keenly than she did feel it had she not fallen over head and ears in love with Alick Mapping. About three hundred pounds, all her mother's savings, came to Dolly; excepting that, and the furniture, she was unprovided for.

"You cannot live upon that: what's a poor three hundred pounds?" spoke Mr. Mapping a day or two after the funeral, his tone full of tender compassion.

"How rich he must be himself!" thought poor Dolly.

"You will have to let me take care of you, child."

"Oh dear!" murmured Dolly.

"We had better be married without delay. Once you are my wife—"

"Please don't go on!" interposed Dolly in a burst of sobs. "My dear mother is hardly buried."

"But what are you to do?" he gently asked. "You will not like to live here alone—and you have no income to live here upon. Your business is worth nothing as yet; it would not keep you in gloves. If I speak of these things prematurely, Dolly, it is for your sake."

Dolly sobbed. The future looked rather desolate.

"You have promised to be my wife, Dolly: remember that."

"Oh, please don't talk of it yet awhile!" sobbed Dolly.

"Leave you here alone I will not; you are not old enough to take care of yourself; you must have a protector. I will take you with me to London, where you will have a good home and be happy as a cricket: but you must know, Dolly, that I cannot do that until we are married. All sensible people must say that you will be quite justified under the circumstances."

Mr. Alick Mapping had a wily tongue, and Dolly was persuaded to listen. The marriage was fixed for the first week in September, and the banns were put up at St. Martin's Church; which, as every one knows, stands in the corn-market. Until then, Mr. Mapping returned to London; to make, as he told Dolly, preparations for his bride. An acquaintance of Mrs. Grape's, who had been staying with Dolly since the death, would remain with her to the last. As soon as Dolly was gone, the furniture would be sold by Mr. Stretch, the auctioneer, and the proceeds transmitted to Dolly in London. Mrs. Grape had given all she possessed to Dolly, in the fixed and firm belief that her son was really no more.

But all this was not to be put in practice without a warning from their neighbour, the Quaker lady; she sent for Dolly, being confined to her own chamber by illness.

"Thee should not be in this haste, Dorothy," she began. "It is not altogether seemly, child, and it may not be well for thee hereafter. Thee art too young to marry; thee should wait a year or two—"

"But I am not able to wait," pleaded poor Dolly, with tears in her eyes. "How could I continue to live alone in the house—all by myself?"

"Nay, but thee need not have done that. Some one of discreet age would have been glad to come and share expenses with thee. I might have helped thee to a suitable person myself: a cousin of mine, an agreeable and kindly woman, would like to live up this way. But the chief objection that I see to this hasty union, Dorothy," continued Miss Deavor, "is that thee knows next to nothing about the young man."

Dolly opened her eyes in surprise. "Why, I know him quite well, dear Miss Rachel. He has told me all about himself."

"That I grant thee. Elizabeth informs me that thee has had a good account from himself as to his means and respectability. But thee has not verified it."

"Verified it!" repeated Dolly.

"Thee has not taken steps to ascertain that the account he gives is true. How does thee know it to be so?"

Dolly's face flushed. "As if he would deceive me! You do not know him, Miss Deavor."

"Nay, child, I wish not to cast undeserved aspersion on him. But thee should ask for proof that what he tells thee is correct. Before thee ties thyself to him for life, Dorothy, thee will do well to get some friend to make inquiries in London. It is my best advice to thee, child; and it is what Mary Ann Grape, thy mother, would have done before giving thee to him."

Dolly thanked Miss Deavor and went away. The advice was well meant, of course; she felt that; but quite needless. Suspect Alick Mapping of deceit! Dolly would rather have suspected herself. And she did nothing.

The morning of the wedding-day arrived in due course. Dolly was attiring herself for the ceremony in a pretty new grey gown, her straw bonnet trimmed with white satin lying on the bed (to resume her black on the morrow), when Elizabeth Deavor came in.

"I have something to say to thee, Dolly," she began, in a grave tone. "I hardly knew whether to speak to thee or not, feeling not altogether sure of the thing myself, so I asked Aunt Rachel, and she thinks thee ought to be told."

"What is it?" cried Dolly.

"I think I saw thy brother Tom last night."

The words gave Dolly a curious shock. She fell back in a chair.

"I will relate it to thee," said Elizabeth. "Last evening I was at Aunt Rachel's window above-stairs, when I saw a boy in dark clothes standing on the pavement outside, just opposite thy gate. It was a bright night, as thee knows. He had his arms folded and stood quite still, gazing at this house. The moonlight shone on his face and I thought how much it was like poor lost Tom's. He still stood on; so I went downstairs and stepped to our gate, to ask whether he was in want of any one: and then, Dolly, I felt queerer than I ever felt in my life, for I saw that it was Tom. At least, I thought so."

"Did he speak?" gasped Dolly.

"He neither spoke nor answered me: he turned off, and went quickly down the road. I think it was Tom; I do indeed."

"What am I to do?" cried Dolly. "Oh, if I could but find him!"

"There's nothing to do, that we can see," answered the young Quakeress. "I have talked it over with Aunt Rachel. It would appear as though he did not care to show himself: else, if it were truly thy brother, why did he not come in? I will look out for him every night and speak to him if he appears again. I promise thee that, Dolly."

"Why do you say 'appears,' Elizabeth?" cried the girl. "You think it was himself, do you not; not his—his spirit?"

"Truly, I can but conclude it was himself."

Dolly, in a state of bewilderment, what with one thing and another, was married to Alick Mapping in St. Martin's Church, by its white-haired Rector, Digby Smith. A yellow post-chaise waited at the church-gates and carried them to Tewkesbury. The following day they went on by coach to Gloucester, where Mr. Mapping intended to stay a few days before proceeding to London.

They took up their quarters at a comfortable country inn on the outskirts of the town. On the second day after their arrival, Dolly, about to take a country walk with her husband, ran downstairs from putting her bonnet on, and could not see him. The barmaid told her he had gone into the town to post a letter, and asked Dolly to step into the bar-parlour to wait.

It was a room chiefly used by commercial travellers. Dolly's attention was caught by something over the mantelpiece. In a small glass-case, locked, there was the portrait of a man cleverly done in pencil; by its side hung a plain silver watch with a seal and key attached to a short black ribbon: and over all was a visiting-card, inscribed in ink, "Mr. Gardner." Dolly looked at this and turned sick and faint: it was her father's likeness, her father's watch, seal, and ribbon. Of an excitable nature, she burst into tears, and the barmaid ran in. There and then, the mystery so long hanging about Robert Grape's fate was cleared up, so far as it ever would be in this world.

He had left Bridgenorth, as may be remembered, on the Thursday morning. Towards the evening of the following day, Friday, as Dolly now heard, he appeared at this very inn. This same barmaid, an obliging, neat, and modest young woman, presenting a rare contrast to the barmaids of the present day, saw him come in. His face had a peculiar, grey shade upon it, which attracted her notice, and she asked him if he felt ill. He answered that he felt pretty well then, but supposed he must have had a fainting-fit when walking into the town, for to his surprise he found himself on the grass by the roadside, waking up from a sort of stupor. He engaged a bedroom for the night, and she thought he said—but she had never been quite sure—that he had come to look out for a horse at the fair to be held in Gloucester the next day. He took no supper, "not feeling up to it," he said, but drank a glass of weak brandy-and-water, and ate a biscuit with it, before going up to bed. The next morning he was found dead; had apparently died quietly in his sleep. An inquest was held, and the medical men testified that he had died of heart disease. Poor Dolly, listening to this, wondered whether the pitch out of the gig at Bridgenorth had fatally injured him.

"We supposed him to be a Mr. Gardner," continued the barmaid, "as that card"—pointing to it—"was found in his pocket-book. But we had no clue as to who he was or whence he came. His stockings were marked with a 'G' in red cotton; and there was a little loose money in his pocket and a bank-note in his pocket-book, just enough to pay the expenses of the funeral."

"But that likeness," said Dolly. "How did you come by it? Who took it?"

"Ah, ma'am, it was a curious thing, that—but such things do not happen by chance. An idle young man of the town used to frequent our inn; he was clever at drawing, and would take off a likeness of any one near him with a few strokes of a pen or pencil in a minute or two, quite surreptitious like and for his own amusement. Wonderful likenesses they were. He was in the bar-parlour, this very room, ma'am, while the stranger was drinking his brandy-and-water, and he dashed off this likeness."

"It is exactly like," said poor Dolly. "But his name was Grape, not Gardner. It must have been the card of some acquaintance."

"When nobody came forward to identify the stranger, the landlord got the sketch given up to him," continued the young woman. "He put it in this case with the watch and seal and card, and hung it where you see, hoping that sometime or other it might be recognized."

"But did you not let it be known abroad that he had died?" sighed Dolly.

"Why, of course we did; and put an advertisement in the Gloucester papers to ask if any Mr. Gardner was missing from his friends. Perhaps the name, not being his, served to mislead people. That's how it was, ma'am."

So that the one disappearance, that of Robert Grape, was now set at rest.

CHAPTER XIV

THE STORY OF DOROTHY GRAPE

IN AFTER YEARS

I

We found her out through Mr. Brandon's nephew, Roger Bevere, a medical student, who gave his people trouble, and one day got his arm and head broken. Mr. Brandon and the Squire were staying in London at the Tavistock Hotel. I, Johnny Ludlow, was also in London, visiting Miss Deveen. News of the accident was brought to Mr. Brandon; the young man had been carried into No. 60, Gibraltar Terrace, Islington, and a doctor named Pitt was attending him.

We went to see him at once. A narrow, quiet street, as I recollected well, this Gibraltar Terrace, the dwellings it contained facing each other, thirty in a row. No. 60 proved to be the same house to which we had gone once before, when inquiring about the illness of Francis Radcliffe, and Pitt was the same doctor. It was the same landlady also; I knew her as soon as she opened the door; a slender, faded woman, long past middle life, with a pink flush on her thin cheeks, and something of the lady about her.

"What an odd thing, Johnny!" whispered the Squire, recognizing the landlady as well as the house. "Mapping, I remember her name was."

Mr. Brandon went upstairs to his nephew. We were shown by her into the small parlour, which looked as faded as it had looked on our last visit, years before: as faded as she was. While relating to us how young Bevere's accident occurred, she had to run away at a call from upstairs.

"Looks uncommonly careworn, doesn't she, Johnny!" remarked the Squire. "Seems a nice sort of person, though."

"Yes, sir. I like her. Does it strike you that her voice has a home-ring in it? I think she must be from Worcestershire."

"A home-ring—Worcestershire!" retorted he. "It wouldn't be you, Johnny, if you did not get up some fancy or other. Here she comes! You are not from Worcestershire, are you, ma'am?" cried the Squire, going to the root of the question at once, in his haste to convict my fancy of its sins.

"Yes, I am, sir," she replied; and I saw the pink flush on her cheeks deepen to crimson. "I knew you, sir, when I was a young girl, many years ago. Though I should not have recognized you when you were last here, but that you left your card. We lived at Islip, sir; at that pretty cottage with the yellow roses round the porch. You must remember Dolly Grape."

"But you are not Dolly Grape!" returned the Squire, pushing up his spectacles.

"Yes, sir, I was Dolly Grape. Your mother knew us well; so did you."

"Goodness bless my heart!" softly cried the Squire, gazing at her as if the news were too much for him. And then, starting up impulsively, he grasped her hand and gave it a hearty shake. A sob seemed to take her throat. The Squire sat back again, and went on staring at her.

"My father disappeared mysteriously on one of his journeys; you may remember us by that, sir."

"To be sure I remember it—Robert Grape!" assented the Squire. "Had to do with the post-horse duty. Got as far as Bridgenorth, and was never heard of again. And it is really you—Dolly Grape! And you are living here—letting lodgings! I'm afraid the world has not been overkind to you."

She shook her head; tears were running down her faded cheeks.

"No, it has not, sir," she answered, as she wiped them away with her handkerchief. "I have had nothing but ups and downs in life since leaving Worcester: sad misfortunes: sometimes, I think, more than my share. Perhaps you heard that I married, sir—one Mr. Mapping?"

The Squire nodded slightly. He was too busy gazing at her to pay attention to much else.

"I am looking at you to see if I can trace the old features of the old days," he said, "and I do now; they grow upon my memory; though you were but a slip of a girl when I used to see you. I wonder I did not recognize you at first."

"And I wonder that you can even recognize me now, sir," she returned: "trouble and grief have so much altered me. I am getting old, too."

"Have you lived in this house long?"

"Nearly ten years, sir. I live by letting my rooms."

The Squire's voice took a tone of compassion.

"It can't be much of a living, once the rent and taxes are paid."

Mrs. Mapping's mild blue eyes, that seemed to the Squire to be of a lighter tinge than of yore, wore a passing sadness. Any one able to read it correctly might have seen she had her struggles.

"Are you a widow?"

"I—call myself one, sir," she replied, with hesitation.

"Call yourself one!" retorted the Squire, for he liked people to be straightforward in their speech. "My good woman, you are a widow, or you are not one."

"I pass for one, sir."

"Now, what on earth do you mean?" demanded he. "Is your husband—Mapping—not dead?"

"He was not dead when I last heard of him, sir; that's a long while ago. But he is not my husband."

"Not your husband!" echoed the Squire, pushing up his spectacles again. "Have you and he quarrelled and parted?"

Any countenance more pitifully sad than Mrs. Mapping's was at that moment, I never wish to see. She stood smoothing down her black silk apron (which had a slit in it) with trembling fingers.

"My history is a very painful one," she said at last in a low voice. "I will tell it if you wish; but not this morning. I should like to tell it you, sir. It is some time since I saw a home-face, and I have often pictured to myself some kind friendly face of those old happy days looking at me while I told it. Different days from these."

"These cannot be much to boast of," repeated the Squire. "It must be a precarious sort of living."

"Of course it fluctuates," she said. "Sometimes my rooms are full, at other times empty. One has to put the one against the other and strive to tide over the hard days. Mr. Pitt is very good to me in recommending the rooms to medical students; he is a good-natured man."

"Oh, indeed! Listen to that, Johnny! Pitt good-natured! Rather a loose man, though, I fancy, ma'am."

"What, Mr. Pitt? Sir, I don't think so. He has a surgery close by, and gets a good bit of practice—"

The rest was interrupted by Mr. Pitt himself; he came to say we might go up to Mr. Brandon in the sick-room. We had reason to think ill enough of Pitt in regard to the Radcliffe business; but the Squire could not tackle him about the past offhand, this not being just the time or place for it. Later, when he did so, it was found that we had been misjudging the man. Pitt had not joined Stephen Radcliffe in any conspiracy; and the false letter, telling of Frank's death at Dr. Dale's, had not been written by him. So we saw that it must have been concocted by Stephen himself.

"Any way, if I did write such a letter, I retained no consciousness of it afterwards," added Pitt, with candour. "I am sorry to say, Mr. Todhetley, that I gave way to drink at that time, and I know I was often not myself. But I do not think it likely that I wrote it; and as to joining Mr. Radcliffe in any conspiracy against his brother, why, I would not do such a thing, drunk or sober, and I never knew it had been done."

"You have had the sense to pull up," cried the Squire, in reference to what Pitt had admitted.

"Yes," answered Pitt, in a voice hardly above a whisper. "And I never think of what I might have become by this time, but for pulling up, but I thank God."

These allusions, however, may perhaps only puzzle the reader. And it is not with Mr. Pitt, his virtues or his failings, that this paper concerns itself, but with the history of Dorothy Grape.

We must take it up from the time Dorothy arrived in London with her husband, Alick Mapping, after their marriage at Worcester, as already narrated. The sum of three hundred pounds, owned by Dolly, passed into Mr. Mapping's possession on the wedding-day, for she never suggested such a thing as that it should be settled on herself. The proceeds, arising from the sale of the furniture, were also transmitted to him later by the auctioneer. Thus he had become the proprietor of Dolly, and of all her worldly goods. After that, he and she faded out of Worcestershire memory, and from the sight of Worcestershire people—except for one brief meeting, to be mentioned presently.

The home in London, to which her husband conveyed her, and of which he had boasted, Dolly found to be lodgings. Lodgings recently engaged by him, a sitting-room and bedroom, in the Blackfriars Road. They were over a shop, kept by one Mrs. Turk, who was their landlady. "I would not fix upon a house, dear, without you," he said; and Dolly thanked him gratefully. All he did was right to her.

She was, as he had told her she would be, happy as a cricket, though bewildered with the noisy bustle of the great town, and hardly daring to venture alone into its busy streets, more crowded than was Worcester Cathedral on the Sundays Mr. Benson preached. The curious elucidation at Gloucester of what her father's fate had been was a relief to her mind, rather than the contrary, once she had got over its sadness; though the still more curious doubt about her brother Tom, whispered to her by Elizabeth Deavor on her wedding morning, was rarely absent from her thoughts. But Dolly was young, Dolly was in love, and Dolly was intensely happy. Her husband took her to the theatres, to Vauxhall, and to other places of amusement; and Dolly began to think life was going to be a happy valley into which care would never penetrate.

This happy state of things changed. Mr. Mapping took to be a great deal away from home, sometimes for weeks together. He laid the fault upon his business; travellers in the wine trade had to go all over England, he said. Dolly was not unreasonable and accepted the explanation cheerfully.

But something else happened now and then that was less satisfactory. Mr. Mapping would appear at home in a condition that frightened Dolly: as if he had made the mistake of tasting the wine samples himself, instead of carrying them to his customers. Never having been brought into contact with anything of the kind in her own home, she regarded it with terror and dismay.

Then another phase of discomfort set in: money seemed to grow short. Dolly could not get from her husband what was needed for their moderate expenses; which were next to nothing when he was away from home. She cried a little one day when she wanted some badly and he told her he had none to give her. Upon which Mr. Mapping turned cross. There was no need of tears, he said: it would all come right if she did not bother. Dolly, in her secret heart, hoped he would not have to break in upon what he called their "nest-egg," that three hundred pounds in the bank. A nest-egg which, as he had more than once assured her, it was his intention to keep intact.

Only in one thing had Mr. Mapping been arbitrary: he would not allow her to hold any communication with Worcester. When they first came to London, he forbade Dolly to write to any of her former friends, or to give them her address. "You have no relatives there," he said, "only a few acquaintances, and I would prefer, Dolly, that you dropped them altogether." Of course she obeyed him: though it prevented her writing to ask Elizabeth Deavor whether she had again seen Tom.

Things, despite Mr. Mapping's assurances, did not come right. As the spring advanced, his absences became more marked and the money less plentiful. Dolly shed many tears. She knew not what to do; for, as the old song says, not e'en love can live on flowers. It was a very favourite song of Dolly's, and her tuneful voice might often be heard trilling it through from beginning to end as she sat at work.

"Young Love lived once in a humble shed,
Where roses breathing
And woodbines wreathing
Around the lattice their tendrils spread,
As wild and as sweet as the life he led.

"The garden flourished, for young Hope nourished,
 And Joy stood by to count the hours:
But lips, though blooming, must still be fed,
And not e'en Love can live on flowers.

"Alas, that Poverty's evil eye
Should e'er come hither   Such sweets to wither;
The flowers laid down their heads to die,
And Love looked pale as the witch drew nigh.

"She came one morning, and Love had warning,
For he stood at the window, peeping for day:
'Oh, oh,' said he, 'is it you,—good-bye'—
And he opened the window and flew away."

Dolly's love did not fly away, though the ugly witch, Poverty, was certainly showing herself. Mrs. Turk grew uneasy. Dolly assured her there was no occasion for that; that if the worst came to the worst, they must break into the "nest-egg" which they had lying by in the Bank of England—the three hundred pounds left her by her mother.

One bright day in May, Dolly, pining for the outdoor sunshine, betook herself to Hyde Park, a penny roll in her pocket for her dinner. The sun glittered in the blue sky, the air was warm, the birds chirped in the trees and hopped on the green grass. Dolly sat on a bench enjoying the sweetness and tranquillity, thinking how very delightful life might be when no evil stepped in to mar it.

Two Quakeress ladies approached arm-in-arm, talking busily. Dolly started up with a cry: for the younger one was Elizabeth Deavor. She had come to London with a friend for the May meetings. The two girls were delighted to see each other, but Elizabeth was pressed for time.

"Why did thee never write to me, Dorothy? I had but one letter from thee, written at Gloucester, telling me, thee knows, all about thy poor father." And, to this question, Dolly murmured some lame excuse.

"I wanted to write to thee, but I had not thy address. I promised thee I would look out for Tom—"

"And have you seen him again?" interrupted Dolly in excitement. "Oh, Elizabeth?"

"I have seen the boy again, but it was not Tom: and I am very sorry that my fancy misled me and caused me to excite thy hopes. It was only recently, in Fourth month. I saw the same boy standing in the same place before thy old gate, his arms folded, and looking at the house as before, in the moonlight. I ran out, and caught his arm, and held it while he told me who he was and why he came there. It was not thy brother, Dorothy, but the likeness to him is marvellous."

"No!—not he?" gasped Dolly, woefully disappointed.

"It is one Richard East," said Elizabeth; "a young sailor. He lived with his mother in that house before she died, when he was a little boy; and when he comes home from a voyage now, and is staying with his friends in Melcheapen Street, he likes to go up there and have a good look at it. This is all. As I say, I am sorry to have misled thee. We think there cannot be a doubt that poor Tom really lost his life that night in the canal. And art thee nicely, Dorothy?—and is thy husband well? Thee art looking thin. Fare thee well."

Summer passed, Dolly hardly knew how. She was often reduced to straits, often and often went dinnerless. Mrs. Turk only had a portion of what was due to her by fits and starts. Mr. Mapping himself made light of troubles; they did not seem to touch him much; he was always in spirits and always well dressed.

"Alick, you should draw a little of that money in the bank," his wife ventured to suggest one day when Mrs. Turk had been rather troublesome. "We cannot go on like this."

"Break in upon our 'nest-egg!'" he answered. "Not if I know it, Dolly. Mrs. Turk must wait."

A little circumstance was to happen that gave some puzzle to Dolly. She had been married about fourteen months, and her husband was, as she believed, on his travels in Yorkshire, when Lord-Mayor's day occurred. Mrs. Gurk, a good woman in the main, and compassionating the loneliness of the young wife, offered to take her to see the show, having been invited to an upper window of a house in Cheapside. Of all the sights in the world that Dolly had heard of, she quite believed that must be the greatest, and felt delighted. They went, took up their station at the window, and the show passed. If it had not quite come up to Dolly's expectation, she did not say so.

"A grand procession, is it not, Mrs. Mapping?" cried her companion, gazing after it with admiring eyes.

"Very," said Dolly. "I wonder—Good gracious!" she broke off, with startling emphasis, "there's my husband!"

"Where?" asked Mrs. Turk, her eyes bent on the surging crowd below.

"There," said Dolly, pointing with her finger; "there! He is arm-in-arm with two others; in the middle of them. How very strange! It was only yesterday I had a letter from him from Bradford, saying he should be detained there for some time to come. How I wish he had looked up at this window!"

Mrs. Turk's sight had failed to single him out amongst the moving crowd. And as Mr. Mapping did not make his appearance at home that evening, or for many evenings to come, she concluded that the young wife must have been mistaken.

When Mr. Mapping did appear, he said the same, telling Dolly she must have "seen double," for that he had not been in London. Dolly did not insist, but she felt staggered and uncomfortable; she felt certain it was her husband she saw.

How long the climax would have been postponed, or in what way it might have disclosed itself, but for something that occurred, cannot be conjectured. This wretched kind of life went on until the next spring. Dolly was reduced to perplexity. She had parted with all the pretty trinkets her mother left her; she would live for days together upon bread-and-butter and tears: and a most unhappy suspicion had instilled itself into her mind—that the nest-egg no longer existed. But even yet she found excuses for her husband; she thought that all doubt might still be explained away. Mrs. Turk was very good, and did not worry; Dolly did some plain sewing for her, and made her a gown or two.

On one of these spring days, when the sun was shining brightly on the pavement outside, Dolly went out on an errand. She had not gone many steps from the door when a lady, very plainly dressed, came up and accosted her quietly.

"Young woman, I wish to ask why you have stolen away my husband?"

"Good gracious!" exclaimed the startled Dolly. "What do you mean?"

"You call yourself Mrs. Mapping."

"I am Mrs. Mapping."

The stranger shook her head. "We cannot converse here," she said. "Allow me to go up to your room"—pointing to it. "I know you lodge there."

"But what is it that you want with me?" objected Dolly, who did not like all this.

"You think yourself the wife of Alick Mapping. You think you were married to him."

Dolly wondered whether the speaker had escaped from that neighbouring stronghold, Bedlam. "I don't know what it is you wish to insinuate," she said. "I was married to Mr. Mapping at St. Martin's Church in Worcester, more than eighteen months ago."

"Ay! But I, his wife, was married to him in London seven years ago. Yours was no marriage; he deceived you."

Dolly's face was turning all manner of colours. She felt frightened almost to death.

"Take me to your room and I will tell you all that you need to know. Do not fear I shall reproach you; I am only sorry for you; it has been no fault of yours. He is a finished deceiver, as I have learnt to my cost."

Dolly led the way. Seated together, face to face, her eyes strained on the stranger's, she listened to the woeful tale, which was gently told. That it was true she could not doubt. Alick Mapping had married her at St. Martin's Church in Worcester, but he had married this young woman some years before it.

"You are thinking that I look older than my husband," said she, misinterpreting Dolly's gaze. "That is true. I am five years older, and am now approaching my fortieth year. He pretended to fall in love with me; I thought he did; but what he really fell in love with was my money."

"How did you come to know about me?—how did you find it out?" gasped Dolly.

"It was through Mrs. Turk, your landlady," answered the true wife. "She has been suspecting that something or other was wrong, and she talked of it to a friend of hers who chances to know my family. This friend was struck with the similarity of name—the Alick Mapping whose wife was here in the Blackfriars Road, and the Alick Mapping whose wife lived at Hackney."

"How long is it since he left you?" asked poor Dolly.

"He has not left me. He has absented himself inexplicably at times for a year or two past, but he is still with me. He is at home now, at this present moment. I have a good home, you must understand, and a good income, which he cannot touch; he would think twice before giving up that. Had you money?" continued the lady abruptly.

"I had three hundred pounds. He told me he had placed it in the Bank of England; I think he did do that; and that he should never draw upon it, but leave it there for a nest-egg."

Mrs. Mapping smiled in pity. "You may rely upon it that there's not a shilling left of it. Money in his hands, when he can get hold of any, runs out of them like water."

"Is it true that he travels for a wine house?"

"Yes—and no. It is his occupation, but he is continually throwing up his situations: pleasure has more attraction for him than work; and he will be a gentleman at large for months together. Yet not a more clever man of business exists than he is known to be, and he can get a place at any time."

"Have you any children?" whispered Dolly.

"No. Shall you prosecute him?" continued the first wife, after a pause.

"Shall I—what?" cried Dolly, aghast.

"Prosecute him for the fraud he has committed on you?"

"Oh dear! the exposure would kill me," shivered the unhappy girl. "I shall only hope to run away and hide myself forever."

"Every syllable I have told you is truth," said the stranger, producing a slip of paper as she rose to depart. "Here are two or three references by which you can verify it, if you doubt me. Mrs. Turk will do it for you if you do not care to stir in it yourself. Will you shake hands with me?"

Dolly assented, and burst into a whirlwind of tears.

Nothing seemed to be left for her, as she said, but to run away and hide herself. All the money was gone, and she was left penniless and helpless. By the aid of Mrs. Turk, who proved a good friend to her, she obtained a situation in a small preparatory school near Croydon, as needle-woman and companion to the mistress. She called herself Mrs. Mapping still, and continued to wear her wedding-ring; she did not know what else to do. She had been married; truly, as she had believed; and what had come of it was surely no fault of hers.

A little good fortune fell to her in time; a little bit. For years and years she remained in that school at Croydon, until, as it seemed to herself, she was middle-aged, and then the mistress of it died. Having no relatives, she left her savings and her furniture to Dolly. With the money Dolly set up the house in Gibraltar Terrace, put the furniture into it, and began to let lodgings. A young woman, who had been teacher in the school, and whom Dolly regarded as her sister, and often called her so, removed to it with her and stayed with her until she married.

Those particulars—which we listened to one evening from her own lips—were gloomy enough. The Squire went into an explosion over Alick Mapping.

"The despicable villain! What has become of him?"

"I never saw him after his wife came to me," she answered, "but Mrs. Turk would get news of him now and then. Since Mrs. Turk's death, I have heard nothing. Sometimes I think he may be dead."

"I hope he was hung!" flashed the Squire.

Well—to hasten on. That was Dorothy Grape's history since she left Worcester; and a cruel one it was!

We saw her once or twice again before quitting London. And the Squire left a substantial present with her, for old remembrance sake.

"She looks as though she needed it, Johnny," said he. "Poor thing! poor thing! And such a pretty, happy little maiden as she used to be, standing in her pinafore amongst the yellow roses in the porch at Islip! Johnny, lad, I hope that vagabond came to be hanged!"

II

It was ever so long afterwards, and the time had gone on by years, when we again fell into the thread of Dorothy Grape's life. The Squire was in London for a few days upon some law business, and had brought me with him.

"I should like to see how that poor woman's getting on, Johnny," he said to me one morning. "Suppose we go down to Gibraltar Terrace?"

It was a dull, damp, misty day at the close of autumn; and when the Squire turned in at No. 60, after dismissing the cab, he stood still and stared, instead of knocking. A plate was on the door, "James Noak, carpenter and joiner."

"Has she left, do you think, Johnny?"

"Well, sir, we can ask. Perhaps the carpenter is only lodging here?"

A tidy young woman, with a baby in her arms, answered the knock. "Does Mrs. Mapping live here still?" asked the Squire.

"No, sir," she answered. "I don't know the name."

"Not know the name!" retorted he, turning crusty; for he disliked, of all things, to be puzzled or thwarted. "Mrs. Mapping lived here for ten or a dozen years, anyhow."

"Oh, stay, sir," she said, "I remember the name now. Mapping; yes, that was it. She lived here before we came in."

"Is she dead?"

"No, sir. She was sold up."

"Sold up?"

"Yes, sir. Her lodging-letting fell off—this neighbourhood's not what it was: people like to get further up, Islington way—and she was badly off for a long while, could not pay her rent, or anything; so at last the landlord was obliged to sell her up. At least, that's what we heard after we came here, but the house lay empty for some months between. I did not hear what became of her."

The people at the next house could not tell anything; they were fresh-comers also; and the Squire stood in a quandary. I thought of Pitt the surgeon; he was sure to know; and ran off to his surgery in the next street.

Changes seemed to be everywhere. Pitt's small surgery had given place to a chemist's shop. The chemist stood behind his counter in a white apron. Pitt? Oh, Pitt had taken to a practice further off, and drove his brougham. "Mrs. Mapping?" added the chemist, in further answer to me. "Oh yes, she lives still in the same terrace. She came to grief at No. 60, poor woman, and lodges now at No. 32. Same side of the way; this end."

No. 32 had a plate on the door: "Miss Kester, dressmaker," and Miss Kester herself—a neat little woman, with a reserved, not to say sour, face and manner, and a cloud of pins sticking out of her brown waistband—answered the knock. She sent us up to a small back-room at the top of the house.

Mrs. Mapping sat sewing near a fireless grate, her bed in one corner; she looked very ill. I had thought her thin enough before; she was a shadow now. The blue eyes had a piteous look in them, the cheeks a hectic.

"Yes," she said, in answer to the Squire, her voice faint and her cough catching her every other minute, "it was a sad misfortune for me to be turned out of my house; it nearly broke my heart. The world is full of trouble, sir."

"How long is it since?"

"Nearly eighteen months, sir. Miss Kester had this room to let, and I came into it. It is quiet and cheap: only half-a-crown a-week."

"And how do you get the half-crown?" questioned the Squire. "And your dinner and breakfast—how do you get that?"

Mrs. Mapping passed her trembling fingers across her brow before she answered—

"I'm sorry to have to tell of these things, sir. I'm sorry you have found me out in my poverty. When I think of the old days at home, the happy and plentiful days when poor mother was living, and what a different life mine might have been but for the dreadful marriage I made, I—I can hardly bear up against it. I'm sure I beg your pardon, gentlemen, for giving way."

For the tears were streaming down her thin cheeks. The Squire set up a cough on his own account; I went to the window and looked down at some grimy back-gardens.

"When I am a little stronger, and able to do a full day's work again, I shall get on, sir, but I've been ill lately through going out in the wet and catching cold," she said, mastering the tears. "Miss Kester is very good in supplying me with as much as I can do."

"A grand 'getting on,'" cried the Squire. "You'd be all the better for some fire in that grate."

"I might be worse off than I am," she answered meekly. "If it is but little that I have, I am thankful for it."

The Squire talked a while longer; then he put a sovereign into her hand, and came away with a gloomy look.

"She wants a bit of regular help," said he. "A few shillings paid to her weekly while she gets up her strength might set her going again. I wonder if we could find any one to undertake it?"

"You would not leave it with herself in a lump, sir?"

"Why, no, I think not; she may have back debts, you see, Johnny, and be tempted to pay them with it; if so, practically it would be no good to her. Wish Pitt lived here still! Wonder if that Miss Kester might be trusted to— There's a cab, lad! Hail it."

The next morning, when we were at breakfast at the hotel—which was not the Tavistock this time—the Squire burst into a state of excitement over his newspaper.

"Goodness me, Johnny! here's the very thing."

I wondered what had taken him, and what he meant; and for some time did not clearly understand. The Squire's eyes had fallen upon an advertisement, and also a leading article, treating of some great philanthropic movement that had recently set itself up in London. Reading the articles, I gathered that it had for its object the distribution of alms on an extensive scale and the comprehensive relieving of the distressed. Some benevolent gentlemen (so far as we could understand the newspaper) had formed themselves into a band for taking the general welfare of the needy into their hands, and devoted their lives to looking after their poverty-stricken brothers and sisters. A sort of universal, benevolent, set-the-world-to-rights invention.

The Squire was in raptures. "If we had but a few more such good men in the world, Johnny! I'll go down at once and shake their hands. If I lived in London, I'd join them."

I could only laugh. Fancy the Squire going about from house to house with a bag of silver to relieve the needy!

Taking note of the office occupied by these good men, we made our way to it. Only two of them were present that morning: a man who looked like a clerk, for he had books and papers before him; and a thin gentleman in spectacles.

The Squire shook him by the hand at once, breaking into an ovation at the good deeds of the benevolent brotherhood, that should have made the spectacles before us, as belonging to a member of it, blush.

"Yes," he said, his cool, calm tones contrasting with the Squire's hot ones, "we intend to effect a work that has never yet been attempted. Why, sir, by our exertions three parts of the complaints of hunger, and what not, will be done away with."

The Squire folded his hands in an ecstasy of reverence. "That is, you will relieve it," he remarked. "Bountiful Samaritans!"

"Relieve it, certainly—where the recipients are found to be deserving," returned the other. "But non-deserving cases—impostors, ill-doers, and the like—will get punishment instead of relief, if we can procure it for them."

"Quite right, too," warmly assented the Squire. "Allow me to shake your hand again, sir. And you gentlemen are out every day upon this good work! Visiting from house to house!"

"Some of us are out every day; we devote our time to it."

"And your money, too, of course!" exclaimed the Squire. "Listen, Johnny Ludlow," he cried, turning to me, his red face glowing more and more with every word, "I hope you'll take a lesson from this, my lad! Their time, and their money too!"

The thin gentleman cleared his throat. "Of course we cannot do all in the way of money ourselves," he said; "some of us, indeed, cannot do anything in that way. Our operations are very large: a great deal is needed, and we have to depend upon a generous public for help."

"By their making subscriptions to it?" cried the Squire.

"Undoubtedly."

The Squire tugged at an inner pocket. "Here, Johnny, help me to get out my cheque-book." And when it was out, he drew a cheque for ten pounds there and then, and laid it on the table.

"Accept this, sir," he said, "and my praises with it. And now I should like to recommend to your notice a case myself—a most deserving one. Will you take it in hand?"

"Certainly."

The Squire gave Mrs. Mapping's address, telling briefly of her present distress and weakly state, and intimated that the best mode of relief would be to allow her a few shillings weekly. "You will be sure to see to her?" was his parting injunction. "She may starve if you do not."

"Have no fear: it is our business to do so," repeated the thin gentleman. "Good-day."

"Johnny," said the Squire, going up the street sideways in his excitement, "it is refreshing to hear of these self-denying deeds. These good men must be going on straight for heaven!"

"Take care, sir! Look where you are going."

The Squire had not been going on straight himself just then, and had bumped up against a foot-passenger who was hurrying along. It was Pitt, the surgeon. After a few words of greeting, the Squire excused his flurry by telling him where he had come from.

"Been there!" exclaimed Pitt, bursting into a laugh. "Wish you joy, sir! We call it Benevolence Hall."

"And a very good name, too," said the Squire. "Such men ought to be canonized, Pitt."

"Hope they will be?" answered Pitt in a curious kind of tone. "I can't stop now, Mr. Todhetley; am on my way to a consultation."

"He slips from one like an eel," cried the Squire, looking after the doctor as he hurried onwards: "I might have spoken to him about Mrs. Mapping. But my mind is at ease with regard to her, Johnny, now that these charitable men have the case in hand: and we shall be up again in a few weeks."

III

It was nearly two months before we were again in London, and winter weather: the same business, connected with a lawsuit, calling the Squire up.

"And now for Mrs. Mapping," he said to me during the afternoon of the second day. So we went to Gibraltar Terrace.

"Yes, she is in her room," said Miss Kester in a resentful tone, when she admitted us. "It is a good thing somebody's come at last to see after her! I don't care to have her alone here on my hands to die."

"To die!" cried the Squire sharply, supposing the dressmaker spoke only in temper. "What is she dying of?"

"Starvation," answered Miss Kester.

"Why, what on earth do you mean, ma'am?" demanded he. "Starvation!"

"I've done what I could for her, so far as a cup of tea might go, and a bit of bread-and-butter once a day, or perhaps a drop of broth," ran on Miss Kester in the same aggrieved tone. "But it has been hard times with myself lately, and I have my old mother to keep and a bedridden sister. What she has wanted is a supply of nourishing food; and she has had as good as none of any sort since you were here, sir, being too weak to work: and so, rapid consumption set in."

She whisked upstairs with the candle, for the short winter day was already closing, and we followed her. Mrs. Mapping sat in an old easy-chair, over a handful of fire, her thin cotton shawl folded round her: white, panting, attenuated, starved; and—there could not be much mistake about it—dying.

"Starved? dying? dear, dear!" ejaculated the Squire, backing to the other chair and sitting down in a sort of terror. "What has become of the good people at Benevolence Hall?"

"They!" cried Miss Kester contemptuously. "You don't suppose those people would spend money to keep a poor woman from dying, do you, sir?"

"Why, it is their business to do it," said the Squire. "I put Mrs. Mapping's case into their hands, and they undertook to see to it."

"To see to it, perhaps, sir, but not to relieve it; I should be surprised if they did that. One of them called here ever so many weeks ago and frightened Mrs. Mapping with his harsh questions; but he gave her nothing."

"I don't understand all this," cried the Squire, rumpling his hair. "Was it a gentleman?"—turning to Mrs. Mapping.

"He was dressed as one," she said, "but he was loud and dictatorial, almost as though he thought me a criminal instead of a poor sick woman. He asked me all kinds of questions about my past life, where I had lived and what I had done, and wrote down the answers."

"Go on," said the Squire, as she paused for breath.

"As they sent me no relief and did not come again, Miss Kester, after two or three weeks had gone by, was good enough to send a messenger to the place: her nephew. He saw the gentlemen there and told them I was getting weaker daily and was in dreadful need, if they would please to give me a trifle; he said he should never have thought of applying to them but for their having come to see after me. The gentlemen answered unfavourably; inquiries had been made, they sternly told him, and the case was found to be one not suitable for relief, that I did not deserve it. I—I—have never done anything wrong willingly," sobbed the poor woman, breaking down.

"I don't think she has, sir; she don't seem like it; and I'm sure she struggled hard enough to get a living at No. 60," said Miss Kester. "Any way, they did nothing for her—they've just left her to starve and die."

I had seen the Squire in many a temper, but never in a worse than now. He flung out of the room, calling upon me to follow him, and climbed into the hansom that waited for us outside.

"To Benevolence Hall," roared he, "and drive like the deuce."

"Yes, sir," said the man. "Where is Benevolence Hall?"

I gave him the address, and the man whirled us to Benevolence Hall in a very short time. The Squire leaped out and indoors, primed. In the office stood a young man, going over some accounts by gaslight. His flaxen hair was parted down the middle, and he looked uncommonly simple. The rest of the benevolent gentlemen had left for the day.

What the Squire said at first, I hardly know: I don't think he knew himself. His words came tumbling out in a way that astonished the clerk.

"Mrs. Mapping," cried the young man, when he could understand a little what the anger was about. "Your ten pounds?—meant for her, you say—"

"Yes, my ten pounds," wrathfully broke in the Squire; "my ten-pound cheque that I paid down here on this very table. What have you done with it?"

"Oh, that ten pounds has been spent, partly so, at least, in making inquiries about the woman, looking-up her back history and all that. Looking-up the back lives of people takes a lot of money, you see."

"But why did you not relieve her with it, or a portion of it? That is the question I've come to ask, young man, and I intend to have it answered."

The young man looked all surprise. "Why, what an idea!" lisped he. "Our association does not profess to help sinners. That would be a go!"

"Sinners!"

"We can't be expected to take up a sinner, you know—and she's a topping one," continued he, keeping just as cool as the Squire was hot. "We found out all sorts of dreadful things against the woman. The name, Mapping, is not hers, to begin with. She went to church with a man who had a living wife—"

"She didn't," burst in the Squire. "It was the man who went to church with her. And I hope with all my heart he came to be hanged!"

The clerk considered. "It comes to the same, doesn't it?" said he, vaguely. "She did go to church with him; and it was ever so long before his proper wife found it out; and she has gone on calling herself Mapping ever since! And she managed so badly in a lodging-house she set up, that she was sold out of it for rent. Consider that! Oh, indeed, then, it is not on such people as these that our good gentlemen would waste their money."

"What do they waste it on?" demanded the Squire.

"Oh, come now! They don't waste it. They spend it."

"What on? The sick and needy?"

"Well, you see, the object of this benevolent association is to discover who is deserving and who is not. When an applicant comes or sends for relief, representing that he is sick and starving, and all the rest of it, we begin by searching out his back sins and misfortunes. The chances are that a whole lot of ill turns up. If the case be really deserving, and—and white, you know, instead of black—we relieve it."

"That is, you relieve about one case in a hundred, I expect?" stormed the Squire.

"Oh, now you can't want me to go into figures," said the clerk, in his simple way. "Anybody might know, if they've some knowledge of the world, that an out-and-out deserving case does not turn up often. Besides, our business is not relief but inquiry. We do relieve sometimes, but we chiefly inquire."

"Now look you here," retorted the Squire. "Your object, inquiring into cases, may be a good one in the main and do some excellent service; I say nothing against it; but the public hold the impression that it is relief your association intends, not inquiry. Why is this erroneous impression not set to rights?"

"Oh, but our system is, I assure you, a grand one," cried the young fellow. "It accomplishes an immense good."

"And how much harm does it accomplish? Hold your tongue, young man! Put it that an applicant is sick, starving, dying, for want of a bit of aid in the shape of food, does your system give that bit of aid, just to keep body and soul together while it makes its inquiries—say only to the value of a few pence?"

The young fellow stared. "What a notion!" cried he. "Give help before finding out whether it ought to be given or not? That would be quite a Utopian way of fixing up the poor, that would."

"And do you suppose I should have given my ten pounds, but for being misled, for being allowed to infer that it would be expended on the distressed?" stamped the Squire. "Not a shilling of it. No money of mine shall aid in turning poor helpless creatures inside out to expose their sins, as you call it. That's not charity. What the sick and the famished want is a little kindly help—and the Bible enjoins us to give it."

"But most of them are such a bad lot, you know," remonstrated the young man.

"All the more need they should be helped," returned the Squire; "they have bodies and souls to be saved, I suppose. Hold your silly tongue, I tell you. I should have seen to this poor sick woman myself, who is just as worthy as you are and your masters, but for their taking the case in hand. As it is she has been left to starve and die. Come along, Johnny! Benevolence Hall, indeed!"

Back to Gibraltar Terrace now, the Squire fretting and fuming. He was hot and hasty, as the world knows, given to saying anything that came uppermost, justifiable or the contrary: but in this affair it did seem that something or somebody must be wrong.

"Johnny," said the Squire, as the cab bowled along, waking up out of a brown study, "it seems to me that this is a serious matter of conscience. It was last Sunday evening, wasn't it, that you read the chapter in St. Matthew which tells of the last judgment?"

"Tod read it, sir. I read the one that followed it."

"Any way, it was one of you. In that chapter Christ charges us to relieve the poor if we would be saved—the hungry and thirsty, the sick, the naked. Now, see here, lad: if I give my alms to this new society that has sprung up, and never a stiver of it to relieve the distress that lies around me, would the blame, rest on me, I wonder? Should I have to answer for it?"

It was too complicated a question for me. But just then we drew up at Miss Kester's door.

Mrs. Mapping had changed in that short time. I thought she was dying, thought so as I looked at her. There was a death-shade on the wan face, never seen but when the world is passing away. The Squire saw it also.

"Yes," said Miss Kester, gravely, in answer to his whisper. "I fear it is the end."

"Goodness bless me!" gasped the Squire. And he was for ordering in pretty nearly every known restorative the shops keep, from turtle-soup to calves'-foot jelly. Miss Kester shook her head.

"Too late, sir; too late. A month ago it would have saved her. Now, unless I am very much mistaken, the end is at hand."

Well, he was in a way. If gold and silver could revive the dying, she'd have had it. He sent me out to buy a bottle of port wine, and got Miss Kester's little apprentice to run for the nearest doctor.

"Not rally again at all, you say! all stuff and nonsense," he was retorting on Miss Kester when I returned. "Here's the wine, at last! Now for a glass, Johnny."

She sipped about a teaspoonful by degrees. The shade on her face was getting darker. Her poor thin fingers kept plucking at the cotton shawl.

"I have never done any harm that I knew of: at least, not wilfully," she slowly panted, looking piteously at the Squire, evidently dwelling upon the accusation made by Benevolence Hall: and it had, Miss Kester said, troubled her frightfully. "I was only silly—and inexperienced—and—and believed in everybody. Oh, sir, it was hard!"

"I'd prosecute them if I could," cried the Squire, fiercely. "There, there; don't think about it any more; it's all over."

"Yes, it is over," she sighed, giving the words a different meaning from his. "Over; over: the struggles and the disappointments, the privations and the pain. Only God sees what mine have been, and how I've tried to bear up in patience. Well, well; He knows best: and I think—I do think, sir—He will make it up to us in heaven. My poor mother thought the same when she was dying."

"To be sure," answered the Squire, soothingly. "One must be a heathen not to know that. Hang that set-the-world-to-rights company!" he muttered in a whisper.

"The bitterness of it all has left me," she whispered, with pauses between the words for want of breath; "this world is fading from my sight, the world to come opening. Only this morning, falling asleep in the chair here, after the fatigue of getting up—and putting on my things—and coughing—I dreamt I saw the Saviour holding out His hand to welcome me, and I knew He was waiting to take me up to God. The clouds round about Him were rose colour; a light, as of gold, lay in the distance. Oh, how lovely it was! nothing but peace. Yes, yes, God will forgive all our trials and our shortcomings, and make it up to us there."

The room had a curious hush upon it. It hardly seemed to be a living person speaking. Any way, she would not be living long.

"Another teaspoonful of wine, Johnny," whispered the Squire. "Dear, dear! Where on earth can that doctor be?"

I don't believe a drop of it went down her throat. Miss Kester wiped away the damp from her brow. A cough took her; and afterwards she lay back again in the chair.

"Do you remember the yellow roses in the porch," she murmured, speaking, as must be supposed, to the Squire, but her eyes were closed: "how the dew on them used to glisten again in the sun on a summer's morning? I was picking such a handful of them last night—beautiful roses, they were; sweet and beautiful as the flowers we shall pick in heaven."

The doctor came upstairs, his shoes creaking. It was Pitt. Pitt! The girl had met him by chance, and told him what was amiss.

"Ah," said he, bending over the chair, "you have called me too late. I should have been here a month or two ago."

"She is dying of starvation," whispered the Squire. "All that money—ten pounds—which I handed over to that blessed fraternity, and they never gave her a sixpence of it—after assuring me they'd see to her!"

"Ah," said Pitt, his mouth taking a comical twist. "They meant they'd see after her antecedents, I take it, not her needs. Quite a blessed fraternity, I'm sure, as you say, Squire."

He turned away to Mrs. Mapping. But nothing could be done for her; even the Squire, with all his impetuosity, saw that. Never another word did she speak, never another recognizing gaze did she give. She just passed quietly away with a sigh as we stood looking at her; passed to that blissful realm we are all travelling to, and which had been the last word upon her lips—Heaven.

And that is the true story of Dorothy Grape.

CHAPTER XV

LADY JENKINS

MINA

I

"Had I better go? I should like to."

"Go! why of course you had better go," answered the Squire, putting down the letter.

"It will be the very thing for you, Johnny," added Mrs. Todhetley. "We were saying yesterday that you ought to have a change."

I had not been well for some time; not strong. My old headaches stuck to me worse than usual; Duffham complained that the pulse was feeble. Therefore a letter from Dr. Knox of Lefford, pressing me to go and stay with them, seemed to have come on purpose. Janet had added a postscript: "You must come, Johnny Ludlow, if it is only to see my two babies, and you must not think of staying less than a month." Tod was from home, visiting in Leicestershire.

Three days, and I was off, bag and baggage. To Worcester first, and then onwards again, direct for Lefford. The very journey seemed to do me good. It was a lovely spring day: the hedges were bursting into bud; primroses and violets nestled in the mossy banks.

You have not forgotten, I dare say, how poor Janet Carey's hard life, her troubles, and the sickness those troubles brought, culminated in a brave ending when Arnold Knox, of Lefford, made her his wife. Some five years had elapsed since then, and we were all of us that much older. They had asked me to visit them over and over again, but until now I had not done it. Mr. Tamlyn, Arnold's former master and present partner, with whom they lived, was growing old; he only attended to a few of the old patients now.

It was a cross-grained kind of route, and much longer than it need have been could we have gone straight as a bird flies. The train made all sorts of detours, and I had to change no less than three times. For the last few miles I had had the carriage to myself, but at Toome Junction, the last station before Lefford, a gentleman got in: a rather elderly man with grey hair. Not a syllable did we say, one to another—Englishmen like—and at length Lefford was gained.

"In to time exactly," cried this gentleman then, peering out at the gas-lighted station. "The clock's on the stroke of eight."

Getting my portmanteau, I looked about for Dr. Knox's brougham, which would be waiting for me, and soon pitched upon one, standing near the flys. But my late fellow-passenger strode on before me.

"I thought I spied you out, Wall," he said to the coachman. "Quite a chance your being here, I suppose?"

"I'm waiting for a gentleman from Worcester, sir," answered the man, looking uncommonly pleased, as he touched his hat. "Dr. Knox couldn't come himself."

"Well, I suppose you can take me as well as the gentleman from Worcester," answered the other, as he turned from patting the old horse, and saw me standing there. And we got into the carriage.

It proved to be Mr. Shuttleworth, he who had been old Tamlyn's partner for a short time, and had married his sister. Tamlyn's people did not know he was coming to-night, he told me. He was on his way to a distant place, to see a relative who was ill; by making a round of it, he could take Lefford, and drop in at Mr. Tamlyn's for the night—and was doing so.

Janet came running to the door, Mr. Tamlyn walking slowly behind her. He had a sad countenance, and scanty grey hair, and looked ever so much older than his actual years. Since his son died, poor Bertie, life's sunshine had gone out for him. Very much surprised were they to see Mr. Shuttleworth as well as me.

Janet gave us a sumptuous high-tea, pouring out unlimited cups of tea and pressing us to eat of all the good things. Except that she had filled out a little from the skeleton she was, and looked as joyous now as she had once looked sad, I saw little difference in her. Her boy, Arnold, was aged three and a half: the little girl, named Margaret, after Miss Deveen, could just walk.

"Never were such children in all the world before, if you listen to Janet," cried old Tamlyn, looking at her fondly—for he had learnt to love Janet as he would a daughter—and she laughed shyly and blushed.

"You don't ask after mine," put in Mr. Shuttleworth, quaintly; "my one girl. She is four years old now. Such a wonder! such a paragon! other babies are nothing to it; so Bessy says. Bessy is silly over that child, Tamlyn."

Old Tamlyn just shook his head. They suddenly remembered the one only child he had lost, and changed the subject.

"And what about everything!" asked Mr. Shuttleworth, lighting a cigar, as we sat round the fire after our repast, Janet having gone out to see to a room for Shuttleworth, or perhaps to contemplate her sleeping babies. "I am glad you have at last given up the parish work."

"There's enough to do without it; the practice increases daily," cried Tamlyn. "Arnold is much liked."

"How are all the old patients?"

"That is a comprehensive question," smiled Tamlyn. "Some are flourishing, and some few are, of course, dead."

"Is Dockett with you still?"

"No. Dockett is in London at St. Thomas's. Sam Jenkins is with us in his place. A clever young fellow; worth two of Dockett."

"Who is Sam Jenkins?"

"A nephew of Lady Jenkins—you remember her? At least, of her late husband's."

"I should think I do remember Lady Jenkins," laughed Shuttleworth. "How is she? Flourishing about the streets as usual in that red-wheeled carriage of hers, dazzling as the rising sun?"

"Lady Jenkins is not well," replied Tamlyn, gravely. "She gives me some concern."

"In what way does she give you concern?"

"Chiefly because I can't find out what it is that's amiss with her?"

"Has she been ill long?"

"For some months now. She is not very ill: goes out in her carriage to dazzle the town, as you observe, and has her regular soirées at home. But I don't like her symptoms: I don't understand them, and they grow worse. She has never been well, really well, since that French journey."

"What French journey?"

"At the end of last summer, my Lady Jenkins must needs get it into her head that she should like to see Paris. Stupid old thing, to go all the way to France for the first time in her life! She did go, taking Mina Knox with her—who is growing up as pretty a girl as you'd wish to see. And, by the way, Shuttleworth, Mina is in luck. She has had a fortune left her. An old gentleman, not related to them at all, except that he was Mina's godfather, left her seven thousand pounds last year in his will. Arnold is trustee."

"I am glad of it. Little Mina and I used to be great friends. Her mother is as disagreeable as ever, I suppose?"

"As if she'd ever change from being that!" returned Tamlyn. "I have no patience with her. She fritters away her own income, and then comes here and worries Arnold's life out with her embarrassments. He does for her more than I should do. Educates young Dicky, for one thing."

"No doubt. Knox always had a soft place in his heart. But about Lady Jenkins?"

"Lady Jenkins went over to Paris with her maid, taking Mina as her companion. It was in August. They stayed three weeks there, racketing about to all kinds of show-places, and overdoing it, of course. When they arrived at Boulogne on their way back, expecting to cross over at once, they found they had to wait. A gale was raging, and the boats could not get out. So they put up at an hotel there; and, that night, Lady Jenkins was taken alarmingly ill—the journey and the racketing and the French living had been too much for her. Young people can stand these things, Johnny Ludlow; old ones can't," added Tamlyn, looking at me across the hearth.

"Very true, sir. How old is Lady Jenkins?"

"Just seventy. But you wouldn't have thought her so much before that French journey. Until then she was a lively, active, bustling woman, with a good-natured, pleasant word for every one. Now she is weary, dull, inanimate; seems to be, half her time, in a sort of lethargy."

"What was the nature of the illness?" asked Shuttleworth. "A seizure?"

"No, nothing of that sort. I'm sure I don't know what it was," added old Tamlyn, rubbing back his scanty grey hair in perplexity. "Any way, they feared she was going to die. The French doctor said her getting well was a miracle. She lay ill ten days, keeping her bed, and was still ill and very weak when she reached home. Mina believes that a lady who was detained at the same hotel by the weather, and who came forward and offered her services as nurse, saved Lady Jenkins's life. She was so kind and attentive; never going to her bed afterwards until Lady Jenkins was up from hers. She came home with them."

"Who did? This lady?"

"Yes; and has since remained with Lady Jenkins as companion. She is a Madame St. Vincent; a young widow—"

"A Frenchwoman!" exclaimed Mr. Shuttleworth.

"Yes; but you wouldn't think it. She speaks English just as we do, and looks English. A very nice, pleasant young woman; as kind and loving to Lady Jenkins as though she were her daughter. I am glad they fell in with her. She— Oh, is it you, Sam?"

A tall smiling young fellow of eighteen, or so, had come in. It was Sam Jenkins: and, somehow, I took to him at once. Mr. Shuttleworth shook hands and said he was glad to hear he promised to be a second Abernethy. Upon which Sam's wide mouth opened in laughter, showing a set of nice teeth.

"I thought Dr. Knox was here, sir," he said to Mr. Tamlyn, as if he would apologize for entering.

"Dr. Knox is gone over to the Brook, but I should think he'd be back soon now. Why? Is he wanted?"

"Only a message, sir, from old Willoughby's. They'd like him to call there as soon as convenient in the morning."

"Now, Sam, don't be irreverent," reproved his master. "Old Willoughby! I should say Mr. Willoughby if I were you. He is no older than I am. You young men of the present day are becoming very disrespectful; it was different in my time."

Sam laughed pleasantly. Close upon that, Dr. Knox came in. He was more altered than Janet, looking graver and older, his light hair as wild as ever. He was just thirty now.

Mr. Shuttleworth left in the morning, and afterwards Dr. Knox took me to see his step-mother. Her house (but it was his house, not hers), Rose Villa, was in a suburb of the town, called the London Road. Mrs. Knox was a dark, unpleasing-looking woman; her voice harsh, her crinkled black hair untidy—it was never anything else in a morning. The two eldest girls were in the room. Mina was seventeen, Charlotte twelve months younger. Mina was the prettiest; a fair girl with a mild face and pleasant blue eyes, her manner and voice as quiet as her face. Charlotte seemed rather strong-minded.

"Are you going to the soirée next door to-night, Arnold?" cried Mrs. Knox, as we were leaving.

"I think not," he answered. "Janet wrote to decline."

"You wished her to decline, I dare say!" retorted Mrs. Knox. "You always did despise the soirées, Arnold."

Dr. Knox laughed pleasantly. "I have never had much time for soirées," he said; "and Janet does not care for them. Besides, we think it unkind to leave Mr. Tamlyn alone." At which latter remark Mrs. Knox tossed her head.

"I must call on Lady Jenkins, as I am up here," observed Dr. Knox to me, when we were leaving. "You don't mind, do you, Johnny?"

"I shall like it. They were talking about her last night."

It was only a few yards higher up. A handsome dwelling, double the size of Rose Villa, with two large iron gates flanked by imposing pillars, on which was written in gold letters, as large as life, "Jenkins House."

Dr. Knox laughed. "Sir Daniel Jenkins re-christened it that," he said, dropping his voice, lest any ears should be behind the open windows: "it used to be called 'Rose Bank.' They moved up here four years ago; he was taken ill soon afterwards and died, leaving nearly all his money to his wife unconditionally: it is over four thousand a-year. He was in business as a drysalter, and was knighted during the time he was mayor."

"Who will come in for the money?"

"That is as Lady Jenkins pleases. There are lots of relations, Jenkinses. Sir Daniel partly brought up two orphan nephews—at least, he paid for their schooling and left each a little money to place them out in life. You have seen the younger of them, Sam, who is with us; the other, Dan, is articled to a solicitor in the town, old Belford. Two other cousins are in the drysalting business; and the ironmonger, Sir Daniel's youngest brother, left several sons and daughters. The old drysalter had no end of nephews and nieces, and might have provided for them all. Perhaps his widow will do so."

Not possessing the faintest idea of what "drysalting" might be, unless it had to do with curing hams, I was about to inquire, when the house-door was thrown open by a pompous-looking gentleman in black—the butler—who showed us into the dining-room, where Lady Jenkins was sitting. I liked her at first sight. She was short and stout, and had pink cheeks and a pink turned-up nose, and wore a "front" of flaxen curls, surmounted by a big smart cap with red roses and blue ribbons in it; but there was not an atom of pretence about her, and her blue eyes were kindly. She took the hands of Dr. Knox in hers, and she shook mine warmly, saying she had heard of Johnny Ludlow.

Turning from her, I caught the eyes of a younger lady fixed upon me. She looked about seven-and-twenty, and wore a fashionable black-and-white muslin gown. Her hair was dark, her eyes were a reddish brown, her cheeks had a fixed bloom upon them. The face was plain, and it struck me that I had seen it somewhere before. Dr. Knox greeted her as Madame St. Vincent.

When we first went in, Lady Jenkins seemed to wake up from a doze. In two minutes she had fallen into a doze again, or as good as one. Her eyelids drooped, she sat perfectly quiet, never speaking unless spoken to, and her face wore a sort of dazed, or stupid look. Madame St. Vincent talked enough for both of them; she appealed frequently to Lady Jenkins—"Was it not so, dear Lady Jenkins?"—or "Don't you remember that, dear Lady Jenkins?" and Lady Jenkins docilely answered "Yes, dear," or "Yes, Patty."

That Madame St. Vincent was a pleasant woman, as Mr. Tamlyn had said, and that she spoke English as we did, as he had also said, there could not be a doubt. Her tongue could not be taken for any but a native tongue; moreover, unless my ears deceived me, it was native Worcestershire. Ever and anon, too, a homely word would be dropped by her in the heat of conversation that belonged to Worcestershire proper, and to no other county.

"You will come to my soirée this evening, Mr. Ludlow," Lady Jenkins woke up to say to me as we were leaving.

"Johnny can come; I dare say he would like to," put in Dr. Knox; "although I and Janet cannot—"

"Which is very churlish of you," interposed Madame St. Vincent.

"Well, you know what impediments lie in our way," he said, smiling. "Sam can come up with Johnny, if you like, Lady Jenkins."

"To be sure; let Sam come," she answered, readily. "How is Sam? and how does he get on?"

"He is very well, and gets on well."

Dr. Knox walked down the road in silence, looking grave. "Every time I see her she seems to me more altered," he observed presently, and I found he was speaking of Lady Jenkins. "Something is amiss with her, and I cannot tell what. I wish Tamlyn would let me take the case in hand!"

Two peculiarities obtained at Lefford. The one was that the universal dinner hour, no-matter how much you might go in for fashion, was in the middle of the day; the other was that every evening gathering, no matter how unpretentious, was invariably called a "soirée." They were the customs of the town.

The soirée was in full swing when I reached Jenkins House that night—at six o'clock. Madame St. Vincent and Charlotte Knox sat behind the tea-table in a cloud of steam, filling the cups as fast as the company emptied them; a footman, displaying large white calves, carried round a tray of bread-and-butter and cake. Lady Jenkins sat near the fire in an easy-chair, wearing a red velvet gown and lofty turban. She nodded to the people as they came in, and smiled at them with quite a silly expression. Mina and Charlotte Knox were in white muslin and pink roses. Mina looked very pretty indeed, and as mild as milk; Charlotte was downright and strong-minded. Every five minutes or so, Madame St. Vincent—the white streamers on her rich black silk dress floating behind her—would leave the tea-table to run up to Lady Jenkins and ask if she wanted anything. Sam had not come with me: he had to go out unexpectedly with Dr. Knox.

"Mr. Jenkins," announced the pompous butler, showing in a tall young fellow of twenty. He had just the same sort of honest, good-natured face that had taken my fancy in Sam, and I guessed that this was his brother, the solicitor. He came up to Lady Jenkins.

"How do you do, aunt?" he said, bending to kiss her. "Hearing of your soirée to-night, I thought I might come."

"Why, my dear, you know you may come; you are always welcome. Which is it?" she added, looking up at him stupidly, "Dan, or Sam?"

"It is Dan," he answered; and if ever I heard pain in a tone, I heard it in his.

"You are Johnny Ludlow, I know!" he said, holding out his hand to me in the warmest manner, as he turned from his aunt. "Sam told me about you this morning." And we were friends from that moment.

Dan brought himself to an anchor by Mina Knox. He was no beauty certainly, but he had a good face. Leaning over Mina's chair, he began whispering to her—and she whispered back again. Was there anything between them? It looked like it—at any rate, on his side—judging by his earnest expression and the loving looks that shot from his honest grey eyes.

"Are you really French?" I asked of Madame St. Vincent, while standing by her side to drink some tea.

"Really," she answered, smiling. "Why?"

"Because you speak English exactly like ourselves."

"I speak it better than I do French," she candidly said. "My mother was English, and her old maid-servant was English, and they educated me between them. It was my father who was French—and he died early."

"Was your mother a native of Worcestershire?"

"Oh dear, no: she came from Wales. What made you think of such a thing?"

"Your accent is just like our Worcestershire accent. I am Worcestershire myself: and I could have thought you were."

She shook her head. "Never was there in my life, Mr. Ludlow. Is that why you looked at me so much when you were here with Dr. Knox this morning?"

"No: I looked at you because your face struck me as being familiar," I frankly said: "I thought I must have seen you somewhere before. Have I, I wonder?"

"Very likely—if you have been much in the South of France," she answered: "at a place called Brétage."

"But I have never been at Brétage."

"Then I don't see how we can have met. I have lived there all my life. My father and mother died there: my poor husband died there. I only came away from it last year."

"It must be my fancy, I suppose. One does see likenesses—"

"Captain Collinson," shouted the butler again.

A military-looking man, got up in the pink of fashion, loomed in with a lordly air; you'd have said the room belonged to him. At first he seemed all hair: bushy curls, bushy whiskers, a moustache, and a fine flowing beard, all purple black. Quite a flutter stirred the room: Captain Collinson was evidently somebody.

After making his bow to Lady Jenkins, he distributed his favours generally, shaking hands with this person, talking with that. At last he turned our way.

"Ah, how do you do, madame?" he said to Madame St. Vincent, his tone ceremonious. "I fear I am late."

It was not a minute that he stood before her, only while he said this: but, strange to say, something in his face or voice struck upon my memory. The face, as much as could be seen of it for hair, seemed familiar to me—just as madame's had seemed.

"Who is he?" I whispered to her, following him with my eyes.

"Captain Collinson."

"Yes, I heard the name. But—do you know anything of him?—who he is?"

She shook her head. "Not much; nothing of my own knowledge. He is in an Indian regiment, and is home on sick leave."

"I wonder which regiment it is? One of our fellows at Dr. Frost's got appointed to one in Madras, I remember."

"The 30th Bengal Cavalry, is Captain Collinson's. By his conversation, he appears to have spent nearly the whole of his life in India. It is said he is of good family, and has a snug private fortune. I don't know any more about him than that," concluded Madame St. Vincent, as she once more rose to go to Lady Jenkins.

"He may have a snug private fortune, and he may have family, but I do not like him," put in Charlotte Knox, in her decisive manner.

"Neither do I, Lotty," added Dan—who was then at the tea-table: and his tone was just as emphatic as Charlotte's.

He had come up for a cup of tea for Mina. Before he could carry it to her, Captain Collinson had taken up the place he had occupied at Mina's elbow, and was whispering to her in a most impressive manner. Mina seemed all in a flutter—and there was certainly no further room for Dan.

"Don't you want it now, Mina?" asked Dan, holding the cup towards her, and holding it in vain, for she was too much occupied to see it.

"Oh, thank you—no—I don't think I do want it now. Sorry you should have had the trouble."

Her words were just as fluttered as her manner. Dan brought the tea back and put it on the tray.

"Of course, she can't spare time to drink tea while he is there," cried Charlotte, resentfully, who had watched what passed. "That man has bewitched her, Dan."

"Not quite yet, I think," said Dan, quietly. "He is trying to do it. There is no love lost between you and him, I see, Lotty."

"Not a ghost of it," nodded Lotty. "The town may be going wild in its admiration of him, but I am not; and the sooner he betakes himself back to India to his regiment, the better."

"I hope he will not take Mina with him," said Dan, gravely.

"I hope not, either. But she is silly enough for anything."

"Who is that, that's silly enough for anything?" cried Madame St. Vincent, whisking back to her place.

"Mina," promptly replied Charlotte. "She asked for a cup of tea, and then said she did not want it."

Some of the people sat down to cards; some to music; some talked. It was the usual routine at these soirées, Mrs. Knox condescended to inform me—and, what more, she added, could be wished for? Conversation, music, and cards—they were the three best diversions of life, she said, not that she herself much cared for music.

Poor Lady Jenkins did not join actively in any one of the three: she for the most part dozed in her chair. When any one spoke to her, she would wake up and say Yes or No; but that was all. Captain Collinson stood in a corner, talking to Mina behind a sheet of music. He appeared to be going over the bars with her, and to be as long doing it as if a whole opera were scored there.

At nine o'clock the supper-room was thrown open, and Captain Collinson handed in Lady Jenkins. Heavy suppers were not the mode at Lefford; neither, as a rule, did the guests sit down, except a few of the elder ones; but the table was covered with dainties. Sandwiches, meats in jelly, rissoles, lobster salad, and similar things that could be eaten with a fork, were supplied in abundance, with sweets and jellies.

"I hope you'll be able to make a supper, my dear," said Lady Jenkins to me in her comfortable way—for supper seemed to wake her up. "You see, if one person began to give a grand sitting-down supper, others would think themselves obliged to do it, and every one can't afford that. So we all confine ourselves to this."

"And I like this best," I said.

"Do you, my dear? I'm glad of that. Dan, is that you? Mind you make a good supper too."

We both made a famous one. At least, I can answer for myself. And, at half-past ten, Dan and I departed together.

"How very good-natured Lady Jenkins seems to be!" I remarked.

"She is good-nature itself, and always was," Dan warmly answered. "She has never been a bit different from what you see her to-night—kind to us all. You should have known her though in her best days, before she grew ill. I never saw any one so altered."

"What is it that's the matter with her?"

"I don't know," answered Dan. "I wish I did know. Sam tells me Tamlyn does not know. I'm afraid he thinks it is the break-up of old age. I should be glad, though, if she did not patronize that fellow Collinson so much."

"Every one seems to patronize him."

"Or to let him patronize them," corrected Dan. "I can't like the fellow. He takes too much upon himself."

"He seems popular. Quite the fashion."

"Yes, he is that. Since he came here, three or four months ago, the women have been running after him. Do you like him, Johnny Ludlow?" abruptly added Dan.

"I hardly know whether I do or not: I've not seen much of him," was my answer. "As a rule, I don't care for those people who take much upon themselves. The truth is, Dan," I laughed jokingly, "you think Collinson shows too much attention to Mina Knox."

Dan walked on for a few moments in silence. "I am not much afraid of that," he presently said. "It is the fellow himself I don't like."

"And you do like Mina?"

"Well—yes; I do. If Mina and I were older and my means justified it, I would make her my wife to-morrow—I don't mind telling you so much. And if the man is after her, it is for the sake of her money, mind, not for herself. I'm sure of it. I can see."

"I thought Collinson had plenty of money of his own."

"So he has, I believe. But money never comes amiss to an extravagant and idle man; and I think that Mina's money makes her attraction in Collinson's eyes. I wish with all my heart she had never had it left her!" continued Dan, energetically. "What did Mina want with seven thousand pounds?"

"I dare say you would not object to it, with herself."

"I'd as soon not have it. I hope I shall make my way in my profession, and make it well, and I would as soon take Mina without money as with it. I'm sure her mother might have it and welcome, for me! She is always hankering after it."

"How do you know she is?"

"We do her business at old Belford's, and she gets talking about the money to him, making no scruple of openly wishing it was hers. She bothers Dr. Knox, who is Mina's trustee, to lend her some of it. As if Knox would!—she might just as well go and bother the moon. No! But for that confounded seven thousand pounds Collinson would let Mina alone."

I shook my head. He could not know it. Mina was very pretty. Dan saw my incredulity.

"I will tell you why I judge so," he resumed, dropping his voice to a lower key. "Unless I am very much mistaken, Collinson likes some one else—and that's Madame St. Vincent. Sam thinks so too."

It was more than I thought. They were cool to one another.

"But we have seen them when no one else was by," contended Dan: "when he and she were talking together alone. And I can tell you that there was an expression on his face, an anxiousness, an eagerness—I hardly know how to word it—that it never wore for Mina. Collinson's love is given to madame. Rely upon that."

"Then why should he not declare it?"

"Ah, I don't know. There may be various reasons. Her poverty perhaps—for she has nothing but the salary Lady Jenkins pays her. Or, he may not care to marry one who is only a companion: they say he is of good family himself. Another reason, and possibly the most weighty one, may be, that madame does not like him."

"I don't think she does like him."

"I am sure she does not. She gives him angry looks, and she turns away from him with ill-disguised coldness. And so, that's about how the state of affairs lies up there," concluded Dan, shaking hands with me as we reached the door of his lodgings. "Captain Collinson's love is given to Madame St. Vincent, on the one hand, and to Mina's money on the other; and I think he is in a pretty puzzle which of the two to choose. Good-night, Johnny Ludlow. Be sure to remember this is only between ourselves."

II

A week or so passed on. Janet was up to her eyes in preparations, expecting a visitor. And the visitor was no other than Miss Cattledon—if you have not forgotten her. Being fearfully particular in all ways, and given to fault-finding, as poor Janet only too well remembered, of course it was necessary to have things in apple-pie order.

"I should never hear the last of it as long as Aunt Jemima stayed, if so much as a speck of dust was in any of the rooms, or a chair out of place," said Janet to me laughingly, as she and the maids dusted and scrubbed away.

"What's she coming for, Janet?"

"She invited herself," replied Janet: "and indeed we shall be glad to see her. Miss Deveen is going to visit some friends in Devonshire, and Aunt Jemima takes the opportunity of coming here the while. I am sorry Arnold is so busy just now. He will not have much time to give to her—and she likes attention."

The cause of Dr. Knox's increased occupation, was Mr. Tamlyn's illness. For the past few days he had had feverish symptoms, and did not go out. Few medical men would have found the indisposition sufficiently grave to remain at home; but Mr. Tamlyn was an exception. He gave in at the least thing now: and it was nothing at all unusual for Arnold Knox to find all the patients thrown on his own hands.

Amongst the patients so thrown this time was Lady Jenkins. She had caught cold at that soirée I have just told of. Going to the door in her old-fashioned, hospitable way, to speed the departure of the last guests, she had stayed there in the draught, talking, and began at once to sneeze and cough.

"There!" cried Madame St. Vincent, when my lady got back again, "you have gone and caught a chill."

"I think I have," admitted Lady Jenkins. "I'll send for Tamlyn in the morning."

"Oh, my dear Lady Jenkins, we shall not want Tamlyn," dissented madame. "I'll take care of you myself, and have you well in no time."

But Lady Jenkins, though very much swayed by her kind companion, who was ever anxious for her, chose to have up Mr. Tamlyn, and sent him a private message herself.

He went up at once—evidently taking madame by surprise—and saw his patient. The cold, being promptly treated, turned out to be a mere nothing, though Madame St. Vincent insisted on keeping the sufferer some days in bed. By the time Mr. Tamlyn was ill, she was well again, and there was not much necessity for Dr. Knox to take her: at least, on the score of her cold. But he did it.

One afternoon, when he was going up there late, he asked me if I would like the drive. And, while he paid his visit to Lady Jenkins, I went in to Rose Villa. It was a fine, warm afternoon, almost like summer, and Mrs. Knox and the girls were sitting in the garden. Dicky was there also. Dicky was generally at school from eight o'clock till six, but this was a half-holiday. Dicky, eleven years old now, but very little for his age, was more troublesome than ever. Just now he was at open war with his two younger sisters and Miss Mack, the governess, who had gone indoors to escape him.

Leaning against the trunk of a tree, as he talked to Mrs. Knox, Mina, and Charlotte, stood Captain Collinson, the rays of the sun, now drawing westward, shining full upon him, bringing out the purple gloss of his hair, whiskers, beard, and moustache deeper than usual. Captain Collinson incautiously made much of Dicky, had told him attractive stories of the glories of war, and promised him a commission when he should be old enough. The result was, that Dicky had been living in the seventh heaven, had bought himself a tin sword, and wore it strapped to his waist, dangling beneath his jacket. Dicky, wild to be a soldier, worshipped Captain Collinson as the prince of heroes, and followed him about like a shadow. An inkling of this ambition of Dicky's, and of Captain Collinson's promise, had only reached Mrs. Knox's ears this very afternoon. It was a ridiculous promise of course, worth nothing, but Mrs. Knox took it up seriously.

"A commission for Dicky!—get Dicky a commission!" she exclaimed in a flutter that set her bracelets jangling, just as I arrived on the scene. "Why, what can you mean, Captain Collinson? Do you think I would have Dicky made into a soldier—to be shot at? Never. He is my only son. How can you put such ideas into his head?"

"Don't mind her," cried Dicky, shaking the captain's coat-tails. "I say, captain, don't you mind her."

Captain Collinson turned to young Dicky, and gave him a reassuring wink. Upon which, Dicky went strutting over the grass-plat, brandishing his sword. I shook hands with Mrs. Knox and the girls, and, turning to salute the captain, found him gone.

"You have frightened him away, Johnny Ludlow," cried Charlotte: but she spoke in jest.

"He was already going," said Mina. "He told me he had an engagement."

"And a good thing too," spoke Mrs. Knox, crossly. "Fancy his giving dangerous notions to Dicky!"

Dicky had just discovered our loss. He came shrieking back to know where the captain was. Gone away for good, his mother told him. Upon which young Dicky plunged into a fit of passion and kicking.

"Do you know how Lady Jenkins is to-day?" I asked of Charlotte, when Dicky's noise had been appeased by a promise of cold apple-pudding for tea.

"Not so well."

"Not so well! I had thought of her as being much better."

"I don't think her so," continued Charlotte. "Madame St. Vincent told Mina this morning that she was all right; but when I went in just now she was in bed and could hardly answer me."

"Is her cold worse?"

"No; I think that is gone, or nearly so. She seemed dazed—stupid, more so than usual."

"I certainly never saw any one alter so greatly as Lady Jenkins has altered in the last few months," spoke Mrs. Knox. "She is not like the same woman."

"I'm sure I wish we had never gone that French journey!" said Mina. "She has never been well since. Oh, here's Arnold!"

Dr. Knox had come straight into the garden from Jenkins House. Dicky rushed up to besiege his arms and legs; but, as Dicky was in a state of flour—which he had just put upon himself in the kitchen, or had had put upon him by the maids—the doctor ordered him to keep at arm's-length; and the doctor was the only person who could make himself obeyed by Dicky.

"You have been to see Lady Jenkins, Arnold," said his step-mother. "How is she?"

"Nothing much to boast of," lightly answered Dr. Knox. "Johnny, are you ready?"

"I am going to be a soldier, Arnold," put in Dicky, dancing a kind of war-dance round him. "Captain Collinson is going to make me a captain like himself."

"All right," said Arnold. "You must grow a little bigger first."

"And, Arnold, the captain says— Oh, my!" broke off Dicky, "what's this? What have I found?"

The boy stooped to pick up something glittering that had caught his eye. It proved to be a curiously-shaped gold watch-key, with a small compass in it. Mina and Lotty both called out that it was Captain Collinson's, and must have dropped from his chain during a recent romp with Dicky.

"I'll take it in to him at Lady Jenkins's," said Dicky.

"You will do nothing of the sort, sir," corrected his mother, taking the key from him: she had been thoroughly put out by the suggestion of the "commission."

"Should you chance to see the captain when you go out," she added to me, "tell him his watch-key is here."

The phaeton waited outside. It was the oldest thing I ever saw in regard to fashion, and might have been in the firm hundreds of years. Its hood could be screwed up and down at will; just as the perch behind, where Thomas, the groom, generally sat, could be closed or opened. I asked Dr. Knox whether it had been built later than the year One.

"Just a little, I suppose," he answered, smiling. "This vehicle was Dockett's special aversion. He christened it the 'conveyance,' and we have mostly called it so since."

We were about to step into it, when Madame St. Vincent came tripping out of the gate up above. Dr. Knox met her.

"I was sorry not to have been in the way when you left, doctor," she said to him in a tone of apology: "I had gone to get the jelly for Lady Jenkins. Do tell me what you think of her?"

"She does not appear very lively," he answered; "but I can't find out that she is in any pain."

"I wish she would get better!—she does give me so much concern," warmly spoke madame. "Not that I think her seriously ill, myself. I'm sure I do everything for her that I possibly can."

"Yes, yes, my dear lady, you cannot do more than you do," replied Arnold. "I will be up in better time to-morrow."

"Is Captain Collinson here?" I stayed behind Dr. Knox to ask.

"Captain Collinson here!" returned Madame St. Vincent, tartly, as if the question offended her. "No, he is not. What should bring Captain Collinson here?"

"I thought he might have called in upon leaving Mrs. Knox's. I only wished to tell him that he dropped his watch-key next door. It was found on the grass."

"I don't know anything of his movements," coldly remarked madame. And as I ran back to Dr. Knox, I remembered what Dan Jenkins had said—that she did not like the captain. And I felt Dan was right.

Dr. Knox drove home in silence, I sitting beside him, and Thomas in the perch. He looked very grave, like a man preoccupied. In passing the railway-station, I made some remark about Miss Cattledon, who was coming by the train then on its way; but he did not appear to hear me.

Sam Jenkins ran out as we drew up at Mr. Tamlyn's gate. An urgent message had come for Dr. Knox: some one taken ill at Cooper's—at the other end of the town.

"Mr. Tamlyn thinks you had better go straight on there at once, sir," said Sam.

"I suppose I must," replied the doctor. "It is awkward, though"—pulling out his watch. "Miss Cattledon will be due presently and Janet wanted me to meet her," he added to me. "Would you do it, Johnny?"

"What—meet Miss Cattledon? Oh yes, certainly."

The conveyance drove on, with the doctor and Thomas. I went indoors with Sam. Janet said I could meet her aunt just as well as Arnold, as I knew her. The brougham was brought round to the gate by the coachman, Wall, and I went away in it.

Smoothly and quietly glided in the train, and out of a first-class carriage stepped Miss Cattledon, thin and prim and upright as ever.

"Dear me! is that you, Johnny Ludlow?" was her greeting to me when I stepped up and spoke to her; and her tone was all vinegar. "What do you do here?"

"I came to meet you. Did you not know I was staying at Lefford?"

"I knew that. But why should they send you to meet me?"

"Dr. Knox was coming himself, but he has just been called out to a patient. How much luggage have you, Miss Cattledon?"

"Never you mind how much, Johnny Ludlow: my luggage does not concern you."

"But cannot I save you the trouble of looking after it? If you will get into the brougham, I will see to the luggage and bring it on in a fly, if it's too much to go on the box with Wall."

"You mean well, Johnny Ludlow, I dare say; but I always see to my luggage myself. I should have lost it times and again, if I did not."

She went pushing about amongst the porters and the trucks, and secured the luggage. One not very large black box went up by Wall; a smaller inside with us. So we drove out of the station in state, luggage and all, Cattledon holding her head bolt upright.

"How is Janet, Johnny Ludlow?"

"Quite well, thank you."

"And those two children of hers—are they very troublesome?"

"Indeed, no; they are the best little things you ever saw. I wanted to bring the boy with me to meet you, but Janet would not let me."

"Um!" grunted Cattledon: "showed a little sense for once. What is that building?"

"That's the Town Hall. I thought you knew Lefford, Miss Cattledon?"

"One cannot be expected to retain the buildings of a town in one's head as if they were photographed there," returned she in a sharp tone of reproof. Which shut me up.

"And, pray, how does that young woman continue to conduct herself?" she asked presently.

"What young woman?" I said, believing she must be irreverently alluding to Janet.

"Lettice Lane."

Had she mentioned the name of some great Indian Begum I could not have been more surprised. That name brought back to memory all the old trouble connected with Miss Deveen's emeralds, their loss and their finding: which, take it for all in all, was nothing short of a romance. But why did she question me about Lettice Lane. I asked her why.

"I asked it to be answered, young man," was Cattledon's grim retort.

"Yes, of course," I said, with deprecation. "But how should I know anything about Lettice Lane?"

"If there's one thing I hate more than another, Johnny Ludlow, it is shuffling. I ask you how that young woman is going on; and I request you to answer me."

"Indeed, I would if I could. I don't understand why you should ask me. Is Lettice Lane not living still with you—with Miss Deveen?"

Cattledon evidently thought I was shuffling, for she looked daggers at me. "Lettice Lane," she said, "is with Janet Knox."

"With Janet Knox! Oh dear, no, she is not."

"Don't you get into a habit of contradicting your elders, Johnny Ludlow. It is very unbecoming in a young man."

"But—see here, Miss Cattledon. If Lettice were living with Janet, I must have seen her. I see the servants every day. I assure you Lettice is not one of them."

She began to see that I was in earnest, and condescended to explain in her stiff way. "Janet came to town last May to spend a week with us," she said. "Before that, Lettice Lane had been complaining of not feeling strong: I thought it was nothing but her restlessness; Miss Deveen and the doctor thought she wanted country air—that London did not agree with her. Janet was parting with her nurse at the time; she engaged Lettice to replace her, and brought her down to Lefford. Is the matter clear to you now, young man?"

"Quite so. But indeed, Miss Cattledon, Lettice is not with Janet now. The nurse is named Harriet, and she is not in the least like Lettice Lane."

"Then Lettice Lane must have gone roving again—unless you are mistaken," said Cattledon, severely. "Wanting country air, forsooth! Change was what she wanted."

Handing over Miss Cattledon, when we arrived, to the care of Janet, who took her upstairs, and told me tea would be ready soon, I went into Mr. Tamlyn's sitting-room. He was in the easy-chair before the fire, dozing, but opened his eyes at my entrance.

"Visitor come all right, Johnny?"

"Yes, sir; she is gone to take her cloaks off. Janet says tea is nearly ready."

"I am quite ready for it," he remarked, and shut his eyes again.

I took up a book I was reading, "Martin Chuzzlewit," and sat down on the broad window-seat, legs up, to catch the now fading light. The folds of the crimson curtain lay between me and Mr. Tamlyn—and I only hoped Mrs. Gamp would not send me into convulsions and disturb him.

Presently Dr. Knox came in. He went up to the fire, and stood at the corner of the mantelpiece, his elbow on it, his back to me; and old Tamlyn woke up.

"Well," began he, "what was the matter at Cooper's, Arnold?"

"Eldest boy fell off a ladder and broke his arm. It is only a simple fracture."

"Been very busy to-day, Arnold?"

"Pretty well."

"Hope I shall be out again in a day or two. How did you find Lady Jenkins?"

"Not at all to my satisfaction. She was in bed, and—and in fact seemed hardly to know me."

Tamlyn said nothing to this, and a silence ensued. Dr. Knox broke it. He turned his eyes from the fire on which they had been fixed, and looked full at his partner.

"Has it ever struck you that there's not quite fair play going on up there?" he asked in a low tone.

"Up where?"

"With Lady Jenkins."

"How do you mean, Arnold?"

"That something is being given to her?"

Tamlyn sat upright in his chair, pushed back his scanty hair, and stared at Dr. Knox.

"What do you mean, Knox? What do you suspect?"

"That she is being habitually drugged; gradually, slowly—"

"Merciful goodness!" interrupted Tamlyn, rising to his feet in excitement. "Do you mean slowly poisoned?"

"Hush!—I hear Janet," cried Dr. Knox.

You might have heard a pin drop in the room. They were listening to the footsteps outside the door, but the footsteps did not make the hush and the nameless horror that pervaded it: the words spoken by Dr. Knox had done that. Old Tamlyn stood, a picture of dismay. For myself, sitting in the window-seat, my feet comfortably stretched out before me, and partially sheltered by the red curtains, I could only gaze at them both.

Janet's footsteps died away. She appeared to have been crossing the hall to the tea-room. And they began to talk again.

"I do not say that Lady Jenkins is being poisoned; absolutely, deliberately poisoned," said Dr. Knox, in the hushed tones to which his voice had dropped; "I do not yet go quite so far as that. But I do think that she is in some way being tampered with."

"In what way?" gasped Tamlyn.

"Drugged."

The doctor's countenance wore a puzzled expression as he spoke; his eyes a far-away look, just as though he did not see his own theory clearly. Mr. Tamlyn's face changed: the astonishment, the alarm, the dismay depicted on it gave place suddenly to relief.

"It cannot be, Arnold. Rely upon it you are mistaken. Who would harm her?"

"No one that I know of; no suspicious person is about her to do it," replied Dr. Knox. "And there lies the puzzle. I suppose she does not take anything herself? Opium, say?"

"Good Heavens, no," warmly spoke old Tamlyn. "No woman living is less likely to do that than Lady Jenkins."

"Less likely than she was. But you know yourself how unaccountably she has changed."

"She does not take opium or any other drug. I could stake my word upon it, Arnold."

"Then it is being given to her—at least, I think so. If not, her state is to me inexplicable. Mind you, Mr. Tamlyn, not a breath of this must transpire beyond our two selves," urged Dr. Knox, his tone and his gaze at his senior partner alike impressively earnest. "If anything is wrong, it is being wilfully and covertly enacted; and our only chance of tracing it home is to conceal our suspicion of it."

"I beg your pardon, Dr. Knox," I interrupted at this juncture, the notion, suddenly flashing into my mind, that he was unaware of my presence, sending me hot all over; "did you know I was here?"

They both turned to me, and Dr. Knox's confused start was a sufficient answer.

"You heard all I said, Johnny Ludlow?" spoke Dr. Knox.

"All. I am very sorry."

"Well, it cannot be helped now. You will not let it transpire?"

"That I certainly will not."

"We shall have to take you into our confidence—to include you in the plot," said Arnold Knox, with a smile. "I believe we might have a less trustworthy adherent."

"You could not have one more true."

"Right, Johnny," added Mr. Tamlyn. "But I do hope Dr. Knox is mistaken. I think you must be, Arnold. What are your grounds for this new theory?"

"I don't tell you that it is quite new," replied Dr. Knox. "A faint idea of it has been floating in my mind for some little time. As to grounds, I have no more to go upon than you have had. Lady Jenkins is in a state that we do not understand; neither you nor I can fathom what is amiss with her; and I need not point out that such a condition of things is unsatisfactory to a medical man, and sets him thinking."

"I am sure I have not been able to tell what it is that ails her," concurred old Tamlyn, in a helpless kind of tone. "She seems always to be in a lethargy, more or less; to possess no proper self-will; to have parted, so to say, with all her interest in life."

"Just so. And I cannot discover, and do not believe, that she is in any condition of health to cause this. I believe that the evil is being daily induced," emphatically continued Dr. Knox. "And if she does not herself induce it, by taking improper things, they are being administered to her by others. You will not admit the first theory, Mr. Tamlyn?"

"No, that I will not. Lady Jenkins no more takes baneful drugs of her own accord than I take them."

"Then the other theory must come up. It draws the point to a narrow compass, but to a more startling one."

"Look here, Arnold. If I did admit the first theory you would be no nearer the light. Lady Jenkins could not obtain drugs, and be everlastingly swallowing them, without detection. Madame St. Vincent would have found her out in a day."

"Yes."

"And would have stopped it at once herself, or handed it over to me to be dealt with. She is truly anxious for Lady Jenkins, and spares no pains, no time, no trouble for her."

"I believe that," said Dr. Knox. "Whatsoever is being done, Madame St. Vincent is kept in the dark—just as much as we are. Who else is about her?"

"No one much but her maid, that I know of," replied old Tamlyn, after a pause of consideration. "And I should think she was as free from suspicion as madame herself. It seems a strange thing."

"It is. But I fear I am right. The question now will be, how are we to set about solving the mystery?"

"She is not quite always in a lethargic state," observed Tamlyn, his thoughts going off at a tangent.

"She is so more or less," dissented Dr. Knox. "Yesterday morning I was there at eight o'clock; I went early purposely, and she was in a more stupidly lethargic state than I had before seen her. Which of course proves one thing."

"What thing? I fail to catch your meaning, Arnold."

"That she is being drugged in the night as well as the day."

"If she is drugged at all," corrected Mr. Tamlyn, shaking his head. "But I do not give in to your fancy yet, Arnold. All this must edify you, Johnny!"

Tamlyn spoke the words in a jesting sense, meaning of course that it had done nothing of the kind. He was wrong, if to edify means to interest. Hardly ever during my life had I been more excited.

"It is a frightful shame if any one is playing with Lady Jenkins," I said to them. "She is as good-hearted an old lady as ever lived. And why should they do it? Where's the motive?"

"There lies one of the difficulties—the motive," observed Dr. Knox. "I cannot see any; any end to be obtained by it. No living being that I know of can have an interest in wishing for Lady Jenkins's death or illness."

"How is her money left?"

"A pertinent question, Johnny. I do not expect any one could answer it, excepting herself and Belford, the lawyer. I suppose her relatives, all the nephews and nieces, will inherit it: and they are not about her, you see, and cannot be dosing her. No; the motive is to me a complete mystery. Meanwhile, Johnny, keep your ears and eyes open when you are up there; there's no telling what chance word or look may be dropped that might serve to give you a clue: and keep your mouth shut."

I laughed.

"If I could put aside my patients for a week, and invent some excuse for taking up my abode at Jenkins House, I know I should soon find out all the mystery," went on Dr. Knox.

"Arnold, why not take Madame St. Vincent into your confidence?"

Dr. Knox turned quickly round at the words to face his senior partner. He held up his finger warningly.

"Things are not ripe for it," he said. "Let me get, or try to get, a little more inkling into matters than I have at present, as touching the domestic economy at Jenkins House. I may have to do as you say, later: but women are only chattering magpies; marplots, often with the best intentions; and Madame St. Vincent may be no exception."

"Will you please come to tea?" interrupted Janet, opening the door.

Miss Cattledon, in a sea-green silk gown that I'm sure I had seen many times before, and the velvet on her thin throat, and a bow of lace on her head, shook hands with Mr. Tamlyn and Dr. Knox, and we sat down to tea. Little Arnold, standing by his mother in his plaid frock and white drawers (for the time to dress little children as men had not come in then by many a year), had a piece of bread-and-butter given to him. While he was eating it, the nurse appeared.

"Are you ready, Master Arnold? It is quite bedtime."

"Yes, he is ready, Harriet; and he has been very good," spoke Janet. And the little fellow went contentedly off without a word.

Miss Cattledon, stirring her tea at the moment, put the spoon down to look at the nurse, staring at her as if she had never seen a nurse before.

"That's not Lettice Lane," she observed sententiously, as the door closed on Harriet. "Where is Lettice Lane?"

"She has left, Aunt Jemima."

If a look could have withered Janet, Cattledon's was severe enough to do it. But the displeasure was meant for Lettice, not for Janet.

"What business had she to leave? Did she misbehave herself?"

"She stayed with me only two months," said Janet. "And she left because she still continued poorly, and the two children were rather too much for her. The baby was cutting her teeth, which disturbed Lettice at night; and I and Arnold both thought we ought to have some one stronger."

"Did you give her warning?" asked Cattledon, who was looking her very grimmest at thought of the absent Lettice; "or did she give it you?"

Janet laughed presently. "I think it was a sort of mutual warning, Aunt Jemima. Lettice acknowledged to me that she was hardly equal to the care of the children; and I told her I thought she was not. We found her another place."

"A rolling-stone gathers no moss," commented Cattledon. "Lettice Lane changes her places too often."

"She stayed some time with Miss Deveen, Aunt Jemima. And she likes her present place. She gets very good wages, better than she had with me, and helps to keep her mother."

"What may her duties be? Is she housemaid again?"

"She is lady's-maid to Lady Jenkins, an old lady who lives up the London Road. Lettice has grown much stronger since she went there. Why, what do you think, Aunt Jemima?" added Janet, laughing, "Lettice has actually been to Paris. Lady Jenkins went there just after engaging Lettice, and took her."

Miss Cattledon tossed her head. "Much good that would do Lettice Lane! Only fill her up with worse conceits than ever. I wonder she is not yet off to Australia! She used always to be talking of it."

"You don't appear to like Lettice Lane, ma'am," smiled old Tamlyn.

"No, I do not, sir. Lettice Lane first became known to me under unfavourable circumstances, and I have not liked her since."

"Indeed! What were they?"

"Some of Miss Deveen's jewels disappeared—were stolen; and Lettice Lane was suspected. It turned out later that she was not guilty; but I could not get over my dislike to her. We cannot help our likes and dislikes, which often come to us without rhyme or reason," acknowledged Miss Cattledon, "and I admit that I am perhaps too persistent in mine."

Not a soul present, myself excepted, had ever heard about the loss of the emeralds: and somehow I felt sorry that Cattledon had spoken of it. Not that she did it in ill-nature—I give her that due. Questions were immediately poured out, and she had to give the full history.

The story interested them all, Dr. Knox especially.

"And who did take the jewels?" he asked.

But Cattledon could not enlighten him, for Miss Deveen had not betrayed Sophie Chalk, even to her.

"I don't know who it was," tartly confessed Cattledon, the point being a sore one with her. "Miss Deveen promised, I believe, to screen the thief; and did so."

"Perhaps it was really Lettice Lane?"

"I believe not. I am sure not. It was a lady, Miss Deveen told me that much. No; of that disgraceful act Lettice Lane was innocent: but I should never be surprised to hear of her falling into trouble. She is capable of it."

"Of poisoning somebody, perhaps?" spoke Dr. Knox.

"Yes," acquiesced Cattledon, grimly.

How prejudiced she was against Lettice Lane! But she had given this last answer only in the same jesting spirit in which it appeared to have been put, not really meaning it.

"To be wrongly suspected, as poor Lettice Lane was, ought to make people all the more considerate to her," remarked Janet, her thoughts no doubt reverting to the time when she herself was falsely suspected—and accused.

"True, my dear," answered old Tamlyn. "Poor Lettice must have had her troubles."

"And she has had her faults," retorted Cattledon.

But this story had made an impression on Dr. Knox that Cattledon never suspected, never intended. He took up the idea that Lettice Lane was guilty. Going into Mr. Tamlyn's sitting-room for "Martin Chuzzlewit," when tea was over, I found his hand on my shoulder. He had silently followed me.

"Johnny Ludlow," he said, looking down into my eyes in the dim room, which was only lighted by the dim fire, "I don't like this that I have heard of Lettice Lane."

And the next to come in was Tamlyn. Closing the door, he walked up to the hearthrug where we stood, and stirred the fire into a blaze.

"I am telling Johnny Ludlow that this story of Miss Deveen's emeralds has made an unfavourable impression on me," quoth Dr. Knox to him. "It does not appear to me to be at all clear that Lettice Lane did not take them; and that Miss Deveen, in her benevolence, screened her from the consequences."

"But, indeed—" I was beginning, when Dr. Knox stopped me.

"A moment, Johnny. I was about to add that a woman who is capable of one crime can sometimes be capable of another; and I should not be surprised if it is Lettice Lane who is tampering with Lady Jenkins."

"But," I repeated, "Lettice Lane did not take the jewels. She knew nothing about it. She was perfectly innocent."

"You cannot answer for it, Johnny."

"Yes, I can; and do. I know who did take them."

"You know, Johnny Ludlow?" cried old Tamlyn, while Dr. Knox looked at me in silence.

"I helped Miss Deveen to find it out. At least, she had me with her during the progress of the discovery. It was a lady who took the jewels—as Miss Cattledon told you. She fainted away when it was brought home to her, and fell on my shoulder."

I believe they hardly knew whether to give me credit or not. Of course it did sound strange that I, young Johnny Ludlow, should have been entrusted by Miss Deveen with a secret she would not disclose even to her many years' companion and friend, Jemima Cattledon.

"Who was it, then, Johnny?" began Mr. Tamlyn.

"I should not like to tell, sir. I do not think it would be right to tell. For the young lady's own sake, Miss Deveen hushed the matter up, hoping it would be a warning to her in future. And I dare say it has been."

"Young, was she?"

"Yes. She has married since then. I could not, in honour, tell you her name."

"Well, I suppose we must believe you, Johnny," said Dr. Knox, making the admission unwillingly. "Lettice Lane did get fingering the jewels, it appears; you admit that."

"But she did not take them. It was—another." And, cautiously choosing my words, so as not to say anything that could direct suspicion to Sophie Chalk—whose name most likely they had never heard in their lives—I gave them an outline of the way in which Miss Deveen had traced the matter out. The blaze lighted up Mr. Tamlyn's grey face as I told it.

"You perceive that it could not have been Lettice Lane, Dr. Knox," I said, in conclusion. "I am sorry Miss Cattledon should have spoken against her."

"Yes, I perceive Lettice could not have been guilty of stealing the jewels," answered Dr. Knox. "Nevertheless, a somewhat unfavourable impression of the girl has been made upon me, and I shall look a little after her. Why does she want to emigrate to Australia?"

"Only because two of her brothers are there. I dare say it is all idle talk—that she will never go."

They said no more to me. I took up my book and quitted the room, leaving them to talk it out between themselves.

II

Mr. Tamlyn might be clever in medicine; he certainly was not in diplomacy. Dr. Knox had particularly impressed upon him the desirability of keeping their suspicion a secret for the present, even from Madame St. Vincent; yet the first use old Tamlyn made of his liberty was to disclose it to her.

Tossed about in the conflict of doubts and suspicions that kept arising in his mind, Mr. Tamlyn, from the night I have just told you of, was more uneasy than a fish out of water, his opinion constantly vacillating. "You must be mistaken, Arnold; I feel sure there's nothing wrong going on," he would say to his junior partner one minute; and, the next minute, decide that it was going on, and that its perpetrator must be Lettice Lane.

The uneasiness took him abroad earlier than he would otherwise have gone. A slight access of fever attacked him the day after the subject had been broached—which fever he had no doubt worried himself into. In the ordinary course of things he would have stayed at home for a week after that: but he now went out on the third day.

"I will walk," he decided, looking up at the sunshine. "It will do me good. What lovely weather we are having."

Betaking himself through the streets to the London Road, he reached Jenkins House. The door stood open; and the doctor, almost as much at home in the house as Lady Jenkins herself, walked in without knocking.

The dining-room, where they mostly sat in the morning, was empty; the drawing-room was empty; and Mr. Tamlyn went on to a third room, that opened to the garden at the back with glass-doors.

"Any one here? or is the house gone a-maying?" cried the surgeon as he entered and came suddenly upon a group of three people, all upon their knees before a pile of old music—Madame St. Vincent, Mina Knox, and Captain Collinson. Two of them got up, laughing. Mina remained where she was.

"We are searching for a manuscript song that is missing," explained madame, as she gave her hand to the doctor. "Mina feels sure she left it here; but I do not remember to have seen it."

"It was not mine," added Mina, looking round at the doctor in her pretty, gentle way. "Caroline Parker lent it to me, and she has sent for it twice."

"I hope you'll find it, my dear."

"I must have left it here," continued Mina, as she rapidly turned over the sheets. "I was singing it yesterday afternoon, you remember," she added, glancing up at the captain. "It was while you were upstairs with Lady Jenkins, Madame St. Vincent."

She came to the end of the pile of music, but could not find the song. Putting it all on a side-table, Mina said a general good-bye, escaped by the glass-doors, and ran home by the little gate that divided the two gardens.

Captain Collinson left next. Perhaps he and Mina had both a sense of being de trop when the doctor was there. Waiting to exchange a few words with Mr. Tamlyn, and bidding Madame St. Vincent an adieu that had more of formality in it than friendship, the captain bowed himself out, taking his tasselled cane with him, madame ringing for one of the men-servants to attend him to the hall-door. Tasselled canes were the fashion then.

"They do not make a practice of meeting here, do they?" began old Tamlyn, when the captain was beyond hearing.

"Who? What?" asked Madame St. Vincent.

"The captain and little Mina Knox."

For a minute or two it appeared that madame could not catch his meaning. She looked at him in perplexity.

"I fail to understand you, dear Mr. Tamlyn."

"The captain is a very attractive man, no doubt; a good match, I dare say, and all that: but still we should not like poor little Mina to be whirled off to India by him. I asked if they often met here."

"Whirled off to India?" repeated madame, in astonishment. "Little Mina? By him? In what capacity?"

"As his wife."

"But—dear me!—what can have put such an idea into your head, my good sir? Mina is a mere child."

"Old enough to take up foolish notions," quoth the doctor, quaintly; "especially if they are put into it by a be-whiskered grenadier, such as he. I hope he is not doing it! I hope you do not give them opportunities of meeting here!"

Madame seemed quite taken aback at the implication. Her voice had a sound of tears in it.

"Do you suppose I could be capable of such a thing, sir? I did think you had a better opinion of me. Such a child as Mina! We were both on our knees, looking for the song, when Captain Collinson came in; and he must needs go down on his great stupid knees too. He but called to inquire after Lady Jenkins."

"Very thoughtful of him, of course. He is often up here, I fancy; at the next house, if not at this."

"Certainly not often at this. He calls on Lady Jenkins occasionally, and she likes it. I don't encourage him. He may be a brave soldier, and a man of wealth and family, and everything else that's desirable; but he is no especial favourite of mine."

"Well, Sam Jenkins has an idea that he would like to get making love to Mina. Sam was laughing about it in the surgery last night with Johnny Ludlow, and I happened to overhear him. Sam thinks they meet here, as well as next door: and you heard Mina say just now that she was singing to him here yesterday afternoon. Stay, my dear lady, don't be put out. I am sure you have thought it no harm, have been innocent of all suspicion of it. Mistaken, you tell me? Well, it may be I am. Mina is but a child, as you observe, and—and perhaps Sam was only jesting. How is our patient to-day?"

"Pretty well. Just a little drowsy."

"In bed, or up?"

"Oh, up."

"Will you tell her I am here?"

Madame St. Vincent, her plumage somewhat ruffled, betook herself to the floor above, Mr. Tamlyn following. Lady Jenkins, in a loose gown of blue quilted silk and a cap with yellow roses in it, sat at the window, nodding.

"Well," said he, sitting down by her and taking her hand, "and how do you feel to-day?"

She opened her eyes and smiled at him. Better, she thought: oh yes, certainly better.

"You are sleepy."

"Rather so. Getting up tired me."

"Are you not going for a drive to-day? It would do you good."

"I don't know. Ask Patty. Patty, are we going out to-day?"

The utter helplessness of mind and body which appeared to be upon her as she thus appealed to another, Mr. Tamlyn had rarely seen equalled. Even while listening to Madame St. Vincent's answer—that they would go if she felt strong enough—her heavy eyelids closed again. In a minute or two she was in a sound sleep. Tamlyn threw caution and Dr. Knox's injunction to the winds, and spoke on the moment's impulse to Madame St. Vincent.

"You see," he observed, pointing to the sleeping face.

"She is only dozing off again."

"Only! My dear, good lady, this perpetual, stupid, lethargic sleepiness is not natural. You are young, perhaps inexperienced, or you would know it to be not so."

"I scarcely think it altogether unnatural," softly dissented madame, with deprecation. "She has really been very poorly."

"But not sufficiently so to induce this helplessness. It has been upon her for months, and is gaining ground."

"She is seventy years of age, remember."

"I know that. But people far older than that are not as she is without some cause: either of natural illness, or—or—something else. Step here a minute, my dear."

Old Tamlyn walked rapidly to the other window, and stood there talking in low tones, his eyes fixed on Madame St. Vincent, his hand, in his eagerness, touching her shoulder.

"Knox thinks, and has imparted his opinion to me—ay, and his doubts also—that something is being given to her."

"That something is being given to her!" echoed Madame St. Vincent, her face flushing with surprise. "Given to her in what way?"

"Or else that she is herself taking it. But I, who have known her longer than Knox has, feel certain that she is not one to do anything of the sort. Besides, you would have found it out long ago."

"I protest I do not understand you," spoke madame, earnestly. "What is it that she could take? She has taken the medicine that comes from your surgery. She has taken nothing else."

"Knox thinks she is being drugged."

"Drugged! Lady Jenkins drugged? How, drugged? What with? What for? Who would drug her?"

"There it is; who would do it?" said the old doctor, interrupting the torrent of words poured forth in surprise. "I confess I think the symptoms point to it. But I don't see how it could be accomplished and you not detect it, considering that you are so much with her."

"Why, I hardly ever leave her, day or night," cried madame. "My bedroom, as you know, is next to hers, and I sleep with the intervening door open. There is no more chance, sir, that she could be drugged than that I could be."

"When Knox first spoke of it to me I was pretty nearly startled out of my senses," went on Tamlyn. "For I caught up a worse notion than he meant to convey—that she was being systematically poisoned."

A dark, vivid, resentful crimson dyed madame's face. The suggestion seemed to be a reproof on her vigilance.

"Poisoned!" she repeated in angry indignation. "How dare Dr. Knox suggest such a thing?"

"My dear, he did not suggest it against you. He and I both look upon you as her best safeguard. It is your being with her, that gives us some sort of security: and it is your watchfulness we shall have to look to for detection."

"Poisoned!" reiterated madame, unable to get over the ugly word. "I think Dr. Knox ought to be made to answer for so wicked a suspicion."

"Knox did not mean to go so far as that: it was my misapprehension. But he feels perfectly convinced that she is being tampered with. In short, drugged."

"It is not possible," reasoned madame. "It could not be done without my knowledge. Indeed, sir, you may dismiss all idea of the kind from your mind; you and Dr. Knox also. I assure you that such a thing would be simply impracticable."

Mr. Tamlyn shook his head. "Any one who sets to work to commit a crime by degrees, usually possesses a large share of innate cunning—more than enough to deceive lookers-on," he remarked. "I can understand how thoroughly repulsive this idea is to you, my good lady; that your mind shrinks from admitting it; but I wish you would, just for argument's sake, allow its possibility."

But madame was harder than adamant. Old Tamlyn saw what it was—that she took this accusation, and would take it, as a reflection on her care.

"Who is there, amidst us all, that would attempt to injure Lady Jenkins?" she asked. "The household consists only of myself and the servants. They would not seek to harm their mistress."

"Not so sure; not so sure. It is amidst those servants that we must look for the culprit. Dr. Knox thinks so, and so do I."

Madame's face of astonishment was too genuine to be doubted. She feebly lifted her hands in disbelief. To suspect the servants seemed, to her, as ridiculous as the suspicion itself.

"Her maid, Lettice, and the housemaid, Sarah, are the only two servants who approach her when she is ill, sir: Sarah but very little. Both of them are kind-hearted young women."

Mr. Tamlyn coughed. Whether he would have gone on to impart his doubt of Lettice cannot be known. During the slight silence Lettice herself entered the room with her mistress's medicine. A quick, dark-eyed young woman, in a light print gown.

The stir aroused Lady Jenkins. Madame St. Vincent measured out the physic, and was handing it to the patient, when Mr. Tamlyn seized the wine-glass.

"It's all right," he observed, after smelling and tasting, speaking apparently to himself: and Lady Jenkins took it.

"That is the young woman you must especially watch," whispered Mr. Tamlyn, as Lettice retired with her waiter.

"What! Lettice?" exclaimed madame, opening her eyes.

"Yes; I should advise you to do so. She is the only one who is much about her mistress," he added, as if he would account for the advice. "Watch her."

Leaving madame at the window to digest the mandate and to get over her astonishment, he sat down by Lady Jenkins again, and began talking of this and that: the fineness of the weather, the gossip passing in the town.

"What do you take?" he asked abruptly.

"Take?" she repeated. "What is it that I take, Patty?" appealing to her companion.

"Nay, but I want you to tell me yourself," hastily interposed the doctor. "Don't trouble madame."

"But I don't know that I can recollect."

"Oh yes, you can. The effort to do so will do you good—wake you out of this stupid sleepiness. Take yesterday: what did you have for breakfast?"

"Yesterday? Well, I think they brought me a poached egg."

"And a very good thing, too. What did you drink with it?"

"Tea. I always take tea."

"Who makes it?"

"I do," said madame, turning her head to Mr. Tamlyn with a meaning smile. "I take my own tea from the same tea-pot."

"Good. What did you take after that, Lady Jenkins?"

"I dare say I had some beef-tea at eleven. Did I, Patty? I generally do have it."

"Yes, dear Lady Jenkins; and delicious beef-tea it is, and it does you good. I should like Mr. Tamlyn to take a cup of it."

"I don't mind if I do."

Perhaps the answer was unexpected: but Madame St. Vincent rang the bell and ordered up a cup of the beef-tea. The beef-tea proved to be "all right," as he had observed of the medicine. Meanwhile he had continued his questions to his patient.

She had eaten some chicken for dinner, and a little sweetbread for supper. There had been interludes of refreshment: an egg beaten up with milk, a cup of tea and bread-and-butter, and so on.

"You don't starve her," laughed Mr. Tamlyn.

"No, indeed," warmly replied madame. "I do what I can to nourish her."

"What do you take to drink?" continued the doctor.

"Nothing to speak of," interposed madame. "A drop of cold brandy-and-water with her dinner."

"Patty thinks it is better for me than wine," put in Lady Jenkins.

"I don't know but it is. You don't take too much of it?"

Lady Jenkins paused. "Patty knows. Do I take too much, Patty?"

Patty was smiling, amused at the very idea. "I measure one table-spoonful of brandy into a tumbler and put three or four table-spoonfuls of water to it. If you think that is too much brandy, Mr. Tamlyn, I will put less."

"Oh, nonsense," said old Tamlyn. "It's hardly enough."

"She has the same with her supper," concluded madame.

Well, old Tamlyn could make nothing of his suspicions. And he came home from Jenkins House and told Knox he thought they must be both mistaken.

"Why did you speak of it to madame?" asked Dr. Knox. "We agreed to be silent for a short time."

"I don't see why she should not be told, Arnold. She is straightforward as the day—and Lettice Lane seems so, too. I tasted the beef-tea they gave her—took a cup of it, in fact—and I tasted the physic.

Madame says it is impossible that anything in the shape of drugs is being given to her; and upon my word I think so too."

"All the same, I wish you had not spoken."

And a little time went on.

The soirée to-night was at Rose Villa; and Mrs. Knox, attired in a striped gauze dress and the jangling ornaments she favoured, stood to receive her guests. Beads on her thin brown neck, beads on her sharp brown wrists, beads in her ears, and beads dropping from her waist. She looked all beads. They were drab beads to-night, each resting in a little cup of gold. Janet and Miss Cattledon went up in the brougham, the latter more stiffly ungracious than usual, for she still resented Mrs. Knox's former behaviour to Janet. I walked.

"Where can the people from next door be?" wondered Mrs. Knox, as the time went on and Lady Jenkins did not appear.

For Lady Jenkins went abroad again. In a day or two after Mr. Tamlyn's interview with her, Lefford had the pleasure of seeing her red-wheeled carriage whirling about the streets, herself and her companion within it. Old Tamlyn said she was getting strong. Dr. Knox said nothing; but he kept his eyes open.

"I hope she is not taken ill again? I hope she is not too drowsy to come!" reiterated Mrs. Knox. "Sometimes madame can't rouse her up from these sleepy fits, do what she will."

Lady Jenkins was the great card of the soirée, and Mrs. Knox grew cross. Captain Collinson had not come either. She drew me aside.

"Johnny Ludlow, I wish you would step into the next door and see whether anything has happened. Do you mind it? So strange that Madame St. Vincent does not send or come."

I did not mind it at all. I rather liked the expedition, and passed out of the noisy and crowded room to the lovely, warm night-air. The sky was clear; the moon radiant.

I was no longer on ceremony at Jenkins House, having been up to it pretty often with Dan or Sam, and on my own score. Lady Jenkins had been pleased to take a fancy to me, had graciously invited me to some drives in her red-wheeled carriage, she dozing at my side pretty nearly all the time. I could not help being struck with the utter abnegation of will she displayed. It was next door to imbecility.

"Patty, Johnny Ludlow would like to go that way, I think, to-day may we?" she would say. "Must we turn back already, Patty?—it has been such a short drive." Thus she deferred to Madame St. Vincent in all things, small and great: if she had a will or choice of her own, it seemed that she never thought of exercising it. Day after day she would say the drives were short: and very short indeed they were made, upon some plea or other, when I made a third in the carriage. "I am so afraid of fatigue for her," madame whispered to me one day, when she seemed especially anxious.

"But you take a much longer drive, when she and you are alone," I answered, that fact having struck me. "What difference does my being in the carriage make?—are you afraid of fatigue for the horses as well?" At which suggestion madame burst out laughing.

"When I am alone with her I take care not to talk," she explained; "but when three of us are here there's sure to be talking going on, and it cannot fail to weary her."

Of course that was madame's opinion: but my impression was that, let us talk as much as we would, in a high key or a low one, that poor nodding woman neither heard nor heeded it.

"Don't you think you are fidgety about it, madame?"

"Well, perhaps I am," she answered. "I assure you, Lady Jenkins is an anxious charge to me."

Therefore, being quite at home now at Jenkins House (to return to the evening and the soirée I was telling of), I ran in the nearest way to do Mrs. Knox's behest. That was through the two back gardens, by the intervening little gate. I knocked at the glass-doors of what was called the garden-room, in which shone a light behind the curtains, and went straight in. Sitting near each other, conversing with an eager look on their faces, and both got up for Mrs. Knox's soirée, were Captain Collinson and Madame St. Vincent.

"Mr. Ludlow!" she exclaimed. "How you startled me!"

"I beg your pardon for entering so abruptly. Mrs. Knox asked me to run in and see whether anything was the matter, and I came the shortest way. She has been expecting you for some time."

"Nothing is the matter," shortly replied madame, who seemed more put out than the occasion called for: she thought me rude, I suppose. "Lady Jenkins is not ready; that is all. She may be half-an-hour yet."

"Half-an-hour! I won't wait longer, then," said Captain Collinson, catching up his crush hat. "I do trust she has not taken another chill. Au revoir, madame."

With a nod to me, he made his exit by the way I had entered. The same peculiarity struck me now that I had observed before: whenever I went into a place, be it Jenkins House or Rose Villa, the gallant captain immediately quitted it.

"Do I frighten Captain Collinson away?" I said to madame on the spur of the moment.

"You frighten him! Why should you?"

"I don't know why. If he happens to be here when I come in, he gets up and goes away. Did you never notice it? It is the same at Mrs. Knox's. It was the same once at Mrs. Hampshire's."

Madame laughed. "Perhaps he is shy," said she, jestingly.

"A man who has travelled to India and back must have rubbed his shyness off, one would think. I wish I knew where I had met him before!—if I have met him. Every now and again his face seems to strike on a chord of my memory."

"It is a handsome face," remarked madame.

"Pretty well. As much as can be seen of it. He has hair enough for a Russian bear or a wild Indian."

"Have wild Indians a superabundance of hair?" asked she gravely.

I laughed. "Seriously speaking, though, Madame St. Vincent, I think I must have met him somewhere."

"Seriously speaking, I don't think that can be," she answered; and her jesting tone had become serious. "I believe he has passed nearly all his life in India."

"Just as you have passed yours in the South of France. And yet there is something in your face also familiar to me."

"I should say you must be just a little fanciful on the subject of likenesses. Some people are."

"I do not think so. If I am I did not know it. I—"

The inner door opened and Lady Jenkins appeared, becloaked and beshawled, with a great green hood over her head, and leaning on Lettice Lane. Madame got up and threw a mantle on her own shoulders.

"Dear Lady Jenkins, I was just coming to see for you. Captain Collinson called in to give you his arm, but he did not wait. And here's Mr. Johnny Ludlow, sent in by Mrs. Knox to ask whether we are all dead."

"Ay," said Lady Jenkins, nodding to me as she sat down on the sofa: "but I should like a cup of tea before we start."

"A cup of tea?"

"Ay; I'm thirsty. Let me have it, Patty."

She spoke the last words in an imploring tone, as if Patty were her mistress. Madame threw off her mantle again, untied the green hood of her lady, and sent Lettice to make some tea.

"You had better go back and tell Mrs. Knox we are coming, though I'm sure I don't know when it will be," she said aside to me.

I did as I was told; and had passed through the garden-gate, when my eye fell upon Master Richard Knox. He was standing on the grass in the moonlight, near the clump of laurels, silently contorting his small form into cranks and angles, after the gleeful manner of Punch in the show when he has been giving his wife a beating. Knowing that agreeable youth could not keep himself out of mischief if he tried, I made up to him.

"Hush—sh—sh!" breathed he, silencing the question on my lips.

"What's the sport, Dicky?"

"She's with him there, beyond the laurels; they are walking round," he whispered. "Oh my! such fun! I have been peeping at 'em. He has his arm round her waist."

Sure enough, at that moment they came into view—Mina and Captain Collinson. Dicky drew back into the shade, as did I. And I, to my very great astonishment, trod upon somebody else's feet, who made, so to say, one of the laurels.

"It's only I," breathed Sam Jenkins. "I'm on the watch as well as Dicky. It looks like a case of two loviers, does it not?"

The "loviers" were parting. Captain Collinson held her hand between both his to give her his final whisper. Then Mina tripped lightly over the grass and stole in at the glass-doors of the garden-room, while the captain stalked round to the front-entrance and boldly rang, making believe he had only then arrived.

"Oh my, my!" repeated the enraptured Dicky, "won't I have the pull of her now! She'd better tell tales of me again!"

"Is it a case, think you?" asked Sam of me, as we slowly followed in the wake of Mina.

"It looks like it," I answered.

Janet was singing one of her charming songs, as we stole in at the glass-doors: "Blow, blow, thou wintry wind:" just as she used to sing it in that house in the years gone by. Her voice had not lost its sweetness. Mina stood near the piano now, a thoughtful look upon her flushed face.

"Where did you and Dicky go just now, Sam?"

Sam turned short round at the query. Charlotte Knox, as she put it, carried suspicion in her low tone.

"Where did I and Dicky go?" repeated Sam, rather taken aback. "I—I only stepped out for a stroll in the moonlight. I don't know anything about Dicky."

"I saw Dicky run out to the garden first, and you went next," persisted Charlotte, who was just as keen as steel. "Dick, what was there to see? I will give you two helpings of trifle at supper if you tell me."

For two helpings of trifle Dick would have sold his birthright. "Such fun!" he cried, beginning to jump. "She was out there with the captain, Lotty: he came to the window here and beckoned to her: I saw him. I dodged them round and round the laurels, and I am pretty nearly sure he kissed her."

"Who was?—who did?" But the indignant glow on Lotty's face proved that she scarcely needed to put the question.

"That nasty Mina. She took and told that it was me who eat up the big bowl of raspberry cream in the larder to-day; and mother went and believed her!"

Charlotte Knox, her brow knit, her head held erect, walked away after giving us all a searching look apiece. "I, like Dicky, saw Collinson call her out, and I thought I might as well see what he wanted to be after," Sam whispered to me. "I did not see Dicky at all, though, until he came into the laurels with you."

"He is talking to her now," I said, directing Sam's attention to the captain.

"I wonder whether I ought to tell Dr. Knox?" resumed Sam. "What do you think, Johnny Ludlow? She is so young, and somehow I don't trust him. Dan doesn't, either."

"Dan told me he did not."

"Dan fancies he is after her money. It would be a temptation to some people,—seven thousand pounds. Yet he seems to have plenty of his own."

"If he did marry her he could not touch the money for three or four years to come."

"Oh, couldn't he, though," answered Sam, taking me up. "He could touch it next day."

"I thought she did not come into it till she was of age, and that Dr. Knox was trustee."

"That's only in case she does not marry. If she marries it goes to her at once. Here comes Aunt Jenkins!"

The old lady, as spruce as you please, in a satin gown, was shaking hands with Mrs. Knox. But she looked half silly: and, may I never be believed again, if she did not begin to nod directly she sat down.

"Do you hail from India? as the Americans phrase it," I suddenly ask of Captain Collinson, when chance pinned us together in a corner of the supper-room, and he could not extricate himself.

"Hail from India!" he repeated. "Was I born there, I conclude you mean?"

"Yes."

"Not exactly. I went there, a child, with my father and mother. And, except for a few years during my teens, when I was home for education, I have been in India ever since. Why do you ask?"

"For no particular reason. I was telling Madame St. Vincent this evening that it seemed to me I had seen you before; but I suppose it could not be. Shall you be going back soon?"

"I am not sure. Possibly in the autumn, when my leave will expire: not till next year if I can get my leave extended. I shall soon be quitting Lefford."

"Shall you?"

"Must do it. I have to make my bow at a levée; and I must be in town for other things as well. I should like to enjoy a little of the season there: it may be years before the opportunity falls to my lot again. Then I have some money to invest: I think of buying an estate. Oh, I have all sorts of business to attend to, once I am in London."

"Where's the use of buying an estate if you are to live in India?"

"I don't intend to live in India always," he answered, with a laugh. "I shall quit the service as soon as ever I can, and settle down comfortably in the old country. A home of my own will be of use to me then."

Now it was that very laugh of Captain Collinson's that seemed more familiar to me than all the rest of him. That I had heard it before, ay, and heard it often, I felt sure. At least, I should have felt sure but for its seeming impossibility.

"You are from Gloucestershire, I think I have heard," he observed to me.

"No; from Worcestershire."

"Worcestershire? That's a nice county, I believe. Are not the Malvern Hills situated in it?"

"Yes. They are eight miles from Worcester."

"I should like to see them. I must see them before I go back. And Worcester is famous for—what is it?—china?—yes, china. And for its cathedral, I believe. I shall get a day or two there if I can. I can do Malvern at the same time."

"Captain Collinson, would you mind giving Lady Jenkins your arm?" cried Mrs. Knox at this juncture. "She is going home."

"There is no necessity for Captain Collinson to disturb himself: I can take good care of Lady Jenkins," hastily spoke Madame St. Vincent, in a tart tone, which the room could not mistake. Evidently she did not favour Captain Collinson.

But the captain had already pushed himself through the throng of people and taken the old lady in tow. The next minute I found myself close to Charlotte Knox, who was standing at the supper-table, with a plate of cold salmon before her.

"Are you a wild bear, Johnny Ludlow?" she asked me privately, under cover of the surrounding clatter.

"Not that I know of. Why?"

"Madame St. Vincent takes you for one."

I laughed. "Has she told you so?"

"She has not told me: I guess it is some secret," returned Charlotte, beginning upon the sandwiches. "I learnt it in a curious way."

A vein of seriousness ran through her half-mocking tone; seriousness lay in her keen and candid eyes, lifted to mine.

"Yes, it was rather curious, the way it came to me: and perhaps on my part not altogether honourable. Early this morning, Johnny, before ten o'clock had struck, mamma made me go in and ask how Lady

Jenkins was, and whether she would be able to come to-night. I ran in the nearest way, by the glass-doors, boisterously of course—mamma is always going on at me for that—and the breeze the doors made as I threw them open blew a piece of paper off the table. I stooped to pick it up, and saw it was a letter just begun in madame's handwriting."

"Well?"

"Well, my eyes fell on the few words written; but I declare that I read them heedlessly, not with any dishonourable intention; such a thought never entered my mind. 'Dear Sissy,' the letter began, 'You must not come yet, for Johnny Ludlow is here, of all people in the world; it would not do for you and him to meet.' That was all."

"I suppose madame had been called away," continued Charlotte, after a pause. "I put the paper on the table, and was going on into the passage, when I found the room-door locked: so I just came out again, ran round to the front-door and went in that way. Now if you are not a bear, Johnny, why should you frighten people?"

I did not answer. She had set me thinking.

"Madame St. Vincent had invited a sister from France to come and stay with her: she does just as she likes here, you know. It must be she who is not allowed to meet you. What is the mystery?"

"Who is talking about mystery?" exclaimed Caroline Parker; who, standing near, must have caught the word. "What is the mystery, Lotty?"

And Lotty, giving her some evasive reply, put down her fork and turned away.

CHAPTER XVII

LADY JENKINS

MADAME

I

"If Aunt Jenkins were the shrewd woman she used to be, I'd lay the whole case before her, and have it out; but she is not," contended Dan Jenkins, tilting the tongs in his hand, as we sat round the dying embers of the surgery fire.

His brother Sam and I had walked home together from Mrs. Knox's soirée, and we overtook Dan in the town. Another soirée had been held in Lefford that night, which Dan had promised himself to before knowing Mrs. Knox would have one. We all three turned into the surgery. Dr. Knox was out with a patient, and Sam had to wait up for him. Sam had been telling his brother what we witnessed up at Rose Villa—the promenade round the laurels that Captain Collinson and Mina had stolen in the moonlight. As for me, though I heard what Sam said, and put in a confirming word here and there, I was thinking my own thoughts. In a small way, nothing had ever puzzled me much more than the letter Charlotte Knox had seen. Who was Madame St. Vincent? and who was her sister, that I, Johnny Ludlow, might not meet her?

"You see," continued Dan, "one reason why I can't help suspecting the fellow, is this—he does not address Mina openly. If he were honest and above board, he would go in for her before all the world. He wouldn't do it in secret."

"What do you suspect him of?" cried Sam.

"I don't know. I do suspect him—that he is somehow not on the square. It's not altogether about Mina; but I have no confidence in the man."

Sam laughed. "Of course you have not, Dan. You want to keep Mina for yourself."

Dan pitched his soft hat at Sam's head, and let fall the tongs with a clatter.

"Collinson seems to be all right," I put in. "He is going up to London to a levée, and he is going to buy an estate. At least, he told me so to-night in the supper-room."

"Oh, in one sense of the word the fellow is all right," acknowledged Dan. "He is what he pretends to be; he is in the army list; and, for all I know to the contrary, he may have enough gold to float an argosy of ships. What I ask is, why he should go sneaking after Mina when he does not care for her."

"That may be just a fallacy of ours, Dan," said his brother.

"No, it's not. Collinson is in love with Madame St. Vincent; not with Mina."

"Then why does he spoon after Mina?"

"That's just it—why?"

"Any way, I don't think madame is in love with him, Dan. It was proposed that he should take aunt home to-night, and madame was as tart as you please over it, letting all the room know that she did not want him."

"Put it down so," agreed Dan, stooping to pick up the tongs. "Say that he is not fond of madame, but of Mina, and would like to make her his wife: why does he not go about it in a proper manner; court her openly, speak to her mother; instead of pursuing her covertly like a sneak?"

"It may be his way of courting."

"May it! It is anything but a right way. He is for ever seeking to meet her on the sly. I know it. He got her out in the garden to-night to a meeting, you say: you and Johnny Ludlow saw it."

"Dicky saw it too, and Charlotte got the truth out of him. There may be something in what you say, Dan."

"There's a great deal in what I say," contended Dan, his honest face full of earnestness. "Look here. Here's an officer and a gentleman; a rich man, as we are given to believe, and we've no reason to doubt it. He seems to spend enough—Carter saw him lose five pounds last night, betting at billiards. If he is in love with a young lady, there's nothing to hinder a man like that from going in for her openly—"

"Except her age," struck in Sam. "He may think they'll refuse Mina to him on that score."

"Stuff! I wish you wouldn't interrupt me, Sam. Every day will help to remedy that—and he might undertake to wait a year or two. But I feel sure and certain he does not really care for Mina; I feel sure that, if he is seeking in this underhand way to get her to promise to marry him, he has some ulterior motive in view. My own belief is he would like to kidnap her."

Sam laughed. "You mean, kidnap her money?"

"Well, I don't see what else it can be. The fellow may have outrun the constable, and need some ready money to put him straight. Rely upon this much, Sam—that his habits are as fast as they can well be. I have been learning a little about him lately."

Sam made no answer. He began to look grave.

"Not at all the sort of man who ought to marry Mina, or any other tender young girl. He'd break her heart in a twelvemonth."

Sam spoke up. "I said to Johnny Ludlow, just now, that it might be better to tell Dr. Knox. Perhaps—"

"What about?" interrupted the doctor himself, pouncing in upon us, and catching the words as he opened the door. "What have you to tell Dr. Knox about, Sam? And why are all you young men sitting up here? You'd be better in bed."

The last straw, you know, breaks the camel's back. Whether Sam would really have disclosed the matter to Dr. Knox, I can't say; the doctor's presence and the doctor's question decided it.

Sam spoke in a low tone, standing behind the drug-counter with the doctor, who had gone round to look at some entry in what they called the day-book, and had lighted a gas-burner to do it by. Dr. Knox made no remark of any kind while he listened, his eyes fixed on the book: one might have thought he did not hear, but his lips were compressed.

"If she were not so young, sir—a child, as may be said—I should not have presumed to speak," concluded Sam. "I don't know whether I have done wrong or right."

"Right," emphatically pronounced the doctor.

But the word had hardly left his lips when there occurred a startling interruption. The outer door of the surgery, the one he had come in by, was violently drummed at, and then thrown open. Charlotte Knox, Miss Mack the governess, and Sally the maid—the same Sally who had been at Rose Villa when the trouble occurred about Janet Carey, and the same Miss Mack who had replaced Janet—came flocking in.

"Dicky's lost, Arnold," exclaimed Charlotte.

"Dicky lost!" repeated Dr. Knox. "How can he be lost at this time of night?"

"He is lost. And we had nearly gone to bed without finding it out. The people had all left, and the doors were locked, when some one—Gerty, I think—began to complain of Dicky—"

"It was I who spoke," interposed the governess; and though she was fat enough for two people she had the meekest little voice in the world, and allowed herself to be made a perfect tool of at Rose Villa. "Dicky did behave very ill at supper, eating rudely of everything, and—"

"Yes, yes," broke in Charlotte, "I remember now, Macky. You said Dicky ought to be restrained, and you wondered he was not ill; and then mamma called out, 'But where is Dicky?' 'Gone to bed to sleep off his supper,' we all told her: and she sent Sally up to see that he had put his candle out."

"And of course," interrupted Sally, thinking it was her turn to begin, "when I found the room empty, and saw by the moonlight that Master Dicky had not come to bed at all, I ran down to say so. And his mamma got angry, accusing us servants of having carelessly locked him out-of-doors. And he can't be found, sir—as Miss Lotty says."

"No, he cannot be found anywhere," added Lotty. "We have searched the house and the gardens, and been in to inquire at Lady Jenkins's; and he is gone. And mamma is frantic, and said we were to come to you, Arnold."

"Master Dicky's playing truant: he has gone off with some of the guests," observed Dr. Knox.

"Well, mamma is putting herself into a frightful fever over him, Arnold. That old well in the field at the back was opened the day before yesterday; she says Dicky may have strayed there and fallen in."

"Dicky's after more mischief than that," said the doctor, sagely. "A well in a solitary field would have no charms for Dicky. I tell you, Lotty, he must have marched home with some one or other. Had you any lads up there to-night?"

"No, not any. You know mamma never will have them. Lads, and Dicky, would be too much."

"If Master Dicky have really gone off, as the doctor thinks, I'd lay my next quarter's wages that it's with Captain Collinson," cried Sally. "He is always wanting to be after the captain."

Lotty lifted her face, a gleam of intelligence flashing across it. "Perhaps that's it," she said; "I should not wonder if it is. He has strayed off after, or with, Captain Collinson. What is to be done, Arnold?"

"Not strayed with him, I should think," observed the doctor. "Captain Collinson, if he possesses any sense or consideration, would order Dicky back at once."

"Won't you come with us to the captain's lodgings, Arnold, and see?" cried Charlotte. "It would not do, would it, for us to go there alone at this time of night? The captain may be in bed."

Arnold Knox looked at his sister; looked at the three of them, as if he thought they were enough without him. He was nearly done up with his long day's work.

"I suppose I had better go with you, Lotty," he said. "Though I don't think Captain Collinson would kidnap any one of you if you went alone."

"Oh dear, no; it is Mina he wants to kidnap, not us," answered Lotty, freely. And Arnold glanced at her keenly as he heard the words.

Did you ever know a fellow in the hey-dey of his health and restlessness who was not ready for any night expedition—especially if it were to search after something lost? Dr. Knox took up his hat to accompany the visitors, and we three took up ours.

We proceeded in a body through the moonlit streets to Collinson's lodgings; the few stragglers we met no doubt taking us all for benighted wayfarers, trudging home from some one or other of the noted Lefford soirées. Collinson had the rooms at the hairdresser's—good rooms, famed as the best lodgings in the town. The gas was alight in his sitting-room over the shop; a pretty fair proof that the captain was yet up.

"Stay, Lotty," said Dr. Knox, arresting her impatient hand, that was lifted to pull the bell. "No need to arouse the house: I dare say Pink and his family are in bed. I will go up to Collinson."

It was easy to say so, but difficult to do it. Dr. Knox turned the handle of the door to enter, and found it fastened. He had to ring, after all.

Nobody answered it. Another ring and another shared the same fate. Dr. Knox then searched for some small loose stones, and flung them up at the window. It brought forth no more than the bell had.

"Dicky can't be there, or that gravel would have brought him to the window," decided Lotty. "I should say Captain Collinson is not there, either."

"He may be in his room at the back," observed Dr. Knox. And he rang again.

Presently, after a spell of at least ten minutes' waiting, and no end of ringing, an upper window was opened and a head appeared—that of the hairdresser.

"Whatever's the matter?" called out he, seeing us all below. "It's not fire, is it?"

"I am sorry to disturb you, Pink," called back Dr. Knox. "It is Captain Collinson I want. Is he in, do you know?"

"Yes, sir; he came in about twenty minutes ago, and somebody with him, for I heard him talking," answered Pink. "He must be in his sitting-room, if he is not gone to bed."

"There is a light in the room, but I don't think he can be in. I have thrown up some gravel, and he does not answer."

"I'll come down and see, sir."

Pink, the most obliging little man in the world, descended to the captain's room and thence to us at the door. Captain Collinson was not in. He had gone out again, and left his gas alight.

"You say some one came in with him, Pink. Was it a young lad?"

"I can't tell, sir. I heard the captain's latch-key, and I heard him come on upstairs, talking to somebody; but I was just dropping off to sleep, so did not take much notice."

That the somebody was young Dick, and that Captain Collinson had gone out to march Dick home again, seemed only probable. There was nothing for it but to go on to Rose Villa and ascertain; and we started for it, after a short consultation.

"I shall not have the remotest idea where to look for Dick if he is not there," remarked Dr. Knox.

"And in that case, I do believe mamma will have a fit," added Charlotte. "A real fit, I mean, Arnold. I wish something could be done with Dicky! The house is always in a commotion."

Captain Collinson was at Rose Villa, whether Dicky was or not. At the garden-gate, talking to Mina in the moonlight, stood he, apparently saying good-night to her.

"Dicky? oh dear, yes; I have just brought Dicky back," laughed the captain, before Dr. Knox had well spoken his young half-brother's name, while Mina ran indoors like a frightened hare. "Upon getting home to my rooms just now I found some small mortal stealing in after me, and it proved to be Dicky. He followed me home to get a top I had promised him, and which I forgot to bring up here when I came to-night."

"I hope you did not give it him," said Dr. Knox.

"Yes, I did. I should never have got him back without," added the captain. "Good-night."

He laughed again as he went away. Dicky's vagaries seemed to be rare fun for him.

Dicky was spinning the top on the kitchen table when we went in—for that's where they had all gathered: Mrs. Knox, Gerty, Kate, and the cook. A big humming-top, nearly as large and as noisy as Dick. Dr. Knox caught up the top and caught Dicky by the hand, and took both into the parlour.

"Now then, sir!" he sternly asked. "What did you mean by this night's escapade?"

"Oh, Arnold, don't scold him," implored Mrs. Knox, following them in with her hands held up. "It was naughty of him, of course, and it gave me a dreadful fright; but it was perhaps excusable, and he is safe at home again. The captain was to bring the top, and did not, and poor Dicky ran after him to get it."

"You be quiet, Arnold; I am not to be scolded," put in cunning Dicky. "You just give me my top."

"As to scolding you, I don't know that it would be of any further use: the time seems to have gone by for it, and I must take other measures," spoke Dr. Knox. "Come up to bed now, sir. I shall see you in it before I leave."

"But I want my top."

"Which you will not have," said the doctor: and he marched off Dicky.

"How cross you are with him, Arnold!" spoke his step-mother when the doctor came down again, leaving Dicky howling on his pillow for the top.

"It needs some one to be cross with him," observed Dr. Knox.

"He is only a little boy, remember."

"He is big enough and old enough to be checked and corrected—if it ever is to be done at all. I will see you to-morrow: I wish to have some conversation with you."

"About Dicky?" she hastily asked.

"About him and other things. Mina," he added in a low tone, as he passed her on his way out, but I, being next to him, caught the words, "I did not like to see you at the gate with Captain Collinson at this hour. Do not let it occur again. Young maidens cannot be too modest."

And, at the reproof, Miss Mina coloured to the very roots of her hair.

II

They sat in the small garden-room, its glass-doors open to the warm spring air. Mrs. Knox wore an untidy cotton gown, of a flaming crimson-and-white pattern, and her dark face looked hot and angry. Dr. Knox, sitting behind the table, was being annoyed as much as he could be annoyed—and no one ever annoyed him but his step-mother—as the lines in his patient brow betrayed.

"It is for his own good that I suggest this; his welfare," urged Dr. Knox. "Left to his own will much longer, he must not be. Therefore I say that he must be placed at school."

"You only propose it to thwart me," cried Mrs. Knox. "A fine expense it will be!"

"It will not be your expense. I pay his schooling now, and I shall pay it then. My father left me, young though I was, Dicky's guardian, and I must do this. I wonder you do not see that it will be the very best thing for Dicky. Every one but yourself sees that, as things are, the boy is being ruined."

Mrs. Knox looked sullenly through the open doors near which she sat; she tapped her foot impatiently upon the worn mat, lying on the threshold.

"I know you won't rest until you have carried your point and separated us, Arnold; it has been in your mind to do it this long while. And my boy is the only thing I care for in life."

"It is for Dicky's own best interest," reiterated Dr. Knox. "Of course he is dear to you; it would be unnatural if he were not; but you surely must wish to see him grow up a good and self-reliant man: not an idle and self-indulgent one."

"Why don't you say outright that your resolve is taken and nothing can alter it; that you are going to banish him to school to-morrow?"

"Not to-morrow, but he shall go at the half-quarter. The child will be ten times happier for it; believe that."

"Do you really mean it?" she questioned, her black eyes flashing fury at Arnold. "Will nothing deter you?"

"Nothing," he replied, in a low, firm tone. "I—bear with me a moment, mother—I cannot let Dicky run riot any longer. He is growing up the very incarnation of selfishness; he thinks the world was made for him alone; you and his sisters are only regarded by him as so many ministers to his pleasure. See how he treats you all. See how he treats the servants. Were I to allow this state of things to continue, how should I be fulfilling my obligation to my dead father?—my father and Dicky's."

"I will hear no more," spoke Mrs. Knox, possibly thinking the argument was getting too strong for her. "I have wanted to speak to you, Arnold, and I may as well do it now. Things must be put on a different footing up here."

"What things?"

"Money matters. I cannot continue to do upon my small income."

Arnold Knox passed his hand across his troubled brow, almost in despair. Oh, what a weary subject this was! Not for long together did she ever give him rest from it.

"Your income is sufficient, mother; I am tired of saying it. It is between three and four hundred a-year; and you are free from house-rent."

"Why don't you remind me that the house is yours, and have done with it!" she cried, her voice harsh and croaking as a raven's.

"Well, it is mine," he said good-humouredly.

"Yes; and instead of settling it upon me when you married, you must needs settle it on your wife! Don't you talk of selfishness, Arnold."

"My wife does not derive any benefit from it. It has made no difference to you."

"She would derive it, though, if you died. Where should I be then?"

"I am not going to die, I hope. Oh, mother, if you only knew how these discussions vex me!"

"Then you should show yourself generous."

"Generous!" he exclaimed, in a pained tone. And, goaded to it by his remembrance of what he had done for her in the present and in the past, he went on to speak more plainly than he had ever spoken yet. "Do you forget that a great portion of what you enjoy should, by right, be mine? Is mine!"

"Yours!" she scornfully said.

"Yes: mine. Not by legal right, but by moral. When my father died he left the whole of his property to you. Considerably more than the half of that property had been brought to him by my mother: some people might have thought that much should have descended to her son."

"He did not leave me the whole. You had a share of it."

"Not of the income. I had a sum of five hundred pounds left me, for a specific purpose—to complete my medical education. Mother, I have never grumbled at this; never. It was my father's will and pleasure that the whole should be yours, and that it should go to your children after you; and I am content to think that he did for the best; the house was obliged to come to me; it had been so settled at my mother's marriage; but you have continued to live in it, and I have not said you nay."

"It is like you to remind me of all this!"

"I could remind you of more," he rejoined, chafing at her unjust words, her resentful manner. "That for years I impoverished myself to help you to augment this income. Three parts of what I earned, before my partnership with Mr. Tamlyn, I gave to you."

"Well, I needed it. Do, for goodness' sake, let the past alone, if you can: where's the use of recalling it? Would you have us starve? Would you see me taken off to prison? And that's what it will come to, unless I can get some money to pay up with. That table-drawer that you've got your elbow on, is full of bills. I've not paid one for these six months."

"I cannot think what it is you do with your money!"

"Do with my money! Why, it goes in a hundred ways. How very ignorant you are, Arnold. Look at what dress costs, for myself and four girls! Look at what the soirées cost! We have to give all sorts of dishes now; lobster salads and raspberry creams, and all kinds of expensive things. Madame St. Vincent introduced that."

"You must put down the soirées and the dress—if you cannot keep them within the bounds of your income."

"Thank you. Just as I had to put down the pony-carriage and James. How cruel you are, Arnold!"

"I hope I am not. I do not wish to be so."

"It will take two hundred pounds to set me straight; and I must have it from you, or from somebody else," avowed Mrs. Knox.

"You certainly cannot have it, or any portion of it, from me. My expenses are heavy now, and I have my own children coming on."

His tone was unmistakably decisive, and Mrs. Knox saw that it was so. For many years she had been in the habit of regarding Arnold as something like a bucket in a well, which brings up water every time it is let down. Just so had he brought up money for her from his pocket every time she worried for it. But that was over now: and he had to bear these reproaches periodically.

"You know that you can let me have it, Arnold. You can lend it me from Mina's money."

His face flushed slightly, he pushed his fair hair back with a gesture of annoyance.

"The last time you spoke of that I begged you never to mention it again," he said in a low tone. "Why, what do you take me for, mother?"

"Take you for?"

"You must know that I could not touch Mina's money without becoming a false trustee. Men have been brought to the criminal bar to answer for a less crime than that would be."

"If Mina married, you would have to hand over the whole of it."

"Of course I should. First of all taking care that it was settled upon her."

"I don't see the necessity of that. Mina could let me have what she pleased of it."

"Talking of Mina," resumed Dr. Knox, passing by her remark, "I think you must look a little closely after her. She is more intimate, I fancy, with Captain Collinson than is desirable, and—"

"Suppose Captain Collinson wants to marry her?" interrupted Mrs. Knox.

"Has he told you that he wants to do so?"

"No; not in so many words. But he evidently likes her. What a good match it would be!"

"Mina is too young to be married yet. And Captain Collinson cannot, I should suppose, have any intention of the sort. If he had, he would speak out: when it would be time enough to consider and discuss his proposal. Unless he does speak, I must beg of you not to allow Mina to be alone with him."

"She never is alone with him."

"I think she is, at odd moments. Only last night I saw her with him at the gate. Before that, while your soirée was going on, Dicky—I believe he could tell you so, if you asked him—saw them walking together in the garden, the captain's arm round her waist."

"Girls are so fond of flirting! And young men think no harm of a little passing familiarity."

"Just so. But for remembering this, I should speak to Captain Collinson. The thought that there may be nothing serious in it prevents me. At any rate, I beg of you to take care of Mina."

"And the money I want?" she asked, as he took up his hat to go.

But Dr. Knox, shortly repeating that he had no money to give her, made his escape. He had been ruffled enough already. One thing was certain: that if some beneficent sprite from fairyland increased Mrs. Knox's annual income cent. per cent. she would still, and ever, be in embarrassment. Arnold knew this.

Mrs. Knox sat on, revolving difficulties. How many similar interviews she had held with her step-son, and how often he had been brought round to pay her bills, she could but remember. Would he do it now? A most unpleasant doubt, that he would not, lay upon her.

Presently the entrance was darkened by some tall form interposing itself between herself and the sunlight. She glanced up and saw Captain Collinson. He stood there smiling, his tasselled cane jauntily swayed in his left hand.

"My dear madam, you looked troubled. Is anything wrong?"

"Troubled! the world's full of trouble, I think," spoke Mrs. Knox, in a pettish kind of way. "Dr. Knox has been here to vex me."

Captain Collinson stepped airily in, and sat down near Mrs. Knox, his eyes expressing proper concern: indignation blended with sympathy.

"Very inconsiderate of Dr. Knox: very wrong! Can I help you in any way, my dear lady?"

"Arnold is always inconsiderate. First, he begins upon me about Dicky, threatening to put him altogether away at school, poor ill-used child! Next, he—"

"Sweet little angel?" interlarded the captain.

"Next, he refuses to lend me a trifling sum of money—and he knows how badly I want it!"

"Paltry!" ejaculated the captain. "When he must be making so much of it!"

"Rolling in it, so to say," confirmed Mrs. Knox. "Look at the practice he has! But if he did not give me any of his, he might advance me a trifle of Mina's."

"Of course he might," warmly acquiesced Captain Collinson.

What with the warmth and the sympathy, Mrs. Knox rather lost her head. Many of us are betrayed on occasion into doing the same. That is, she said more than she should have said.

"You see, if Mina married, as I pointed out to Arnold, the money would no longer be under his control at all. It would be hers to do as she pleased with. She is a dear, good, generous girl, and would not scruple to let me have one or two hundred pounds. What would such a trifle be out of the whole seven thousand?"

"Very true; nothing at all," cried the captain, toying with his handsome beard.

"But no; Arnold will not hear of it: he answered me in a way that I should not like to repeat. He also said he should take care, if Mina did marry before she was of age, that her money was settled upon her; said it on purpose to thwart me."

"Cruel!" aspirated the captain.

"Some girls might be tempted to marry off-hand, and say nothing to him, if only to get her fortune out of his control. I don't say Mina would."

"Miser! My dear madam, rely upon it that whenever Miss Mina does marry, her husband will join with her in letting you have as much money as you wish. I am sure it would be his pride and pleasure to do so."

Was it an implied promise? meant to be so understood? Mrs. Knox took it for one. She came out of her dumps, and felt exalted to the seventh heaven.

Meanwhile, Arnold Knox was with Lady Jenkins, to whom he had gone on quitting his step-mother. The old lady, up and dressed, sat in her dining-room. There appeared to be no change in her condition: drowsy, lethargic, gentle, yielding; imbecile, or not many shades removed from it. And yet, neither Dr. Knox nor his fellow-practitioner could see any cause to account for this. Of bodily illness she had none: except that she seemed feeble.

"I wish you would tell me what it is you are taking," said Dr. Knox, bending over her and speaking in low, persuasive tones. "I fear that you are taking something that does you harm."

Lady Jenkins looked up at him, apparently trying to consider. "I've not had anything since I took the physic," she said.

"What physic?"

"The bottles that Mr. Tamlyn sent me."

"But that was when you were ill. Are you sure you have not taken anything else?—that you are not taking anything? Any"—he dropped his voice to a still lower key—"opiates? Laudanum, for instance?"

Lady Jenkins shook her head. "I never took any sort of opiate in my life."

"Then it is being given to her without her knowledge," mentally decided the doctor. "I hear you were at the next door last night, as gay as the best of them," he resumed aloud, changing his tone to a light one.

"Ay. I put on my new bronze satin gown: Patty said I was to. Janet sang her pretty songs."

"Did she? When are you coming to spend an evening with us? She will sing them again for you."

"I should like to come—if I may."

"If you may! There's nothing to prevent it. You are quite well enough."

"There's Patty. We shall have to ask her whether I may."

Anything Arnold Knox might have rejoined to this was stopped by the entrance of Patty herself, a light blue shawl on her shoulders. A momentary surprise crossed her face at sight of the doctor.

"Oh, Dr. Knox! I did not know you were here," she said, as she threw off the shawl. "I was running about the garden for a few minutes. What a lovely day it is!—the sun so warm."

"It is that. Lady Jenkins ought to be out in it. Should you not like to take a run in the garden?" he laughingly added to her.

"Should I, Patty?"

The utter abnegation of will, both of tone and look, as she cast an appealing glance at her companion, struck Dr. Knox forcibly. He looked at both of them from under his rather overhanging eyebrows. Did Madame St. Vincent extort this obedience?—or was it simply the old lady's imbecility? Surely it must be the latter.

"I think," said madame, "a walk in the garden will be very pleasant for you, dear Lady Jenkins. Lettice shall bring down your things. The may-tree is budding beautifully."

"Already!" said the doctor: "I should like to see it. Will you go with me, madame? I have two minutes to spare."

Madame St. Vincent, showing no surprise, though she may have felt it, put the blue shawl on her shoulders again and followed Dr. Knox. The may-tree was nearly at the end of the garden, down by the shrubbery.

"Mr. Tamlyn mentioned to you, I believe, that we suspected something improper, in the shape of opiates, was being given to Lady Jenkins," began Dr. Knox, never as much as lifting his eyes to the budding may-tree.

"Yes; I remember that he did," replied Madame St. Vincent. "I hardly gave it a second thought."

"Tamlyn said you had a difficulty in believing it. Nevertheless, I feel assured that it is so."

"Impossible, Dr. Knox."

"It seems impossible to you, I dare say. But that it is being done, I would stake my head upon. Lady Jenkins is being stupefied in some way: and I have brought you out here to tell you so, and to ask your co-operation in tracing the culprit."

"But—I beg your pardon, Dr. Knox—who would give her anything of the kind? You don't suspect me, I hope?"

"If I suspected you, my dear lady, I should not be talking to you as I am. The person we must suspect is Lettice Lane."

"Lettice Lane!"

"I have reason to think it. Lettice Lane's antecedents are not, I fear, quite so clear as they might be: though it is only recently I have known this. At any rate, she is the personal attendant of Lady Jenkins; the only one of them who has the opportunity of being alone with her. I must beg of you to watch Lettice Lane."

Madame St. Vincent looked a little bewildered; perhaps felt so. Stretching up her hand, she plucked one of the budding may-blossoms.

"Mr. Tamlyn hinted at Lettice also. I have always felt confidence in Lettice. As to drugs—Dr. Knox, I don't believe a word of it."

"Lady Jenkins is being drugged," emphatically pronounced Dr. Knox. "And you must watch Lettice Lane. If Lettice is innocent, we must look elsewhere."

"Shall I tax Lettice with it?"

"Certainly not. You would make a good detective," he added, with a laugh; "showing your hand to the enemy. Surely, Madame St. Vincent, you must yourself see that Lady Jenkins is being tampered with. Look at her state this morning: though she is not quite as bad as she is sometimes."

"I have known some old people sleep almost constantly."

"So have I. But theirs is simply natural sleep, induced by exhausted nature: hers is not natural. She is stupefied."

"Stupefied with the natural decay of her powers," dissented madame. "But—to drug her! No, I cannot believe it. And where would be the motive?"

"That I know not. But I am sure I am not mistaken," he added decisively. "You will watch Lettice Lane?"

"I will," she answered, after a pause. "Of course it may be as you say; I now see it. I will watch her to the very utmost of my ability from this hour."

III

"DEAR JOHNNY,

"I expect your stay at Lefford is drawing towards a close; mine is, here. It might be pleasant if we travelled home together. I could take Lefford on my way—starting by an early train—and pick you up. You need some one to take care of you, you know. Let me hear when you intend to be ready. I will arrange my departure accordingly.

"Hope you have enjoyed yourself, old fellow."

"Ever yours,

"J. T."

The above letter from Tod, who was still in Leicestershire, reached me one morning at breakfast-time. Dr. Knox and Janet, old Tamlyn—all the lot of them—called out that they could not spare me yet. Even Cattledon graciously intimated that she should miss me. Janet wrote to Tod, telling him he was to take Lefford on his way, as he proposed, and to stay a week when he did come.

It was, I think, that same day that some news reached us touching Captain Collinson—that he was going to be married. At least that he had made an offer, and was accepted. Not to Mina Knox; but to an old girl (the epithet was Sam's) named Belmont. Miss Belmont lived with her father at a nice place on the London Road, half-a-mile beyond Jenkins House; he had a great deal of money, and she was his only child. She was very plain, very dowdy, and quite forty years of age; but very good, going about amongst the poor with tracts and soup. If the tidings were true, and Captain Collinson had made Miss Belmont an offer, it appeared pretty evident that his object was her money: he could not well have fallen in love with her, or court a wife so much older than himself.

When taxed with the fact—and it was old Tamlyn who did it, meeting him opposite the market-house—Collinson simpered, and stroked his dark beard, and said Lefford was fond of marvels. But he did not deny it. Half-an-hour later he and Miss Belmont were seen together in the High Street. She had her old cloth mantle on and her brown bonnet, as close as a Quaker's, and carried her flat district basket in her hand. The captain presented a contrast, with his superb dandy-cut clothes and flourishing his ebony cane.

"I think it must be quite true," Janet observed, as we watched them pass the house. "And I shall be glad if it is: Arnold has been tormenting himself with the fancy that the gallant captain was thinking of little Mina."

A day or two after this, it chanced that Dr. Knox had to visit Sir Henry Westmorland, who had managed to give a twist to his ankle. Sir Henry was one of those sociable, good-hearted men that no one can help liking; a rather elderly bachelor. He and Tamlyn were old friends, and we had all dined at Foxgrove about a week before.

"Would you like to go over with me, Johnny?" asked Dr. Knox, when he was starting.

I said I should like it very much, and got into the "conveyance," the doctor letting me drive. Thomas was not with us. We soon reached Foxgrove: a low, straggling, red-brick mansion, standing in a small park, about two miles and a half from Lefford.

Dr. Knox went in; leaving me and the conveyance on the smooth wide gravel-drive before the house. Presently a groom came up to take charge of it, saying Sir Henry was asking for me. He had seen me from the window.

Sir Henry was lying on a sofa near the window, and Knox was already beginning upon the ankle. A gentlemanly little man, nearly bald, sat on the ottoman in the middle of the room. I found it was one Major Leckie.

Some trifle—are these trifles chance?—turned the conversation upon India. I think Knox spoke of some snake-bite in a man's ankle that had laid him by for a month or two: it was no other than the late whilom mayor, Sir Daniel Jenkins. Upon which, Major Leckie began relating his experience of some reptile bites in India. The major had been home nearly two years upon sick leave, he said, and was now going back again.

"The 30th Bengal Cavalry!" repeated Dr. Knox, as Major Leckie happened to mention that regiment—which was his, and the doctor remembered that it was Captain Collinson's. "One of the officers of that regiment is staying here now."

"Is he!" cried the major, briskly. "Which of them?"

"Captain Collinson."

"Collinson!" echoed the major, his whole face alight with pleasure. "Where is he? How long has he been here? I did not know he had left India."

"He came home last autumn, I fancy; was not well, and got twelve months' leave. He has been staying at Lefford for some time."

"I should like to see him! Good old Collinson! He and I were close friends. He is a nice fellow."

"Old, you style him!" cried Dr. Knox. "I should rather call him young—of the two."

Major Leckie laughed. "It is a word we are all given to using, doctor. Of course Collinson's not old in years. Why is he staying at Lefford?"

"I'm sure I don't know. Unless it is that he has fallen in love. I heard him remark one day that the air of the place suited him."

"Ah ah, Master Collinson!" laughed the major. "In love, are you, sir! Caught at last, are you! Who is the lady?"

"Nay, I spoke only in jest," returned Dr. Knox. "He seems to be a general admirer; but I don't know that it is any one in particular. Report has mentioned one or two ladies, but report is often a false town-crier."

"Well, she will be in luck—whoever gets him. He is one of the nicest, truest fellows I know; and will make a rare good husband."

"It is said he has private means. Do you know whether that's true?"

"He has very good private means. His father left him a fortune. Sometimes we fancy he will not stay with us long. I should not be surprised if he sells out while he is at home, and settles down."

"Johnny Ludlow heard him say something the other night to that effect," observed the doctor, looking at me.

"Yes," I said, confirming the words. "He is about buying an estate now, I believe. But he talked of going back to India for a few years."

"I hope he will. There's not a man amongst us, that I would not rather spare than Collinson. I should like to see him. I might walk into Lefford now—if you will give me his address, doctor. Will you spare me for an hour or two, Sir Henry?"

"Well, I must, I suppose," grumbled Sir Henry. "It's rather bad of you, though, Leckie; and after putting me off with so miserably short a stay. You get here at ten o'clock last night, and you go off at ten o'clock to-night! Fine behaviour that!"

"I am obliged to go to-night, Westmorland; you know I am, and I could not get to you earlier, although I tried. I won't be away a minute longer than I can help. I can walk into Lefford in half-an-hour—my pace is a quick one. No; and I won't stay an unconscionable time with Collinson," he added, in answer to a growl of the baronet's. "Trust me. I'll be back under two hours."

"Bring him back with you for the rest of the day," said Sir Henry.

"Oh, thank you. And I am sure you will say he is the best fellow going. I wonder you and he have not found out one another before."

"If you don't mind taking a seat in yonder nondescript vehicle—that Mr. Johnny Ludlow here has the audacity to say must have been built in the year One," laughed Dr. Knox, pointing outside, "I can drive you to Captain Collinson's lodgings."

"A friend in need is a friend indeed," cried the major, laughing also. "What style of vehicle do you call it?"

"We call it the conveyance. As to its style—well I never had the opportunity of asking that of the builder. I believe my father bought it second-hand when he first went into practice many a year ago."

The doctor drove this time; Major Leckie sitting beside him, I in the perch behind. Leaving the major at the hairdresser's, upon reaching Lefford, Dr. Knox and I went home. And this is what occurred—as we heard later.

Ringing at the private door, which was Captain Collinson's proper entrance, a young servant-girl appeared, and—after the manner of many young country servants—sent Major Leckie alone up to Captain Collinson's rooms, saying she supposed the captain was at home. It turned out that he was not at home. Seated before the fire was a gentleman in a crimson dressing-gown and slippers, smoking a huge pipe.

"Come in," cried out he, in answer to the major's knock.

"I beg your pardon," said the major, entering. "I understood that Captain Collinson lodged here."

"He does lodge here," replied he of the dressing-gown, putting his pipe into the fender, as he rose. "What is it that you want with him?"

"I only called to see him. I am one of his brother-officers—home on sick leave; as I understand he is."

"Collinson is out," said the gentleman. "I am sorry it should happen so. Can you leave any message?"

"Will he be long? I should much like to see him."

"He will be back to dinner to-night; not much before that, I think. He is gone by train to—to—some place a few miles off. Boom—or Room—or Doom—or some such name. I am a stranger here."

"Toome, I suppose," remarked the major. "It's the last station before you get to Lefford—I noticed the name last night. I am very sorry. I should liked to have seen Collinson. Tell him so, will you. I am Major Leckie."

"You will be calling again, perhaps?"

"I can't do that. I must spend the rest of this day with my friend, Sir Henry Westmorland, and I leave to-night. Tell Collinson that I embark in a few days. Stay: this is my address in London, if he will write to me. I wonder he did not attempt to find me out—I came home before he did: and he knew that he could always get my address at my bankers'."

"I will tell Collinson all you say, Major Leckie," said the stranger, glancing at the card. "It is a pity he is out."

"Should he come back in time—though I fear, by what you say, there's little chance of it—be so good as to say that Sir Henry Westmorland will be happy to see him to dinner this evening at Foxgrove, at six o'clock—and to come over as much earlier as he can."

With the last words, Major Leckie left, Collinson's friend politely attending him down to the front-door. I was standing at Mr. Tamlyn's gate as he passed it on his way back to Foxgrove. Dr. Knox, then going off on foot to see a patient, came across the yard from the surgery at the same moment.

"Such a mischance!" the major stopped in his rapid walk to say to us. "Collinson has gone to Toome to-day. I saw a friend of his, who is staying with him, and he thinks he won't be back before night."

"I did not know Collinson had any one staying with him," remarked the doctor. "Some one called in upon him, probably."

"This man is evidently staying with him; making himself at home too," said the major. "He was in a dressing-gown and slippers, and had his feet on the fender, smoking a pipe. A tall, dark fellow, face all hair."

"Why, that is Collinson himself," cried I.

"Not a bit of it," said the major. "This man is no more like Collinson—except that Collinson is dark and has a beard—than he is like me. He said he was a stranger in the place."

A rapid conclusion crossed me that it must be a brother of Collinson's—for a resemblance to himself, according to the major's description, there no doubt was. Major Leckie wished me good-day, and continued his way up the street, Dr. Knox with him.

"What are you gazing at, Johnny Ludlow?"

I turned at the question, and saw Charlotte Knox. She was coming to call on Janet. We stood there talking of one thing and another. I told Charlotte that Collinson's brother, as I took it to be, was staying with him; and Charlotte told me of a quarrel she had just had with Mina on the score of the captain.

"Mina won't believe a word against him, Johnny. When I say he is nothing but a flirt, that he is only playing with her, she bids me hold my tongue. She quite scorns the notion that he would like to marry Miss Belmont."

"Have you seen any more letters, that concern me, in at Madame St. Vincent's?" I asked.

"Do you think I should be likely to?—or that such letters are as plentiful as blackberries?" retorted Charlotte. "And you?—have you discovered the key to that letter?"

"I have not discovered it, Charlotte. I have taxed my memory in vain. Never a girl, no matter whose sister she may be, can I recall to mind as being likely to owe me a grudge."

"It was not that the girl owed you a grudge," quickly spoke Charlotte. "It was that she must not meet you."

"Does not the one thing imply the other? I can't think of any one. There was a young lady, indeed, in the years gone by, when I was not much more than a lad, who—may—have—taken up a prejudice against me," I added slowly and thoughtfully, for I was hardly sure of what I said. "But she cannot have anything to do with the present matter, and I am quite sure she was not a sister of Madame St. Vincent."

"What was her name?" asked Charlotte.

"Sophie Chalk."

CHAPTER XVIII

LADY JENKINS

LIGHT

I

Tod arrived at Lefford. I met him at the train, just as I had met Miss Cattledon, who was with us still. As we walked out of the station together, many a man cast a glance after the tall, fine young fellow—who looked strong enough to move the world, if, like Archimedes, the geometrician of Syracuse, he had only possessed the necessary lever.

"Shall you be able to stay a week, Tod?"

"Two weeks if they'd like it, Johnny. How you have picked up, lad!"

"Picked up?"

"In looks. They are all your own again. Glad to see it, old fellow."

Some few days had elapsed since the latest event recorded in this veritable little history—the call that Major Leckie made on Captain Collinson, and found his brother there, instead of himself—but no change worth noting to the reader had occurred in the town politics. Lady Jenkins was ailing as much as ever, and Madame St. Vincent was keeping a sharp watch on the maid, Lettice Lane, without, as yet, detecting her in any evil practices: the soirées were numerous, one being held at some house or other every night in the work-a-day week: and the engagement of Captain Collinson to Miss Belmont was now talked of as an assured fact. Collinson himself had been away from Lefford during these intervening days. Pink, the hairdresser, thought he had taken a run up to London, on some little matter of business. As to the brother, we had heard no more of him.

But, if Captain Collinson had taken a run up to London, he had unquestionably run down again, though not to Lefford. On the day but one before the coming of Tod, Janet and Miss Cattledon went over by train to do some shopping at the county town, which stood fifteen miles from Lefford, I being with them. Turning into a pastry-cook's in the middle of the day to get something to eat, we turned in upon Captain Collinson. He sat at a white marble-topped table in the corner of the shop, eating an oyster patty.

"We heard you were in London," said Janet, shaking hands with him, as he rose to offer her his seat.

"Got back this morning. Shall be at Lefford to-morrow: perhaps to-night," he answered.

He stood gobbling up his patty quickly. I said something to him, just because the recollection came into my mind, about the visit of his brother.

"My brother!" he exclaimed in answer, staring at me with all his eyes. "What brother? How do you know anything about my brother?"

"Major Leckie saw him when he called at your lodgings. Saw him instead of you. You had gone to Toome. We took it to be your brother, from the description; he was so like yourself."

The captain smiled. "I forgot that," he said. "We are much alike. Ned told me of Leckie's call. A pity I could not see him! Things always happen cross and contrary. Has Leckie left Foxgrove yet?"

"Oh, he left it that same night. I should think he is on his way back to India by this time."

"His visit to Lefford seems to have been as flying a one as my brother's was, and his did not last a day. How much?" to the girl behind the counter. "Sixpence? There it is." And, with a general adieu nodded to the rest of us, the captain left the shop.

"I don't like that dandy," spoke Cattledon, in her severest tone. "I have said so before. I'm sure he is a man who cannot be trusted."

I answered nothing: but I had for a little time now thought the same. There was that about him that gave you the idea he was in some way or other not true. And it may as well be mentioned here that

Captain Collinson got back to Lefford that same evening, in time to make his appearance at Mrs. Parker's soirée, at which both Miss Belmont and Mina Knox were present.

So now we come to Tod again, and to the day of his arrival. Talking of one thing and another, telling him of this and that, of the native politics, as we all like to do when a stranger comes to set himself down, however temporarily, amidst us, I mentioned the familiarity that in two of the people struck upon my memory. Never did I see this same Captain Collinson, never did I see Madame St. Vincent, or hear them speak, or listen to their laugh, but the feeling that I had met them before—had been, so to say, intimate with both one and the other—came forcibly upon me.

"And yet it would seem, upon the face of things, that I never have been," I continued to Tod, when telling of this. "Madame St. Vincent says she never left the South of France until last year; and the captain has been nearly all his life in India."

"You know you do take fancies, Johnny."

"True. But, are not those fancies generally borne out by the result? Any way, they puzzle me, both of them: and there's a ring in their voices that—"

"A ring in their voices!" put in Tod, laughing.

"Say an accent, then; especially in madame's; and it sounds, to my ears, unmistakably Worcestershire."

"Johnny, you are fanciful!"

I never got anything better from Tod. "You will have the honour of meeting them both here to-night," I said to him, "for it is Janet's turn to give the soirée, and I know they are expected."

Evening came. At six o'clock the first instalment of guests knocked at the door; by half-past six the soirée was in full glory: a regular crowd. Every one seemed to have come, with the exception of the ladies from Jenkins House. Sam Jenkins brought in their excuses.

Sam had run up to Jenkins House with some physic for the butler, who said he had a surfeit (from drinking too much old ale, Tamlyn thought), and Sam had made use of the opportunity to see his aunt. Madame St. Vincent objected. It would try the dear old lady too much, madame said. She was lying in a sweet sleep on the sofa in her own room; had been quite blithe and lively all day, but was drowsy now; and she had better not be disturbed until bedtime. Perhaps Mr. Sam would kindly make their excuses to Mrs. Arnold Knox.

"Can't you come yourself, madame?" asked Sam, politely. "If Aunt Jenkins is asleep, and means to keep asleep till bed-time, she can't want you."

"I could not think of leaving her," objected madame. "She looks for me the moment she wakes."

So Sam, I say, brought back the message. Putting himself into his evening-coat, he came into the room while tea was going on, and delivered madame's excuses to Janet as distinctly as the rattle of cups and saucers allowed. You should have seen Cattledon that evening:—in a grey silk gown that stood on end, a gold necklace, and dancing shoes.

"This is the second soirée this week that Lady Jenkins has failed to appear at," spoke Mrs. Knox—not Janet—in a resentful tone. "My firm opinion is that Madame St. Vincent keeps her away."

"Keeps her away," cried Arnold. "Why should she do that?"

"Well, yes; gives way to her fads and fancies about being ill, instead of rousing her out of them. As to why she does it," continued Mrs. Knox, "I suppose she is beginning to grow nervous about her. As if an innocent, quiet soirée could hurt Lady Jenkins!"

"Johnny," whispered Sam, subsiding into the background after delivering his message, "may I never stir again if I didn't see Collinson hiding in aunt's garden!"

"Hiding in your aunt's garden!" I exclaimed. "What was he doing that for?"

"Goodness knows. Did you ever notice a big bay-tree that you pass on the left, between the door and the gate? Well, he was standing behind it. I came out of the house at a double quick pace, knowing I should be late for the soirée, cleared the steps at a leap, and the path to the gate at another. Too quick, I suppose, for Collinson. He was bending forward to look at the parlour windows, and drew back as I passed."

"Did you speak, Sam?"

"No, I came flying on, taking no notice. I dare say he thinks I did not see him. One does not like, you know, to speak to a man who evidently wants to avoid you. But now—I wonder what he was doing there?" continued Sam, reflectively. "Watching Madame St. Vincent, I should say, through the lace curtains."

"But for what purpose?"

"I can't even imagine. There he was."

To my mind this sounded curious. But that Mina Knox was before my eyes—just at the moment listening to the whispers of Dan Jenkins—I should have thought the captain was looking after her. Or, rather, not listening to Dan. Mina had a pained, restless look on her face, not in the least natural to it, and kept her head turned away. And the more Dan whispered, the more she turned it from him.

"Here he is, Sam."

Sam looked round at my words, and saw Captain Collinson, then coming in. He was got up to perfection as usual, and wore a white rose in his button-hole. His purple-black hair, beard, whiskers and moustache were grand; his voice had its ordinary fashionable drawl. I saw Tod—at the opposite side of the room— cease talking with old Tamlyn, to fix his keen eyes on the captain.

"Very sorry to be so late," apologized the captain, bowing over Janet's hand. "Been detained at home writing letters for India. Overland mail goes out to-morrow night."

Sam gave me a knock with his elbow. "What a confounded story!" he whispered. "Wonder what the gallant captain means, Johnny! Wonder what game he is up to?"

It was, I dare say, nearly an hour after this that I came across Tod. He was standing against the wall, laughing slightly to himself, evidently in some glee. Captain Collinson was at the piano opposite, his back to us, turning over the leaves for Caroline Parker, who was singing.

"What are you amused at, Tod?"

"At you, lad. Thinking what a muff you are."

"I always am a muff, I know. But why am I one just now in particular?"

"For not knowing that man," nodding towards Collinson. "I thought I recognized him as he came in; felt sure of him when I heard him speak. Men may disguise their faces almost at will; but not their voices, Johnny."

"Why, who is he?" I asked in surprise.

"I'll tell you when we are alone. I should have known him had we met amid the Hottentots. I thought he was over in Australia; knew he went there."

"But—is he not Captain Collinson?"

Tod laughed. "Just as much as I am, Johnny. Of course he may have assumed the name of Collinson in place of his own: if so, nobody has a right, I take it, to say him nay. But, as to his being a captain in the Bengal Cavalry—well, I don't think he is."

"And you say I know him!"

"I say you ought to—but for being a muff. I suppose it is the hair he is adorned with that has thrown you off the scent."

"But, where have I seen him, Tod? Who—"

"Hush, lad. We may be overheard."

As a general rule, all the guests at these soirées left together. They did so to-night. The last to file out at the door were the Hampshires, with Mrs. Knox, her daughter, and Miss Mack—for Janet had made a point of inviting poor hard-worked, put-upon Macky. Both families lived in the London Road, and would go home in company. Dan had meant to escort Mina, but she pointedly told him he was not wanted, and took the offered arm of Captain Collinson. Upon which, Dan turned back in a huff. Sam laughed at that, and ran after them himself.

How long a time had elapsed afterwards, I hardly know. Perhaps half-an-hour; perhaps not so much. We had not parted for the night: in fact, Mr. Tamlyn and Tod were still over the game at chess they had begun since supper; which game seemed in no mood to be finished. I watched it: Dr. Knox and Miss Cattledon stood talking over the fire; while Janet, ever an active housekeeper, was in the supper-room, helping the maids to clear the table. In the midst of this, Charlotte Knox came back, rushing into the room in a state of intense excitement, with the news that Mina and Captain Collinson were eloping together.

The account she gave was this—though just at first nothing clear could be made out of her. Upon starting, the Hampshires, Mrs. Knox, and Miss Mack went on in front; Captain Collinson and Mina walked next, and Charlotte fell behind with Sam. Fell very much behind, as it appeared; for when people are talking of what interests them, their steps are apt to linger; and Sam was telling her of having seen Captain Collinson behind the bay-tree. It was a beautiful night, warm and pleasant.

Charlotte and Sam let the captain and Mina get pretty nearly the length of a street before them; and they, in their turn, were as much behind the party in advance. Suddenly Sam exclaimed that the captain was taking the wrong way. His good eyes had discerned that, instead of keeping straight on, which was the proper (and only) route to the London Road, he and Mina had turned down the lane leading to the railway-station. "Halloa!" he exclaimed to Charlotte, "what's that for?" "They must be dreaming," was Charlotte's laughing reply: "or, perhaps the captain wants to take an excursion by a night-train!" Whether anything in the last remark, spoken in jest, struck particularly on the mind of Sam, Charlotte did not know: away he started as if he had been shot, Charlotte running after him in curiosity. Arrived at the lane, Sam saw the other two flying along, just as if they wanted to catch a train and had not a minute to do it in. Onward went Sam's long legs in pursuit; but the captain's legs were long also, and he was pulling Mina with him: altogether Sam did not gain much upon them. The half-past eleven o'clock train was then gliding into the station, where it was timed to halt two minutes. The captain and Mina dashed on to the platform, and, when Sam got up, he was putting her into the nearest carriage. Such was Charlotte's statement: and her eyes looked wild, and her breath was laboured as she made it.

"Have they gone?—gone on by the train?" questioned Dr. Knox, who seemed unnaturally calm.

"Goodness, no!" panted the excited Charlotte. "Sam managed to get his arm round Mina's waist, and the captain could not pull her away from him. It was a regular struggle on the platform, Arnold. I appealed to the station-master, who stood by. I told him it was my sister, and that she was being kidnapped against her will; Sam also appealed to him. So he gave the signal when the time was up, and let the train go on."

"Not against her will, I fear," spoke Arnold Knox from between his condemning lips. "Where are they now, Lotty?"

"On the platform, quarrelling; and still struggling which shall keep possession of Mina. I came running here to fetch you, Arnold, and I believe I shall never get my breath again."

With one accord we all, Cattledon excepted, set off to the station; even old Tamlyn proved he had some go in his legs yet. Tod reached it first: few young men could come up to him at running.

Sam Jenkins had exchanged his hold of Mina for a hold on Captain Collinson. The two were struggling together; but Sam's grasp was firm, and he held him as in a vice. "No, no," he was saying, "you don't escape me, captain, until some one comes here to take charge of Mina." As to Mina, little simpleton, she cowered in the shade of the corner, shivering and crying. The station-master and the two night-porters stood about, gaping and staring.

Tod put his hand on the captain's shoulder; his other hand momentarily holding back Dr. Knox. "Since when have you been Captain Collinson," he quietly asked.

The captain turned his angry eyes upon him. "What is that to you?" he retorted. "I am Captain Collinson; that is enough for you."

"Enough for me, and welcome. Not enough, as I judge, for this gentleman here," indicating the doctor. "When I knew you your name was not Collinson."

"How dare you insult me?" hissed the captain. "My name not Collinson!"

"Not at all!" was Tod's equable answer. "It used to be FABIAN PELL."

II

The history of the Clement-Pells and their downfall was given in the First Series of these stories, and the reader can have no difficulty in recalling Fabian to his memory. There are times, even to this day, when it seems to me that I must have been a muff, as Tod said, not to know him. But, some years had elapsed since I saw him; and those years, with their ill-fortune and exposure, and the hard life he had led in Australia, had served to change him greatly; above all, there was now the mass of hair disguising the greater part of his face. Bit by bit my recollection came to me, and I knew that he was, beyond all shadow of doubt, Fabian Pell.

How long we sat up that night at Mr. Tamlyn's, talking over its events, I cannot precisely tell. For quite the half of what was left of it. Mina, brought to his own home by Arnold for safety, was consigned to Cattledon's charge and bed, and retired to the latter in a state of humiliation and collapse.

The scene on the platform had soon come to a conclusion. With the security of Mina assured by the presence of her brother and the rest of us, Sam let go his hold of the captain. It had been a nice little plot this, that the captain had set on foot in secret, and persuaded that silly girl, not much better than a child, to accede to. They were to have run away to London that night, and been married there the next day; the captain, as was found out later, having already managed to procure a licence. You see, if Mina became his wife without any settlement, her money at once lapsed to him and he could do what he would with it. How, as Captain Collinson, he would have braved the matter out to Dr. Knox that night, and excused himself for his treachery, he best knew. Tod checkmated him by proclaiming him as Fabian Pell. A lame attempt at denial, which Tod, secure in his assertion, laughed at; a little bravado, and Captain Collinson collapsed. Against the truth—that he was Fabian Pell—brought home to him so suddenly and clearly, he could not hold out; the man's hardihood deserted him; and he turned tail and went off the platform, calling back that Mr. Todhetley should hear from him in the morning.

We came away then, bringing Mina. Sam went to escort Charlotte home, where they would have the pleasure of imparting the news to Mrs. Knox, who probably by that time was thinking that Lotty had eloped as well as Mina. And now we were sitting round the fire in old Tamlyn's room, discussing what had happened. Sam came back in the midst of it. Arnold was down in the mouth, and no mistake.

"Did you see Mrs. Knox?" he asked of Sam.

"Not to speak to, sir. I saw her through the kitchen window. She was spreading bread-and-jam for Dicky, who had come down in his night-gown and would not be coaxed back to bed."

"What an injudicious woman she is!" put in old Tamlyn. "Enough to ruin the boy."

Perhaps Dr. Knox was thinking, as he sat there, his hand pressed upon his brow, that if she had been a less injudicious woman, a different mother altogether, Mina might not have been in danger of falling into the present escapade: but he said nothing.

"I remember hearing of the notorious break-up of the Clement-Pells at the time it took place," observed old Tamlyn to Tod. "And to think that this man should be one of them!"

"He must carry his impudence about with him," was Tod's remark.

"They ruined hundreds of poor men and women, if not thousands," continued old Tamlyn. "I conclude your people knew all about it?"

"Indeed, yes. We were in the midst of it. My father lost—how much was it, Johnny?"

"Two hundred pounds," I answered; the question bringing vividly back to me our adventures in Boulogne, when the pater and Mr. Brandon went over there to try to get the money back.

"I suppose," resumed the surgeon, "your father had that much balance lying in their hands, and lost it all?"

"No," said Tod, "he did not bank with them. A day or two before Clement-Pell burst up, he drove to our house as bold as brass, asking my father in the most off-hand manner to let him have a cheque for two hundred pounds until the next day. The Squire did let him have it, without scruple, and of course lost it. He would have let him have two thousand had Pell asked for it."

"But that was a fraud. Pell might have been punished for it."

"I don't know that it was so much a fraud as many other things Pell did, and might have been punished for," observed Tod. "At any rate, not as great a one. He escaped out of the way, as I dare say you know, sir, and his family escaped with him. It was hard on them. They had been brought up in the greatest possible extravagance, in all kinds of luxury. This one, Fabian, was in the army. He, of course, had to retire. His own debts would have forced that step upon him, apart from the family disgrace."

"Did he re-enter it, I wonder."

Tod laughed. "I should say not. He went to Australia. Not above a year ago I heard that he was still there. He must have come back here fortune-hunting; bread-hunting; and passed himself off as Captain Collinson the better to do it. Miss Mina Knox's seven thousand pounds was a prize to fight for."

"That's it!" cried Sam. "Dan has said all along it was the money he was after, dishonourable wretch, not Mina herself. He cares too much for Madame St. Vincent to care for Mina: at least we think so. How did he get the funds, I wonder, that he has been flourishing about upon?"

"Won them at billiards," suggested Tod.

"No," said Sam, "I don't think that. By all accounts he lost more than he won in the billiard-rooms."

Dr. Knox looked up from a reverie. "Was it himself that Major Leckie saw?—and did he pass himself off as another man to escape detection? Did he go off for the remainder of the week lest the major should look him up again?"

And we knew it must have been so.

Little sleep did I get that night, or, rather, morning, for the small hours had struck when we went to bed. The association of ideas is a great thing in this world; a help in many an emergency. This association led me from Fabian Pell to his sisters: and the mysterious memory of Madame St. Vincent that had so puzzled my mind cleared itself up. As though a veil had been withdrawn from my eyes, leaving the recollection unclouded and distinct, I saw she was one of those sisters: the eldest of them, Martha Jane. And, let not the reader call me a muff, as Tod again did later, for not having found her out before. When I knew her she was an angular, raw-boned girl, with rather a haggard and very pale face, and nothing to say for herself. Now she was a filled-out woman, her face round, her colour healthy, and one of the most self-possessed talkers I ever listened to. In the old days her hair was reddish and fell in curls: now it was dark, and worn in braids and plaits fashionably incomprehensible. Whether the intervening years had darkened the hair, or whether madame cunningly dyed it, must remain a question.

Dan Jenkins and his brother were right. They no doubt had seen looks of anxious interest given to Madame St. Vincent by Captain Collinson. Not as a lover, however; they were mistaken there; but as a brother who was living in a state of peril, and whom she was doubtless protecting and trying to aid. But how far had her aid gone? That she kept up the ball, as to his being Captain Collinson, the rich, honourable, and well-connected Indian officer, went without saying, as the French have it; and no one could expect her to proclaim him as Fabian Pell, the swindler; but had she been helping him in his schemes upon Mina? As to her display of formal coolness to him, it must have been put on to mislead the public.

And what was I to do? Must I quietly bury my discovery within me and say nothing? or must I tell Dr. Knox that Madame St. Vincent was no other than Martha Jane Pell? What ought I to do? It was that question that kept me awake. Never liking to do harm where I could not do good, I asked myself whether I had any right to ruin her. It might be that she was not able to help herself; that she had done no worse than keep Fabian's secret: it might be that she had wanted him gone just as much as Dan Jenkins had wanted it.

"I'll tell Tod in the morning," was my final conclusion, "and hear what he thinks."

When I got downstairs they were beginning breakfast, and Miss Cattledon was turning from the table to carry up Mina's tea. Mina remained in the depths of tears and contrition, and Cattledon had graciously told her she might lie in bed. Breakfast was taken very late that morning, the result of the previous night's disturbance, and the clock was striking ten when we rose from it.

"Tod, I want to speak to you," I said in his ear. "I want to tell you something."

"All right, lad. Tell away."

"Not here. Won't you come out with me somewhere? We must be alone."

"Then it must wait, Johnny. I am going round to the stables with Tamlyn. He wishes me to see the horse they have got on trial. By the description, I don't think much of him: should give him a pretty long trial before I bought him."

They went out. Not long after that, I was strolling across the court-yard with Sam Jenkins, who had been despatched on some professional errand, when we saw Sir Henry Westmorland ride up and rein in his horse. He asked for Dr. Knox. Sam went back to the house to say so, while Sir Henry talked to me.

"Look here," said Sir Henry to the doctor, after they had shaken hands, "I have had a curious letter from Major Leckie this morning. At least"—taking the letter from his pocket and opening it—"it contains an odd bit of news. He says—where is it?—stand still, sir,"—to the horse. "Here it is; just listen, doctor. 'Dr. Knox must have made a mistake in saying Collinson was at Lefford. Collinson is in India; has not been home at all. I have had a letter from him by the overland mail just in, asking me to do a commission for him. Tell Dr. Knox this. If the man he spoke of is passing himself off for Collinson of ours, he must be an impostor.' What do you think of that, doctor?" concluded Sir Henry, folding the letter again.

"He is an impostor," replied Dr. Knox. "We found him out last night."

"What a rogue! Has he been taking people in—fleecing them?"

"He has taken us all in, Sir Henry, in one sense of the word; he was on the point of doing it more effectually, when he was stopped. As to fleecing people, I don't know about that. He seems to have had plenty of money at his command—whence obtained is another question."

"Cheated some one out of it; rely upon that," remarked the baronet, as he nodded a good-day to us, and rode off.

Mina was downstairs when we returned indoors. Anything more pitiful than her state of contrition and distress I should not care to see. No doubt the discovery, just made, tended to strengthen her repentance. In a silly girl's mind some romance might attach to the notion of an elopement with a gallant captain of consideration, brave in Her Majesty's service; but to elope with Mr. Fabian Pell, the chevalier d'industrie, was quite another affair. Mina was mild in temperament, gentle in manners, yet she might have flown at the ex-captain's face with sharp nails, had he come in her way.

"I did not really like him," she sobbed forth: and there was no doubt that she spoke truth. "But they were always on at me, persuading me; they never let me alone."

"Who persuaded you, my dear?" asked Janet.

"He did. He was for ever meeting me in private, and urging me. I could not go out for a walk, or just cross the garden, or run into the next door, but he would be there. Madame St. Vincent persuaded me. She did not say to me, in words, 'you had better do as he asks you and run away,' but all her counsels tended towards it. She would say to me how happy his wife would be; what a fine position it was for any young lady lucky enough to be chosen by him; and that all the world thought me old enough to marry, though Arnold did not, and for that reason Arnold would do his best to prevent it. And so—and so—"

"And so they persuaded you against your better judgment," added Janet pityingly, as Mina broke down in a burst of tears.

"There, child, take this, and don't cry your eyes out," interposed Cattledon, bringing in a beaten-up egg.

Cattledon was coming out uncommonly strong in the way of compassion, all her tartness gone. She certainly did not look with an eye of favour on elopements; but she was ready to take up Mina's cause against the man who had deceived her. Cattledon hated the Pells: for Cattledon had been done out of fifty pounds at the time of old Pell's failure, money she had rashly entrusted to him. She could not very well afford to lose it, and she had been bitter on the Pells, one and all, ever since.

That morning was destined to be one of elucidation. Mr. Tamlyn was in the surgery, saying a last word to Dr. Knox before the latter went out to visit his patients, when Lettice Lane marched in. She looked so fresh and innocent that three parts of Tamlyn's suspicions of her melted away.

"Anything amiss at home?" asked he.

"No, sir," replied Lettice, "I have only brought this note"—handing one in. "Madame St. Vincent told the butler to bring it; but his pains are worse this morning; and, as I chanced to be coming out at the moment, he asked me to leave it here for him."

"Wait an instant," said Mr. Tamlyn, as he opened the note.

It contained nothing of consequence. Madame St. Vincent had written to say that Lady Jenkins was pretty well, but had finished her medicine: perhaps Mr. Tamlyn would send her some more. Old Tamlyn's injunction to wait an instant had been given in consequence of a sudden resolution he had then come to (as he phrased it in his mind), to "tackle" Lettice.

"Lettice Lane," he began, winking at Dr. Knox, "your mistress's state is giving us concern. She seems to be always sleeping."

"She is nearly always dozing off, sir," replied Lettice, her tone and looks open and honest as the day.

"Ay. I can't quite come to the bottom of it," returned old Tamlyn, making believe to be confidential. "To me, it looks just as though she took—took opiates."

"Opiates, sir?" repeated Lettice, as if she hardly understood the word: while Dr. Knox, behind the desk, was glancing keenly at her from underneath his compressed eyebrows.

"Opium. Laudanum."

Lettice shook her head. "No, sir, my mistress does not take anything of that sort, I am sure; we have nothing of the kind in the house. But Madame St. Vincent is for ever dosing her with brandy-and-water."

"What?" shouted old Tamlyn.

"I have said a long while, sir, that I thought you ought to know it; I've said so to the housemaid. I don't believe an hour hardly passes, day or night, but madame administers to her a drop of brandy-and-water. Half a wine-glass, maybe, or a full wine-glass, as the case may happen; and sometimes I know it's pretty strong."

"That's it," said Dr. Knox quietly: and a curious smile crossed his face.

Mr. Tamlyn sat down on the stool in consternation. "Brandy-and-water!" he repeated, more than once, "Perpetually dosed with brandy-and-water! And now, Lettice Lane, how is it you have not come here before to tell me of this?"

"I did not come to tell you now, sir," returned Lettice. "Madame St. Vincent says that Lady Jenkins needs it: she seems to give it her for her good. It is only lately that I have doubted whether it can be right, I have not liked to say anything: servants don't care to interfere. Ten times a-day she will give her these drops of cold brandy-and-water: and I know she gets up for the same purpose once or twice in the night."

"Does Lady Jenkins take it without remonstrance?" asked Dr. Knox, speaking for the first time.

"She does, sir, now. At first she did not. Many a time I have heard my lady say, 'Do you think so much brandy can be good for me, Patty? I feel so dull after it,' and Madame St. Vincent has replied, that it is the only thing that can get her strength back and bring her round."

"The jade!" spoke Dr. Knox, between his teeth. "And to assure us both that all the old lady took was a drop of it weak twice a-day at her meals! Lettice Lane," he added aloud, and there was a great sternness in his tone, "you are to blame for not having spoken of this. A little longer silence, and it might have cost your mistress her life." And Lettice went out in contrition.

"What can the woman's motive be, for thus dosing her into stupidity?" spoke the one doctor to the other when they were shut in together.

"That: the dosing her into it," said Dr. Knox.

"But the motive, Arnold?—the reason? She must have had a motive."

"That remains to be found out."

It turned out to be too true. The culprit was Madame St. Vincent. She had been administering these constant doses of brandy-and-water for months. Not giving enough at a time to put Lady Jenkins into a state of intoxication; only to reduce her to a chronic state of semi-stupidity.

Tod called me, as I tell you, a muff: first for not knowing Madame St. Vincent; and next for thinking to screen her. Of course this revelation of Lettice Lane's had put a new complexion upon things. I left the matter with Tod, and he told the doctors at once: Madame St. Vincent was, or used to be, Martha Jane Pell, own sister to Captain Collinson the false.

Quietly knocking at the door of Jenkins House this same sunny morning went three gentlemen: old Tamlyn, Mr. Lawrence, and Joseph Todhetley. Mr. Lawrence was a magistrate and ex-mayor; he had preceded the late Sir Daniel Jenkins in the civic chair, and was intimate with him as a brother. Just as old Tamlyn tackled Lettice, so they were now about to tackle Madame St. Vincent on the score of the brandy-and-water; and they had deemed it advisable to take Tod with them.

Lady Jenkins was better than usual; rather less stupid. She was seated with madame in the cheerful garden-room, its glass-doors standing open to the sunshine and the flowers. The visitors were cordially received; it was supposed they had only come to pay a morning visit. Madame St. Vincent sat behind a table in the corner, writing notes of invitation for a soirée, to be held that day week. Tod, who had his wits about him, went straight up to her. It must be remembered that they had not yet met.

"Ah! how are you?" cried he, holding out his hand. "Surprised to see you here." And she turned white, and stared, uncertain how to take his words, or whether he had really recognized her, and bowed stiffly as to a stranger, and never put out her own hand in answer.

I cannot tell you much about the interview: Tod's account to me was not very clear. Lady Jenkins began talking about Captain Collinson—that he had turned out to be some unworthy man of the name of Pell, and had endeavoured to kidnap poor little Mina. Charlotte Knox imparted the news to her that morning, in defiance of Madame St. Vincent, who had tried to prevent her. Madame had said it must be altogether some mistake, and that no doubt Captain Collinson would be able to explain: but she, Lady Jenkins, did not know. After that there was a pause; Lady Jenkins shut her eyes, and madame went on writing her notes.

It was old Tamlyn who opened the ball. He drew his chair nearer the old lady, and spoke out without circumlocution.

"What is this that we hear about your taking so much brandy-and-water?"

"Eh?" cried the old lady, opening her eyes. Madame paused in her writing, and looked up. Tamlyn waited for an answer.

"Lady Jenkins does not take much brandy-and-water," cried madame.

"I am speaking to Lady Jenkins, madame," returned old Tamlyn, severely: "be so kind as not to interfere. My dear lady, listen to me"—taking her hand; "I am come here with your life-long old friend, William Lawrence, to talk to you. We have reason to believe that you continually take, and have taken for some time past, small doses of brandy-and-water. Is it so?"

"Patty gives it me," cried Lady Jenkins, looking first at them and then at Patty, in a helpless sort of manner.

"Just so: we know she does. But, are you aware that brandy-and-water, taken in this way, is so much poison?"

"Tell them, Patty, that you give it me for my good," said the poor lady, in affectionate appeal.

"Yes, it is for your good, dear Lady Jenkins," resentfully affirmed Madame St. Vincent, regarding the company with flashing eyes. "Does any one dare to suppose that I should give Lady Jenkins sufficient to hurt her? I may be allowed, I presume, as her ladyship's close companion, constantly watching her, to be the best judge of what is proper for her to take."

Well, a shindy ensued—as Tod called it—all of them talking altogether, except himself and poor Lady Jenkins: and madame defying every one and everything. They told her that she could no longer be trusted with Lady Jenkins; that she must leave the house that day; and when madame defied this with a double defiance, the magistrate intimated that he had come up to enforce the measure, if necessary, and he meant to stay there until she was gone.

She saw it was serious then, and the defiant tone changed. "What I have given Lady Jenkins has been for her good," she said; "to do her good. But for being supported by a little brandy-and-water, the system could never have held out after that serious attack she had in Boulogne. I have prolonged her life."

"No, madame, you have been doing your best to shorten her life," corrected old Tamlyn. "A little brandy-and-water, as you term it, might have been good for her while she was recovering her strength, but you have gone beyond the little; you have made her life a constant lethargy; you would shortly have killed her. What your motive was, Heaven knows."

"My motive was a kind one," flashed madame. "Out of this house I will not go."

So, upon that, they played their trump card, and informed Lady Jenkins, who was crying softly, that this lady was the sister of the impostor, Collinson. The very helplessness, the utter docility to which the treatment had reduced her, prevented her expressing (and most probably feeling) any dissent. She yielded passively to all, like a child, and told Patty that she must go, as her old friends said so.

A bitter pill for madame to take. But she could not help herself.

"You will be as well as ever in a little time," Tamlyn said to Lady Jenkins. "You would have died, had this gone on: it must have induced some malady or other from which you could not have rallied."

Madame St. Vincent went out of the house that afternoon, and Cattledon entered it. She had offered herself to Lady Jenkins for a few days in the emergency.

It was, perhaps, curious that I should meet Madame St. Vincent before she left the town. Janet was in trouble over a basket of butter and fowls that had been sent her by one of the country patients, and of which the railway people denied the arrival. I went again to the station in the afternoon to see whether they had news of it: and there, seated on the platform bench, her boxes around her, and waiting for the London train, was madame.

I showed myself as respectful to her as ever, for you can't humiliate fallen people to their faces, telling her, in the pleasantest way I could, that I was sorry things had turned out so. The tone seemed to tell upon her, and she burst into tears. I never saw a woman so subdued in the space of a few hours.

"I have been treated shamefully, Johnny Ludlow," she said, gulping down her sobs. "Day and night for the past nine months have I been about Lady Jenkins, wearing myself out in attendance on her. The poor old lady had learnt to love me and to depend upon me. I was like a daughter to her."

"I dare say," I answered, conveniently ignoring the dosing.

"And what I gave her, I gave her for the best," went on madame. "It was for the best. People seventy years old need it. Their nerves and system require soothing: to induce sleep now and then is a boon to them. It was a boon to her, poor old thing. And this is my recompense!—turned from the house like a dog!"

"It does seem hard."

"Seem! It is hard. I have had nothing but hardships all my life," she continued, lifting her veil to wipe away the tears. "Where I am to go now, or how make a living, I know not. They told me I need not apply to Lady Jenkins for references: and ladies won't engage a companion who has none."

"Is your husband really dead?" I ventured to ask.

"My poor husband is really dead, Johnny Ludlow—I don't know why you should imply a doubt of it. He left me nothing: he had nothing to leave. He was only a master in the college at Brétage—a place in the South of France—and he died, I verily believe, of poor living. We had not been married twelve months. I had a little baby, and that died. Oh, I assure you I have had my troubles."

"How are—Mr. and Mrs. Clement-Pell?" I next asked, with hesitation. "And Conny?—and the rest of them?"

"Oh, they were well when I last heard," she answered, slightingly. "I don't hear often. Foreign postage is expensive. Conny was to have come here shortly on a visit."

"Where is Gusty? Is—"

"I know nothing at all about my brothers," she interrupted sharply. "And this, I suppose, is my train. Good-bye, Johnny Ludlow; you and I at least can part friends. You are always kind. I wish the world was like you."

I saw her into the carriage—first-class—and her boxes into the van. And thus she disappeared from Lefford. And her brother, "Captain Collinson," as we found later, had taken his departure for London by an early morning train, telling little Pink, his landlord, as he paid his week's rent, that he was going up to attend a levee.

It was found that the rumour of his engagement to Miss Belmont was altogether untrue. Miss Belmont was rather indignant about it, freely saying that she was ten years his senior. He had never hinted at such a thing to her, and she should have stopped him if he had. We concluded that the report had been set afloat by himself, to take attention from his pursuit of Mina Knox.

Madame St. Vincent had feathered her nest. As the days went on, and Lady Jenkins grew clearer, better able to see a little into matters, she could not at all account for the money that had been drawn from the bank. Cheque after cheque had been presented and cashed; and not one-tenth of the money could have been spent upon home expenses. Lady Jenkins had been always signing cheques; she remembered that much; never so much as asking, in her loss of will, what they were needed for. "I want a cheque to-day, dear Lady Jenkins," her companion would say, producing the cheque-book from her desk; and Lady Jenkins would docilely sign it. That a great portion of the proceeds had found their way to Mr. Fabian Pell was looked upon as a certainty.

And to obtaining this money might be traced the motive for dosing Lady Jenkins. Once let her intellect become clear, her will reassert itself, and the game would be stopped. Madame St. Vincent had also another scheme in her head—for the past month or two she had been trying to persuade Lady Jenkins to make a codicil to her will, leaving her a few thousand pounds. Lady Jenkins might have fallen blindly into that; but they had not as yet been able to agree upon the details: Madame St. Vincent urging that a lawyer should be called in from a distance; Lady Jenkins clinging to old Belford. That this codicil would have been made in time, and by the remote lawyer, there existed no doubt whatever.

Ah, well: it was a deep-laid plot altogether. And my visit to Lefford, with Tod's later one, had served, under Heaven, to frustrate it.

Lady Jenkins grew rapidly better, now that she was no longer drugged. In a few days she was herself again. Cattledon came out amazingly strong in the way of care and kindness, and was gracious to every one, even to Lettice.

"She always forbade me to say that I took the brandy-and-water," Lady Jenkins said to me one day when I was sitting with her under the laburnum tree on her lawn, talking of the past, her bright green silk dress and pink cap ribbons glistening in the sun. "She made my will hers. In other respects she was as kind as she could be to me."

"That must have been part of her plan," I answered. "It was the great kindness that won you to her. After that, she took care that you should have no will of your own."

"And the poor thing might have been so happy with me had she only chosen to be straightforward, and not try to play tricks! I gave her a handsome salary, and new gowns besides; and I don't suppose I should have forgotten her at my death."

"Well, it is all over, dear Lady Jenkins, and you will be just as well and brisk as you used to be."

"Not quite that, Johnny," she said, shaking her head; "I cannot expect that. At seventy, grim old age is laying its hand upon us. What we need then, my dear," she added, turning her kindly blue eyes upon me, in which the tears were gathering, "is to go to the mill to be ground young again. And that is a mill that does not exist in this world."

"Ah no!"

"I thank God for the mercy He has shown me," she continued, the tears overflowing. "I might have gone to the grave in the half-witted state to which I was reduced. And, Johnny, I often wonder, as I lie awake at night thinking, whether I should have been held responsible for it."

The first use Lady Jenkins made of her liberty was to invite all her relations, the young nephews and nieces, up to dinner, as she used to do. Madame St. Vincent had set her face against these family entertainments, and they had fallen through. The ex-mayor, William Lawrence, and his good old wife, made part of the company, as did Dr. Knox and Janet. Lady Jenkins beamed on them once more from her place at the head of the table, and Tamlyn sat at the foot and served the big plum-pudding.

"Never more, I trust, shall I be estranged from you, my dears, until it pleases Heaven to bring about the final estrangement," she said to the young people when they were leaving. And she gave them all a sovereign a-piece.

Cattledon could not remain on for ever. Miss Deveen wanted her: so Mina Knox went to stay at Jenkins House, until a suitable lady should be found to replace Madame St. Vincent. Upon that, Dan Jenkins was taken with an anxious solicitude for his aunt's health, and was for ever finding his way up to inquire after it.

"You will never care to notice me again, Dan," Mina said to him, with a swelling heart and throat, one day when he was tilting himself by her on the arm of the sofa.

"Shan't I!" returned Dan.

"Oh, I am so ashamed of my folly; I feel more ashamed of it, day by day," cried Mina, bursting into tears. "I shall never, never get over the mortification."

"Won't you!" added Dan.

"And I never liked him much: I think I dis-liked him. At first I did dislike him; only he kept saying how fond he was of me; and Madame St. Vincent was always praising him up. And you know he was all the fashion."

"Quite so," assented Dan.

"Don't you think it would be almost as well if I were dead, Dan—for all the use I am likely to be to any one?"

"Almost, perhaps; not quite," laughed Dan; and he suddenly stooped and kissed her.

That's all. And now, at the time I write this, Dan Jenkins is a flourishing lawyer at Lefford, and Mina is his wife. Little feet patter up and down the staircase and along the passages that good old Lady Jenkins used to tread. She treads them no more. There was no mill to grind her young again here; but she is gone to that better land where such mills are not needed.

Her will was a just one. She left her property to her nephews and nieces; a substantial sum to each. Dan had Jenkins House in addition. But it is no longer Jenkins House; for he had that name taken off the entrance pillars forthwith, replacing it by the one that had been there before—Rose Bank.

CHAPTER XIX

THE ANGELS' MUSIC

How the Squire came to give in to it, was beyond the ken of mortal man. Tod turned crusty; called the young ones all the hard names in the dictionary, and said he should go out for the night. But he did not.

"Just like her!" cried he, with a fling at Mrs. Todhetley. "Always devising some rubbish or other to gratify the little reptiles!"

The "little reptiles" applied to the school children at North Crabb. They generally had a treat at Christmas; and this year Mrs. Todhetley said she would like it to be given by us, at Crabb Cot, if the Squire did not object to stand the evening's uproar. After vowing for a day that he wouldn't hear of it, the Squire (to our astonishment) gave in, and said they might come. It was only the girls: the boys had their treat later on, when they could go in for out-of-door sports. After the pater's concession, she and the school-mistress, Miss Timmens, were as busy planning-out the arrangements as two bees in a honeysuckle field.

The evening fixed upon was the last in the old year—a Thursday. And the preparations seemed to me to be in full flow from the previous Monday. Molly made her plum-cakes and loaves on the Wednesday; on the Thursday after breakfast, her mistress went to the kitchen to help her with the pork-pies and the tartlets. To judge by the quantity provided, the school would require nothing more for a week to come.

The Squire went over to Islip on some matter of business, taking Tod with him. Our children, Hugh and Lena, were spending the day with the little Letsoms, who would come back with them for the treat; so we had the house to ourselves. The white deal ironing-board under the kitchen window was raised on its iron legs; before it stood Mrs. Todhetley and Molly, busy with the mysteries of pastry-making and patty-pan filling. I sat on the edge of the board, looking on. The small savoury pies were done, and in the act of baking, a tray-load at a time; every now and then Molly darted into the back kitchen, where the oven was, to look after them. For two days the snow had come down thickly; it was falling still in great flakes; far and near, the landscape showed white and bright.

"Johnny, if you will persist in eating the jam, I shall have to send you away."

"Put the jar on the other side then, good mother."

"Ugh! Much jam Master Johnny would leave for the tarts, let him have his way," struck in Molly, more crusty than her own pastry, when I declare I had only dipped the wrong end of the fork in three or four times. The jam was not hers.

"Mind you don't give the young ones bread-and-scrape, Molly," I retorted, catching sight of no end of butter-pats through the open door. At which advice she only threw up her head.

"Who is this, coming up through the snow?" cried the mater.

I turned to the window and made it out to be Mrs. Trewin: a meek little woman who had seen better days, and tried to get her living as a dressmaker since the death of her husband. She had not been good for very much since: never seemed quite to get over the shock. Going out one morning, as usual, to his duties as an office clerk, he was brought home dead. Killed by an accident. It was eighteen months ago now, but Mrs. Trewin wore deep mourning still.

Not standing upon ceremony down in our country, Mrs. Todhetley had her brought into the kitchen, going on with the tartlets all the same, while she talked. Mrs. Trewin was making a frock for Lena, and had come up to say that the trimming ran short. The mater told her she was too busy to see to it then, and was very sorry she had come through the snow for such a trifle.

"'Twas not much further, ma'am," was her answer: "I had to go out to the school to fetch home Nettie. The path is so slippery, through the boys making slides, that I don't altogether like to trust the child to go to and fro to school by herself."

"As if Nettie would come to any harm, Mrs. Trewin!" I put in. "If she went down, it would only be a Christmas gambol."

"Accidents happen so unexpectedly, sir," she answered, a shadow crossing her sad face. And I was sorry to have said it: it had put her in mind of her husband.

"You are coming up this evening, you know, Mrs. Trewin," said mother. "Don't be late."

"It is very good of you to have asked me, ma'am," she answered gratefully. "I said so to Miss Timmens. I'm sure it will be something new to have such a treat. Nettie, poor child, will enjoy it too."

Molly came banging in with a tray of pork-pies, just out of the oven. The mater told Mrs. Trewin to take one, and offered her a glass of beer.

But, instead of eating the pie, she wrapped it in paper to take with her home, and declined the beer, lest it should give her a headache for the evening.

So Mrs. Trewin took her departure; and, under cover of it, I helped myself to another of the pork-pies. Weren't they good! After that the morning went on again, and the tart-making with it.

The last of the paste was being used up, the last of the jam jars stood open, and the clock told us that it was getting on for one, when we had another visitor: Miss Timmens, the schoolmistress. She came in, stamping the snow from her shoes on the mat, her thin figure clad in an old long cloth cloak, and the chronic redness in her face turned purple.

"My word! It is a day, ma'am, this is!" she exclaimed.

"And what have you come through it for?" asked Mrs. Todhetley. "About the forms? Why, I sent word to you by Luke Mackintosh that they would be fetched at two o'clock."

"He never came, then," said Miss Timmens, irate at Luke's negligence. "That Mackintosh is not worth his salt. What delicious-looking tartlets!" exclaimed she, as she sat down. "And what a lot of them!"

"Try one," said the mother. "Johnny, hand them to Miss Timmens, and a plate."

"That silly Sarah Trewin has gone and tumbled down," cried Miss Timmens, as she thanked me and took the plate and one of the tartlets. "Went and slipped upon a slide near the school-house. What a delicious tart!"

"Sarah Trewin!" cried the mater, turning round from the board. "Why, she was here an hour ago. Has she hurt herself?"

"Just bruised all the one side of her black and blue, from her shoulder to her ankle," answered Miss Timmens. "Those unruly boys have made slides all over the place, ma'am; and Sarah Trewin must needs go down upon one, not looking, I suppose, to her feet. She had only just turned out of the schoolroom with Nettie."

"Dear, dear! And she is so unable to bear a fall!"

"Of course it might have been worse, for there are no bones broken," remarked Miss Timmens. "As to Nettie, the child was nearly frightened out of her senses; she's sobbing and crying still. Never was such a timid child as that."

"Will Sarah Trewin be able to come this evening?"

"Not she, ma'am. She'll be as stiff as buckram for days to come. I'd like to pay out those boys—making their slides on the pathway and endangering people's lives! Nicol's not half strict enough with them; and I'm tired of telling him so. Tiresome, rude monkeys! Not that my girls are a degree better: they'd go down all the slides in the parish, let 'em have their way. What with them, and what with these fantastical notions of the new parson, I'm sure my life's a martyrdom."

The mother smiled over her pastry. Miss Timmens and the parson, civilly polite to one another, were mentally at daggers drawn.

The time I am writing of was before the movement, set in of later years, for giving the masses the same kind of education as their betters; but our new parson at Crabb was before his age in these ideas. To experienced Miss Timmens, and to a great many more clear-sighted people, the best word that could be given to the movement was "fantastical."

"He came in yesterday afternoon at dusk," she resumed, "when I was holding my Bible Class. 'And what has been the course of instruction to-day, Miss Timmens?' asked he, as mild as new milk, all the girls gaping and staring around him. 'It has been reading, and writing, and summing, and spelling, and sewing,' said I, giving him the catalogue in full: 'and now I'm trying to teach them their duty to Heaven and to one another. And according to my old-fashioned notion, sir,' I summed up, 'if a poor girl acquires these matters thoroughly, she is a deal more fitted to go through life in the station to which God has called her (as the catechism says), than she would be if you gave her a course of fine mincing uppishness, with your poetry and your drawing and your embroidery.' Oh, he gets his answer from me, ma'am."

"Mr. Bruce may be kind and enlightened, and all that," spoke Mrs. Todhetley, "but he certainly seems inclined to carry his ideas beyond reasonable bounds, so far as regards these poor peasant children."

"Reasonable!" repeated Miss Timmens, catching up the word, and rubbing her sharp nose with excitement: "why, the worst is, that there's no reason in it. Not a jot. The parson's mind has gone a little bit off its balance, ma'am; that's my firm conviction. This exalted education applied to young ladies would be all right and proper: but where can be the use of it to these poor girls? What good will his accomplishments, his branches of grand learning do them? His conchology and meteorology, and all the rest of his ologies? Of what service will it be to them in future?"

"I'd have got my living nicely, I guess, if I'd been taught them things," satirically struck in Molly, unable to keep her tongue still any longer. "A fine cook I should ha' made!—kept all my places a beautiful length of time; I wouldn't come with such flighty talk to the Squire, Miss Timmens, if 'twas me."

"The talk's other people's; it isn't mine," fired Miss Timmens, turning her wrath on Molly. "That is, the notions are. You had better attend to your baking, Molly."

"So I had," said Molly. "Baking's more in my line than them other foreign jerks. But well I should have knowed how to do it if my mind had been cocketed up with the learning that's only fit for lords and ladies."

"Is not that my argument?" retorted Miss Timmens, flinging the last word after her as she went out to her oven. "Poor girls were sent into the world to work, ma'am, not to play at being fine scholars," she added to Mrs. Todhetley, as she got up to leave. "And, as sure as we are born, this new dodge of education, if it ever gets a footing, will turn the country upside down."

"I'm sure I hope not," replied the mother in her mild way. "Take another tart, Miss Timmens. These are currant and raspberry."

II

The company began to arrive at four o'clock. The snow had ceased to fall; it was a fine, cold, clear evening, the moon very bright. A large store-room at the back of the house had been cleared out, and a huge fire made in it. The walls were decorated with evergreens, and tin sconces holding candles; benches from the school-house were ranged underneath them. This was to be the principal play-room, but the other rooms were open. Mrs. Hill (formerly Mrs. Garth, who had not so very long before lost poor David) and Maria Lease came up by invitation to help Miss Timmens with the children; and Mrs. Trewin would have come but for her fall on the slide. Miss Timmens appeared in full feather: a purple gown of shot silk, with a red waist-band, and red holly berries in her lace cap. The children, timid at first, sat round on the forms in prim stillness, just like so many mice.

By far the most timid of all was a gentle little thing of seven years old, got up like a lady; white frock, black sash and sleeve ribbons. She was delicate-featured, blue-eyed, had curling flaxen hair. It was Nettie Trewin. Far superior she looked to all of them; out of place, in fact, amongst so many coarser natures. Her little arm and hand trembled as she clung to Miss Timmens' gown.

"Senseless little thing," cried Miss Timmens, "to be afraid in a beautiful room like this, and with all these kind friends around her! Would you believe it, Mr. Johnny, that I could hardly get her here? Afraid, she said, to come without mother!"

"Oh, Nettie! Why, you are going to have lots of fun! Is mother better this evening?"

"Yes," whispered Nettie, venturing to take a peep at me through her wet eyelashes.

The order of the day was this. Tea at once, consisting of as much bread-and-butter and plum-cake as they could eat; games afterwards. The savoury pies and tartlets later on; more cake to wind up with, which, if they had no room for, they might carry home.

After all signs of tea had disappeared, and our neighbours, the Coneys, had come in, and several round rings were seated on the floor at "Hunt-the-Slipper," I, chancing to draw within earshot, found Miss Timmens had opened out her grievance to the Squire—the parson's interference with the school.

"It would be reversing the proper and natural order of things, as I look upon it," she was saying, "to give an exalted education to those who must get their living by the sweat of their brow; as servants, and what not. Do you think so, sir?"

"Think so! of course I think so," spluttered the Squire, taking up the subject hotly as usual. "It's good for them to read and write well, to add up figures, and know how to sew and clean, and wash and iron. That's the learning they want, whether they are to pass their lives serving in families, or as the wives of working men."

"Yes, sir," acquiesced Miss Timmens, in a glow of satisfaction; "but you may as well try to beat common sense into a broomstick as into Mr. Bruce. The other day—what, is it you again, Nettie!" she broke off, as the little white-robed child sidled up and hid her head in what appeared to be her haven of refuge— the folds of the purple gown. "Never was such a child as this, for shyness. When put to play with the rest, she'll not stay with them. What do you think you are good for?"—rather wrathfully. "Do you suppose the gentlefolk are going to eat you, Nettie?"

"There's nothing to be afraid of, little lassie. What child is it?" added the Squire, struck with her appearance.

"Tell your name to the Squire," said Miss Timmens, with authority. And the little one lifted her pretty blue eyes appealingly to his face, as if beseeching him not to bite her.

"It's Nettie Trewin, sir," she said in a whisper.

"Dear me! Is that poor Trewin's child! She has a look of her father too. A delicate little maid."

"And silly also," added Miss Timmens. "You came here to play, you know, Nettie; not hide your face. What are they all stirring at, now? Oh, going to have 'Puss-in-the-corner.' You can play at that, Nettie. Here, Jane Bright! Take Nettie with you and attend to her. Find her a corner: she has not had any play at all."

A tall, awkward girl stepped up: slouching shoulders, narrow forehead, stolid features, coarse hair all ruffled; thick legs, thick boots—Miss Jane Bright. She seized Nettie's hand.

"Yes, sir, you are right: the child is a delicate, dainty little thing, quite a contrast to most of these other girls," resumed Miss Timmens, in answer to the Squire. "Look at that one who has just fetched Nettie away: she is only a type of the rest. They come, most of them, of coarse, stupid parents, and will be no better to the end of the chapter, whatever education you may try to hammer into them. As I said to Mr. Bruce the other day when— Well, I never! There he is!"

The young parson caught her eye, as he was looming in. Long coat, clerical waistcoat, no white tie to speak of round his bare neck; quite à la mode. The new fashions and the new notions that Mr. Bruce went in for, were not at all understood at North Crabb.

The Squire had gone on at first against the party; but no face was more sunshiny than his, now that he was in the thick of it. A select few of the children, with ours and the little Lawsons, had appropriated the dining-room for "Hunt-the-Whistle." The pater chanced to look in just before it began, and we got him to be the hunter. I shall never forget it as long as I live. I don't believe I had ever laughed as much before. He did not know the play, or the trick of it: and to see him whirling himself about in search of the whistle as it was blown behind his back, now seizing on this bold whistler, believing he or she must be in possession of the whistle, and now on that one, all unconscious that the whistle was fastened to the back button of his own coat; and to look at the puzzled wonder of his face as to where the whistle could possibly be, and how it contrived to elude his grasp, was something to be remembered. The shrieks of laughter might have been heard down at the Ravine. Tod had to sit on the floor and hold his sides; Tom Coney was in convulsions.

"Ah—I—ah—what do you think, Mr. Todhetley?" began Bruce, with his courteous drawl, catching the Squire, as he emerged later, red and steaming, from the whistle-hunt. "Suppose I collect these young ones around me and give them a quarter-of-an-hour's lecture on pneumatics? I've been getting up the subject a little."

"Pneumatics be hanged!" burst forth the pater, more emphatically than politely, when he had taken a puzzled stare at the parson. "The young ones have come here to play, not to have their brains addled. Be shot if I quite know myself what 'pneumatics' means. I beg your pardon, Bruce. You mean well, I know."

"Pneumatics!" repeated old Coney, taking time to digest the word. "Don't you think, parson, that's more in the department of the Astronomer Royal?"

One required a respite after the whistle-hunt. I put my back against the wall in the large room, and watched the different sets of long tails, then pulling fiercely at "Oranges and Lemons." Mrs. Hill and Maria Lease sat side by side on one of the benches, both looking as sad as might be, their memories, no doubt, buried in the past. Maria Lease had never, so to say, worn a smiling countenance since the dreadful end of Daniel Ferrar.

A commotion! Half-a-dozen of the "lemons," pulling too fiercely, had come to grief on the ground. Maria went to the rescue.

"I was just thinking of poor David, sir," Mrs. Hill said to me, with a sigh. "How he would have enjoyed this scene: so merry and bright!"

"But he is in a brighter scene than this, you know."

"Yes, Master Johnny, I do know it," she said, tears trickling slowly down her cheeks. "Where he is, all things are beautiful."

In her palmy days Mrs. Todhetley used to sing a song, of which this was the first verse:—

"All that's bright must fade,
The brightest still the fleetest;
All that's sweet was made
But to be lost when sweetest."

Mrs. Hill's words brought this song to my memory, and with it the damping reminder that nothing lasts in this world, whether of pleasure or brightness. All things must fade, or die: but in that better life to come they will last for ever. And David had entered upon it.

"Now, where's that senseless little Nettie?"

The words, spoken sharply, came from Miss Timmens. But if she did possess a sharp-toned tongue, she was good and kind at heart. The young crew were sitting down at the long table to the savoury pies and tartlets; Miss Timmens, taking stock of them, missed Nettie.

"Jane Bright, go and find Nettie Trewin."

Not daring to disobey the curt command, but looking as though she feared her portion of the good things would be eaten up during her absence, Jane Bright disappeared. Back she came in a brace of shakes, saying Nettie "was not there."

"Maria Lease, where's Nettie Trewin?" asked Miss Timmens.

Maria turned from the table. "Nettie Trewin?" she repeated, looking about her. "I don't know. She must be somewhere or other."

"I wish to goodness you'd find her then."

Maria Lease could not see anything of the child. "Nettie Trewin" was called out high and low; but it brought forth no response. The servants were sent to look over the house, with no better result.

"She is hiding somewhere in her shyness," said Miss Timmens. "I have a great mind to punish her for this."

"She can't have got into the rain-water butt?" suggested the Squire. "Molly, go and look."

It was not very likely: as the barrel was quite six feet high. But, as the Squire once got into the water-butt to hid himself when he was a climbing youngster, and had reasons for anticipating a whipping, his thoughts naturally flew to it.

"Well, she must be somewhere," cried he when we laughed at him. "She could not sink through the floor."

"Who saw her last?" repeated Miss Timmens. "Do you hear, children? Just stop eating for a minute, and answer."

Much discussion—doubt—cross-questioning. The whole lot seemed to be nearly as stupid as owls. At last, so far as could be gathered, none of them had noticed Nettie since they began "Puss-in-the-corner."

"Jane Bright, I told you to take Nettie to play with the rest, and to find her a corner. What did you do with her?"

Jane Bright commenced her answer by essaying to take a sly bite at her pie. Miss Timmens stopped her midway, and turned her from the table to face the company.

"Do you hear me? Now don't stand staring like a gaby! Just answer."

Like a "gaby" did Jane Bright stand: mouth wide open, eyes round, countenance bewildered.

"Please, governess, I didn't do nothing with her."

"You must have done something with her: you held her hand."

"I didn't do nothing," repeated the girl, shaking her head stolidly.

"Now, that won't do, Jane Bright. Where did you leave her?"

"'Twas in the corner," answered Jane Bright, apparently making desperate efforts of memory. "When I was Puss, and runned across and came back again, I didn't see her there."

"Surely, the child has not stolen out by herself and run off home!" cried Mrs. Coney: and the schoolmistress took up the suggestion.

"It is the very thought that has been in my mind the last minute or two," avowed she. "Yes, Mrs. Coney, that's it, depend upon it. She has decamped through the snow and gone back to her mother's."

"Then she has gone without her things," interposed Maria Lease, who was entering the room with a little black cloak and bonnet in her hand. "Are not these Nettie's things, children?" And a dozen voices all speaking together, hastened to say Yes, they were Nettie's.

"Then she must be in the house," decided Miss Timmens. "She wouldn't be silly enough to go out this cold night with her neck and arms bare. The child has her share of sense. She has run away to hide herself, and may have dropped asleep."

"It must be in the chimbleys, then," cried free Molly from the back of the room. "We've looked everywhere else."

"You had better look again," said the Squire. "Take plenty of light—two or three candles."

It seemed rather a queer thing. And, while this talking had been going on, there flashed into my mind the old Modena story, related by the poet Rogers, of the lovely young heiress of the Donatis: and which has been embodied in our song "The Mistletoe Bough." Could this timid child have imprisoned herself in any place that she was unable to get out of? Going to the kitchen for a candle, I went upstairs, taking the garret first, with its boxes and lumber, and then the rooms. And nowhere could I find the least trace or sign of Nettie.

Stepping into the kitchen to leave the candle, there stood Luke Mackintosh, whiter than death; his back propped against Molly's press, his hands trembling, his hair on end. Tod stood in front of him suppressing his laughter. Mackintosh had just burst in at the back-door in a desperate state of fright, declaring he had seen a ghost.

It's not the first time I have mentioned the man's cowardice. Believing in ghosts and goblins, wraiths and witches, he could hardly be persuaded to cross Crabb Ravine at night, on account of the light sometimes seen there. Sensible people told him that this light (which, it was true, no one had ever traced to its source) was nothing but a will-o'-the-wisp, an ignis-fatuus arising from the vapour; but Luke could not be brought to reason. On this evening it chanced that the Squire had occasion to send Mackintosh to the Timberdale post-office, and the man had now just come in from the errand.

"I see the light, too, sir," he was saying to Tod in a scared voice, as he ran his shaking hand through his hair. "It be dodging about on the banks of the Ravine for all the world like a corpse-candle. Well, sir, I didn't like that, and I got up out of the Ravine as fast as my legs would bring me, and were making straight for home here, with my head down'ards, not wanting to see nothing more, when something dreadful met me. All in white, it was."

"A man in his shroud, who had left his grave to take a moonlight walk," said Tod, gravely, biting his lips.

"'Twere in grave-clothes, for sure; a long, white garment, whiter than the snow. I'd not say but it was Daniel Ferrar," added Luke, in the low dread tones that befitted the dismal subject. "His ghost do walk, you know, sir."

"And where did his ghost go to?"

"Blest if I saw, sir," replied Mackintosh, shaking his head. "I'd not have looked after it for all the world. 'Twarn't a slow pace I come at, over the field, after that, and right inside this here house."

"Rushing like the wind, I suppose."

"My heart was all a-throbbing and a-skeering. Mr. Joseph, I hope the Squire won't send me through the Ravine after dark again! I couldn't stand it, sir; I'd a'most rather give up my place."

"You'll not be fit for this place, or any other, I should say, Mackintosh, if you let this sort of fear run away with your senses," I put in. "You saw nothing; it was all fancy."

"Saw nothing!" repeated Mackintosh in the excess of desperation. "Why, Mr. Johnny, I never saw a sight plainer in all my born days. A great, white, awesome apparition it were, that went rushing past me with a wailing sound. I hope you won't ever have the ill-luck to see such a thing yourself, sir."

"I'm sure I shan't."

"What's to do here?" asked Tom Coney, putting in his head.

"Mackintosh has seen a ghost."

"Seen a ghost!" cried Tom, beginning to grin.

Mackintosh, trembling yet, entered afresh on the recital, rather improving it by borrowing Tod's mocking suggestion. "A dead man in his shroud come out walking from his grave in the churchyard—which he feared might be Ferrar, lying on the edge on't, just beyond consecrated ground. I never could abear to go by the spot where he was put in, and never a prayer said over him, Mr. Tom!"

But, in spite of the solemnity of the subject, touching Ferrar, Tom Coney could only have his laugh out. The servants came in from their fruitless search of the dairy and cellars, and started to see the state of Mackintosh.

"Give him a cup of warm ale, Molly," was Tod's command. And we left them gathered round the man, listening to his tale with open mouths.

From the fact that Nettie Trewin was certainly not in the house, one only deduction could be drawn—that the timid child had run home to her mother. Bare-headed, bare-necked, bare-armed, she had gone through the snow; and, as Miss Timmens expressed it, might just have caught her death.

"Senseless little idiot!" exclaimed Miss Timmens in a passion. "Sarah Trewin is sure to blame me; she'll say I might have taken better care of her."

But one of the elder girls, named Emma Stone, whose recollection only appeared to come to her when digesting her supper, spoke up at this juncture, and declared that long after "Puss-in-the-corner" was over, and also "Oranges and Lemons," which had succeeded it, she had seen and spoken to Nettie Trewin. Her account was, that in crossing the passage leading from the store-room, she saw Nettie "scrouged against the wall, half-way down the passage, like anybody afeared of being seen."

"Did you speak to her, Emma Stone?" asked Miss Timmens, after listening to these concluding words.

"Yes, governess. I asked her why she was not at play, and why she was hiding there."

"Well, what did she say?"

"Not anything," replied Emma Stone. "She turned her head away as if she didn't want to be talked to."

Miss Timmens took a long, keen look at Emma Stone. This young lady, it appeared, was rather in the habit of romancing; and the governess thought she might be doing it then.

"I vow to goodness I saw her," interrupted the girl, before Miss Timmens had got out more than half a doubt: and her tone was truthful enough. "I'm not telling no story, 'm. I thought Nettie was crying."

"Well, it is a strange thing you should have forgotten it until this moment, Emma Stone."

"Please, 'm, it were through the pies," pleaded Emma.

It was time to depart. Bonnets and shawls were put on, and the whole of them filed out, accompanied by Miss Timmens, Mrs. Hill, and Maria Lease: good old motherly Dame Coney saying she hoped they would find the child safe in bed between the blankets, and that her mother would have given her some hot drink.

Our turn for supper came now. We took it partly standing, just the fare that the others had had, with bread-and-cheese added for the Squire and old Coney. After that, we all gathered round the fire in the dining-room, those two lighting their pipes.

And I think you might almost have knocked some of us down with a feather in our surprise, when, in the midst of one of old Coney's stories, we turned round at the sudden opening of the door, and saw Miss Timmens amongst us. A prevision of evil seemed to seize Mrs. Todhetley, and she rose up.

"The child! Is she not at home?"

"No, ma'am; neither has she been there," answered Miss Timmens, ignoring ceremony (as people are apt to do at seasons of anxiety or commotion) and sitting down uninvited. "I came back to tell you so, and to ask what you thought had better be done."

"The child must have started for home and lost her way in the snow," cried the Squire, putting down his pipe in consternation. "What does the mother think?"

"I did not tell her of it," said Miss Timmens. "I went on by myself to her house; and the first thing I saw there, on opening the door, was a little pair of slippers warming on the fender. 'Oh, have you brought Nettie?' began the mother, before I could speak: 'I've got her shoes warm for her. Is she very, very cold?—and has she enjoyed herself and been good?' Well, sir, seeing how it was—that the child had not got home—I answered lightly: 'Oh, the children are not here yet; my sister and Maria Lease are with them. I've just stepped on to see how your bruises are getting on.' For that poor Sarah Trewin is good for so little that one does not care to alarm her," concluded Miss Timmens, as if she would apologize for her deceit.

The Squire nodded approval, and told me to give Miss Timmens something hot to drink. Mrs. Todhetley, looking three parts frightened out of her wits, asked what was to be done.

Yes; what was to be done? What could be done? A sort of council was held amongst them, some saying one thing, some another. It seemed impossible to suggest anything.

"Had harm come to her in running home, had she fallen into the snow, for instance, or anything of that sort, we should have seen or heard her," observed Miss Timmens. "She would be sure to take the direct path—the way we came here and returned."

"It might be easy enough for the child to lose her way—the roads and fields are like a wide white plain," observed Mrs. Coney. "She might have strayed aside amongst the trees in the triangle."

Miss Timmens shook her head in dissent.

"She'd not do that, ma'am. Since Daniel Ferrar was found there, the children don't like the three-cornered grove."

"Look here," said old Coney, suddenly speaking up. "Let us search all these places, and any others that she could have strayed to, right or left, on her road home."

He rose up, and we rose with him. It was the best thing that could be done: and no end of a relief, besides, to pitch upon something to do. The Squire ordered Mackintosh (who had not recovered himself yet) to bring a lantern, and we all put on our great-coats and went forth, leaving the mater and Mrs. Coney to keep the fire warm. A black party we looked, in the white snow, Miss Timmens making one of us.

"I can't rest," she whispered to me. "If the child has been lying on the snow all this while, we shall find her dead."

It was a still, cold, lovely night; the moon high in the sky, the snow lying white and pure beneath her beams. Tom Coney and Tod, all their better feelings and their fears aroused, plunged on fiercely, now amidst the deep snow by the hedges, now on the more level path. The grove, which had been so fatal to poor Daniel Ferrar, was examined first. And now we saw the use of the lantern ordered by the Squire, at which order we had secretly laughed: for it served to light up the darker parts where the trunks of the trees grew thick. Mackintosh, who hated that grove, did not particularly relish his task of searching it, though he was in good company. But it did not appear to contain Nettie.

"She would not turn in here," repeated Miss Timmens, from the depth of her strong conviction; "I'm sure she wouldn't. She would rather bear onwards towards her mother's."

Bounding here, trudging there, calling her name softly, shouting loudly, we continued our search after Nettie Trewin. It was past twelve when we got back home and met Mrs. Todhetley and Mrs. Coney at the door, both standing there in their uneasiness, enveloped in woollen shawls.

"No. No success. Can't find her anywhere."

Down sank the Squire on one of the hall-chairs as he spoke, as though he could not hold himself up a minute longer, but was dead beat with tramping and disappointment. Perhaps he was. What was to be done next? What could be done? We stood round the dining-room fire, looking at one another like so many helpless mummies.

"Well," said the pater, "the first thing is to have a drop of something hot. I am half-frozen. What time's that?"—as the clock over the mantelpiece chimed one stroke. "Half-past twelve."

"And she's dead by this time," gasped Miss Timmens, in a faint voice, its sharpness gone clean out of it. "I'm thinking of the poor widowed mother."

Mrs. Coney (often an invalid) said she could do no good by staying longer, and wanted to be in bed. Old Coney said he was not going in yet; so Tom took her over. It might have been ten minutes after this—but I was not taking any particular account of the time—that I saw Tom Coney put his head in at the parlour-door, and beckon Tod out. I went also.

"Look here," said Coney to us. "After I left mother indoors, I thought I'd search a bit about the back-ground here: and I fancy I can see the marks of a child's footsteps in the snow."

"No!" cried Tod, rushing out at the back-door and crossing the premises to the field.

Yes, it was so. Just for a little way along the path leading to Crabb Ravine the snow was much trodden and scattered by the footsteps of a man, both to and fro. Presently some little footsteps, evidently of a child, seemed to diverge from this path and go onwards in rather a slanting direction through the deeper snow, as if their owner had lost the direct way. When we had tracked these steps half-way across the field. Tod brought himself to a halt.

"I'm sure they are Nettie's," he said. "They look like hers. Whose else should they be? She may have fallen down the Ravine. One of you had better go back and bring a blanket—and tell them to get hot water ready."

Eager to be of use, Tom Coney and I ran back together. Tod continued his tracking. Presently the little steps diverged towards the path, as if they had suddenly discovered their wanderings from it; and then they seemed to be lost in those other and larger footsteps which had kept steadily to the path.

"I wonder," thought Tod, halting as he lost the clue, "whether Mackintosh's big ghost could have been this poor little white-robed child? What an idiotic coward the fellow is! These are his footmarks. A slashing pace he must have travelled at, to fling the snow up in this manner!"

At that moment, as Tod stood facing the Ravine, a light, looking like the flame of a candle, small and clear and bright as that of a glow-worm, appeared on the opposite bank, and seemed to dodge about the snow-clad brushwood around the trunks of the wintry trees. What was this light?—whence did it proceed?—what caused it? It seemed we were never tired of putting these useless questions to ourselves. Tod did not know; never had known. He thought of Mack's fright and of the ghost, as he stood watching it, now disappearing in some particular spot, now coming again at ever so many yards' distance. But ghosts had no charms for Tod: by which I mean no alarms: and he went forward again, trying to find another trace of the little footsteps.

"I don't see what should bring Nettie out here, though," ran his thoughts. "Hope she has not pitched head foremost down the Ravine! Confound the poltroon!—kicking up the snow like this!"

But now, in another minute, there were traces again. The little feet seemed to have turned aside at a tangent, and once more sought the deep snow. From that point he did not again lose them; they carried him to the low and narrow dell (not much better than a ditch) which just there skirted the hedge bordering the Ravine.

At first Tod could see nothing. Nothing but the drifted snow. But—looking closely—what was that, almost at his feet? Was it only a dent in the snow?—or was anything lying on it? Tod knelt down on the deep soft white carpet (sinking nearly up to his waist) and peered and felt.

There she was: Nettie Trewin! With her flaxen curls fallen about her head and mingling with the snow, and her little arms and neck exposed, and her pretty white frock all wet, she lay there in the deep hole. Tod, his breast heaving with all manner of emotion, gathered her into his arms, as gently as an infant is hushed to rest by its mother. The white face had no life in it; the heart seemed to have stopped beating.

"Wake up, you poor little mite!" he cried, pressing her against his warm side. "Wake up, little one! Wake up, little frozen snow-bird!"

But there came no response. The child lay still and white in his arms.

"Hope she's not frozen to death!" he murmured, a queer sensation taking him. "Nettie, don't you hear me? My goodness, what's to be done?"

He set off across the field with the child, meeting me almost directly. I ran straight up to him.

"Get out, Johnny Ludlow!" he cried roughly, in his haste and fear. "Don't stop me! Oh, a blanket, is it? That's good. Fold it round her, lad."

"Is she dead?"

"I'll be shot if I know."

He went along swiftly, holding her to him in the blanket. And a fine commotion they all made when he got her indoors.

The silly little thing, unable to get over her shyness, had taken the opportunity, when the back-door was open, to steal out of it, with the view of running home to her mother. Confused, perhaps, by the bare white plain; or it may be by her own timidity; or probably confounding the back-door and its approaches with the front, by which she had entered, she went straight across the field, unconscious that this was taking her in just the opposite direction to her home. It was she whom Luke Mackintosh had met—the great idiot!—and he frightened her with his rough appearance and the bellow of fear he gave, just as much as she had frightened him. Onwards she went, blindly terrified, was stopped by the hedge, fell into the ditch, and lay buried in the snow. Whether she could be brought back to life, or whether death had really taken her, was a momentous question.

I went off for Cole, flying all the way. He sent me back again, saying he'd be there as soon as I—and that Nettie Trewin must be a born simpleton.

"Master Johnny!—Mr. Ludlow!—Is it you?"

The words greeted me in a weak panting voice, just as I reached the corner by the store barn, and I recognized Mrs. Trewin. Alarmed at Nettie's prolonged stay, she had come out, all bruised as she was, and extorted the fact—that the child was missing—from Maria Lease. I told her that the child was found—and where.

"Dead or alive, sir?"

I stammered in my answer. Cole would be up directly, I said, and we must hope for the best. But she drew a worse conclusion.

"It was all I had," she murmured. "My one little ewe lamb."

"Don't cry, Mrs. Trewin. It may turn out to be all right, you know."

"If I could only have laid her poor little face on my bosom to die, and said good-bye to her!" she wailed, the tears falling. "I have had so much trouble in the world, Master Johnny!—and she was all of comfort left to me in it."

We went in. Cole came rushing like a whirlwind. By-and-by they got some warmth into the child, lying so still on the bed; and she was saved.

"Were you cold, dear, in the snow?—were you frightened?" gently asked the mother, when Nettie could answer questions.

"I was very cold and frightened till I heard the angels' music, mother."

"The angels' music?"

"Yes. I knew they played it for me. After that, I felt happy and went to sleep. Oh, mother, there's nothing so sweet as angels' music."

The "music" had been that of the church bells, wafted over the Ravine by the rarefied air; the sweet bells of Timberdale, ringing in the New Year.

MRS HENRY WOOD (aka ELLEN WOOD) – A CONCISE BIBLIOGRAPHY

Danesbury House (1860)
East Lynne (1861)
The Elchester College Boys (1861)
A Life's Secret (1862)
Mrs. Halliburton's Troubles (1862)
The Channings (1862)
The Foggy Night at Offord: A Christmas Gift for the Lancashire Fund (1863)
The Shadow of Ashlydyat (1863)
Verner's Pride (1863)
Lord Oakburn's Daughters (1864)
Oswald Cray (1864)
Trevlyn Hold; or, Squire Trevlyn's Heir (1864)
William Allair; or, Running away to Sea (1864)
Mildred Arkell: A Novel (1865)
The Argosy (1865)
Elster's Folly: A Novel (1866)
St. Martin's Eve: A Novel (1866)
Lady Adelaide's Oath (1867)
Orville College: A Story (1867)
The Ghost of the Hollow Field (1867)
Anne Hereford: A Novel (1868)
Castle Wafer; or, The Plain Gold Ring (1868)
The Red Court Farm: A Novel (1868)

Roland Yorke: A Novel (1869)
Bessy Rane: A Novel (1870)
George Canterbury's Will (1870)
Dene Hollow (1871)
Within the Maze: A Novel (1872)
The Master of Greylands (1872)
Johnny Ludlow (1874)
Bessy Wells (1875)
Told in the Twilight: Containing 'Parkwater' and nine short stories (1875)
Adam Grainger: A Tale (1876)
Edina (1876)
Our Children (1876)
Parkwater: With four other tales (1876)
Pomeroy Abbey (1878)
Lady Adelaide (1879)
Johnny Ludlow, Second Series (1880)
A Tale of Sin and Other Tales (1881)
Court Netherleigh: A Novel (1881)
About Ourselves (1883)
Johnny Ludlow. Third Series (1885)
Lady Grace and Other Stories (1887)
The Story of Charles Strange (1888)
Featherston's Story. A Tale by Johnny Ludlow (1889)
The Unholy Wish and Other Stories (1890)
The House of Halliwell. A Novel (1890)
Ashley and Other Stories (1897)
Victor Serenus (1898)
Johnny Ludlow. Fifth series (1899)
Johnny Ludlow. Sixth series (1899)

Translations
Les Channing. Traduit de l'Anglais par Mme Abric-Encontre (1864)
Les Filles de Lord Oakburn: Roman traduit de l'anglais par L. Bochet (1876)
La Gloire des Verner: Roman traduit de l'anglais par L. de L'Estrive (1878)
Le Serment de Lady Adelaïde: Roman traduit de l'anglais par Léon Bochet (1878)